The Disguises of Whitbury Manor

Jo Jo Hanbury

Joella Siatalan

To Marty, for your brilliance, and the inspiration to write (and finish) a book.
And Adam, whose courage and kindness are unmatched.

Both better brothers than imagination could create.

Chapter One

"I think I shall marry old Mr. March," Lady Celeste Honeychurch declared. She flopped onto the receiving room settee the way she often did after any event among the *ton*, despite the room being swathed in darkness. She could navigate the familiar space with ease by the scent of the flowers placed around the room, refreshed each day from their small townhouse garden. The motion caused the deflated golden curls of her coiffure to flop into her face. She brushed them aside, grinning. "How everyone would laugh!"

Celeste's parents, the Marquess and Marchioness of Kingstone, did not appear amused as they handed off their outerwear to Mr. Graves, the butler, before following her into the well-known space.

"Marry Mr. March? He is almost eighty years old!" her mother sputtered.

"Should you like the fire lit, My lord?" Mr. Graves offered in a soft voice.

Celeste's father yawned. "No, thank you, Graves. I cannot imagine we will be in here long. You may see yourself to bed."

The butler nodded and lit a few candles about the room before bowing out. It was tastefully decorated with furniture in the directoire style, framed for the most part in white. The soft settee Celeste lounged on was a favorite of hers on at-home days. It was the prettiest in the room, upholstered with gold and blue stripes, but that was not its main attraction. It sat nearer the door than the other chairs, giving her a ready escape if required. As pleasant as the aspect from this room out into the street was during the day, she had used the proximity to the door a time or two when their visitors were the kind who could make even the flowers droop from boredom.

Celeste's mother frowned, not distracted by the furnishings as Celeste was.

"Do sit up, Celeste. If we are going to indulge your sudden desire to discuss marriage prospects in the middle of the night, we will do so with the proper decorum."

"Think of how it would read in the news sheets, Mother." Celeste contained a giggle, making no move to sit as she ought. "*'Lady Celeste Honey*church *to wed the vicar'*. Can you imagine?"

Across from Celeste on a golden velvet wingback chair, her father's eyes, blue like hers, twinkled in the candlelight. Though to his credit he kept his expression blank. If he showed his humor in a moment such as this, his wife would no doubt have a fit of the vapors, but he was well practiced at containing himself.

"Besides, he is a vicar," Celeste continued. "That must mean he is a good sort of man and would not begrudge me my inheritance, even if he does boast in his sermons of being a self-made man. It could be used to help the poor...and all that." Celeste waved a hand to imply her etcetera.

"Do be serious," her mother implored, content to stand in the center of the room. "Has something occurred this evening at the ball that has induced these thoughts?"

Celeste groaned. "I am tired of being serious. I have been so all evening. What is the point of a ball if one is expected to be so reserved? Is it not supposed to be an entertainment? If so, then why may I not appear entertained?"

Her father coughed into his hand, but it sounded suspiciously like a laugh. She would break his composure yet. He reached out for the book resting on a side table near his chair but retracted his hand at a narrow-eyed glance from his wife. Celeste wondered if it would be possible to read in such low light anyway. She could not even make out the subjects of the paintings hanging on the walls, though she knew them well enough.

She wished that her mother would relax, but she just stood there, opening and closing her fan over and over. Though Celeste did enjoy thinking up new ways to produce that expression of shock on her face, she also did it out of a sense of confusion. Her mother was always so highly strung when they were in Town, and yet she insisted on dragging the family there every Season.

At least the ball they had just attended would be their last in London until the following year. Celeste had grown weary of the endless pursuit of decorum, amongst other things, and was looking forward to returning to Willoworth, their home in the country.

"Do not smirk, it is unladylike," her mother chastised before sighing. "I know you are very pleased with your own wit, but if you ever wish to marry, you will need to learn to watch your tongue. I very much doubt even your Mr. March would enjoy your repartee."

"Perhaps, but his right mind will soon go begging, and then I shall be left in my own company. It is a perfect situation." Celeste grinned, showing off the dimple in her left cheek.

"Do not be unkind," her father spoke with gentleness, but his brow dropped, along with his chin.

Celeste frowned a little as the sting in the center of her chest shifted her demeanor and colored her cheeks. She acquiesced, knowing she ought not to have spoken ill of her elder.

"You are right, Father. I apologize," she offered in all seriousness and adjusted her position. Not enough to be considered demure, mind you. Celeste was not demure; she just pretended at it when necessary, but her remorse was sincere.

Her mother sat down beside her, wrapping her hands around her closed fan. "I do not understand you, Celeste. You are capable of great maturity, your behavior in public is impeccable. Why this rebellion as soon as we arrive at home?"

Celeste softened a little as her mother searched her face with her brows pulled together.

"Because keeping up appearances is exhausting," Celeste huffed, more irritation escaping through her voice than she had intended. "I behave for the sake of the family, but surely I am allowed to be myself when I am at home."

"A lady ought to behave with respectability in every circumstance." Her mother's brow lowered in disapproval. Mother was indeed a lady at all times. Her very posture, straight and poised, showed her conviction in the statement. She had probably never misbehaved in her entire life. "Even if you receive a respectable offer, how do you expect to keep it once the gentleman learns of this contrary nature of yours?"

"Unlike every other young lady in the social whirl, I do not wish to snare some gentleman stupid enough to be won by shallow acquaintance, insipid conversation, and fluttering eyelashes. In fact, I should rather not marry at all." Celeste folded her arms across her chest.

The horror on her mother's face would have been something to relish a few moments earlier, but Celeste could not meet her gaze to enjoy it. She had been more open than she had intended, and her heart was thudding in her chest as if she were being chased. Her dry eyes blinked more times than was required as she awaited her mother's reaction.

"But why ever not?" The softness of the reply caught Celeste off guard enough that she returned her gaze to her mother, whose head was cocked to the side.

It was a rather unusual notion among ladies of the *ton*, including her own friends, most of whom were unmarried, but Celeste had known for a long time that she need not marry to ensure her comfort. She did, after all, have the benefit of a doting father, the only truly sensible man of her acquaintance, as well as the security of her inheritance. Besides, the closest of Celeste's London friends had just confided in her that evening that the man she had courted last season was far less agreeable as a husband than anticipated, and Celeste had no desire to endure the same fate. As it was, she had received too much attention from Mr. Tullford all season, an empty-headed peacock if ever she saw one.

"Because gentlemen are all vapid, indolent creatures, far too obsessed with themselves, the lot of them," Celeste huffed, slouching once again.

To her surprise, Celeste saw concern on her parents' faces rather than censure.

"No one is as good as Father," she admitted in a low voice when the silence began to feel awkward.

Celeste's parents exchanged a loving glance. If Celeste could not achieve the same, then she was not interested at all. Nor did she need to be; her fortune saw to that.

"There are other worthy men out there, dearest." Her mother reached out and patted her hand. Celeste was almost mollified until she added, "And your father and I have found such a gentleman for you."

Celeste straightened her spine and withdrew her hand, instead gripping the edge of her seat.

"I beg your pardon. Did you just say that you found one *for* me?" Incredulity and surprise warred with the beginning spark of anger.

"As you have asserted, your father is indeed a very good man, and we believe you will find Mr. Bellmoore to be one also. We have arranged—"

Celeste cut off her mother's sentence by standing, her fists clenched at her sides. "You have arranged what, Mother? Father? Have you sold me to the highest bidder?" The room seemed to be shrinking around them and growing warmer by the minute. Had Mr. Graves lit the fire after all? Celeste glanced around, but the hearth in the ornate French fireplace was dark. What then, explained this sudden oppressive heat she was feeling? She snatched the fan from her mother's hands without thinking, but met no resistance or even surprise. She flicked it open in one swift movement and began fluttering the air about her face, welcoming the scent of roses that came with it.

"Celeste." Father always knew the exact tone to invoke respect. It was never harsh but was laced with genuine concern. If any censure accompanied it, it was always deserved. "Sit down."

Celeste obeyed with reluctance but continued fanning herself and took a slow, deliberate breath.

"Now, Lord Whitbury, whom you may or may not recall having been introduced to last season, has a brother, a Mr. Bellmoore," Celeste's mother explained. "As he is a younger son, his only real hope is to marry well himself."

"How mercenary."

The last thing Celeste wanted was a fortune hunter for a husband. She could lose her money and her independence, possibly her will to live.

"It is quite an ordinary situation," her mother reasoned. "However, if it will put you at ease to know, when last we heard from his mother, Lady Whitbury, she had not yet informed him of our plans. I am quite assured of his integrity in the matter."

"And have I even met this paragon?" Celeste asked through her teeth, glancing at the door. The escape was so close, it would take her but a moment to be free of this conversation. She had only to drop the fan and run, but her father wished for her to listen, and so she would. Embracing the topic, however, would be asking too much.

"No. He has been on the continent these two years at least and has missed the Season. I believe he is due to return presently. I met with his mother this week past at the Harrington's ball."

"My, you work quickly, Mother," Celeste muttered, making an effort to not look at her father's face. She did not wish to see the disapproval she knew would be there in response to her disrespect.

Celeste had always wished for a sibling to confide in and commiserate with, but never more so than at this moment. She could not even blame her parents for the lack, because she knew that they had tried to produce more children than herself. She did not wish to feel sympathy for them just now, so she shook those thoughts away.

"Are you so desperate to see me wed that you would pledge me to a penniless younger son without so much as a proper introduction?" She infused the question with as much ridicule as possible.

"I never said anything of the sort," her mother retorted. "All we are suggesting is that you attend a house party at Whitbury Manor for that very purpose. You will be introduced, and if you find that you suit each other, well, the matter will be settled."

"I never heard of anything so ridiculous!" Celeste refuted.

In truth, she could think of no legitimate argument against attending something as innocuous as a house party, but she refused to admit that aloud. The awareness that the suggestion was not ridiculous at all, and that her reaction was rather rash, only served to restrict Celeste's breathing and make her legs spasm as if they would take off running without her command.

"May I remind you that a moment ago you were ready to propose marriage to an octogenarian clergyman?" Celeste's mother pointed out.

"He is not an octogenarian, he is only seventy-eight," Celeste shot back, although it lacked the bite she would have liked. Her head was spinning with increasing speed. She could think of no way out of this that did not border on the dramatic. "I have not received an introduction, nor an invitation. I could not possibly attend!"

Celeste's feeling of victory lasted a mere moment until her mother retrieved a folded piece of embellished paper from her reticule. It had a frightening likeness to an invitation. Celeste pinched her eyes shut, hoping to force the offending item to vanish from existence.

"You were, as I mentioned, introduced to Lord Whitbury last year," Celeste's mother reminded her. "His mother, Lady Whitbury, is a dear friend of mine going back many years, since your father and I..." She stopped, emotion thick in her voice. It was such a rare display that Celeste opened her eyes with curiosity. Celeste's mother recovered herself with some effort and patted Celeste on the hand. "No one would have any reason to doubt your connection to the family."

"How does everyone else know of such a connection, if even I did not?" Celeste asked, side-tracked for a moment.

Celeste's father lowered himself almost to the floor in front of her. He reached for her hand with such kindness that she could not deny him. It reminded her of when she was a child, and he would do the same to soften some bad news.

"I fear there is far too much for us to discuss in one conversation in the dead of night in this cold room. However, with regard to us assisting you to find a suitable marriage partner, we have not explained things adequately. You see, my dear, part of your inheritance is yours to do with as you will following your twenty-first birthday, which was, of course, over a year ago. That is from your mother's family, and you may draw on it even now, but it is not enough to live on well, even for a vicar."

This was new. Celeste had always assumed she would inherit everything from both sides of her family and travel the world. Or at least go on a grand tour of the continent.

"What of the rest?" she had to ask. "What of your fortune, Father?"

Celeste already knew that their country home at Willoworth near the Welsh border, as well as the other family holdings, would pass to her husband should she have one, on her father's death. If she did not marry, the title and lands would pass to some other relative, while the money at least was supposed to be hers. Or so she thought. It was a substantial sum, over forty thousand pounds in cash and investments, although she was not certain of the particulars. It seemed those details now meant to torment her.

"You will inherit a portion upon my demise as you know, but since most of the wealth is tied to the estates and titles that have been held by the family for several generations, there are...stipulations," he answered.

"Stipulations?" Celeste blurted, panic rising in her chest. "An entail?"

Her father gave her a sympathetic nod. "Yes." He shifted his weight, his lips pursing before he continued. "I will be direct, my dear. In order to inherit the main portion tied to the estates, you need to marry by your twenty-third birthday, which only gives you until the beginning of the Season next year. Should that not occur, you will forfeit the entirety, and it will pass to a distant cousin. We have tried to introduce you to a number of suitable gentlemen over the years, but you have not desired any of them. That is why we introduced you to Mr. Tullford. We felt it prudent to see you wed this year, rather than risk running it too close."

"And Mr. Forely, and Mr. Hargrave, and Lord Tardington, and—" Celeste's mother ceased her distressing list at a look from Celeste's father.

"Well, it is your fault I have not found a suitor yet," Celeste burst out, making her mother jump. "You gave me this French name that everyone comments on." She rolled her eyes. In truth, she knew she was clutching at straws. The comments were only occasional, but she needed something to grasp onto.

"Celeste, we do not discuss the French!" her mother gasped, a hand flying to her chest. "That ghastly revolution business began several months after your christening, and it was too late by then. Besides, it is the British spelling, and you may tell anyone who asks that you were named for your grandmother. On the Italian side." She sniffed into her handkerchief and shifted in her seat.

Celeste knew all of this already, but it did not make her feel any better, nor did it make their designs any more desirable, despite their kind intentions.

"What of the twenty thousand from you directly, apart from the estates?"

Celeste was beginning to feel detached from her body, and the patterns on the rug at her feet seemed to be weaving together by themselves.

This time, her mother's gentle voice echoed from far away. "Dearest, that is your dowry. You must be married to obtain that part of your fortune as well."

Of course. Celeste knew that dowries were attached to marriage, just not the rest of it.

"Why have you never told me? How have I never heard of these entails before?" She tried to shake the encroaching stupor. "I have squandered my seasons when I could have been..." The appropriate phrase escaped her spiraling mind. It had not bothered Celeste that she was approaching spinsterhood, but now...

"We had hoped for you to find a match of your own liking, with minimal interference from us." Again, Father gave her hand a gentle squeeze as he spoke. "It seems we were mistaken in not making you aware of the situation sooner."

All Celeste could manage was a silent, somewhat detached nod.

"Perhaps you ought to retire. A receiving room in the middle of the night is hardly the place for this discussion anyway; the servants will hear everything. We may resume in the morning." Her mother phrased the words like a suggestion, but her tone was firm. Without a word, Celeste nodded, absently kissed each parent on the cheek, and walked to her room in a daze.

Owens, Celeste's lady's maid, must have been waiting for her because Celeste found herself being made ready for bed. Celeste had never liked Honeychurch House as much as Willoworth. Although her bedroom had all the same basic comforts, like a soft bed and an ornate dressing table, and was decorated in the lilac paper she liked, it lacked the space and feel of Willoworth. However, she did not notice any of those things as Owens adeptly guided her through her ablutions, navigating her around the small room. Somehow, Owens managed to do so without so much as a strand of her auburn hair falling out of place. She even kept Celeste from bumping a toe on the heavy bed frame, despite her absentmindedness.

Celeste often took the time to breathe in the scent from the sprigs of lavender set in a small vase beside the bed that Owens refreshed from the garden each day. Instead, she slumped before the mirror, the luxury of the warmed bed and pillows she would soon sink into, for the moment lost on her.

"Are you all right, My lady?" Owens asked in a small voice.

"I hardly know," Celeste answered, still dazed. "My parents have informed me that my inheritance is conditional upon my being married by next year."

Owens' fingers paused from unpinning Celeste's hair.

"That's plenty of time for a beauty like you to find someone, especially one as clever as you are. Even with the Season closing, there is the little season, or perhaps someone closer to home might suit."

She could have been saying what she assumed her mistress would like to hear, but Celeste thought she sounded sincere. She had shared confidences with Owens before, and in her own mind, considered them to be friends. She did not know if Owens shared that notion, but they often conversed on any number of topics.

"Unfortunately, men do not appreciate clever ladies," Celeste stated, resurrecting some of the fire in her midsection, making her breathe faster. "They often have little sense of humor and prefer a witless servant for a wife."

Owens gaped for a moment, her green eyes wide, before recovering enough to continue her task.

"Do you truly think so?" she asked, not maintaining the eye contact.

"Yes, I do," Celeste nodded. "My father is the only man I have ever met who enjoys stimulating conversation or a good-natured set-down, from male or female alike."

The thought of a husband who would deprive her of herself was terrifying. Celeste knew that people married for convenience all the time, but she doubted her own ability to endure it.

When Owens said nothing, Celeste continued. "My parents would have me marry immediately. I believe they lack confidence in my ability to manage it myself without frightening any potential suitors away." She almost smiled at that and would have if not for the new reality crushing her ability to breathe. "They have even chosen someone."

The words preceded a wave of nausea that necessitated Celeste grabbing onto the sides of the chair for balance as she considered how many *someones* her parents had nudged her way without even mild suspicion on her part that it had anything to do with inheritance. She had never given serious thought to any of them. Without intention, her mind began to catalogue and review every man she had ever met.

Celeste wondered for a moment if perhaps Mr. March ought to be considered as more than just a means to vex her mother.

"Who?" Owens asked. It took Celeste a moment to realize that Owens was not reading her thoughts but responding to the news of her parents' plot.

In her surprise, Owens had locked her green eyes with Celeste's blue ones in the reflection again, forgetting her usual deference. Celeste found herself smiling a little. If her parents had their way, Owens would be the only lifeline she would have, provided Celeste would be allowed to keep her. No, she would insist upon it.

"A Mr. Bellmoore. I have never even met him, at least not that I recall." Celeste dropped her face into her hands.

"Would you like me to fetch you a cup of tea, My lady? My mum always says that a good cup of tea fixes everything."

Celeste looked up at Owens with a small half smile. "I do not think tea will solve this one, unfortunately." Owens and Celeste shared a gentle chuckle, and Celeste's smile softened. "Thank you, though. You are so good to me."

"It is a pleasure, truly." She bobbed a curtsy.

"Owens," Celeste bit her lip. "I have no idea where I am going to be settled, whether I go along with my parents' mad scheme or not. Would you mind coming with me, even if it is very far away?"

"It's not for me to decide," she inclined her chin.

"I would never take you away against your wishes, Owens. I would not have you unhappy. Or feeling that you need to search for another position. Please be open with me."

It occurred to Celeste that she did not know Owens' age, but she guessed that they could not be more than a year or two apart. Owens could find a position elsewhere with relative ease if she chose to, or even stay at Willoworth, but Celeste would still lose her.

"I wouldn't mind an adventure someplace new," Owens answered with a small smile.

"Thank you." Celeste smiled with a sigh of relief, then teetered on the edge of the seat.

"It's off to bed with you now, My lady," Owens commanded, catching her by the shoulders. Celeste did not resist being led by her maid. If she were going to survive this house party, she would need the familiar comfort of Owens.

As she tossed and turned throughout the night, Celeste imagined manifold scenarios in which everything would go wrong. By morning she had concluded that this plan of her parents' making, though well intentioned, was doomed to be a humiliating failure. She had to find a way out of it.

Chapter Two

Whitbury Manor, Berkshire, 1815

Jacob Bellmoore could not believe his ears. His mother could not honestly believe she was helping him. Being a bachelor at twenty-five hardly constituted the need for a matchmaker. What could she even know about what he sought for in a wife when he was not certain of that himself, having never tried? He had just begun fencing when his mother had requested a private word with him, and he had come down in his shirtsleeves. He was beginning to wish he had kept her waiting.

"Are you quite mad?" he inquired, considering at least a little, the possibility of senility as he paced the perimeter of the parlor. Despite being large, there were too many small tables with vases and small ornaments on them, next to chairs of every size to allow distracted pacing. The space also felt more confined due to the deep red decorative linen paper lining the walls.

Not to mention the large rug Jacob continued to trip on.

"Hardly." His mother rolled her blue eyes from her seat in the center of the room, also red. "There is no need for theatrics. I have arranged a wife for you, not an execution."

"Is there a difference?" Jacob flung out. He had nothing against marriage in general, but this nonsense his mother spoke of was not what he had in mind.

"My dear boy, your brother is about to marry, and with that will come heirs. Why should you think your allowance from him will continue forever?" she posed. "I am simply being practical."

"Because the allowance is set out in Father's will. Besides, what is wrong with having a profession like any other second son? Indeed, I would prefer it to living in idleness."

As it was, Jacob had been vacillating between his options that very morning. He had been away on a grand tour for the past two years, returning a fortnight past and so had missed the entire social season. He had been happy to meet his brother's new fiancée and her family upon his return. They had come from London directly, along with Jacob's mother and his brother, the day before Jacob's arrival, to stay at Whitbury Manor for a visit.

Jacob was surprised when his mother did not immediately concede. Under normal circumstances, he could count on her to be a good balance of humor and sense, but she was beginning to seem uncharacteristically ill at ease.

"You need a stable situation now." She seemed intent on ignoring everything Jacob had said. "Your brother could decide to cut you off at any moment. No, it will not do. You must marry as soon as possible," she concluded.

It took Jacob a moment to wade through his confusion and form a reply. He interrupted his latest circuit of the room to face her.

"Mother, Whitbury cannot cut me off. Nor has he ever indicated to me that he wished to. And even if he could, how then could I support a wife without a profession? Even a farmer's daughter would have some expectation of an income."

"A farmer's daughter, Jacob?" She raised an eyebrow, but a corner of her mouth rose with it. "In answer to your question though, I have betrothed you to an heiress."

"You—what? An heiress? What would an heiress want with me? I have no title and very little income. I am not even sufficiently handsome to be worth her notice," he argued, trying in vain to keep up with this conversation that was taking on a strange, dreamlike quality. He turned back toward the large gothic windows overlooking the gardens and tripped on the rug again.

"Nonsense!" his mother refuted without hesitation. "You are more pleasing to look upon than any other gentleman of our acquaintance, and that includes your brother."

"Coming from my mother," Jacob retorted before returning to the center of the room to stand beside her chair. "What possible benefit could an heiress gain by an alliance of this nature? I cannot believe you are in earnest."

For the first time in the conversation, Jacob's mother's façade slipped enough to show real distress. What she was not saying began to worry him even more than what she was. Perhaps he would have been better off remaining at the windows.

"Lady Celeste Honeychurch is..." She paused to consider her words.

"So, my betrothed has a name," Jacob remarked, "and a title apparently." Jacob stopped, realizing for the first time the reality of that particular word choice. If his mother had made promises on his behalf, no matter that he was not obligated by law, he was a gentleman and would therefore be expected to fulfill them.

"You have not discussed this idea of yours with anyone else, have you?" he asked, as his breathing increased.

In all his life, Jacob had never seen his mother squirm. "Mother?"

Panic rose in his chest. He resisted the urge to run to the windows and fling them open. Had he just thought of this room as large?

"Well, the engagement is a formality. The wedding, I am sure, will take place as soon as possible once you meet her." She twisted whatever unfortunate object was clutched in her hand.

"What have you done?" Jacob felt the color drain from his face and was no longer certain he was in possession of a pulse.

"I may have announced the happy news to a few of our friends...in anticipation of your relief to have your situation so comfortably resolved."

"How absurd! What do you mean you have told a few friends? Which few?"

"W—well, only our acquaintances attending Sunday services and the vicar. There was the matter of preparing the man for the upcoming necessities."

"What?!" Jacob gasped with far less volume than the effort warranted. Breathing felt like a foreign practice. If she had announced it to the parish, he was as good as engaged. To a complete stranger.

Jacob pulled at his cravat until his fingers hurt, and he was certain he was not fit to be seen. Not that he cared. He could not in good conscience ruin this Lady Celeste Honeychurch, whoever she was, by canceling the ostensible engagement. And he could not know how far the gossip trail had taken the misinformation. Nor did he wish to make a laughingstock of his mother, despite her high-handedness.

Jacob had an easy and amiable temperament, but this was beyond the pale. He resisted the urge to pick apart the nearest bouquet. Then a terrifying thought struck him.

"Have *you* even met her?" he demanded. His mother fidgeted in silence but eventually shook her head, looking down. Jacob dropped to the seat beside her and ran his hands through his long, dark brown hair. He ought to cut it, but he preferred to keep it in the same style that his late father had.

"No, I have not yet had the pleasure, but her mother was a dear friend of mine during our debutant season, and we were reacquainted by providence a week past at Lady Harrington's ball. Naturally, we spoke at length of the welfare of our children and—"

"Are you telling me that you may have just shackled me to a tooth-less spinster?" Jacob's voice cracked.

"Oh no, she is not yet three and twenty. She may be approaching spinsterhood if you ask the stuffier matrons in Town, but she is not toothless. Her mother and father are quite adamant that she is well of body, and I saw a lovely portrait of her at Honeychurch House in Grosvenor Street. She is quite pretty."

"Well of body? Whatever do you mean?" he asked, but the answer dawned on him before she had a chance to reply. "Oh, this gets better and better, doesn't it?" he asked no one. "You mean that you made certain she is healthy enough to give you plenty of grandchildren, don't you!" It was not a question.

The moment Jacob's brother had announced his own engagement, their mother had been in raptures over the possibility of little lords and ladies running about.

"It isn't as selfish as all that—don't look at me that way," she defend-ed. "I will not deny that the idea of grandchildren pleases me, but I do worry about you, my boy. You are not just a spare to me."

Jacob had been staring at the clouds through the windows from his seat but turned his head back toward his mother with a sigh. She had indeed always made a point that while society viewed having two sons as insurance for the title, she did not see him that way. She was very attentive as a mother, and he knew that not everyone was so fortunate. He took several slow, deliberate breaths.

"You do not really think that Whitbury wishes to find a way to cut me off, do you? Why go to these lengths if not for that?"

"Your brother is not as attentive to the situations of others as you are. He has made some comments of concern of late."

"Anything specific?" He forced his brow to relax by rubbing it with his fingers. Having it creased for so long was beginning to give him a headache.

Jacob was certain his brother would allow him to choose his own livelihood, and had been considering his options between the Church or perhaps even a physician's apprentice. He had planned to speak to Whitbury on the subject soon enough, once he was decided. All he was certain about was that he was happiest when helping people. Like when he would assist his brother with the Whitbury tenants and their needs, be it organizing repairs, or playing with the children, while their parents spoke with Whitbury. His brother would grant him whatever time he required for that, he was certain. Jacob had noticed an increasing aloofness in him since he had inherited the Whitbury title, but he assumed that was a natural reaction to losing their father and gaining the responsibilities of the earldom.

No, his mother's interference was entirely superfluous.

"Your brother indicated that, well, that the army..." She left the sentence unfinished and took a deep breath. After a moment, she turned away from him and retrieved a lacy handkerchief from her sleeve to dab at the corner of her eye.

Jacob sighed. He never stayed cross for long. Angst, on the other hand, was likely to remain awhile. He reached out and placed a gentle hand on his mother's to offer comfort.

"The army is a noble profession, Mother," he tried to reassure her. He had no desire for battle but would serve England with pride if that were his lot. "Whitbury would purchase a commission for me, so I would be an officer. That is not so bad."

His words seemed to have little effect as her shoulders shook. Neither of them believed his trivialization of so grave a matter as marching off to war. Too many men had returned from the fight against Napoleon wounded in body and mind, or not at all. He wished he could think of something to say that would comfort her, but his mind was blank.

"I know it isn't very patriotic, but..." an audible sob hiccupped through her restraint. "What, with this business of Napoleon returning to France. I know he has been defeated, but what if he were to return again? I do not want some battlefield to take you. I wish to keep you for myself."

"Oh, Mother." He shuffled closer and gave her shoulders a squeeze. She turned and buried her face in his tortured cravat for a long moment. He did not rush her, and when she was ready, she leaned back and patted his cheek.

"You are so like your father." Her words made him smile. "He was also very dashing." She pretended to swoon to lighten the mood, making him laugh and cringe at the same time.

"That is enough of that, Your Ladyship." He hugged her again and sighed in defeat. "Tell me more about this magnificent solution you've conjured."

"Conjured? You make me sound like a witch."

"If the broom fits..." he muttered. With that, she hit him quite soundly with her fan. He had not even noticed that she had been holding one.

"That hurt!" he yelped.

"Well, you watch yourself. I am not too old to lock you in the nursery, you know," she mock-threatened. He shook his head in wonder. Most women of his acquaintance would faint dead away at a jest like that, rather than engaging with it.

Jacob wondered if this heiress his mother had chosen had a sense of humor, although he doubted it. Anyone foolhardy enough to marry him sight unseen had to be out of her wits.

"She isn't a lunatic, is she?" he blurted.

"What? Oh, the girl." It took Jacob's mother a moment to follow where his mind had taken him. "No, I do not believe so. In any case, you shall judge for yourself this afternoon."

"Today?" Fresh panic increased Jacob's heart rate and its volume in his ears.

"Yes. As you may recall, your brother and I arranged a house party in honor of his engagement to Lady Adelle. I do believe I told you about it. Not to worry though, it will only be a fortnight long, and—"

"A fortnight?!" Jacob almost leaped out of his chair. "Why so long? We do not live that far into the country."

"—the guest list is not so very great," she went on, ignoring him. "I have invited Lady Celeste to attend. Her parents are not able to come away at present, so I shall take her under my wing while she is here, and she will be under the protection of your brother. Are you well, Jacob? You do look pale." She placed the back of her hand on his forehead as he broke out in a cold sweat.

It was becoming a real possibility that Jacob's breakfast could return to haunt him at any moment.

"If you do not mind my asking, Mother, why the rush?" Jacob was not sure he would hear the answer over the blood rushing in his ears.

"The invitations had already been accepted. Adding her to the guest list was quite simple. Doing so at the last moment was so that, well, I did not want to give you the opportunity to... ah...cry off." She at least had the decency to blush.

The parlor suddenly felt stifling.

"I need to go for a ride."

Without waiting for more information on the house party, or who else would be in attendance, Jacob fled out the door.

The wind in Jacob's face as he gave Thor his head and let him fly to his heart's content was just what he needed. The stallion's hooves thundered on the ground as he galloped at an impressive speed. Jacob's first look at the horse had inspired the name, the way he ran with such strength, hammering the ground.

Jacob had left his hat and coat behind in his desperation for freedom, but he could not make himself care. He had probably horrified his mother to leave the house in such a state, but she would recover. His hair had long since come loose and was whipping around him as he rode, but somehow that made him feel all the better for it.

Jacob had no solutions by the time he neared the stable house once again and dismounted to walk Thor the rest of the way an hour later, but he felt more like himself. He had not asked what time the guests would begin to arrive and so was not prepared to greet the carriages rolling up the drive in his current state of undress. Instead, he avoided them and approached the stalls.

"You there," one of the guests called out to a groom. Jacob continued until the man called out again. "Here, see to my horse or I shall have you whipped!"

Jacob turned, looking around, but no one else was present. As the gentleman with dark hair, dark eyes, and a dark coat thrust his reins at him, Jacob was startled to realize that the scoundrel was addressing him. He had been mistaken for a servant. Indignation rose in his chest, not only at the insinuation, but the impertinence of the man presuming to whip someone employed by his family. The Bellmoore's had never been violent toward their staff, and he took exception to anyone who would be.

"I beg your..." Jacob paused as another thought illuminated. This could be the answer to everything. He affected a more common accent. "That is, beggin' your pardon, sir. I's a bit 'ard of 'earin'. Allow me to tend tha' beast for ye." He bobbed his head in what he hoped was a deferential manner, having never impersonated a servant before. He had no idea if his accent was correct, but he hoped the man would not notice either way.

As it was, his apology was ignored. The man, a similar height and age to Jacob, did not even look him in the face.

"See that he is brushed and fed if you can manage that," the man demanded. The implication was insulting. If Jacob were indeed employed in the stables, to have his abilities mocked would have rankled. However, instead of expressing any offense, he took the reins, dipped a slight bow, and led both mounts to the stalls as the gentleman strode away.

"'Ard of 'earin' are ye, guv'nah?" Tom McInnes, the stable master, had Jacob leaping out of his skin. A grin quirked the side of his unrepentant mouth as he stood nearby with his arms folded.

"Tom! I didn't see you there," Jacob flushed.

"No, I'd wager you dinnae." The man's native Scottish brogue returned. "Would you mind tellin' me what you're about, young Jack?"

The nickname made Jacob smile. Tom and Mrs. Thatcher, the housekeeper, were the only ones who still called him that. They had been with the family for all of Jacob's life, as unusual as that was. His brother had replaced most of the servants when he inherited the title, but even he could not bear to let these two go.

"Just avoiding my own funeral," Jacob half joked. When concern replaced the older man's expression, though, he felt that he ought to explain. "My mother has announced my engagement to the world."

"Where I come from, that's somethin' to celebrate." Tom raised a brow, expecting more.

"Perhaps it would be if I had ever met the woman," Jacob quipped, "but I have not, and she is arriving this afternoon for this farce of a house party. I was considering what was to be done about it when I was mistaken for one of your boys there by that fiend, which gave me an idea."

"I dinnae ken Mrs. Thatcher'll go along with it, let alone her ladyship."

At least Tom did not dismiss it out of hand.

"I have not thought it through yet. The idea struck me just now," Jacob admitted. "If I can lie low until the house party is over, I might be able to avoid this whole thing without damaging Lady Celeste's reputation. Perhaps it will be assumed that it was all just misinformation if we are never seen together."

"If you say so." Tom's face scrunched up on one side, with the eyebrow on the opposite side rising.

"I will have to think of a story or come down with a fever or something."

"How convenient." Tom's expression did not change. Nevertheless,

Jacob was not deterred. He had perfected the art of pretending sickness, he just had not employed those particular skills in over a decade. He did not yet know what he wanted for himself, but having a life forced upon him wasn't it. Even in the army, his family's status would allow him some choices. His closest friend had been in the army and seemed to enjoy it, before a family tragedy called him back. Being beholden to a snobby heiress would mean that Jacob would always be subject to her whims or those of her parents.

If he could convince the staff to go along with him, there was the potential for Jacob to avoid the whole snare. He could hide out in the stables, working alongside Tom. The chores might even keep him busy enough to prevent driving himself mad by overthinking the situation.

"I think it just might work!" He made to leave, but Tom cleared his throat. Jacob turned, folding his arms across his chest as he did so. "Yes, Tom, what is it?

"Well, you'll need to affect that accent the entire time." Tom shook his head and made a sound that was half exhale and half chuckle.

"My accent cannot be that bad," Jacob smiled.

"If you say so." Tom fought a grin. "And you'll need some homespun clothes. If that gentleman had glanced your way for long, he would have seen that you're togged too fine for a servant, no matter that you look like a faerie dog right now."

Jacob opened his mouth to protest but then looked down at his disheveled shirt. Tom was right.

"I have some at the cottage you can use," Tom offered, then scratched at his jaw. "You'll also need a name and a good splinter bar."

"The name is easy enough, but a splinter bar? From a carriage? Whatever for?" Jacob cocked his head to the side.

"Aye, not an actual splinter bar, but someone in a position to support you and take the questions from the staff. Dinnae forget that as well as the people employed by the Whitbury Estate, there'll be servants from all over accompanying the guests. I'd suggest Mrs. Thatcher for that job. If she agrees to help you, then the rest'll go along with it, but if not, you'll have a mess of gossip, the likes of which have not been heard since the poor king lost his marbles. No doubt it'll find its way to the ears of your dear mother, not to mention the rest of society." Tom had a point there.

Jacob thought for a moment, his arms folded across his chest, before snapping his fingers. "I have it! I shall be Jack McKnell."

"McKnell?" Tom asked, raising a skeptical eyebrow.

"Yes, since I am avoiding a fate worse than death," Jacob shrugged, "it is appropriate."

"Well, aren't you just a ray of sunshine...Mr. McKnell," Tom tried it out, then chuckled, "It does have a sort of morbid ring to it, if you'll excuse the joke. I'll have the boys informed that they are to refer to you as McKnell until further notice. 'Though I must caution you, Jack, some of the other servants who know you may talk either way."

Jacob nodded, not very concerned. He was grateful that his parents had always taught him that those employed by their family were real people, deserving of respect. Were it not for that, he would have had no allies at such an unforeseeable moment.

Chapter Three

En route to Whitbury Manor, England

Celeste felt the sway of the carriage but did not notice it. She was aware of very little outside of her own thoughts. An hour or two into her journey toward Berkshire, she had realized that she had been pulling at a loose thread on the blue pelisse she wore over her gown and had to pick up a book to occupy her hands, else risk actual damage to her clothing.

It was only Celeste and Owens in the carriage. Celeste's parents were not joining her yet. It was odd and disconcerting. They had made excuses about her father needing to stay in Town a little longer but had avoided giving her a worthy reason for their neglect. She suspected it was to give her a little more freedom to grow attached to the unknown gentleman they had procured for her, without the resistance she would no doubt put up should they be present. They had evaded every attempt by Celeste to draw out a confession during the week since she had learned of the house party.

Along with her parents' other sins, allowing Celeste so little time to prepare was ridiculous. There had been little time to visit Bond Street for a rush order on a new gown or two to impress the dreaded Mr. Bellmoore.

She wanted to throw her luggage over the nearest bridge.

Celeste glanced at Owens, wondering if she should make a present of them. They were of a size, but it was nonsense. It was not uncommon for an abigail to be gifted her lady's castoffs, but not when they were brand new and at the height of fashion.

"You're awfully quiet, My lady." Owens made Celeste jump with her cautious expression of concern.

"I suppose I have been woolgathering." Celeste shrugged, still staring at nothing out of the carriage window.

"Everything will be all right, you'll see," Owens tried to reassure her, bless her heart.

"I fear that you are wrong, Owens. There is little I desire less than to attend this house party." Celeste continued to mutter to herself a moment longer before noticing the wistful smile on her maid's face. "What is it?"

Owens' eyes widened, and she blushed. With her red hair and fair complexion, it was easy to accomplish.

"Oh, nothing." Owens looked down. Her knees knocked together a little with the sway of the carriage.

"Now I must know!" Celeste smiled. It may have been sheer boredom, but she was grateful for someone else to focus on. "Do tell me, Owens. It is just you and I in this carriage; the driver and footman will not overhear."

"Very well, but it is nothing of consequence," Owens laughed. "I was just thinking of how wonderful it must be to dress in those fancy gowns and dance with all those fine gentlemen." She stared out of the window, smiling.

Celeste did not wish to spoil her naïvety but could not help the sarcasm from escaping. "Yes, it is wonderful to be a piece of meat sold at market."

Resentment toward the unacquainted Mr. Bellmoore brought the sting of tears that Celeste refused to cry. She did not know what the man looked like, sounded like, behaved like. She did not even know how old he was, although she had some indistinct memory of who Lord Whitbury may be. Presuming there was no great difference in their ages, that gave her some idea at least. Her comparison to a market made her wonder vaguely if he smelled like fish.

"I know you're frightened, but perhaps it won't be as bad as all that." Owens looked back at Celeste.

"You try it." Celeste did not mean to bite back like that, but she was growing more panicked with every mile that drew her nearer to her fate. She had no idea who the other guests were, or if they were aware of her reason for attendance. She did not know if she would be expected to explain her out-of-place presence there. Or how she could even explain that her mother was such wonderful friends with Lady Whitbury when the countess was a stranger to her.

Celeste shook her head. The whole trip was unnecessary. Celeste felt quite capable of finding her own husband without assistance. True, she had never tried to look for one before, but once she began putting an effort into it, it could not be so difficult within a year. She had acquaintances with brothers. Very well, perhaps she was not so confident as that, but no one needed to know it. Her fists clenched in her lap.

As the nondescript scenery moved by, Celeste felt the pangs of longing for a friend who would understand, but all of her friends were in town, or in Kingstone, and none of them were people she thought would understand her position. The only person she had to comfort her was Owens. At least Owens seemed too wrapped up in her fantasies to have been affected by Celeste's sharpness.

Celeste fought the urge to shake her head in wonder, even as a sardonic grin pulled at one side of her mouth. Owens likely *would* enjoy being in her place if the circumstances were reversed. That thought made Celeste chuckle until she stumbled over it again.

"Are you well, My lady?" Owens' eyes shot to Celeste, who burst into a fit of laughter.

"Yes, quite well. Better than well actually," Celeste answered, leaving Owens confused. "You are brilliant, Owens!"

"We can stop the carriage if you need to rest," Owens suggested, her eyebrows pulling together whilst reaching for her hairline.

"Yes! What a wonderful idea!" Celeste agreed. "Stop the carriage!" she called out as she thumped on the roof with the book she had been neglecting all morning, dropping it in the process, and laughing some more.

The carriage rolled to a halt in the middle of nowhere, and James, the footman, opened the door.

"Is everything all right, My lady?" he asked with his eyes wide and searching.

"Yes, everything is in order, or it will be. I need some fresh air. Come, Owens."

Celeste allowed James to hand her down, followed by Owens, and stepped from the side of the road into an apple orchard. She picked a low-hanging apple for herself and one for Owens. She even threw one to James and then the coachman, whose eyes widened just before they caught them. There was nothing around for miles but fields and orchards and fresh air. It was invigorating.

After pacing for a few minutes, enjoying the pilfered fruit, Celeste swung around to face Owens.

"You are very well spoken for a servant—why is that?" she asked, although it sounded more like an accusation.

"I... ah..." Owens choked a little on her apple.

"Come on then, out with it," Celeste insisted.

"It is expected of a lady's maid."

"No, beyond that. You could easily pass for a member of the gentry," Celeste pressed.

"Well, my-my father is Welsh, but my mother is English." When Celeste waited for more, Owens continued, "Before marrying, she was a governess, so she believed in education. She hoped it would set-set us up to find better positions."

"Your mother is a clever woman. Tell me, what is your Christian name?" Celeste could not remember ever having asked before, and it gave her pause.

"Bryn, My lady."

"That is quite lovely. I shall call you that from now on...that is, if it is all right with you."

"O—of course."

"Hmm..." Celeste peered at her through a narrowed gaze. "Perfect!"

"Begging your pardon, My lady, but..." Bryn took a fortifying breath before asking with a hint of that Welsh accent, "what are you going on about?"

Celeste smiled like a cat with a face full of cream. Bryn gaped and blinked, leaning away.

"I am so glad you asked that, Bryn. You see, we are going to switch places!" She laughed out loud at her own ingenuity.

"I—what?" Bryn's voice shook.

"I have no desire to marry, or even meet, Mr. What's-his-name. I can find my own match on my own terms without all this fuss and bother. And you deserve to experience all those wonderful diversions of society," Celeste reasoned, palms up. She was a genius!

"Why go to all the trouble at all? Could you not decide not to marry him if you do not like him?" Bryn asked the perfectly rational question.

"I am more concerned that I *will* like him," Celeste answered.

Bryn's face scrunched.

"Do you not see, Bryn? He is obviously a fortune hunter. He must be. Everything he does will be designed to charm and entice me to accept him so that he may acquire my fortune. I cannot rely on my own judgment, especially if he turns out to be handsome. I must avoid the man at all costs."

"I think I understand, but then why are you going to the house party at all? If it isn't too bold to ask. Your reputation could be ruined." Bryn tilted her chin down, but her eyes flitted up often as though her curiosity were engaged in a battle with her deference.

"I do need to satisfy my parents by going, but no one in attendance knows me so no one will know the difference." Celeste tapped her lip.

Bryn cocked her head, her lips pursed.

"What is it? I do not mind hearing your opinion," Celeste encouraged.

"Thank you, My lady. It is just that, well, what will you do if there has already been talk in society of the arrangement?"

"Then I may have to cry off of the engagement, but until we know that, you will be free to enjoy your first house party, and I will be free to find my own husband. And if I should fail at that, then I shall have to marry Mr. March or learn to economize." Celeste shrugged, not really believing it would come to that. She was not so desperate just yet with the best part of a year ahead of her.

"I know I am just a poor servant, but please reconsider," Bryn pleaded, stopping Celeste in her tracks. "I am sorry for speaking out of turn, My lady, but if we are found out..."

"Yes, I know. It would be a terrific scandal," Celeste admitted.

"I would be dismissed, or worse." Bryn's eyes widened.

"We shall be inordinately careful, and think how wonderful it could be, for me too, to see the life of a servant." She was not above begging.

"I do not think you will find it all that wonderful," Bryn cautioned.

"Does that mean you will do it?" Celeste pulled Bryn's hands toward her chest, still clasped, and held her breath. She could not tell what Bryn was thinking, but then Bryn gave a tentative nod.

Celeste smiled in a way that her mother would have told her was too wide to be considered refined and led Bryn back into the carriage. She was feeling much more herself now that she had an idea of how to proceed.

"I think it would be best for you to pretend to be me and for me to use a false name. And we should use them all the time, even in private, so there is less chance of discovery," Celeste suggested. "How about Elsie? That is similar enough to my real name, and then from Honeychurch to...honey-bear...honeybee...aha, I know!" Celeste clapped her hands. "Coombe. Like a variation on honeycomb." She giggled again.

"I think I will need to tutor you a little," Bryn ventured.

"Yes, please do," Celeste agreed. "You are sounding more assertive already. You will need that if you are to begin addressing me as your lady's maid."

Bryn's face blanched again. The poor girl might swoon if Celeste were not careful. She hoped Bryn could rally enough to be convincing.

For the remainder of the journey, Bryn tutored Celeste on various aspects of being a lady's maid, all the while speaking well but with wide eyes and rigid shoulders.

After a few hours, the carriage pulled onto the long drive leading to Whitbury Manor. As soon as the house came into view, smiling too much ceased to be an issue as nerves made Celeste's stomach drop, along with her mouth.

The house was beautiful. With pale stone walls and tall windows aplenty, it was a very pleasant prospect. The grounds were immaculate, but it was clear from the architecture and the gothic windows that formed the main center of the building, that the estate was not of modern construction. Celeste wondered how long it had been in the family. It appeared to be Elizabethan at least. The east and west wings of the manor were modern by comparison with stone terraces and porticos, but most distinctive was the classic endless symmetrical sea of sash windows. Celeste wondered if the renovations were a recent project of the current Lord Whitbury, or the Earl before him. All in all, it was quite large.

A gasping sound brought Celeste's attention away from herself. Bryn was taking rapid breaths and appeared to be on the brink of hysterics. She turned wide eyes on Celeste.

"It isn't going to work!" she exclaimed, her eyes unfocused. "No one is going to believe that I'm a Lady, I can't do it!"

Celeste drew a deep, calming breath. She swallowed her own misgivings in order to calm her maid. She knew her plan was a brilliant one, and she would not back down now. Neither could she, since they had already swapped clothing the last time they had stopped to change the horses. Not to mention paying every coin in her small reticule to the coachman and James for their discretion.

"Owens...Bryn." Celeste reached out and took her hands. They were shaking. "You will have time to become accustomed to your new position. There will not be any planned activities today aside from dinner, as all of the guests will be arriving at varying times. You may even claim tiredness from your journey and request a tray in your room. Nothing will be required of you but to endure introductions." She paused, unsure whether she had made any real difference. "You may do anything you wish. As of this moment, you *are* a lady!"

Celeste's encouragement did not seem very effective, based on Bryn's lack of response, so, she drew herself up with a confidence she did not feel and began to play her own part. She hoped it was the right way to assist Bryn. They had to be united, or this whole thing would collapse.

"My lady, we have arrived," Celeste announced. Her accent could use a little work, but she was grateful for her deficiency as she saw a spark of amusement in Bryn's eyes and a little color returning to her lips. A subtle nod of reassurance was all Celeste allowed herself to give before committing fully to her role.

It took a conscious effort for Celeste not to descend from the carriage first, and James, who was not a gifted actor, just stood there agape for a moment before assisting Bryn down. Celeste wanted to acknowledge his efforts but dared not risk even a silent communication with the Whitbury butler's hawk-eyes on them. She was so distracted by her own nerves that Bryn had to pretend to trip in order to whisper, "servants' entrance," before Celeste followed her to the front door.

Mortified, Celeste turned to James as he handed her a bag. With her back to the butler, she took the opportunity to mouth the words "thank you" to James. To say he gave her a subtle grin, or a nod would be to exaggerate. It was more that his eyes grew lighter, lifted by an infinitesimal rise in his cheekbones, and his lips twitched by the tiniest degree. Celeste had never known before that clear communication could be had with such minute gestures.

James carried Celeste's trunk, now to be Bryn's, toward the side of the house and hinted for her to follow. She trailed behind him, grateful for the guidance.

Once inside, Celeste tried to take in her surroundings without being too obvious about looking around. For some reason, she had assumed that the servants' hallways would be dark and heavy, but the walls were light in color, rendering the crowded passage a little less intimidating. It could not dispel her anxiety, the space being abuzz with the comings and goings of the servants. Though it did help some.

It struck Celeste as odd that the areas of the house with the least space were those of greatest activity. The crowded hallway she was squeezing through as she hurried to keep up was nothing like the grand entrance Bryn had used. She would be even then in a large open room, full of quiet politeness and space to breathe. Whereas the sheer number of bodies moving about below stairs was overwhelming.

It was not long before Celeste was separated from James. She felt her heart rate increase with the sensation that the population in the hallway had suddenly doubled. She did her best to ignore it, but the feeling of her lungs being caught in a vice increased until she had to fight the urge to flee. She had known that James would soon be gone, and she would be alone, but the reality felt quite different from her fanciful anticipation of it.

When she was approached by one of the Whitbury maids to show her where she needed to go, she found that her tongue would not obey her commands to speak. It felt swollen in her dry mouth.

"Are you well?" the maid asked, reaching out to take Celeste's bag.

"I..." Celeste took as deep a breath as she could manage and tried again. "I have just now realized that I left one of Lady Celeste's bags in the carriage." She did not wait for the girl's reply before pushing back through the crowd toward the exit.

As soon as she was outside, Celeste gasped for air. It took her a moment to catch her breath, but she did not stop for long. She had to act out the lie she had just told, so she made her way toward the stable house where the carriage would be, telling herself to enjoy the blissful fresh air while it lasted.

When Celeste stepped into the open yard, she paused, glancing around, unable to make a decision. She could ask for directions from one of the grooms, but her hands were already shaking, and she did not trust her ability to speak. Instead, she walked with her head held high as if she knew where she was going.

It did not take long to find the coach house, as large as it was, with several open archways in a row that could accommodate any number of guests and was situated right beside the stable. With a glance around to see if anyone was paying attention, she darted inside. The carriages were lined up in neat rows, and with the light flowing in through the large open arch, it took her very little time to find the Kingstone crest. She slipped inside where she could draw the blinds down for a moment of privacy.

The familiar pale pink upholstery and the faint smell of home calmed Celeste's mind and helped her to remember why she was going through this in the first place. She had to last long enough to satisfy her parents, discover Mr. Bellmoore's true character, and ascertain how many people had an expectation of a union between them. That would influence what she planned to do next.

Once she had regained her equilibrium, Celeste felt a little silly to have reacted the way she had. Even Bryn, as frightened as she was, had not fled from the house. Still, Celeste decided that a few more minutes to herself would be beneficial, so she closed her eyes and massaged her temples, drawing slow deep breaths.

When the door opened to reveal a large silhouette blocking the light, Celeste opened her mouth to scream, but only a hoarse whimper came out. Her heart was thumping so loud and fast that she thought the silhouette could hear it. She could not afford to bring attention to herself by getting into trouble.

"What are you doing in here?" a deep voice with an odd accent demanded.

Chapter Four

Whitbury Manor, Berkshire

Jacob had been brushing down his horse in the stable yard when out of the corner of his eye, he caught sight of a maid walking alone through the place. He had left what he was doing with the intention of finding someone to assist her, but then she had slipped into the coach house.

Jacob hesitated, waiting to see if she would emerge. He had not spent enough time with the servants in the stables to know if maids often frequented the coach house, but he doubted it. He could either follow her and make a fool of himself if it were all innocent, or he could neglect an opportunity to catch someone up to no good. Not that she looked much like a thief, but the coach house was part of his home, and whether she was skulking around or in distress, he could not ignore it. He glanced around, but no other servants were in the immediate vicinity for him to call on with any efficiency.

Jacob went inside. The carriages appeared to be undisturbed, so he made his way along the line, looking underneath and around each one. He had passed a few when he came to a carriage whose crest he did not recognize, the only one with its shades pulled down. As far as hiding places went, it was not the most inventive.

Jacob opened the door, catching the girl doing...nothing. She was just sitting there. It was clear that she was startled, the blush stealing across her cheeks visible even in the dim carriage, and her wide blue eyes made her appear much younger than her more mature frame. Jacob almost jumped back a step himself. It appeared as though the maid were about to scream, but nothing followed.

"What are you doing in here?" he asked, attempting some kind of accent other than his own. It took a conscious effort to remember he had a role to play here as a servant, and not a son of an earl.

The maid's eyes darted toward the exit as she tilted her head to see around him, no doubt assessing escape routes. He couldn't help a small sigh from escaping. She had said nothing, but her thoughts were so obvious that they may as well have been audible.

"I mean you no harm. I just wish to know what you are doing in the carriage house." He softened his voice, not wanting to frighten her more.

She sat staring agape at him for several moments before answering in a quiet voice.

"I forgot something. My lady sent me to fetch it. We arrived a half hour ago."

Jacob found that he did not have to put in a lot of effort to offer a reassuring smile. This maid's face was so open in her expressions that it would be more difficult not to smile. Besides, her reasons were sound enough.

"Did you find it?" he asked, offering her a hand down.

"Pardon?" she asked, staring at his hand and then up at his face once again.

"Your lady's item. Did you find it?"

"Oh yes, of course." She sucked in an awkward laugh and turned a darker shade of red. That was an odd reaction.

After a deep breath, the maid took Jacob's offered hand and alighted from the carriage, which he closed behind her. Strange, she did not appear to have any item on her person. She stood facing him for a moment, those wide eyes studying him.

With her out of the carriage and the sunlight showing her features, Jacob forgot for a moment why they were standing there. She was quite pretty. The blue of her eyes was complemented by the contrast in color from the even blush across her cheeks. Some of her golden hair was poking out from under her white cap. It was neither curly nor straight, but somewhere in between. He found himself curious as to what it would look like without the hindrance.

It wasn't until a horse whinnied from the stable beside them that

Jacob realized he was still touching her hand. Her un-gloved hand. He jumped back, unsure what madness had just overcome him. She seemed to startle out of the strange moment herself.

"I should return to the house. Thank you for your assistance, sir." She bobbed a quick curtsy and turned to leave.

"Wait," Jacob called, not sure why he was stopping her.

"Yes?" She turned only her head back toward him as if her body still wished to flee.

"Ah…" He searched for something to justify delaying her. "Do you have the item you forgot?"

The maid stared at Jacob for a moment or two with a blank expression before she uttered a strained sound halfway between a laugh and a gasp.

"Oh dear, what a state I am in today. I left it in the carriage again. I had best fetch it," she rambled as she hurried past him back in the direction they had come.

It was not long before she returned, her blush deeper than ever, with a book in her hand. A book? She was sent all the way back out to the carriage for a book?

"Whitbury Manor has a well-stocked library if your Lady wishes for something to read," Jacob could not help offering as the maid passed by again.

"Yes, I am certain you are right, but she is most particular in her choice of books." She waved a hand and shook her head.

"And what has her so enraptured? I am most curious." Jacob reached out, but she pulled back, holding the volume against herself.

"You are most impertinent!" She stood back, with her chin held high. "What my lady reads is her business. Getting this book back to her is my business, and you…" she looked him up and down. "Well, I do not precisely know your business, but I suggest you get on with it."

And with that, she gave an emphatic nod and left Jacob standing alone between the coach house and the stable in bewilderment. Whilst doing the right thing had been more important to him than his disguise, he did wonder if he should be stricter in avoiding interaction with the visiting servants in the future.

Chapter Five

When Celeste was free of the manservant near the coach house, she breathed a sigh of relief. She was convinced that could not have gone much worse. What if he asked someone about her, or recognized the Kingstone crest? No, that was unlikely. She had never been to Whitbury Manor before. She paused just a moment outside the door that led back into the main house through the kitchens. Taking a few measured breaths, she glanced down at the book she had taken from the carriage. In her haste, she had knocked the novel she had been reading during the journey onto the floor, and in the dim light, retrieved *Roadside Wheel Repairs* in its place. There was no way she would have been able to explain *that* had the inquisitive servant seen through her evasions.

As Celeste made her way back inside, she tried to avoid thinking back on the embarrassing turn of events, but failed. Being caught by that servant had given her quite the fright, but then she had lost all sensible thought when his attractive features were illuminated by the sunlight. He had an angular face with kind brown eyes under his well-defined brow. His windblown dark hair, hanging loose to his shoulders, was longer than was fashionable and could have used some attention, but it suited him well. Celeste had never considered laughter lines a feature of note before, but his lent his face an aura of safety.

Celeste sighed. Even before she had seen the man with any clarity, she had made a cake of herself. With any luck, he worked in the stables and would have no reason to come to the Manor, then they would never see each other again. The thought caused a pang of disappointment that she chastised herself for. She most emphatically was not willing to dwell on the attractiveness of any servant. It would be most inconvenient.

With her mind made up, and her mettle restored, Celeste sought out the maid who had approached her before, careful to conceal the title of her book once again.

The room she was shown to was, in truth, more akin to the size of a closet. And she was expected to share it with another maid. The beds were close enough that they would hear each other breathe. She held back a shudder, hoping her assigned roommate would be amiable.

"This is one of the good rooms," the maid informed her with a smile. "You'll just be sharin' with Betsy. If you need anything afore she returns, I'll be happy to assist you."

"Thank you." Celeste's voice came out in a whisper, and she had neglected to use her accent, but she did not think it was noted.

It was not lost on Celeste that the maid considered her to be very fortunate to be in that particular room. She had never considered how her servants lived, and so it was quite the shock. Bryn had not covered sleeping quarters in Celeste's brief education along the way, although she was aware that Bryn had her own room at Willoworth and Honeychurch House. Perhaps things were a little tighter during a house party. It had not seemed at all unreasonable to Celeste that the staff shared their living spaces with others until she was facing the lack of privacy herself.

Sitting down on the bed, Celeste clutched the book to her chest as she again fought that sense of panic she had felt in the hallway. The bed was not as hard as she expected, but neither was it as soft as she was accustomed to. She looked around the room and its sparse furnishings. It was dim, with only a small window, and barely enough space to walk around the beds. A small chest squeezed into the corner and a little round table sat under the window. With a pang of guilt, she did her best to not concern herself with what the worst rooms might look like if this were one of the best.

Celeste was not left to consider her surroundings for long, as she was soon joined by the housekeeper. Jumping to her feet, she almost tripped over the bag she had already forgotten was there, dropping the carriage book to the floor in the process. She kicked it under the bed, hoping the housekeeper would not notice.

"I am Mrs. Thatcher," the housekeeper greeted with neither a smile nor a frown. Her voice was neutral, with no emotional inflections, but also lacking the hardness Celeste had not known she was expecting.

"I am L...Elsie Coombe," Celeste fumbled, her mouth feeling like it was full of bread dough. She resisted the urge to roll her eyes at herself. Mrs. Thatcher did not seem to notice and went on.

"Should you have any queries, Miss Coombe, Betsy is the upstairs maid at your disposal, but you may come to me if she is unable to help you. Come, I'll introduce you."

Celeste nodded and followed the housekeeper. She was somewhat aware of the separation of up and downstairs servants, but a little vague on the details. As they made their way through the passage, Celeste spied James. She almost smiled at him but remembered what Bryn had said in the carriage. Another burly-looking manservant with oily black hair down past his ears, shoved past James then glared at him. Either Mrs. Thatcher did not notice, or it was not a part of her job to intervene, because she continued walking, and Celeste was forced to keep up. A quick glance back told her nothing about whether James was alright.

Celeste had no idea where they were headed, but as they ventured higher into the house, she figured they must be going toward the bedrooms. Once they made it to the upper levels, there was space to breathe, but only a little because Mrs. Thatcher kept up a rather fast pace. Celeste found herself struggling to maintain a dignified posture as she almost chased after the woman.

"Ah, Betsy," Mrs. Thatcher stopped to greet a maid walking in the opposite direction down one of the wide upstairs hallways. Celeste took advantage of the pause to catch her breath. The maid was much shorter than Celeste, with a round, childlike face and tight brown curls poking out from under her cap. Her brown eyes widened in alarm.

"I'm sorry, Mrs. Thatcher, I were on my way to tend to those garments, but Lady Adelle called for me again, this time it were for—" she rushed on, flustered, until Mrs. Thatcher held up a hand, interrupting her.

"Do calm yourself," she instructed, her tone a little short. "I stopped you to introduce you to Lady Celeste Honeychurch's maid, Miss Elsie Coombe."

Betsy's expression changed, and she gave Celeste an open, broad smile.

"Oh, I've heard all about Lady Celeste. Is it true—"

Again, Mrs. Thatcher had to silence Betsy, this time using a look of warning. Betsy bit her bottom lip enough to swallow it. Celeste withheld a giggle.

"Betsy, Miss Coombe is to be sharing your room for the duration of the party. Do you remember what we discussed?" Mrs. Thatcher's wide eyes and raised eyebrows made her look as though she were speaking to a child in a school. Betsy's eyes mirrored hers in recognition, and she nodded. Celeste had to suppress another smile at the childlike exchange. She almost had to bite her own lip to prevent herself from asking what it was they had discussed.

Once Betsy was sent to finish whatever she had been about, and Celeste was in Bryn's room, Mrs. Thatcher spoke again.

"Betsy is..." her lip twitched before she covered it with her neutral expression and continued, "please be discreet with anything she confides in you, for the respect of the house."

"Of course," Celeste agreed, surprised. "Is she likely to confide in me?"

"Oh yes," Mrs. Thatcher affirmed, smothering another twitch. Perhaps she was not so serious as she seemed. Without another word, she left Celeste to unpack Bryn's things.

Celeste took a moment to orient herself in the room. The walls were papered in mauve and featured a large tapestry depicting a country landscape above the fireplace to Celeste's right as she entered the room. They lent it a more feminine feel than the heavy mahogany four-post bed frame that dominated the center of the room and backed against the wall to her left. Three gothic windows welcomed a surprising amount of sunlight into the room from straight ahead, highlighting the floral arrangement on the mantel. Celeste took a few steps forward to better enjoy the fragrance and almost fell over her trunk on the floor at her feet, or Bryn's trunk, as she reminded herself. She had never been so clumsy in all her days. She shook her head, determined to pull herself together.

Before tending to the unpacking at her feet, Celeste gave in to the temptation to lay down on the large soft bed, giving herself leave to doubt, for a moment, her decision to switch places. When the door opened, she leapt to her feet, her heart beating a wild rhythm. She did not realize she had been holding her breath until she saw that it was Bryn. She stepped back over to the trunk, aware that she ought to have been unpacking dresses, rather than bidding farewell to feather down. When she opened it, it was empty save for a small scrap of paper at the bottom signed with a J. James had done her job for her. The kindness inspired a swelling warmth to grow in her chest, even as she wondered how he knew the feminine chores.

Bryn closed the door and stood with her hands clasped in front of her.

"How was your reception, My lady?" Celeste curtseyed.

Bryn smiled and looked down before sucking in her cheek and affecting a neutral expression. "Not as terrible as I feared. Lady Whitbury and her son, Lord Whitbury, greeted me and then made the proper introductions to those who have already arrived. Mr. Bellmoore wasn't there though, which I thought strange."

"It is a little," Celeste agreed. "Good manners would dictate that he be there to greet the woman he is supposed to marry. Perhaps he is yet unaware of the arrangement our parents have concocted. Mama did say that at least a week ago he did not know."

Celeste bit her lip. Part of her, that she did not share with Bryn, worried that Mr. Bellmoore did indeed know and meant to slight her. That could place her reputation in a precarious position. She needed to somehow find out.

"I will try to be discrete and find out what I can for you," Bryn offered. At first, Celeste thought she had voiced her thoughts aloud but then realized that Bryn was speaking of Mr. Bellmoore's absence.

"Thank you," Celeste nodded, clearing her head with a deep breath.

"Lady Adelle Poppery was one of the first ladies I was introduced to," Bryn picked up. "She is engaged to Lord Whitbury. Her sister and parents were with her, Lord and Lady...somebody, and there was also a Lord Mortcastle, who was a bit of an odd duck. Then we had tea in the front room. Did you have a chance to eat anything?"

"No, not yet, I will have something later." Celeste shook her head. She could not have eaten anyway for the sick feeling in her stomach. "Was anyone of my acquaintance present? Did the family appear to suspect anything?"

"Lady Whitbury did mention that she had seen your portrait in Honeychurch House and that I looked quite different. That was a little awkward."

Celeste almost fell over. It was too soon for a loose thread to pull their plan apart.

Bryn continued. "There were no other names in the introductions that I recognized."

"What did you say to Lady Whitbury?" Celeste asked, not daring to breathe.

"I said that the painter changed my hair color because auburn is not fashionable." Bryn bit her lip and appeared to hold her breath.

"Did she believe you?" Celeste had heard of such things but had to ask.

Bryn nodded.

"Oh Bryn, you scared me!" Celeste laughed and took several dramatic deep breaths.

After an awkward silence, Bryn asked, "What do we do now?"

"You have an hour or so to rest before making ready for dinner, but I should be asking you that question. What would you normally do at this time?" She wanted Bryn to experience life as a lady, even if that meant getting herself out of the way for a while.

"I press the gown for the evening and make sure everything is in order and that no mending is required. Which gown do you think I ought to wear?" She looked herself over.

Celeste moved to the armoire and selected a gown the color of spring grass that matched Bryn's eyes. She had never seen eyes that color on anyone else. They ought to be highlighted. Her dark auburn hair would further complement the overall look.

"I have never pressed a gown before. How is it done?" Celeste asked. Bryn's eyes widened until there was a white border around each iris.

"No, My lady, I will do it. I cannot have you doing my chores!"

Bryn reached forward for the dress, but Celeste held it away.

"Your presence in the scullery would cause the housekeeper to swoon, so you had best begin giving me some instruction," she laughed.

Celeste was surprised to find that she was keen to learn the new skill as Bryn explained as best she could without being able to demonstrate. Bryn spent the entire lesson switching between shaking her head and rubbing it, showing her discomfort, but in the end she had very little choice.

Chapter Six

Once Jacob had recovered from his stupor by the coach house, he wasted no more time moving his plan along to avoid the house party by becoming Mr. McKnell.

He entered the house through the kitchens to find Mrs. Thatcher, but she was busy somewhere else, so he left a message with Mrs. Cooper, the cook, saying that Tom wished to see her instead of having her come to Jacob. She could show up in the middle of his performance for his mother, and that would spoil the whole thing. Delegating Tom the task of explaining the situation to her was just being practical.

Half of Mrs. Cooper's brow scrunched, and her mouth hung open when Jacob bent down and leaned his face as close to her stove as he could stand and stayed there.

"Beggin' your pardon, Mr. Bellmoore..." she began in her thick northern accent. He grinned up at her, making her pause before she continued, "but 'ave you taken leave of your senses, sir? Are you quite well?"

Jacob's response was to laugh at the odd picture he must make. Mrs. Cooper looked as though she were about to speak again when Mrs. Thatcher entered the kitchens, stopping dead in her tracks at the sight of him. Her wide eyes and dangling jaw made her expression almost identical to Mrs. Cooper's. In that moment, Jacob wished he were an artist and could recreate the expression. They were most entertaining.

Mrs. Thatcher looked at Mrs. Cooper.

"Don't look at me, 'e just came in and star'ed roastin' 'imself," Mrs. Cooper attempted to explain. "I think 'e's quite gone mad. It 'appened to a cousin o' mine last year. 'eaded right to Bedlam 'e is."

"Thank you, Mrs. Cooper," Mrs. Thatcher said, her calm demeanor fixed in place. "Come away from there, young Jack. You're turning quite red; you'll do yourself a harm." She reached out a hand to assist him should he need it.

Jacob stood, his grin never shifting. It occurred to him that he could tell his mother he refused to participate in her little scheme and meet Lady Celeste on his own terms once he had some time to acclimatize to the idea that he was tied to the lady. That option involved facing a reality he was not yet prepared for. Besides, it lacked the sense of adventure he felt at the idea of becoming someone new. Not that burning one's head to appear feverish was all that adventurous. Perhaps he had cracked up, as his cook believed.

"I must say, you appear much happier than you did when you left on your ride. Are you resigned to the marriage, then?" Mrs. Thatcher observed, having seen him leave the house earlier. Despite the impertinence of the question from a servant, Jacob snorted in response.

"Hardly. I have a plan. I am occupied at the moment, but Tom will speak with you about it."

"If this nonsense is the occupation you speak of, I would suggest that you reconsider. Why do I need to hear it from Tom?"

"Ah..." Jacob was unsure what to say. On the one hand, she had a point. He could lay out the plan for her himself. On the other hand, Tom had a way of breaking through her armor that Jacob did not understand. She seemed to conclude that Tom would be the better source of information when Jacob took a full minute to decide how to answer her.

"Mrs. Cooper, would you be so kind as to prepare a cup of tea for Mr. Bellmoore? I shall have it sent up," Mrs. Thatcher instructed.

Jacob opened his mouth, but before he could speak, Mrs. Thatcher closed her eyes and nodded with a small sigh. "Alright, I will go and speak with Tom, but I don't want to catch you at that stove again." She wagged a finger at him as she had when he was young and left, making him smile. Jacob found it endearing that she still seemed to see the child version of him. It reminded him of a time when his father was still alive. How he would love to turn to him for advice in this situation.

With a sigh, he sought out the items he needed for a good theatrical performance of being ill before heading up to his bedroom.

When Mrs. Thatcher returned from speaking with Tom, she found Jacob in his bedroom, placing a pan of coals under the sheets of his bed, despite the warm weather. He had already splashed himself with warm water to mimic sweat and had been about to send for his valet to bring him into the scheme.

"Are you mad, boy?" Mrs. Thatcher demanded upon entering the room. He could not be sure if she referred to his plan to become a servant or the fact that she had caught him toasting himself earlier.

"You spoke to Tom?" he asked.

"Aye, and I think you're daft. It won't work. You will be recognized, for one. And people will talk. They're expecting you to make your engagement official, not disappear. Or suddenly happen to fall ill." She rolled her eyes.

"I am honor-bound to see this through, and I will do what duty requires if I cannot find a way out of this, but it is too soon. I need to see her from a distance first, find out what I can about her real character, not just what she presents in a drawing room."

"And how do you plan on finding anything out from the stables working for Tom? You won't even see her unless she rides," Mrs. Thatcher retorted all too reasonably.

"There will be time to sort that out. For now, I need to hide and avoid this party." Jacob willed his eyes to convey his desperation as his hands grasped at thin air.

"You can't hide from everyone unless you intend to stay up here."

"I would not last two days being confined like that." He shook his head. "Besides, I do not need to hide from everyone—just my family and whichever guests might recognize me."

"And what if you're caught?"

"Then I will be forced to join the party. But this will buy me some time to work out my situation." He did not realize he was holding his hands out in a plea.

Mrs. Thatcher sighed half a dozen times as she considered. "I can't keep everyone silent forever with something as hare-brained as this." She threw up her hands in exasperation.

"You will do it, though? You will help me?" he asked, feeling the beginning spark of hope.

Mrs. Thatcher sighed. "I suppose if you're quite determined to make a fool out of yourself, I can have a word to each of the maids. And I'll have to speak to Mr. Norman, but I won't be doing any lying for you, least of all to your mother, you understand?" She built up to a stern shaking of that finger again in his direction.

Jacob had not intended to involve Mr. Norman. The butler had only been with the household since Jacob's brother had become the Earl, but he trusted Mrs. Thatcher's judgment.

"Thank you, Mrs. Thatcher," he said with sincerity. "I shall need your advice on the matter. I have several questions."

Mrs. Thatcher sighed in disapproval, but it seemed like she would go along with it, nonetheless.

"We'll have plenty of time for that, but first you ought to be going to bed before you cool down too much if you want to be convincing. Just keep in mind that you will need to follow any cues I deign to give you when you're amongst the other servants. Besides, I don't want you baking whatever is left of your brains," she quipped under her breath, shaking her head, but Jacob heard her and laughed.

The next thing Jacob did was call for his valet.

After explaining his plans thus far, he had hoped to see some kind of reaction, but the man was too professional, so Jacob could not tell what he thought.

"You are an integral part of my plan, Giles," Jacob reiterated as he climbed into bed. "Oh, and I shan't be shaving."

Giles' eyes grew wide at that, but he said nothing. It seemed that having once been the late Lord Whitbury's valet meant that he would honor the eccentric wishes of his son.

Like many gentlemen, when Charles had become the new Lord

Whitbury, he had preferred to be addressed by his title at all times, including by his family, and he maintained a professional distance from the servants. He had not liked the idea of retaining anyone who had known him as a child, but Jacob liked the older servants. They were familiar. Jacob had asked to retain Giles, Tom, and Mrs. Thatcher, who were now the only original servants left at Whitbury Manor. Although Giles would soon be requiring a pension.

"As you wish, sir," Giles answered, his brow creased in either concern or disapproval, maybe both. Jacob nodded. It seemed his servants at least would not hinder his strategy.

When Jacob was ready, he asked Giles to send for his mother. He had climbed into the sweltering bed in preparation, any good he had done at the stove worn off by the time he was ready. Perhaps Mrs. Cooper and Mrs. Thatcher were right, and that had been a fool's errand.

When footsteps could be heard approaching the room, he hopped out of the bed and straightened it up. The relief from the heat was immediate. He went and stood by the window as if contemplating something very important.

"There you are, dear, I have been worried," Lady Whitbury greeted him upon entering the room. "Where have you been? You have not greeted any of the guests."

Jacob did not waste any time in confirming which guest's introduction in particular she lamented the loss of his company for. The lady his mother wanted him to marry all of a sudden was in his house. He shuddered without having to pretend.

"I..." he muttered before touching his head and dropping like a sack of potatoes. He hit his shin on the leg of his bed as he went down but managed not to react as the pain shot up and down his leg. He was certain to find an instant bruise there.

"Jacob!" His mother hurried over to him, summoning Giles to help him back to his bed, where he delivered his best performance in years. He groaned at random intervals and squeezed his eyes shut, not having to pretend at being in pain.

Jacob's poor mother fell for it hook, line and sinker. He had the decency to feel guilty about the worry line he had created between her eyes, but he had come too far to stop now. She felt his forehead but was not as alarmed as he would have liked. However, as she pulled back the blanket to reach for his wrist, the warming pan did its job, and her eyes widened at the rush of heat.

"Your hands are very warm," she commented. "How do you feel?"

"I'm perfectly...argh!" Jacob curled in on himself.

"Oh dear. Here, drink some water." She brought a cup to his lips.

Jacob sipped a little before giving an exhausted sigh and lying back.

"I am all right, Mother. I just need a little rest," he pretended to protest. "Could you please have the fire stoked? It's terribly cold in here." He pulled the blanket up to his chin and curled as close around the warming pan as he could without touching it under the blanket.

Jacob knew the sun was bright outside, and the room had been hot before he came in, so he was not surprised when his mother's brow puckered in concern. She felt his head again, and he seemed to be warming up. He could feel the beads of sweat rolling from his hairline down his face.

Without warning, Jacob's mother pulled on the blanket. Jacob managed to grip it just in time before she succeeded.

"Sweetheart, you need to cool down. Allow me to remove this blanket." She tried again.

"I am fine, Mother, just a little cold. Please, just allow me a little rest and privacy, and I shall be down directly." He pulled the blanket tighter and rolled away from her, closing his eyes.

"Well, I suppose it is a good thing I just made your excuses downstairs." She sighed and sat down on his bed beside him. She didn't speak for a few moments. "I had worried that you were overwrought by the news we spoke of earlier."

Jacob was not expecting the regretful tone in his mother's voice. He felt another pang of guilt and considered turning over and telling her the truth, but he knew that he would then be required to join the party. His only hope of creating sufficient distance to dispel the wedding rumors was to follow through with his plan.

After a short time, Jacob relaxed his shoulders and deepened his breathing. He even managed a faint snore, surprising himself.

When his mother left to allow him to rest, Jacob leaped out of his steaming hot bed, gasping, and splashed the remaining water from the cup onto his face. His valet was at his side in an instant with a towel and a fresh basin of water, much to Jacob's relief.

Jacob could stay in the sickroom until he was ready to face his future, but he worried that he might go mad in truth. He opened the window, but there was not much of a breeze, and he was craving the outdoors. He also wanted to be unobtrusive in his observation of Lady Celeste as much as possible, and being a servant was the perfect disguise for it. He was unsure how long he planned to pretend sickness. He did not know any real details of the activities planned for the house party, having escaped on his ride before asking. He would have to be very careful not to walk right into an outdoor activity, or someone taking a walk or ride around the estate. He still could not suppress the urge to get himself outside as soon as possible.

After cleaning himself up, scruffing up his hair, and then checking that the coast was clear outside his bedroom door, Jacob slipped out. Giles locked the room behind him to prevent anyone discovering his absence. He headed for the servants' stairs, wondering if the staff were yet aware of his temporary change in status. As he passed by maids he recognized and flashed smiles at them for reassurance, they blushed and turned away. Odd. They had never behaved that way before. He hoped none of them would break his confidence after all. He was not the most authoritative member of the household, so he supposed that pledging loyalty to him could carry some risk if they thought it might land them in any trouble.

As Jacob descended into the kitchens, Mrs. Thatcher rolled her eyes discreetly before scolding with a raised voice, "And what's a stablehand doing shirking his chores in the middle of the day? Don't think I don't know about you and Betsy." She waggled her imperious finger in his direction. His eyebrows shot up in a moment of surprise before her brief head tilt and intense stare instructed him to play his part better. She was looking at him like he was a few pence short of a crown. Right.

Jacob tried to look embarrassed at being 'caught' above stairs when he ought to have been in the stables. And for rendezvousing with a maid, apparently. That was creative. A few of the maids giggled behind their hands.

"I—I'm sorry, Missus. It won't 'appen again." He shuffled his feet for good measure.

"See that it doesn't, or I'll be speaking with Mr. McInnes." She always referred to Tom by his surname in front of the other servants. She maintained her gaze of steel, a natural thespian. Jacob had to fight hard not to smile at her dedication. He glanced around, trying for a look of chagrin.

The kitchens were full of servants Jacob had never seen before. They would be the staff of Whitbury's guests. He hoped that none of them who worked for his brother's friends would notice him. He had to return to the stables and get away from all the eyes on him as soon as possible, but just as Jacob was about to perform a humiliated exit, he stopped in his tracks. He recognized one of the maids as the one he had found in the carriage earlier. Her cheeks were bright as she stared at him with unmasked disapproval. He wondered if her blush was due to the way they had met, or the mock accusation. He hoped for a moment that her name was Betsy.

"Off with you now, or I'll be telling the stable master." Mrs. Thatcher snapped Jacob out of his reverie, her eyes boring into him as her lips pursed. He made a hurried exit, real heat in his cheeks this time. As he jogged toward the stables, he considered that whatever reputation Mrs. Thatcher had concocted for him, he had, in all likelihood, helped it along by gawking at the prettiest woman in the room.

Chapter Seven

～～⁂～～

At first, Celeste paid little attention to the servant standing in the shadowed entry to the kitchens. She could not see his face well, but as he stepped further into the room and was reprimanded by Mrs. Thatcher, Celeste's breath caught, and she averted her eyes. It was the man from the stables who had appeared at her carriage door. She felt heat fill her cheeks and hoped it was not obvious from the outside.

When she hazarded a glance in the man's direction, he was staring right at her. Her eyebrows lowered, and her chin pulled back. How dare he ogle her like that? Moments after being caught with another maid and appearing so disheveled, the scoundrel. Well, ogle was a strong word. He gaped at her as if he had never seen a woman before. He, a groundskeeper no less. Or groom, or footman, or whatever sort of manservant he was, staring at her like that. She had to remind herself that she was playing the part of a servant to prevent her from taking action that would give her away.

Celeste looked around at the other people in the room and noticed a few of them glancing between her and the servant. She could not afford to draw undue attention, so she forced down her indignation and relaxed her expression.

The maid, who had been introduced to Celeste as Betsy, came down the stairs and into the kitchens just as the manservant was leaving through the outer door. She stopped and looked around the room in confusion as several of the other servants began whispering and staring at her. All giggles and gossiping ceased with a stern look from Mrs. Thatcher.

Behind Betsy was the manservant Celeste had seen pushing James earlier. For the most part, Celeste had enjoyed meeting the other servants and found them to be quite friendly. He had been the exception to that. He turned out to be the valet of one of the guests. He only stayed in the kitchens long enough to demand a tea tray for his master, then looked on the rest of them with his lips pulled up on one side in distain before returning above stairs. At least with him around, no one would be accusing her of putting on airs.

Lost in her thoughts, Celeste could not remember what she was about. It took Mrs. Cooper handing her a cup of water and a scone to remind her. The cook had offered her a little something to tide her over until the much later dinner hour the servants had to wait for. Celeste thanked her and sat at the large wooden table to eat. She knew she did not have much time, so she attempted to keep her silent observations to a minimum. It was difficult with all the activity about her. She had never had any awareness of how alive below-stairs could be. There was as much bustle amongst the servants as any London street, with everybody seeing to their tasks and smiling at acquaintances as they passed, delicious aromas wafting through.

With reluctance, Celeste paused her musings when she was finished and stood. However, as she began to move away from the table, Mrs. Cooper's loud reprimand startled her into immobility. "'ere. What d'you think this is? I'll tell ye right now, I'll not be cleanin' up after ye like ye mam, no matter wha' hoity toity guest ye work for. Put tha' over there." She gave directions with her wooden spoon, waving it like a scepter. "Ye clean up after yeself in my kitchens."

Celeste nodded in embarrassment and did as she was instructed while all the other servants in the room stared at her.

"I'm so sorry, Mrs. Cooper, I forgo' my manners," she tried to recover by following the instructions straight away, with Mrs. Cooper all the while muttering away her displeasure.

"'ere I am, slaving away for all these ingrates, as well as the likes of them upstairs, and wha' do I get? 'er high an' migh'y Majesty 'erself leaving 'er crumbs and all sorts all over my kitchens, the cheek…"

Celeste did not wait to hear the remainder of the cook's tirade but headed down to the scullery, where there was a flurry of activity as the other ladies' maids pressed and primped and perfected their lady's gowns. Celeste just stood there, overwhelmed once again until Betsy noticed her.

"Miss Coombe? Or do you prefer Elsie?" she inquired.

"Pardon?" was all Celeste managed to squeak out.

"You're liable to be run down if you just stand there like a babe in the wood." Betsy carried on as if Celeste had answered her question. "That happened to me on my first week, me bein' scared stiff of all the other maids and such. Is that what has you all addlepated? Is this your first house party with your lady? Dear me. Pass me that gown, and I'll have you bang up to the mark. Don't you fret."

Celeste was so distracted that she had not even noticed that she'd retrieved Bryn's gown from where she had left it a few minutes before. She handed it to Betsy with a brief nod and an unconvincing smile. When she began to feel lightheaded, she gasped in a sudden breath. How had she forgotten to breathe? Giving herself a good shake, she followed Betsy, who was already pressing the gown, but only in places it was needed. Celeste would have wasted time going over the entire thing. Betsy's hands moved so fast as she fluffed and primped and checked the gown that Celeste could not follow every movement. She made a mental note to spend some time watching the other maids each day.

"There. Your lady'll shine everyone else down," Betsy smiled with kindness.

Celeste felt her eyes fill for reasons unknown.

"Thank you, Betsy."

"Not to worry, I'll keep you up to snuff," Betsy winked.

Celeste smiled at the expression and opened her mouth to ask where Betsy learned so much cant, but then closed it again, predicting that the answer could take some time. Instead, she smiled again and hurried up to Bryn's room, being very careful not to disturb the gown in her arms.

To say that Celeste helped Bryn dress for dinner would have been a falsehood. When the time came, Bryn did most of the work, avoiding Celeste's help unless she could not reach. Celeste followed her instructions with care, determined to learn. It was quite the adventure to see the other side of the manor, so to speak.

The time passed easier than Celeste expected. After her stressful introduction into being a servant, it was a welcome relief to be back in Bryn's company. She even found herself chatting about the day and what had transpired in the kitchens with that manservant who had been caught with Betsy, to which Bryn just gave a knowing nod. Such things must have been encountered by her before.

When it was time to style Bryn's hair, Celeste again found herself standing behind Bryn, with her hands suspended in the air awaiting instructions while Bryn did all the work. When Bryn did ask for some assistance attaching a hairpin at the back, Celeste's excitement froze, along with her body.

"I have no idea what to do," she admitted with horror. Aside from playing with dolls' hair as a child, she had very little experience in the matter. The disappointment she felt was a sharp stab in the bottom of her chest that seemed disproportionate to the situation.

"It will be alright," Bryn shrugged. "I don't need it."

She began readjusting, but Celeste did not wish for her to compromise her experience on the first night.

"No, I will ask one of the other maids for help. I'll pretend I injured my hand," Celeste suggested.

"It is not important, My lady," Bryn insisted.

Celeste pursed her lips. They had discussed this. Someone might overhear them if they were not well practiced at addressing each other by their assumed roles. Bryn mouthed a 'sorry' and bobbed her head.

"They will help me, won't they?" Celeste asked, unsure.

"Of course, they will. They must assist a lady's maid, but it really is not necessary."

Celeste cocked her head at this new information. There was a lot she did not know.

"Once you have someone, watch what they do, then we can practice some more tomorrow," Bryn sighed.

Celeste's frown turned into a smile, and she hurried to find Betsy. She found her carrying a dinner tray up for one of the other guests.

"Betsy, could you please help me?" Celeste whispered.

"Oh, for sure an' certain, once I've delivered this tray to Lady Adelle. What do you need, Elsie?" Betsy continued walking but inclined her head for Celeste to follow.

"You see, I—I have injured my hand, and I cannot seem to manage my lady's coiffure."

"Oh, dearie me, is it bad? Are you at risk of dismissal?" Betsy gave Celeste her whole attention.

"No, it was just a hairpin." Celeste had no notion of whether that was a believable story or not. "I expect to be recovered tomorrow."

Betsy nodded and then continued a story that Celeste did not remember her starting. "...then my cousin were working for a cantankerous ol' hen who sacked her for a hair in her tea. It's right hard to find work in that village, so she were done for..." She kept up her monologue until approaching the assigned door.

Celeste waited in the hall while Betsy delivered the tray, then led Betsy toward Bryn's room when she was done.

"You work for the Lady Celeste Honeychurch, don't you, Elsie? I heard she's a spitfire—is it true? I don't suppose you're allowed to say, being her maid and all. Still, I long to know all about..."

Celeste was not certain how to respond, or if she was even required to as Betsy went on. She had never heard of herself being referred to as a spitfire before, and it both confused and concerned her. She always took great pains to appear the very picture of a decorous young lady when in company.

"How did you know? About her reputation, I mean?" Celeste had to interrupt. It seemed the only way to get a word in. Betsy appeared not to mind, though.

"I have a brother, who works in Guildford, and their gardener is from Caterham on the Hill, where his brother's wife's father works as a coachman for the estate over the hill from hers."

Celeste gave up trying to keep an accurate picture of the thread of gossip. That was quite a network.

"Does the entire country speak ill of me? Er, her?" She blurted the question without thinking.

"Oh no, Elsie! Beggin' your pardon, I meant that as a compliment." Betsy touched her arm for reassurance. "We're all in awe of her, that is all. She's a right proper lady; what takes charge and don't let no one tell her what for. What it must be like working for 'er..." Betsy mused, staring off at nothing.

Celeste was dumbstruck. That did not happen often. The servants liked that she spoke her mind? Since she reserved that for the privacy of her home, it had to be someone among her own family's staff spreading the gossip. Whilst the sentiment was flattering, she was not certain she approved. She also did not like that it supported her mother's ideas of untrustworthy servants. For the time being though, there was nothing to be done but benefit from being privy to such things.

When they arrived, Bryn was attempting to see the back of her own head in the mirror.

"Here, My lady, let me fix that for you." Betsy went right to work without needing more than five words between them to know what Bryn wanted.

"Thank you. What is your name?" Bryn asked her, focusing more than usual on her speech.

"I'm Betsy, My lady." She bobbed a quick curtsy without releasing the hair in her hands, "and if it's not speakin' out of turn, may I say what a right honor it is to make your acquaintance."

Celeste was surprised. She did not expect Betsy to be brave enough to chat with her, or Bryn pretending to be her; this was getting confusing. It went against what Bryn had taught her in the carriage about being a servant. Celeste hoped that Betsy would not ask too many questions, or Bryn would eventually stumble over an answer she did not know.

"Thank you. It is nice to meet you too, Betsy."

Recognition dawned on Bryn's face as she spoke the name. After a few moments of silence, she asked, "Betsy, did I hear that you have a beau among the staff? That must be very exciting!"

Betsy made eye contact through the mirror Bryn sat in front of.

"Aye..." She paused with a dreamy look in her eyes for a moment before continuing. "He's the uh... stablehand. He's ever so handsome. Sometimes I get caught dreamin' about 'im when I'm s'posed to be doing my work, but he does make my heart go somethin' fast. First time it happened, I thought I was ill, but Mrs. Thatcher sorted me out. What a fella..." and on she went.

No wonder Mrs. Thatcher had been certain she would share confidences. Getting her to stop would be the problem.

"Did you hear? He was chastised in the kitchens earlier? I hope you did not find yourself in hot water with Mrs. Thatcher as well," Celeste asked with genuine concern. Despite her propensity to talk, she liked Betsy. She had saved Celeste a couple of times now, out of nothing but kindness.

Betsy laughed. "Naw, everyone knows I fancy him. I don't 'spect it'll change nothin'."

"If you are meeting during work hours, it could mean trouble," Celeste probed.

"He hasn't kissed me or nothin' misbehavin' like that, but my, I wish he would..." Again, she was lost in that dreamy stare, maybe imagining that very thing. Celeste felt her cheeks warm, uncertain whether the last part of that sentence was meant to be voiced aloud.

"Betsy, that is scandalous." Bryn's wide eyes flitted between Betsy and Celeste, and her brows drew upwards together in a steeple. She need not have worried. Whilst Celeste did worry a little for Betsy, she found her openness refreshing and amusing. In truth, she could understand the sentiment, having seen the man herself. Her estimation of him increased a little, knowing that he at least had not been taking liberties with the poor girl, and then staring at another in that bold manner. That did not mean he would not, but she could not rightly judge a man on something he had not done.

Celeste wished to put Bryn's mind at ease, so she said to Betsy, "Do tell us if he does kiss you. It is terribly exciting!"

Celeste was puzzled to find that she had to put in an effort to sound enthusiastic about such a report. She could not fathom why she would have any trepidation in hearing the information. There was no reason for her to care at all other than worry over Betsy's poor heart.

Once Bryn was ready and off enjoying her first evening as a lady, Celeste stayed in her bedroom, unsure of where she was supposed to be. Bryn had refused to give her any tasks to complete, and Betsy had excused herself to see to other chores, scarcely drawing breath between speeches as she left. Celeste wondered if Betsy would continue her monologue with only herself for company. She was verbose enough. When in the room they shared, Celeste would have to pretend to sleep, although there were no guarantees that would deter Betsy from chattering. She considered whether this might be the reason Betsy had her own space, rather than residing in the larger room with the other upper maids. It could be a temporary situation, due to the influx of guests and their servants, but she had to wonder.

ഏ····•····ഏ

Celeste had never been so bored. She ought to be enjoying having a night off from having to behave herself for company, but she was anxious for Bryn's return. When she did, all the tedium was worth it to see Bryn's full smile. That starry-eyed look from the carriage had intensified, and she took a moment to spin. Even in her dreamy state, Bryn did most of the undressing herself, but she did not resist Celeste's assistance quite so much.

"Do I need to ask if you had an enjoyable evening?" Celeste chuckled.

"Oh, it was wonderful! How can you ever tire of such luxuries? Do you know I did not have to stand once during dinner? And then there were the conversations without interruption in the drawing room, not to mention this fine gown, I fair felt like a proper lady..." Her eyes went out of focus.

Celeste smiled, biting one side of her lip, enjoying Bryn's delight more than she had anticipated.

"Who are the other guests? I presume they have all arrived now." Celeste was hungry for the details she was forfeiting.

Bryn thought for a moment, no doubt trying to recall names and so forth.

"I already mentioned Lady Adelle Poppery and her family. They were not at dinner, but I have learned who they are now. Her father is the Earl of Waverley, and the other guests were all arrived as far as I could tell. Oh, except for Mr. Bellmoore. His mother—"

"He was absent again?" Celeste interrupted with some alarm. Perhaps he had no intention of showing up at all. Not knowing if that would be a good or a bad thing had Celeste's stomach tying up in knots.

Bryn reached out a hand, then pulled it back, the other hand fidgeting with her skirt. Celeste offered a smile of reassurance.

Bryn continued in a gentle tone. "Lady Whitbury said that Mr. Bellmoore is not feeling quite the thing tonight. He kept to his room."

"He is ill?" Celeste clarified. All of her scheming would be for nothing if the gentleman were abed for the entire party.

"Yes, his mother apologized to me, er you. She said she expects him to recover soon, so I do not think it is anything serious."

"I suppose we will find out soon enough," Celeste sighed. She could feel the beginnings of a headache. "Who else was present?"

"There was a Mr. Goldsmith and his two sisters. They did not react as though there is a prior acquaintance. Do you know them at all?" Bryn paused. Celeste shook her head, relieved that she had never heard of them. "Other than those, there were two other gentlemen, Lord Tardington—"

Celeste gave a little gasp, causing Bryn to pause in alarm.

"What could Lord Tardington be doing here?" Celeste wondered aloud.

"Do you know him, My lady?" Bryn asked, holding her breath.

"We were introduced, but it was during my first season, and I have not seen much of him since. I have danced with him once or twice. With any luck, he will not remember me, 'though it is possible that he may," Celeste explained, tapping her mouth with her finger. They would have to be cautious around him, but he was often aloof, so they could keep interactions to a minimum.

"He is a rather fearsome gentleman, if I may be so bold," Bryn grimaced.

"I thought so too," Celeste agreed.

"He did not react when I was introduced to him as you, if that is any comfort. In fact, he barely spared me a glance," Bryn offered with a shrug.

"Then we may yet be safe. He has a reputation for being somewhat austere, socializing with his political peers for the most part. He appears to consider himself above the rest of society, but in our case, his reticence may be an asset." Celeste pursed her lips in thought.

"Yes, I believe you're right, My lady," Bryn agreed, her shoulders relaxing.

"That is enough of that 'My lady' business. I am Elsie, your humble maid." Celeste affected her accent and bobbed a curtsy to emphasize her point, making Bryn smile.

"I keep forgetting that, My—Elsie."

"Hmm," Celeste narrowed her eyes at Bryn with a smile, making them both chuckle. "Who was the last gentleman?"

"Oh! Lord Blakely—" Again, Bryn waited for Celeste to indicate if the name was familiar before continuing.

"I have heard of Lord Blakely, but we have never met." Celeste shrugged, beginning to relax. It appeared that they may get away with the swap after all.

"He is a friend of Mr. Bellmoore's from school," Bryn added in.

Celeste nodded and gave a sigh of relief. It appeared they had little to fear from the guest list. It was a great relief indeed.

"Have you enjoyed yourself tonight?" she asked Bryn, confident in the answer.

To Celeste's knowledge, Bryn had never giggled in her adult life, but she did so as she described her evening. It sounded enchanting, and the fresh perspective made Celeste miss it a little, since the pressure of meeting Mr. Bellmoore was not even present with him being unwell. Still, she was very happy for Bryn and looked forward to her animated retelling of each event to come. She might even dare a peek if she could think of a way to do so without drawing attention to herself.

Chapter Eight

Early-morning chores in a stable house were not activities the people in Jacob's usual circles of acquaintance would consider entertaining, but to his surprise, he was enjoying the work. The complex was already alive with activity when Jacob arrived. He had thought he had risen early with the dawn, but the yard already had horses being exercised in it, and all the arched doors to the coach house were open with coachmen preparing for the day ahead. He intended to head for the stalls to offer his help with the horses, since his lack of knowledge would be a hindrance anywhere else. His mere presence caused enough whispering to slow the morning almost to a halt, despite them all knowing he would be there.

He had snuck out of the house wearing some borrowed clothes of Tom's, including a floppy old tricorn. He suspected the hat may have been Tom's way of having a little fun with his wardrobe. It was so well-worn that it may have even belonged to Tom's father. Despite the ridiculousness of wearing something so far out of fashion that even the servants had cast him sidelong glances, it made Jacob smile. He appreciated Tom's humor, not to mention his help.

Tom noticed the lack of activity and cracked a joke about Jacob sleepwalking out to the stables, and that was that. The men had a laugh, and work moved on. Tom had Jacob feeding and running errands to begin with, but as he proved himself willing, he was given more to do. He had no idea how Tom kept everything running so smoothly every day.

Before the guests were ready to depart for church services, Jacob had a quiet word with Tom and excused himself with a borrowed length of rope in hand. He needed to return to his room to continue his ruse for his mother, but entering and exiting the house was causing a bit of a stir if Mrs. Thatcher's reactions were anything to go by. He could try to learn the appropriate timings for the comings and goings of the servants and where he ought to fit into that, but in the meantime, he needed easy access to his bedroom. The rope would give him that.

As a boy, Jacob had always loved the added attention from his mother when he was ill, but this time it was proving to be exhausting. Rushing back from the stables to his room and leaping into bed with that stifling warming pan was more than a little unpleasant. However, she insisted on visiting to see how he fared, and Giles could only put her off for so long under the pretense that he was sleeping. At least he did not need to wet his face to pretend to be in a sweat after his mad dash. It was still preferable to being stuck up there all day with nothing to do.

"Hmm. You are not feverish, but you are warm. We shall have to see how you fare. I am sorry if I have brought this upon you, Jacob." She examined his forehead and cheeks with the back of her hand. As she shifted her weight on his bed, it forced Jacob uncomfortably close to the warming pan under the blanket. His heart raced of its own accord in line with the anticipation of a nasty burn.

"Do not make yourself uneasy, Mother," Jacob tried to reassure her, but he gasped as she moved again, forcing his knee to connect with a hot edge.

"Oh dear," she fussed, standing up to better assess his condition. "Perhaps I had better send for Doctor Fitzpatrick."

Jacob closed his eyes to block the sight of the worry lines appearing on his mother's face.

"I will be well, Mother," he reassured her. "Just don't have the first banns read in church before I have the chance to speak with Lady Celeste, will you?"

"Oh, my dear boy, of course not! We do not have to make it official just yet." She reached down and stroked his cheek. "You do feel a little cooler already. That must be a good sign," she mumbled.

"I will watch over him while you are at services, My lady," Giles hinted with a gentle nod.

"Yes, of course. Thank you, Giles," she acknowledged, glancing at the clock on the mantel. After a few more pleasantries, she finally left.

Jacob wasted no time in leaping out of the bed and heading for the open window.

"Are you certain this course of action is worth the difficulty?" Giles asked, his voice soft. It was so unlike him to offer anything by way of an opinion that it left Jacob stunned a moment, but he covered it by focusing on recovering his breath with the gentle breeze coming in.

The truth was that Jacob was not sure, but the freedom he had felt all morning in the stables was worth pursuing it a little longer.

By the time Jacob washed up and returned to the stable house, things had begun to settle into a nice rhythm. Then the guests returned from church, and the chaos began all over again. People bustled about as horses and carriages were disembarked, taken care of and returned to their proper places. He avoided being near any of the guests and kept his head down in the washing bay, content to be another pair of hands for Tom. He may not be familiar with all the goings-on in the stable house, but at least brushing down and cleaning horses was something he knew well. From a young age, Jacob's father had insisted on teaching him that, gentleman or not, if he were going to have a horse, he ought to learn how to keep it.

As the day wore on, the weather had the audacity to be very fine, inspiring several of the guests to go on a late afternoon ride. Tom seemed to have no issue with using Jacob's extra hands while he had them, and after all of Tom's cooperation, Jacob was determined to help as much as he was able.

Tom began barking orders in every direction so that the guests would not need to wait, and Jacob leaped into action, almost startling the mare whose stall he had invaded. He settled his movements and soothed her as he worked to make her ready.

"Jack, take Aphrodite to the block for Lady Celeste. Peter, dinnae send Maggie out today, she needs to be re-shoed. Saddle Juniper instead..."

Tom continued to hurl instructions. but one name stood out, Lady

Celeste. It was obvious that Tom had assigned him to that lady on purpose.

Ignoring the urge to run in the opposite direction, Jacob led Aphrodite out to the yard, speaking to her as he did so, and lined her up for Lady Celeste, who waited by the mounting block. He reminded himself that this was what he wanted, an opportunity to see what she was like. He glanced at her from under the brim of the old hat he had pulled low to avoid detection. His first impression was one of relief. She smiled with fondness at her maid, obstructed from his view by the hat, who must have been saying something amusing. She was not the cold harpy he had feared. She had red hair styled neatly under a bonnet adorned with fewer ribbons than he would expect from someone of her status and wore a pale blue riding habit. He did not expect to feel any kind of instant connection, but he was a little disappointed to feel nothing at all aside from relief.

He gave Aphrodite another pat and approached the women.

"Good afternoon, My lady, Miss." He nodded to them both in turn, not certain if he was supposed to be greeting them or just handing over the horse. Being so friendly with the servants himself, he found that he was unsure of the proper protocol.

As he took a tentative glance up, the maid turned her face to him. Jacob froze. She was the one from the coach house, whom he had seen later in the kitchens the previous afternoon. Her blue eyes narrowed at him. It was not unlike the look she had given him then, so it was not difficult to ascertain the source of her reaction. It would be tied up in that story propagated by Mrs. Thatcher. Wonderful. Mr. McKnell had existed for a day, and he already had an unsavory reputation.

Lady Celeste looked at her maid, probably noting the same expression Jacob saw, her eyebrows rising in surprise. Her attention then turned to him.

"Good afternoon, Mr....?" She waited for his name. What was it again? Oh, yes.

"McKnell." His voice cracked.

"Thank you, Mr. McKnell." Lady Celeste nodded toward him as she mounted the horse and settled herself in the saddle. "My maid, Miss

Coombe, is fascinated by horses."

"Is she?" He was surprised, but unaccountably pleased. "Perhaps she would like to see the stables once everyone is away." Too late, Jacob realized that he had neglected his phony accent. Blast.

"I am sure she would be delighted, thank you," Lady Celeste accepted for her maid.

Miss Coombe cast her mistress a look of disbelief. The way she cocked her head with her eyes widened almost looked like a glare. It was odd, but they behaved more like friends than mistress and maid. He had never seen a servant cast such a bold expression before, nor the reaction. Lady Celeste blushed and looked down at the ground. The horse seemed to feel the sudden tension and began to shift her weight around. Jacob was about to reach out, but Lady Celeste was faster and adjusted her demeanor in an instant, speaking softly to Aphrodite whist stroking her neck.

A prickling on the back of Jacob's neck had him looking around toward the entrance to the stable yard. Mounted on a black stallion a few feet away was the vile fellow from the previous day, the one who had inspired Jacob's disguise. His gaze raked over the women, and Jacob felt his own eyes narrowing, and his muscles tense in response.

"Mortcastle!" Another gentleman approached from behind. Jacob knew that voice and averted his face, holding his breath. A moment later, Zachariah Carringham, Lord Blakely now, rode up beside the man Jacob had just been sizing up.

"Blakely," Mortcastle acknowledged without a glance. Jacob was unsure whether Mortcastle was his name or title, but it mattered little.

Jacob hoped the gentlemen would soon be done with their pleasantries and leave without looking down at him. All it would take would be a glance for Jacob's best friend since childhood to recognize him, no matter Jacob's unshaven face and poor state of dress. Jacob had been worried that there might be a few guests he might be acquainted with attending the party, but he had not been aware that Zach was coming. His elder brother, Nathaniel, had been close friends with Jacob's brother when they were at school and had died of an accident a year earlier. Had Jacob given it any thought, he might have anticipated that Zach might attend in his place, out of duty.

"Jack?"

Drat. Jacob looked up, certain the grimace he felt was clear on his face. He hoped it was sufficient silent communication to implore Zach not to draw attention to him.

"Yes, My lord?" Jacob made the accent a little thicker. Zach's lips twitched, and his blue eyes became brighter.

"Uh, see that my horse has a proper brushing next time. He was shockingly dusty this morning."

Jacob let out a sigh of relief that was more audible than he intended, but no one reacted to it.

Zach turned to the man beside him, who had the presence of a vampire. "Lord Mortcastle, let us unite with our party. Are you joining us, Lady Celeste?" Both the lady and her maid looked up.

"Do say you will, Lady Celeste," Lord Mortcastle begged, with a smile that Jacob thought was meant to resemble delight.

"Yes, thank you," Lady Celeste answered with a small nod. Zach smiled and waited for her as they joined the others for their excursion.

Despite Jacob's hesitation in wishing to marry Lady Celeste himself, he did not care for the marked attention this Lord Mortcastle gave her as they rode away. There was no reason to feel that way, but Jacob had a sudden urge to protect every lady at the party. It made no sense. There was nothing obviously sinister in the man's address, but the sudden pumping of blood through Jacob's veins and the tensing of his gut tempted him to abandon his disguise and go after them. Were it not for Zach's presence, he may have done just that, but Zach was a true gentleman, and Jacob felt confident in the lady's safety with him there.

It took Jacob longer than it should have to realize that he had been left alone beside Lady Celeste's maid. When Miss Coombe made to leave, he ought to have let her go. It was stressful enough that he expected Zach would return later for an explanation. Jacob did not want to complicate his situation further by spending extra time with a maid who might see through his disguise.

Despite his very sensible thoughts, Jacob found himself voicing the opposite.

"Are you ready fer ye tour, Miss?" Jacob offered a bow and gestured toward the door to the empty loose boxes. He could not miss the eyebrow Miss Coombe raised at his accent. It was woeful even to his ears that time. He forced a smile to cover the grimace that was trying to occupy his face.

"Certainly, Mr. McKnell." She flashed him a smile that was both condescending and amused. Was she reacting to her impression of him from the day before or indicating that she was aware of his pretense? Jacob was all of a sudden unsure of himself. The accent might have given away that he did not belong there at all, but he also could not be certain that the maids had not gossiped about his odd request to be addressed as a servant either. He should have allowed her to return to the house. He was already going to be forced to confide in Zach. He did not want to widen his circle to anyone else outside of his household. He inhaled a fortifying breath. He was in way over his head.

Miss Coombe was still standing there, waiting. Jacob pulled himself from his thoughts, but he was not sure what to do next. He felt his chest tighten and his heart rate increase as he tried to think fast. On a normal day, he would offer his arm, but he had no idea if that was something a real stablehand would do. The feeling of imminent drowning intensified. She already knew something was off, so he had to be careful.

"McKnell. Would you care to show your guest around?" Tom startled him from the stall he was clearing. Bless the man, he was offering a lifeline. Jacob almost gasped in relief.

"Aye, if you'll come this way, Miss." Jacob gestured for Miss Coombe to precede him. As she passed by him, her hand brushed against his with a whisper of a touch. It was purely accidental, but it sent a jolt through him that reminded him of an evening amusement with Zach's family involving an electrifying machine. Though, the contact with Miss Coombe lacked the unpleasant bite the device had produced. Jacob had more pressing things on his mind though, so he shook his head and followed behind.

With the patience of a saint, Tom ended up laying aside his work and guiding them around the well-kept stable complex. It was large enough to keep them walking for over half an hour. He took the time to explain things Jacob knew a little about, and did a far greater job of it than he ever could. Those details would help him with his tasks later, so he paid particular attention.

At the end of the tour, Miss Coombe turned a blinding smile on Tom.

"Thank you so very much, Mr. McInnes, for the lovely tour."

Tom blinked a few times, mumbled something in return, then went whistling back to his work. Jacob chuckled at his reaction to a smile and a few kind words from a beautiful lady.

"Is something amusing, Mr. McKnell?" Miss Coombe turned her wide blue eyes on him.

"Yes," he answered with a wide smile but offered nothing more.

Miss Coombe's eyes narrowed, and her expression turned calculating. What had he said? Jacob's smile dropped, and his blink rate increased as he watched her face. He was unaccustomed to someone scrutinizing him with that intensity. The ladies he usually conversed with were practiced at coy glances rather than staring through his soul. They were also often far more interested in his brother, or at least his title.

"Would it have something to do with your ridiculous accent, or is that a secondary amusement?"

Jacob's eyebrows shot up. Miss Coombe had a sharp wit. Wielding it in his direction meant trouble. Jacob did not wish to give anything away, but he needed to guide her attention away from him. He did want to learn more about his potential bride; perhaps Lady Celeste's maid could help him with that.

"Alright, I confess that my accent was a farce," he answered with a shrug. "I was raised a gentleman but am a younger son and obliged to earn a living, if you must pry. The accent helps me to blend in." A little truth might help his redirection, even if the context was made up.

Miss Coombe believed him if the blush stealing across her face was anything to go by. Or the way all of her facial muscles seemed to fall a little at once. Jacob felt a small pang of guilt for that. When she did not answer, he changed the subject. "I was amused by that weapon you used on poor Tom. He may never recover."

"Whatever do you mean?" she asked, her brow creased in what appeared to be genuine confusion.

"You honestly do not know?" He peered into her eyes, searching for false modesty, but found none. Perhaps genuine humility came with being a real servant.

"Did I do something wrong?" she asked, swiping some golden hair out of her eyes that had escaped the white cap she wore. "I thought I was being everything congenial. I really am grateful for his taking the time to lead me on such an informative tour." She shifted her weight from foot to foot and fidgeted with her apron. The pink spread in an attractive gradient across her cheeks, but Jacob could only enjoy that for a moment before good manners won out.

"I refer to your smile," he said with a gentle smile, hoping it would reassure her. "I meant it as a compliment."

"Hmm." She peered back at him, those eyes narrowing again.

Jacob squirmed under her scrutiny, back in the place he had diverted her from, hoping he were not transparent. He could not help thinking that she had missed her calling and ought to have become a governess. She would have no difficulty in eliciting confessions of misbehavior out of her charges or inspiring circumspection to avoid that interrogating gaze.

Jacob tried to think of something clever to say, but his mouth had gone dry, and his wit seemed to have left him to fend for himself.

"I see," Miss Coombe mumbled, and he hoped she didn't.

"Do you always take praise so well?" he asked with false arrogance, his heart in his throat. To his immense satisfaction, the pink already in her cheeks rose to highlight most of her face, making her look like a painting. It made his heartbeat slightly erratic.

"Forgive me, I did not believe it to be genuine." The color on her face intensified into more of a red and her eyes widened. "That is to say..."

Despite being reasonably certain he had just been insulted, Jacob was also amused by her thoughts spilling out aloud.

"Do you believe the compliment to be untrue, or me insincere?" He wished the question unsaid as soon as it was spoken. Believing she had insulted him was preferable to having it confirmed after all, and his voice did not carry any hint of the amusement he felt in the background.

Miss Coombe's eyes widened.

"I am surprised you would ask such a question." She crossed her arms over her chest as she pulled her chin in and spoke with the same arrogance he had affected a moment before. He was surprised too. The question was not one a gentleman ought to ask, it was far too direct.

Miss Coombe continued to glare at him. Jacob had never found defensiveness endearing before, but he was enjoying their banter, and whilst he did not wish for her to discover the truth about him, he also did not want the repartee to stop, even as he felt himself tense. "And I am surprised you would insult my character on so short an acquaintance."

Jacob could see as he said it that he had been correct. Her inability to stand still as she looked up and down his face told him that she had indeed assumed him to be the kind of man who gave out meaningless compliments for whatever purpose she thought he had. It was a small thing, and he knew she had more reason to doubt his character than not. Why he should care what she thought of him was anybody's guess. Nevertheless, the sting was real. She thought him a rake.

"Forgive me." Miss Coombe looked at the ground. "I am prone to hasty judgment. It is a fault of mine. I—forgive me." She offered a minute curtsy and fled in the direction of the house, leaving Jacob once again staring after her. He was uncertain when the teasing had turned serious, or what had just happened, but he was confident that it was his fault.

Chapter Nine

Celeste ran into the manor and hid like a frightened cat in the sleeping quarters she shared with Betsy. She had to catch her breath. How had she allowed Mr. McKnell to disarm her so? She did believe him to be a flirt but had not intended to offend him. She had meant it when she asked his forgiveness, and yet she could sense that there was something off about him. His boorish boldness for one. Then there was his lackluster accent, although he did have a good reason for that.

Mr. McKnell had said that he used his false accent to fit in, which was quite boring and believable. However, Celeste questioned whether that was all there was to his story. He was hiding something, she was sure of it. He was as defensive as she was, and she was hiding something herself. Perhaps he really was higher born, but in addition to being a younger son, the family had fallen on hard times. Or maybe he was a gambler or hiding from the law. He could be a pirate in disguise. No, that one would make the whole accent subterfuge backwards.

Celeste shook her head. She was becoming more fanciful with every suspicion. She had an unfortunate habit of believing things before finding out that they had been exaggerated. Although in this case, it had not been idle gossip but a scolding from the housekeeper that led to her impression of him being a Romeo. That was only supported by Mr. McKnell's constant use of charming smiles during conversation. She felt her face warm just thinking about it.

One thing was certain; Mr. McKnell seemed to see through Celeste with his amber gaze. Not that she had noted the color of his eyes. She squeezed her eyes shut and shook her head, but that solidified the image of his face in her mind.

She thought back on the compliment he issued of her smile. She knew full well that flattery could be a devil's trick, but the hurt she had seen in his eyes when she accused him of being shallow made her question her assumption that flattery was all it was. If she were honest, she would admit that part of her wanted him to have meant it. That was what made him dangerous. His face appeared to be both strong and sincere, his eyes sparked with intelligence when he spoke, and his voice was just the right balance of depth and warmth. She could well see how Betsy or any other maid might dream of meeting someone so handsome and engaging as him in the stairwell or some other secluded spot.

Celeste stopped her mind in its tracks and calmed her breathing. Her thoughts were reprehensible. Had she not, only that morning, attended church services with the other servants? She offered a silent repentant prayer and promised that she would read twice as much as usual from the Bible before bed, as penance for her thoughts.

Celeste took a moment to breathe and solidify her resolve. She would not think of Mr. McKnell any more than any other person she encountered, and certainly not entertain even an errant notion of a stairwell. She could not risk drawing attention to herself. More than her reputation alone was on the line if her secret were to be discovered. As much as Celeste had tried to reassure Bryn that all would be well, the consequences could be disastrous if they were found out. Just as she feared.

With a sigh, Celeste rallied herself and went into the kitchens to find out if Mrs. Thatcher needed her anywhere. She imagined she was supposed to be mending or some such. She had already looked at the gown Bryn planned to wear to dinner earlier in the day and could see nothing amiss. In the meantime, she might as well be useful to someone and gain some practice in her new skills.

When Mrs. Thatcher insisted that the party would return at any moment and that she ought to be waiting in her mistress's room, she looked at Celeste with confusion. Celeste had committed another faux pas she knew nothing about. She rubbed her face with both hands, feeling weary. Why did she ever come up with this folly?

When the party returned from their exercise, it was a welcome diversion from Celeste's thoughts. Bryn needed to change out of her riding habit, and Celeste was waiting for her as she entered the room.

"Oh, Lady—Elsie!" she exclaimed with a lightness Celeste had not seen before. "I have not been on horseback for many a year. I had forgotten how much I enjoyed riding!"

"Did you ride as a child?" Celeste asked, surprised.

"Oh, yes." Bryn smiled at a memory. "Papa taught all of us how to ride, but I haven't had the chance of it since going into service."

Celeste smiled, unable to help but be pulled along by her enthusiasm. Bryn had lifted her mood in an instant.

"We shall have to ride together more often when we return," she determined. Bryn's face lit up at the idea.

"I would love that, My—Elsie," she corrected herself again at a look from Celeste. "Are you enjoying your time as a maid?" Bryn bit her lip and fidgeted with her fingers.

"Yes, although I am in desperate need of some tutelage. I am making a cake of myself at every opportunity. I have no idea what I am supposed to be doing. I only know that I am doing it wrong."

There was a stretch of silence between them for a few moments.

"I have a little time now before dinner. I can help you," Bryn offered.

"I am desperate to accept, but are you not fatigued?" Celeste asked.

"I am a little, I will admit it, but not so much that I will draw attention to myself. After dinner, I should have some time also."

"As long as it is no bother. I am quite lost," Celeste laughed. "I am earning myself some very odd looks, so I will have to first tell you my woes, even though they are quite embarrassing."

"Of course, it is no bother."

Bryn smiled and listened as Celeste told a theatrical version of all that had happened, finishing with her suspicions regarding Mr. McKnell. She did not include that she found his smile charming, or that her heart had fluttered when he had explained his compliment. Those things were not necessary since she had no intention of ever experiencing them again.

Once Bryn had explained to Celeste that she did not answer to the housekeeper, but directly to her lady, Mrs. Thatcher's reaction, and a few other details, began to make more sense. Celeste should have known that since Bryn answered to her, but her mother had the run of their home. Had Celeste been taught these things and tuned them out, or was her education in household management so lacking?

Afterwards, Bryn walked Celeste through more of the basic duties she would perform at that time of day. Celeste noticed that Bryn often used it as an excuse to save Celeste from the work and do it herself. There were so many chores. She had no idea how Bryn achieved so much every day, and she knew that no matter what their plan was, Bryn had no intention of allowing Celeste a greater workload than was necessary.

After about an hour, Bryn mentioned with an apology that it was time to make ready for dinner.

"I am sorry, My lady. If I could stay..." She looked as if she expected an instruction to do just that, but Celeste would have none of it.

"Nonsense. You must go and enjoy yourself. I insist upon it. And no more of this 'My lady.' I thought we agreed that you are the lady now."

"I'm sorry...Elsie." Bryn shook her head. "It seems awfully presumptuous to call you anything else." She blushed bright red, matching her hair.

Celeste smiled in understanding. "Yes, it does take some getting used to, but I like using our Christian names, even though mine is not real. Now, let us make you presentable to all those gentlemen out there."

"Very well."

Celeste thought she noticed a slight blush return to Bryn's face. "Or is there one in particular?"

Bryn began to fidget.

Celeste said nothing more as she attempted to assist Bryn but noticed that the blush did not recede, and Bryn's eyes looked everywhere but at Celeste. By the time they were working on Bryn's hair together, Celeste was grinning at her through the mirror she was seated in front of.

"I know nothing can ever be between myself and a gentleman—I haven't forgotten my place," Bryn broke the silence, speaking faster than usual.

"Bryn," Celeste took her lightly by the shoulders, "you have only two weeks for this house party, so I suggest you do forget your place and enjoy it."

Celeste did not release her until Bryn's wide-eyed expression softened enough to appear less like a frightened animal.

"Thank you, My—I mean, Elsie. I know I cannot forget entirely, though." Bryn managed a shaky smile. Celeste leaned down and rested her chin on Bryn's shoulder.

"Bryn, I know we did not start out as friends, because you are my maid, but I hope we shall be now, after this. And I truly do wish you the best. If some gentleman did fall in love with you, it would make me very happy."

Bryn looked through the reflection into Celeste's eyes for longer than a few seconds, perhaps for the first time since they had met. Celeste's smile held a gentleness, often foreign between lady and servant, and Bryn had to swipe at the corner of her eye.

"Do not get emotional, or I shall cry." Celeste stood, reaching out to Bryn as she did. When she also stood, Celeste offered her a light squeeze and sent her off to dinner feeling for the first time in her life like she had a real friend.

As Celeste gathered with the other specialized servants for their evening meal, she was preoccupied with all she had learned from Bryn already about her role. She noticed, as Bryn had mentioned would be the case, that most of the servants were not there, due to differing mealtimes based on hierarchy. Also, Mrs. Thatcher had organized all the visiting staff according to the rank of their masters and mistresses so that everyone knew their place. All of that proved to be helpful to know so that Celeste did not find herself sitting amiss or at the wrong time.

Betsy was an upper maid and so was not among those eating, but she happened to be passing by behind Celeste and let out a sigh that was fit for the stage. Celeste followed her lovesick gaze to see Mr. McKnell entering the kitchens from the outer door that led to the side of the house. Mrs. Thatcher's brow lowered in consternation as he picked up a plate and sat down beside a valet Celeste was not familiar with. Celeste expected Mr. McKnell to be addressed for sitting at the table at the wrong time, but after he settled into amiable conversation with the man beside him, the housekeeper merely shook her head and turned away. Celeste looked in the direction of Mr. Norman. Perhaps it was the butler's job to scold him. Or the stable master's. Was he even meant to be eating in the manor, or was he supposed to take his meals in the stable house? She had no idea. Either way, Mr. Norman did nothing more than purse his lips and pause a moment in his conversation. It seemed that Mr. McKnell was beyond reproach.

Celeste did her best not to stare, or notice Mr. McKnell at all, as intriguing as the situation may be. Noticing anything about him was counterproductive. Wondering if he had noticed her was not a thought she could dismiss with ease. It made her self-conscious. She hoped that no one else noticed how she adjusted her tired posture to one of advantage, not that any posture would be attractive in such an ugly dress as the very plain and practical brown one she had chosen to wear to be as invisible as possible. She berated herself for caring at all what he might see if he happened to glance her way.

Celeste jumped a little as Betsy spoke close to her ear, afraid her thoughts had been transparent. As it was, she became aware that she had been sitting there with her fork suspended in mid-air halfway to her mouth. She finished the journey and almost choked on her food.

"Is he not the handsomest man in all the world?" Betsy breathed. Celeste was mortified to be caught, but as she looked at Betsy, the maid was not paying even the slightest attention to her. She was gazing at Mr. McKnell himself and seemed oblivious to all else. Celeste had to smother a smile with the back of her hand at the wistful expression.

"Yes, he is," she agreed without thinking. She looked in the direction of Mr. McKnell, not two spaces removed from the man across the table, and was mortified to see him watching her. She felt every degree of warmth in her body rush to her face; from so short a distance it was impossible that he had missed her agreement. He would have also seen her staring like a fool who did not know how to eat a moment ago too. She looked away, not wanting him to think she was the kind of maid who would welcome his attention. Indeed, as handsome as he may be, she desired far more in a man than a handsome face and the ability to make one's heart dance about. She wanted freedom more than anything. To be herself without always being told what to do. And she wanted to laugh.

A sudden shriek and the distinctive sound of crockery breaking drove all other thoughts from Celeste's head, and she was on her feet in an instant. She saw a commotion between the cook and a kitchen maid by the stove, and hurried over to offer assistance.

"I'm sorry, I'm sorry." The young girl was weeping as she clambered to pick up pieces of broken crockery. Mrs. Thatcher was there even before Celeste closed the short distance.

"What happened this time?" She sounded exhausted. The girl stood, clutching her bloodied left hand, pieces of the bowl still held captive in her grip.

"This child is useless!" Mrs. Cooper growled.

From nowhere, Mr. McKnell was standing there, investigating the scene. "Mrs. Thatcher, do you have any linen I can wrap around her hand?"

Rather than being put out by his taking charge, Mrs. Thatcher seemed oddly relieved and nodded as she rushed to retrieve it. The poor kitchen maid looked to be quite young, perhaps thirteen, and sobbed without stopping while the cook continued her tirade. Celeste tried to think of how she could help, feeling useless. If it were a ball and she saw someone in distress, she would know precisely how to act. In this place though, where she held no authority, she was lost.

At first, Mr. McKnell ignored the shouting, speaking in low, soothing tones to the girl while he pried the loose pieces of crockery from her grip, but eventually he turned to the cook.

"Mrs. Cooper," his voice was like velvet, "you are so kind to mentor young...?"

"Sally," the girl whimpered.

"Young Sally 'ere," he continued, sounding as if he meant what he said, his accent firmly in place this time. "I know she's young, and few would 'ave the patience you so graciously bestow upon 'er." He smiled at the gnarled woman, and to Celeste's surprise, her scowl softened. "I also understand that yer worried about countless things at once, so please, allow us to take care of Sally 'ere and we'll 'ave 'er back to you, ready to resume 'er work before you can say 'best apple dumplings in England.'"

Celeste would not have believed it had she not seen it with her own eyes, but the implacable cook actually smiled under the power of his charm and easy manner.

As soon as Mrs. Thatcher returned, Celeste offered to help wash and wrap Sally's hand. It seemed a maid-like thing to do, and while she hoped it would help to offset the incompetence she could not help displaying for all to see, she had also noted the worshipful way the young girl gazed at Mr. McKnell. Although quite understandable, having him hold her hand like that, even to bandage it, would no doubt leave a scar on the poor dear's heart.

Amidst the fuss, Mr. McKnell managed a half smile of gratitude toward Celeste with a short purse of his lips, seeming to appreciate her interference. Perhaps this meant that he was more aware of the feelings of others than she had given him credit for. She remembered his hurt at her assumptions in the stable yard and had to concede that as gifted as he was at being charming, she may have misjudged his character, but she was by no means settled on that opinion.

When Sally managed to tear her eyes away from Mr. McKnell, she noticed the frown on Mrs. Thatcher's face.

"I sure is sorry, Mrs. Thatcher," she pleaded. "Please don't give me the sack."

"Sally, it's the third time this week, and I can't run this household with clumsy staff." Despite the hard words, the housekeeper did not look as gruff as she was trying to sound. She even appeared regretful.

"Don't worry, Sally." Mr. McKnell turned to her, looking how Celeste would imagine an elder brother might. "Mrs. Thatcher won't take your position. Will you?" He looked up suddenly uncertain.

Who was this man who had no sense of stratum? Mrs. Thatcher

did not even chastise him as Celeste expected. Was no one immune to him? Celeste wondered how many people this man had wrapped around his little finger that allowed him such leniency with his place.

"No, girl, I won't sack you. It's up to Mrs. Cooper anyway."

All eyes turned to the red-faced cook. Celeste held her breath, caring very much over young Sally's fate. After a long pause, Mrs. Cooper sighed.

"It ain't cause they're all lookin' at me like a litter o' puppies," she relented, "but this is your last chance. Even ol' Tom won't expect 'nother one."

Sally gave a cautious little smile up at her. Mrs. Cooper returned it before realizing, then rolled her eyes and muttered as she turned away.

Celeste smiled, both amused by the cook and happier than she ever expected to be over the fate of a kitchen girl.

Chapter Ten

Jacob knew he was in for it. The look Mrs. Thatcher had given him when he sat down to eat had told him he had done something out of place, but unable to figure out what, he had remained next to Giles. He had not appeared pleased either, but neither did he protest. Then, when the kitchen maid had dropped a dish, Jacob had behaved as he would have if it were to happen in a drawing room. He was glad to have been of help but was now afraid of the cost. At least he had kept his accent intact this time.

Jacob knew that Sally would not lose her position because of his interference, since both Mrs. Cooper and Mrs. Thatcher knew who he was. That went a long way toward calming tempers, but in the eyes of the visiting servants, taking orders from a stablehand may have diminished their authority. One of those visitors, Miss Coombe, had been right there to witness it all. The hierarchy of servants was not something he had ever had to consider before, and it seemed social expectation was relative to whatever sphere one was a part of, not only the upper classes. He felt a pang of regret at causing Mrs. Thatcher any embarrassment. He had been grateful for Miss Coombe's assistance, though. What she lacked in confidence she made up for with kindness.

When the kitchens were empty except for the scullery maids, who all knew Jacob, Mrs. Thatcher approached him.

"Stablehands do not eat with valets," she chastised.

"Oh." was all he managed. Even though he suspected he'd broken some rule of etiquette, that had not even crossed his mind.

After a moment, Mrs. Thatcher's expression softened. "It's not that I'm ungrateful for your help with Sally; that girl can use all the help she can get, but there are ways of doing things."

"I apologize most humbly. I had no idea. I smelled food and came running. I hope my interference has no ill-effect on your running of the household. I should not have overruled you with Miss Coombe present." Jacob rubbed at the two-day stubble on his jaw.

"Perhaps you should tell her the truth. From what I've seen of her so far, she hasn't engaged in any gossip or spoken much to anyone. She might be persuaded to keep your confidence," Mrs. Thatcher thought out loud.

"I would rather not," Jacob dismissed. "She is Lady Celeste's abigail after all. If she has any loyalty, she would expose me to the very person I am trying to avoid. It would not be fair to expect otherwise."

"On that subject, why are you bothering with this at all? Why not just meet the lady and decide for yourself? It is not wise to have secrets."

"It will not be for long, just this house party. And in all likelihood, I will come clean before it is through. I just need a little more time."

"Well, I'll not be lying to your mother if she catches wind of your little game is all I'm saying." She waited with narrowed eyes for that to sink in.

Jacob nodded. He moved to another topic to prevent progression of the headache that was forming.

"What was Mrs. Cooper saying about Tom?"

"Tom is Sally's uncle. Her parents are tenants. Being the youngest in her family, she lacks the experience an older child would have of being useful around the house, and a clumsier person I never saw." She shook her head, but the edges of her mouth were turned up.

"You're a good woman for giving her another chance. I'll speak to Tom to save you the trouble," Jacob promised as he made ready to leave through the side door. He would head to the stables before climbing back up to his bedroom and the stifling bed warmer that awaited him there.

"It's thanks to you she has another chance," Mrs. Thatcher corrected.

Jacob smiled, happy for that outcome at least.

By the time he had finished his errand and returned to his room, by standing below the window and calling up to Giles to throw the rope down, he was a little out of breath and questioning the necessity of such measures.

In the morning, Jacob's mother caught him by surprise, coming in before he had a chance to raise his temperature with the warming pan. At least he was still abed. She smiled when she felt his head.

"You are doing much better today. How are you feeling?" she asked with a maternal hand on his cheek.

"I am much improved, but still very tired. I think it best if I keep to my room again today. I would not wish to risk any of the guests." He tried to make his yawn sound authentic.

"Hmm. Perhaps you are right," she agreed. "I shall have a tray sent up, and I will visit you again this afternoon."

"Thank you, Mother." He smiled at her, hoping she did not detect the energy he felt at having won another day. How he was going to pretend a turn for the worse, he was uncertain. At least he had the morning to come up with something.

In the stables, Tom's smile broadened every time he ordered Jacob about. It was the hardest Jacob had ever worked in his life, and the glimmer in the older man's eye was enough to make him want to throw himself into every task, to prove that he could do anything Tom would assign. Being an imposter with no qualifications meant that he did not have much opportunity of leaving the stalls or wash box—or smell of anything fresher than manure—while he was outside. Tom had him doing simple tasks that required less know-how but more strength than the younger stable boys were capable of. But the work was plentiful, and he was not in anybody's way as far as he was aware. Although he did wonder if anyone would tell him if he were being a nuisance.

Jacob had been concerned that he would not be welcomed among the real servants, but it appeared that they were too busy to care about his presence with all the extra bodies. Thus far, the visiting servants he had encountered had shown no indication of knowing that he did not belong, and his own family's servants had ignored him for the most part. They were likely wary of how to behave around him during this temporary change in status.

As the day progressed, Jacob became so busy competing with the tasks Tom set for him that he forgot to expect a visit from his friend, until the gentlemen returned and was striding into the stable.

"Jacob Bellmoore," boomed a voice that could only belong to Zachariah Carringham. Jacob stepped out of the stall he was mucking out to shush him and was met with a grin.

Jacob would prefer to avoid the inevitable conversation, but it was of little use, so he led his friend to an empty stall away from the other staff.

"Blakely," Jacob greeted.

"Come, come now, we are not in London. Can I not simply be Zach to one person still? At least in private? Please?" Zach sighed, a mournful, tired sound. "Besides, truth be told, I am not quite used to the title yet."

"If you insist, old friend. I do not envy you the responsibilities or the grief. We all miss Nathaniel." Jacob grasped his shoulder in commiseration.

"Thank you," Zach nodded.

In appearance, they were opposites of each other. Zach, with his bright blue eyes and blonde hair, cropped short in a fashionable style. Then Jacob, with his brown eyes and brown hair. He wore it shoulder length and tied back the way his father used to, not caring one bit that he was a generation out of fashion. And now, adding to that, his very out of fashion facial hair. Zach was also taller than Jacob, though not by much. Within their personalities though, they had much in common.

"How is Esther doing? Do we have good news yet?" Jacob asked, referring to Zach's sister. She was younger than Nathaniel, but older than Zach and expecting her first child.

"She is well. Langley takes good care of her. I have not yet received any news of the baby. It should be soon though," he answered with a fond smile.

There was a comfortable silence, and Jacob hoped that talk of Zach's sister was a sufficient distraction from Jacob himself.

"Well, Jacob, would you care to explain yourself? I'm quite at a loss as to why I find you dressed as a servant and mucking out stalls? Has Whitbury demoted you from brother to stable boy?" Zach laughed, but the sincerity of the question was in his eyes. So much for that.

"You did not mention seeing me here to him, did you?" Jacob asked, his smile dropping.

"No..." Zach drew out, his affable brow creased with fresh concern.

Jacob sighed. This was it. "You're going to have a hard time believing this..."

When he finished explaining all the relevant details of his brilliant plan to his friend, the earl surprised him by bursting out in great guffaws.

"So, you mean to tell me that you feign illness like a schoolboy, then you climb out of your window every day and hide in the stables? From a woman?" He did not stop laughing to breathe, clutching his middle as he doubled over.

"Well, when you put it that way..." Jacob felt like an imbecile and a coward.

"Who is the unfortunate lady?" Zach slowed his laughter enough to ask the question, but it did not stop.

"Lady Celeste Honeychurch, did I not mention that?"

"No, you did not." Zach's brow knit, and he sobered somewhat. "Why on earth would you wish to hide from her?"

"I had never met the woman in my life before yesterday, and to tell you the truth, I was expecting someone more...humble in years and appearance," Jacob admitted. Rather than helping his case though, it only served to bring back Zach's laughter.

"You thought that she could be a spinster or such, but instead of being introduced and deciding for yourself if you liked her, you hid away behind the rear end of a horse?"

"It is not that funny," Jacob defended, resisting the urge to plant him a facer.

"Yes, it is!" Zach guffawed.

"Well, if it were not for that Mortcastle fellow demanding I take his horse, I would never have had the idea and would be in there, sipping tea and dancing with her like you."

Saying it out loud confirmed to Jacob that he had made the right choice. He had nothing in particular against the lady, but the whole affair of being forced into marriage did not sit well with him. He was yet to come up with a plan to deal with the situation without damaging anyone's reputations, so in the meantime he would continue to enjoy the simple pleasure of being of use in the stables.

"She is quite lovely. Not the most polished conversationalist, but delightful company."

Zach seemed to be lost in a memory with a smile on his face long enough to give Jacob an idea.

"Care to take her off my hands?" he asked.

Zach looked startled. "Slow down, old boy. I have only known the lady a day."

Jacob held up his hands in surrender. "Alright. You cannot blame me for trying."

"No, I suppose not. You may not have to worry though; she appears to be very sweet and quite popular already. Mr. Goldsmith has been rather attentive, as well as Lord Mortcastle." Zach shrugged, but the crease in his brow belied his nonchalance.

"Mortcastle?" Jacob sat up straight. "I cannot like the sound of that."

"No, neither do I. I mean, I do not know him from Adam myself, but there is something disquieting about him. Your Lady Celeste did not seem all that comfortable with his conversation either, but it is still early days yet."

"Would you do me a favor, Zach?" Jacob asked.

"Of course. Name it," he agreed without reserve.

"Just stay near her when Mortcastle is around. I cannot like the idea of him causing her any distress," Jacob entreated.

Zach raised an eyebrow. "I would be happy to, of course, but why not just come out of hiding and look after her yourself? If you are already so invested in her welfare, perhaps you are not so indifferent as you claim."

"It isn't that." Jacob could not place exactly what *it* was. How was he to explain that any gentleman giving Lady Celeste too marked attention could damage her reputation if others believed her to be engaged to him? Even casting that aside, the idea of Lord Mortcastle paying her his addresses seemed worse somehow.

He should take Zach's very sound advice, and he knew it.

Zach peered at Jacob with suspicion. "It really is a little too early to tell if we would suit. Besides, women have a tendency of showing you only what they think you'd like to see before snaring you in the parson's trap." He laughed uneasily, misinterpreting Jacob's hesitation, then added, "'though I do not know any man who chooses a wife because her comments on the weather are more appropriate than the next lady's. Baffles me, what women think is impressive conversation." he shook his head.

"Is that all Lady Celeste has spoken to you about?" Jacob asked. He had to admit to being a little curious about the woman he may still end up being obliged by honor to marry.

"No, although we have not yet spoken at length." He chuckled at what must have been an amusing memory.

Jacob watched his friend, who at least liked Lady Celeste. Perhaps she might not be so bad after all. Or perhaps, given time, Zach's feelings might develop further until they allowed Jacob off the hook.

Chapter Eleven

Celeste burned another dress.

She was beginning to be grateful for that extra trip to the modiste before leaving London. She had already rendered two day-gowns unusable with her lack of skill at pressing, despite Betsy's tutelage. Now she had damaged a third, this time an evening one, in as many days. She had no idea how anyone became used to using the heavy tools required for such work with any kind of finesse. She also knew that her latest blemishes were going to bother Bryn, even though she would say nothing. She had begun to notice the way Bryn's eyes would tense around the edges, and her fingers would flex as though she were itching to rescue the garments from Celeste's abuse.

Celeste was considering how to break the news to Bryn as she held the poor offended garment in her hand, just as she heard a whisper from elsewhere in the scullery that sounded like "Elsie." She looked up to see a couple of pairs of eyes darting away from her. Her cheeks flushed and her eyes burned for reasons she did not understand. She was only playacting after all, and would be done with all of this before the fortnight was through, but sting it did.

With as much dignity as an embarrassed pretend maid could hope to muster, she gathered up her bundle and left the scullery, holding her head as high as she dared.

Once in Bryn's bedroom, Celeste sighed and looked down at herself. All the clothes at her disposal as Elsie the maid had been hers as Lady Celeste a couple of years prior. They were no longer new, but the fabrics were soft and comfortable. Even the ugly ones. If she did not learn how to press the gowns without damaging them soon, Bryn would be wearing them once again by the end of the party. At least Bryn could have her hair free of this mobcap. Celeste was already tired of pinning her hair tight so that it could fit underneath.

She laid out the burned gown on the bed to take a better look. The mark was smaller than the others, and very close to the bodice. She might be able to conceal it with a ribbon and a little embroidery. At least she knew how to do that.

Bryn found Celeste sitting by the window after luncheon, humming to herself whist stitching.

"I burnt another one," she admitted, looking up, when Bryn said nothing. Finishing the stitch, she held the gown up for inspection. "What do you think?"

"I cannot even see the scorch mark this time." Bryn sounded impressed.

"I never thought I would be grateful for all that endless embroidery my mother forced upon me," Celeste admitted with a sigh. "Don't ever tell her, will you? She will be insufferable if she knows that I think she was right about something." Celeste rolled her eyes in the precise way her mother disapproved of, even though she was not there to react.

Bryn concealed a grin, making Celeste wonder what Bryn's family was like, but that conversation could wait for another time.

"Are you ready to change into your afternoon gown?" Celeste asked. Bryn nodded. Celeste stood and hung the newly mended gown for later, then retrieved the pale blue afternoon dress she had laid out on the bed.

"I am sorry that I do not have more gowns to match your hair and complexion better," Celeste offered.

"Of course they would match your coloring; they are yours." Bryn gave a short laugh as if the notion of considering her were absurd. She slipped into the dress. "I will admit, it is nice to wear so many fine new things." Bryn smiled as she swished the skirt back and forth.

"Yes, I quite took that part of being a lady for granted," Celeste admitted. She was missing the feel of a soft muslin and a pretty bonnet, as opposed to the old brown dress she was wearing with an unflattering mobcap. When she saw herself in the mirror and noticed the way her lip was curled up in distaste, she corrected her reflection. Perhaps she was a little too used to being pretty.

She did have some of her nicer out of fashion garments among Bryn's things, but she was saving them for if they went into town, rather than the dangerous work of burning gowns.

"Would you care to go for a walk in the gardens with me?" Bryn asked.

"Yes! It would be splendid to be outside. Are there no activities planned for this afternoon?" Celeste accepted with a happy sigh, not even attempting to hide the enthusiasm in her voice.

"Only endless embroidery," Bryn grinned as she quoted Celeste, who could not help a laugh from escaping.

"Then I shall be pleased to rescue you from it."

The gardens of Whitbury Manor were some of the finest Celeste had ever seen. Nothing compared to her home at Willoworth in Hereford-shire, but the roses and hyacinths surrounding neatly shaped artistic lawns were the very definition of an English garden. There was even a high hedge maze that she was itching to explore.

"It is splendid out here." Celeste filled her lungs with the scented air, relishing being out of doors. She had even put on one of the nicer dresses. After spending so much time feeling confined and anxious under the watchful stares of servants who knew their tasks, it was a welcome reprieve.

"Yes, indeed," Bryn agreed. She seemed more relaxed than Celeste had yet seen her. "What do you say? Shall we follow the path to admire these flowers, or shall we venture into that maze there?"

"I confess I was hoping you would wish to see the maze." Celeste tried not to sound as eager as she felt.

"Very well, the maze it is," Bryn agreed with a broad smile.

When Celeste and Bryn had been wandering through the maze for a few minutes, Bryn spoke. "You do not need to pretend while we are alone, you know. You are not really—"

Celeste held up a hand to stop her.

"Do not say it. You never know who might be within hearing," she cautioned.

As if to prove her point, Celeste and Bryn heard low voices as they drew deeper. The gentle sounds of a water fountain obscured the voices somewhat. Both women stopped before reaching the leafy archway, not wishing to intrude on another's conversation.

As they were about to leave and turn back, Celeste paused as one of the voices carried on the breeze toward them.

"...and if you weren't the sniveling cur you are, I wouldn't be stuck here tending to you like a nursemaid."

The voice was familiar, but Celeste could not place it. The accent sounded different, maybe even American.

"Do not forget to whom you are speaking, or reporting back to your *employer* will be the least of your concerns."

The retort, distinctly British, came from another masculine voice with a definite note of threat to the tone. A chill went up Celeste's spine as she listened. She wanted to hear the rest of the conversation, but Bryn tugged on her arm, her eyes wide. Celeste could see the sense in not being caught eavesdropping on a heated conversation, but she was also very curious. Who were these men, and what were they arguing about?

"Are you threatening me?"

The low growl had enough menace in it to frighten Celeste into complete stillness. Bryn's tugging on her sleeve became incessant to the point that Celeste was no longer able to ignore it.

"Please, My lady," Bryn whispered with as little volume as possible, but her rapid breathing was becoming rather loud.

"Very well," Celeste whispered back, swatting at her hands.

As luck would have it, they heard nothing more as they tiptoed away as fast as they were able and thought themselves undetected.

Then one of the men called out, "Who is there? Show yourself!"

Revealing themselves was the last thing either of them was prepared to do. Without having to communicate it, they broke into an instant run away from the garden.

Celeste paused for a moment at the garden's entrance. Bryn looked as though she would run the most direct and obvious way back to the house, but Celeste had read enough novels to consider that to be a bad idea. It was the first direction anyone chasing after them would look. They had managed to keep their footfalls somewhat quiet considering the speed of their flight and the loose gravel, but it would be too much to hope that they could make it to the house without being spotted. Instead, she grasped Bryn's hand and headed around through the trees toward the stable house, where there was more cover if the men were to come searching for anyone. They could claim any number of reasons for being there if questions were asked by anyone they encountered once they caught their breath.

As they entered the stable yard, Celeste realized that they needed to slow down if they did not wish to draw serious attention. The problem was that Bryn ran straight into Celeste's back and stepped on her own ankle as she bounced off. Then, as Celeste spun to assist her, she tripped herself and tangled them both up in a flurry of arms, legs and skirts, landing them in a heap in the dirt.

It was mere seconds before they were surrounded by grooms and the like, all offering kind assistance but also giving them no room to hide from their embarrassment. Celeste did not know whose hands belonged to whom as their elbows were grasped and they were hoisted up like toy soldiers by their group of rescuers. Her bonnet fell down the back of her head as she was assisted, and the knotted ribbons choked her throat for a moment before she could right herself. She was not succeeding in being invisible, which was made worse by the blush she could feel on her cheeks, making her even more conspicuous.

"Are you alright, Miss Coombe?"

It took Celeste a moment to understand that the pleasant deep voice she could hear was addressing her. In the confusion, she forgot her assumed name and that Bryn would be addressed as 'My lady.'

"Yes, I am quite well, thank you, Mister…" She turned as she spoke to the man who still held her elbow, only to lose all coherent thought when she saw his face.

"McKnell," he finished for her with a half-grin when she did nothing but stare at him for the space of four whole heartbeats. And he had called *her* smile a weapon.

"Yes, of course. I know who you are," she stuttered through an awkward laugh.

Celeste had no idea what came over her in that moment. Sudden awareness of how warm his hand felt on her elbow as he steadied her held her entire focus, and she found that some invisible force was preventing her from looking anywhere near his eyes. Each of the seven times she tried, her cheeks ignited, and her gaze darted to some random place around his face but never at them. She could not explain it. She had embarrassed herself in front of gentlemen before and never reacted like this. She was further puzzled as she considered that there were several men around her and Bryn who had all witnessed their tangle, and yet she only behaved like a blushing debutante around this one.

"Are you hurt?" Mr. McKnell asked, a worry line appearing between his eyebrows as they drew together. "You're frowning."

"Oh, am I?" She felt around her mouth with her fingertips to verify his words. He was right. Now her eyes fixed on his, and she could not look away. What madness was this?

"Perhaps we had best find you somewhere to rest," he suggested, looking at her is if he feared she might collapse. Her behavior was rather odd.

"But Bryn—" She cut herself off immediately as she realized her mistake. She had used Bryn's real name. Celeste did her best not to show any reaction, but her attention skittered over to Bryn, who managed to keep her eyes from going wide, but her jaw was tight and her shoulders rigid. She was standing but favoring one foot over the other and holding tight to the arms of the two men on either side of her. Celeste felt her brow furrow in concern. Bryn had been injured.

"What was that?" Mr. McKnell asked. Either he had not heard what she said, or he was unfamiliar with the name. Either way, it gave Celeste a chance to cover her slip.

"Brun, broon, blub…" she mumbled, rubbing a hand across her

forehead and following it with a delicate moan.

"Did you hit yer head, love?" one of the other stablemen asked.

"I..." She began to answer but thought better of it and just nodded. She had not, in fact, and hated to burden anyone with unnecessary worry, but she could not risk exposure.

"Please, if you would be so good as to assist us to the house. I will see to it that Miss Coombe is able to rest for a spell," Bryn instructed, taking the cue. Her assertiveness sounded convincing. Celeste was impressed, though she made a conscious effort not to change her facial expression from what she hoped conveyed pain and confusion. She knew Bryn could not have been feeling so unflappable on the inside, yet she'd had the presence of mind to secure them an escort inside. They would be safe from whomever they had stumbled upon in the garden maze thanks to her fast thinking.

Celeste groaned. She was now obliged to feign a head injury, reducing the chances of anyone believing her about the voices she had overheard in the garden. It would be attributed to being overwrought or a hallucination. As inconvenient as that was, though, she knew she ought not complain, even to herself, because Bryn was limping a lot. Her injury was obviously real.

Mr. McKnell appeared to notice as well, and just as he had with young Sally, he organized everyone else and soon had them conveyed back to the house. He even procured a gentleman out of nowhere to carry Bryn. By the way she was blushing, Celeste wondered if he might be the one-in-particular she had avoided discussing.

Over the course of the evening and the following day, it became difficult for Celeste not to feel insulted by the lagging concern over her welfare. Their assisted entry into the house had caused quite a stir, and soon it seemed that everyone knew of Bryn's ankle and Celeste's nonsensical blathering. After a short rest, however, the house party guests, as well as the other servants, spoke as if her rest had been a holiday. Well, truth be told, she did not speak to the other guests, but at least one of them inquired after Bryn and managed to leave Celeste feeling like an insignificant insect at the same time. She was an older woman, who Celeste thought must have been Lady Waverley based on her age. She had a certain knack for asking after a person in a tone devoid of any feeling.

It was surprising that the house servants were worse with their barely hidden gossip. There she was with a head injury—very well, a pretended head injury, but they did not know that—and no one seemed bothered by it at all. As long as she was still able to perform her duties, she ought to. The valet, who had pushed James at the beginning of the house party, an American whose name turned out to be Reeves, had a sarcastic question to ask about her injury every time he passed her in the halls. Somehow, his sneering directness felt worse than the whispering gossips. Since she could not escape the attention, she wished it were nicer.

Bryn, on the other hand, was receiving all the consideration owed to the both of them put together. Celeste could not stop the wave of jealousy that rolled over her. She was not upset with Bryn, it was not her fault. Besides, she had seen how swollen Bryn's ankle had been. She was most certainly deserving of all the solicitations she received. Celeste was just not accustomed to being disregarded.

Were all servants treated with such indifference? Celeste tried to think back and remember if there had been a time when she might have been guilty of this sort of neglect, but she recalled nothing. That was no comfort however, as all it may mean was that she had paid little mind.

The one good thing to come out of the situation was that Lady Whitbury had insisted Bryn rest for the evening and have a tray brought to her room. Aside from the difficulty in learning to balance the thing whist walking up the stairs, Celeste had been pleased to have some time alone with Bryn to hear more about the parts of the party she was missing. At least she was having a marvelous time.

Bryn had been reluctant to accept that she could not tend to the lady's maid duties since the beginning. She had acquiesced only because she could not afford to be seen below stairs doing maid's work, but Celeste was beginning to suspect that she had somehow been finding a way. There was not nearly as much to be done as there ought to have been, and the gowns were surprisingly wrinkle-free. Until Bryn injured her ankle. Celeste wondered if Bryn had been doing clandestine chores late in the night after even the scullery maids were abed. It bothered Celeste that she found the work, reduced as it may be, so difficult. Or that she was already relishing a little time away from those duties and the other servants. She was always out of place. Not to mention her growing resentment toward the mobcap she was wearing all the day long. Although she ought not complain. The lower servants' workload of all the cleaning, scrubbing and carting items, big and small about for longer hours than the upper servants, did not bear contemplation. She was ashamed to feel so grateful that she had switched lives with a lady's maid.

She would not admit it aloud, but Celeste was beginning to regret her decision to try out the life of a servant. Bryn's words of warning—that it would not be as glamorous as she thought—were often at the forefront of her mind. Nevertheless, she was urged on by a stubborn need to prove that she was not one of the pampered creatures she knew herself to be. That alone motivated Celeste not to give in or allow her fatigue to show. That she had never before even considered what Bryn's life looked like was becoming a sore spot on her conscience. She knew that nobody else of her acquaintance would be bothered by such things, but Celeste had always considered herself to be more conscientious than her peers. The gap between stations had never been more obvious to Celeste than it was now.

Still, Celeste had every intention of remaining Elsie the Lady's maid until the end of the party, if only for Bryn's sake. And if Celeste's parents did make an appearance...well, she would have to do some very clever thinking. Perhaps elope with a stablehand to distract them. There was one in particular who immediately came to mind, and she lingered on the image of his handsome features and brown eyes longer than was prudent.

Chapter Twelve

Jacob was learning that there were several pros and cons to living a double life at home. His time in the stable house was far more fulfilling than he expected. There was something about working with his hands, as well as the particular variety of tiredness he was experiencing at the end of a long day of using every last muscle in his body. It was enlivening, despite the exhaustion. The camaraderie of the men was also an unexpected boon. Even the horses made for excellent company, and he was surprised to find that he would prefer a conversation with one of them to many a person of his acquaintance. He could be quite content to continue in his assumed role for the remainder of the house party. The main drawback of being out in the open in the stable yard was the risk of Jacob's disguise being discovered, exposing his family to ridicule. Were it not for that consideration, he would shed this façade and ask Whitbury for a position under Tom. He did not know why his brother wanted to send him away to the army after he had been away so long on his grand tour, but perhaps the stables were far enough.

Feigning illness also had certain disadvantages. One was that Jacob was not free to roam the house as he saw fit. Another, that he would admit to no one, was that his brilliant plan was not working.

The fifth day of the house party was half gone, yet impersonating a stable boy was giving Jacob very little access to Lady Celeste, so he was not getting to know her, surreptitiously or otherwise. He may be forced to admit that Mrs. Thatcher had been right in that regard. What he had seen in the way Lady celeste treated her maid led him to believe that she was a kind lady, but that did not mean he was content to be forced into marriage with her. Though, it was still prudent to learn what he could in case that did yet become his fate. He had seen Lady Celeste's maid a number of times, but they had not thus far had a lot of conversation, so he had gleaned no useful insights from her. His attraction to said maid was also a complication he needed to resolve.

With any luck, Lady Celeste may not be settled on him, and he could find himself disentangled with a little patience. If Zach was right about her popularity, and she accepted an offer from someone else, her reputation would no longer be his responsibility. Perhaps all he needed to do to be free of this mess was to remain absent a while longer. He could do that.

Jacob knew that he needed to work on staying in the background to achieve any of his intentions. He tried to remain aware of all that occurred around him so that he could become scarce at a moment's notice. However, he had already risked exposure more than once when he saw someone in distress. He just could not justify prioritizing his own designs over assisting someone who was hurt.

Two days prior, Lady Celeste and Miss Coombe had come stumbling into the stable complex and had toppled over each other. Lady Celeste had injured an ankle, but Zach was already in the stable house. That Jacob suggested he carry Lady Celeste was purely practical. It had nothing at all to do with his wishing for Zach to form a stronger attachment to the lady.

He was concerned by what had inspired such haste as to make them fall over themselves like that.

Jacob had been one of the first to go to their aid, but even if he had been able to suppress the instinct to assist, the rest of the nearby stable staff had rushed in. He would have been more conspicuous by hanging back.

Jacob had fancied for a moment that he might have rendered Miss Coombe a little speechless. She had been blushing and stammering and holding his forearm with a lighter touch than he would expect one would for support. He was just beginning to enjoy the feeling, though he knew he should not, when it became apparent that it had been a side effect from being knocked a little insensible by the fall. Jacob's disappointment had been like a splash of water in the face. It had been a welcome reminder that he was indeed a gentleman, and as such, he was not free to enjoy the admiration, real or imagined, of a maid.

Jacob's reflections were interrupted by the return of a group of guests who had gone into town earlier. One gentleman Jacob had not seen the arrival of at the onset of the house party was Lord Tardington, a man he had a passing acquaintance with through his association with Whitbury. He certainly saw him now as he approached the stable on horseback in line with the rest of the party. There was a good chance that he would be recognized if the gentleman were to glance in his direction. The stubble on Jacob's face, not even a week's worth, would not disguise him from someone he had met several times in London.

As Jacob froze and spun away from the oncoming assemblage, Tom's attention turned to him.

"Do you need to make yourself scarce, lad?" he offered in a low tone as he approached.

Jacob looked up, feeling his face lift in hope. Taking the hint, Tom cleared his throat and spoke louder.

"McKnell, my grandson, young William here, is needed at home. Would you walk him for me? He has a habit of wanderin' off."

Jacob nodded toward Tom in gratitude, but William pulled his twelve-year-old head back and looked from one side to the other, appearing confused. He opened his mouth to ask, but Tom cut him off before he began.

"Away with you now," was all Tom offered, before returning his attention to his workers.

Jacob waited for William and pulled the tricorn he wore low over his eyes before they slipped away in the direction of the cottage where William lived with his parents and siblings.

Once they were well away from the guests, Jacob began to relax.

"What was that about?" William asked, with no trace of his grand-father's Scottish accent.

"I just needed to avoid some of the guests." Jacob shrugged.

"Why are you pretending to be a servant anyway?" William asked with the boldness of youth.

"It is a long story," Jacob brushed off, having no desire to explain his situation to yet another person, especially one so young who had no compunctions about discussing whatever popped into his head. The less information he had, the better.

"I'm twelve, I like stories," William persisted.

"This one is boring."

"I don't mind."

"It's about *girls*." Jacob scrunched his face.

"We have nothing else to do." The boy shrugged. He was relentless.

Jacob sighed. He was unsure how to get out of the uncomfortable conversation. As luck would have it, he was spared further torment by the blessed sound of his nom de plume being called from somewhere in the distance.

As he looked around to find the source of the sound, he saw two ladies approaching from further down the road. Without thought to consequence, or the possibility that they might know him, Jacob quickened his pace to approach, trusting William to follow. It did not matter to him in that moment who had saved him from the awkward conversation. When he realized that it was Lady Celeste, he was more pleased than he ought to have been that her maid was with her. He sighed to himself. He would have to remind himself to feel guilty about that later.

The ladies must have been returning from shopping in the nearby village of Whitbury, but it was odd that they were not with the rest of the party. It was just over half a mile away but would not be an easy distance on foot after their injuries from only two days before.

"Good morning, My lady. Miss Coombe." He bowed.

"Good morning, Mr. McKnell, isn't it?" Lady Celeste responded with a genuine smile that surprised him. Not everyone treated the stable staff with such respect.

"Yes, My lady. And how is your ankle today?" he inquired, re-membering at the last moment to affect some kind of accent. One profession he would never be at liberty to consider was the stage.

"It is much improved, I thank you. Although it is the reason we called out to you." She blushed as she spoke, though there was no false modesty or coyness about her. "You see, we were distracted by...some very fine lace. And we were late to our meeting place." She seemed to fidget more with each sentence.

"Do you mean to tell me that they abandoned you?" Jacob could not cover the incredulity in his voice. "Who was in the party?" Too late, he remembered that he had once again neglected his accent.

"Really, it was my own fault," she rushed, waving it away. "They must have thought we had already returned to the Manor."

Jacob stood agape with his arms folded across his chest. He could not believe that whoever was on the shopping excursion would leave a lady alone to find her own way across unfamiliar hills and fields. Especially Zach, although Jacob did not recall seeing him in the party when the coaches were called.

It may have been plausible to assume that the ladies had returned on foot were it not for Lady Celeste's injury, something that was common knowledge. His mother had even informed him of it during one of her visits to check on him. He would like to know who was responsible for this neglect.

"Are these the girls in your story?" William asked, shifting Jacob's attention like a bolt of lightning. His stomach lurched into his throat, and he hoped his expression was not showing the depth of his panic.

"I do not have any notion of what you are saying." He sounded in his own ears exactly as nervous as he felt at being caught out in such a way. He would be willing to do a great many undignified things to escape from having to explain such a question.

William looked confused for a moment, but then the clever lad seemed to catch on somehow. A distinctive gleam came into his eyes.

"You know, the one about the girl who lost her shoe at some ball. Didn't someone hurt their feet in that one?" William's eyes grew wide as his expression shifted, making him look to all the world like an innocent child. He had clearly used that tactic before. Whatever reason William had for suddenly assisting Jacob with the subterfuge, he would not complain.

"Oh, right, the fairy tale we read to your sister," Jacob played along. It did not help that William winked at him in response as he nodded.

The ladies looked at each other, but Jacob could not tell what passed between them.

"Perhaps you ought to rest your ankle, My lady, while I send William here back to the manor for a carriage," Jacob suggested, changing the subject.

"That is a splendid idea, thank you," Miss Coombe accepted.

Something was not quite right. Not only was it out of place for Miss Coombe to speak for her mistress, but the Lady did not even bat an eye at the impertinence. No matter how close a Lady and her maid were, that was downright odd. And why did they not seem to be in the slightest distress at having been left behind? At the expense of their injuries, no less.

Come to think of it, Jacob recalled that on Monday afternoon, just prior to their collision, they had seemed in a great hurry. He wondered if something had happened or if they were avoiding someone in the party.

"Will he be alright on his own, do you think? Should you stay with him?" Miss Coombe asked with concern.

William looked as though someone had just challenged his grand-mother to a duel, then took off like a shot before anyone else could insult his sense of independence further.

"He knows these lands as well as anyone. He lives just over that rise." Jacob pointed in the direction of the cottage.

"I meant no offense." Miss Coombe watched after the shrinking figure, biting her lip distractingly.

"I am certain that by the time he reaches Whitbury Manor, he will have forgotten all about it, Elsie," Lady Celeste offered by way of comfort.

Elsie. It was a pretty name.

"I hope you are right," Miss Coombe answered, then seemed to notice her Lady struggling to sit down on a log.

Jacob stepped over to assist as he ought to have done in the first place, chastising himself for his neglect. He should never have allowed his own musings to blind him to a lady requiring assistance. To make up for his inattention, he made an extra effort to see to her comfort by searching out an obliging rock for her to rest her foot on and rolled his coat to cushion it a little.

"Thank you, you are most kind." She smiled at him. He waited, hoping for some spark of something to happen as he looked into her eyes, but there was nothing.

Jacob's stomach dropped. He liked Lady Celeste Honeychurch well enough, as he would any new acquaintance with kind manners. However, if he hoped for her good character to be enough to make him feel something more, he was destined for disappointment. The temptation in that moment to reveal the truth of who he was and have it over with almost pushed the words out of his mouth.

Lady Celeste blinked for a long moment, then her breathing was long and controlled. It was possible that her ankle was paining her more than she wanted to show. He bit his tongue. It was not the time to add confusion and potential indignation to her present distress by forcing his confessions upon her.

"Mr. McKnell," Lady Celeste said, snapping him out of his thoughts. "I see a patch of daisies over there. Would you be so kind as to fetch me some?"

"Of course, I would be happy to," he agreed, a little surprised. "I mean, yes, My lady," he fumbled, having forgotten that he was not supposed to be responding as a gentleman would to a request from a lady, but as a servant would to an instruction, but they did not appear to notice anything amiss.

Jacob removed himself to a patch of the little yellow flowers far enough away that it would afford him a little time to re-establish his persona of Mr. McKnell in his mind before returning. He did not notice Elsie, *Miss Coombe,* walking with him until she stooped down beside him to pick some of the flowers herself.

"Ought you to leave the lady on her own?" he asked, not wishing her to be reprimanded.

"She is hardly ten yards from us," Miss Coombe said with a raised eyebrow. "I am certain it is alright. Besides, these flowers are her favorites."

She continued examining the weeds as though some were superior to others. Jacob could not tell the difference. They were not even long enough to pick without feeling like he had a hand full of grass.

"Truly? I would not have thought such a tiny common flower to be favored above the more impressive varieties," he voiced his confusion out loud.

"And which of the *more impressive* varieties are your favorites, Mr. McKnell?"

Jacob did not miss the challenge in her voice. He knew nothing about flowers, nor why a lady might prefer one above another.

"Alright, I concede," he laughed. "I am no expert on the subject of flowers." After a moment of contemplation, he could not help but ask, "Which are your favorites, Miss Coombe?"

When she did not give an immediate answer, Jacob looked up and was surprised to see her biting that lip again, a look of chagrin on her face. How odd. It was not a personal question. Indeed, it was the acceptable kind asked in drawing rooms and gardens.

When she finally looked up, a small smile played at the corner of her mouth.

"Would I seem the greatest hypocrite in the world if I were to admit that I prefer one of your more *impressive varieties*?" she asked, sounding timid.

Jacob felt a smile pulling at the corner of his mouth. "Oh?"

"Roses," she admitted, her face moving into her shoulder.

Jacob laughed out loud. He could not help it. Miss Coombe had chastised him with her tone for his surprise over the choice of a common weed as a favorite flower, when all the while she preferred the cultivated, or more *impressive varieties* all along.

Miss Coombe threw a daisy at him and joined in his laughter. Hers was not musical or delicate, but neither was it harsh. It was such a joyous, happy sound as to render any listener incapable of feeling anything heavier than the wisp of a dandelion. Jacob found himself enveloped by it and was loath to speak as the moment ebbed, content for it to linger as long as possible.

After a moment of comfortable silence, Miss Coombe spoke.

"Mr. McKnell, may I ask you something, servant to servant?" she posed, not taking her eyes off of the flowers in her hands.

Jacob was not certain how to answer that. He did not want her to ask him anything about being a servant but could not politely refuse such an innocent request either. Instead of answering at all, he settled on waiting for her to continue.

"My lady is a very kind mistress and allows me to be more of a friend sometimes than is normal," she began.

"Yes, so, I have seen." He nodded, wondering at the fleeting look of alarm that passed over Miss Coombe's face before she continued.

"Tell me if you would, do you also enjoy friendship with the family of Lord Whitbury? His mother, and brother, and so forth." She seemed to struggle to say the last part of her sentence, and Jacob wondered what Lady Celeste had shared with her maid about their situation. Part of him wanted to pepper her with questions of his own, but the other part wanted to run for the stables and 'hide' there as Zach had suggested he was already doing.

Jacob was also struck by the oddness of being asked, in effect, if he were on friendly terms with himself.

"I think I may say that the family and I share mutual respect, although I have wondered how secure my place here is from time to time."

He could not say what possessed him to be so honest. Perhaps his uncertainty over his future and his brother's intentions to send him away were weighing on his mind more than he himself realized.

"Oh?" Miss Coombe asked, looking at him with concern. The blue of her eyes seemed to deepen, and the innocent kindness in them rendered her more beautiful than he had first thought. *Oh dear.* A man could be persuaded to share a great many secrets when looking upon a face like that. He looked away, clearing his throat.

"It is nothing, I am sure." He waved a dismissive hand and looked at the fragile daisies in his palm. He almost jumped when he felt her gentle hand rest on his forearm.

"If you ever find yourself in need of employment, I am certain Lady Celeste's family would assist you."

Again, Jacob was disarmed by the gentleness in Miss Coombe's eyes as he looked up. He wondered how that expression might change if she were to find out his real identity. His conscience began its annoying pestering in the back of his mind, trying to make its way to the forefront.

It was time to change the subject.

"I thank you, but I am certain all will be well." He spoke quickly so she would not have a chance to offer him any more generosity that he did not deserve. He stood, ready to return to Lady Celeste with his pathetic offering. "Out of curiosity, why do you ask? About the family, I mean?"

"Oh. Yes. I heard a rumor and wanted to find out if it were true," she explained, also standing. "And since it concerned the family, I wanted to find out from someone employed by the family."

"You want gossip?" Jacob could not believe his ears. Had his assessment of her character been entirely incorrect? Miss Coombe's face turned scarlet.

"Not at all! Please, you misunderstand me, sir. It is not an idle report I am seeking, but to have such a report refuted. The subject could be damaging to my lady Celeste's reputation; my purpose is to find out if I need be concerned for her."

Jacob felt the color drain from his face. This could only mean one thing. If the report circulating around the visiting servants concerned both his family and Lady Celeste...

"Pray, what is it you have heard?" he asked with urgency, seeming to startle her a little with his intensity. He was barely breathing. He made a conscious effort to soften his features and resume blinking, even though the panic was rising in his throat. She studied him for a moment as if to ascertain *his* trustworthiness. He would have laughed out loud if he were not fighting the urge to hold on to something.

"It has been said that there is to be a union between a member of the household and Lady Celeste, 'though I cannot imagine how since they have never met."

It was as Jacob had feared. He may not escape his fate after all. Unless Lord Blakely or someone else fell in rapturous love with Lady Celeste in the next few days, he was hopelessly stuck.

"May I ask where you heard such rumors?" he asked, tasting bile.

Miss Coombe did not answer but seemed to be searching for something to say. She opened and closed her mouth several times whilst looking anywhere but at him.

"You do not mean to tell me that you intend to protect whoever is circulating such things?" he demanded, incensed. That she would devote her loyalty to a gossiping servant above the reputations of his family and her own mistress was nothing short of abhorrent. She gaped at him but had no chance to reply as the carriage arrived from the house. Jacob had been so invested in their conversation that he had not even noticed its approach.

As Lady Celeste and her maid were loaded into the carriage, Jacob took a deep breath to clear his mind. He had much to consider. Among which was that he had been far too distracted by Miss Coombe and her revelations. The wisest course of action would be to avoid her from now on, but he needed to find out more about the gossip she had shared.

Jacob opted to walk back to the house rather than ride on the back of the carriage. He had a great deal on his mind, and the sunshine and fresh air were all he could think of to aid him in untangling it.

Chapter Thirteen

Despite her ankle being tender, Bryn had still been able to participate in the party to some degree, following their mishap. Celeste could not help but relish the reports of activities Bryn had never imagined she would be free to enjoy. Like the picnic the previous morning, where she had not been required to lift a finger. The shopping trip had also been a highlight until Lord Tardington had joined the party on horseback. Celeste was not confident that he would not recognize her if she and Bryn were side by side, so they had insisted that they would find their own way back and abandoned their group as soon as civility would allow. Celeste had kept her head down the entire time and stayed as inconspicuous as she could. It was the most maid-like behavior she had achieved thus far. Then Bryn and Celeste had attempted to walk back to Whitbury Manor. It should have only taken half an hour or so. They could have chosen the simple option of hiring a carriage, but neither of them thought of that for so short a distance. Bryn's ankle had not been bothering her too much, but became quite a hindrance after walking along the uneven road for twenty minutes.

Celeste had been certain they were lost when they had spotted Mr. McKnell. She was still unsure what to make of her conversation with him. He seemed such an odd fellow at times, switching between affability and intensity, and she still always felt that all was not as it seemed when she was around him. Yet it bothered her that they had not parted well, with him no doubt thinking the worst of her. She had frozen when he had asked her where she had heard the rumor about Lady Celeste and a member of the Bellmoore family. Such a reasonable question ought to have been expected, but she found herself unprepared for it. It would not do to tell him that she had heard it from the Marchioness of Kingstone. She had bungled the whole thing and did not even gain any answers. All she had done was discover yet another ineptitude to add to her growing list.

Celeste felt torn. On the one hand, she wanted to speak with Mr. McKnell again, to repair his opinion of her and to try to achieve something useful. The urge to seek him out for those very reasons also frightened her a little. His character seemed so at odds with her first impression of him from the housekeeper, but then his character was at odds with his very existence as a servant. He had admitted to being raised a gentleman, though. It must be terribly difficult, as she was discovering, to adjust to such social decline.

Celeste thought back on her offer to assist him with employment should he need it. She had meant every word. The smile he affected when he insisted that all would be well was in such contrast to the sincerity from the previous moment that it was the opposite of reassuring. His chin was flexed a little, making him look sad. She had not meant to reach out and grasp his arm in that moment, but when she did, the simple contact made her breath catch. It was an inexplicable feeling, but it felt like her hand belonged there. It was vain to imagine that her small offer of assistance could be anything more than a passing kindness to him, but somehow it felt *right*.

Celeste nodded to herself as she picked up a petticoat that required some mending and situated herself beside the window of Bryn's bedroom. She would find a moment to seek Mr. McKnell out and speak with him again. She needed to finish her task first so that Bryn would not feel minded to do it herself, but she would head to the stables at her earliest opportunity.

Celeste's basic mending was not such a far cry from the needlework she was used to. She was required to work faster than she would when sitting down to a piece of embroidery, which she could accomplish at her leisure or never complete at all. When Bryn joined her in her spare hour before dinner, she picked up a headpiece to work on and they sat together, chatting as Celeste imagined sisters might. Bryn seemed more open than usual, sharing an animated retelling of everything she was experiencing as a lady. Lord Blakely featured in Bryn's anecdotes more than once, and Celeste suspected a growing attachment there. She did not interrupt, except to ask if Lord Blakely was the gentleman who had carried Bryn into the house. When Bryn looked down, her easy blush betraying her, Celeste could not keep her smile bitten back, much as she tried. It was not very likely that anything would come of it. Even if the gentleman did show an interest in her, they would have to tell the man the truth at some point. For now though, both Bryn and Celeste could enjoy a moment of fancy. No need for reality to ruin their evening.

Celeste would never have believed even a week before that she would miss being in society, but hearing all about the dinners, games, and picnics from Bryn's unique perspective triggered a longing in Celeste. Bryn made drawing room conversations sound like opportunities to form genuine friendships rather than meeting expectations. She made a normal dinner sound like an enchanting dream and reminded Celeste of the great joy to be had from the saddle of a horse. She had not been unhappy in her life, but she had never understood the privilege she had, to be able to enjoy those things the way Bryn did.

It was a unique feeling for Celeste to be envious of her own life.

By the time the upper servants had finished their evening meal, Celeste could bear it no longer and snuck outside through the kitchens to watch the party through the drawing room window. There was a convenient wide stone terrace outside with an external staircase leading up the side of it. Were it not for that, she would have had to try something as undignified as climbing. Though once the thought entered her head, she had to admit it sounded adventurous.

Keeping to the shadows at the side of the terrace, Celeste leaned around a tall potted plant to see inside through the large French windows. At first, she was hard-pressed to find Bryn, but when she did, it was quite a shock. The girl was radiant in her pale pink gown, wearing the floral hairpiece she had constructed earlier. She did not do anything conspicuous except smile at every person she spoke to as if her day had been brightened by their presence. It was not the aloofness expected by society that Celeste had been forced to practice, but she could not disapprove. It was how she had wished to behave, were her parents not always monitoring her. It was also what she had wanted for Bryn all along. She could not tell as yet which of the three gentlemen surrounding her might have been Lord Blakely, but Celeste was gratified that she was receiving so much attention. There were several ladies present also, none of whom appeared to be anything less than cordial toward her, which was a tremendous relief, society being what it was. It was obvious who the matrons were, but Celeste had no idea which of the younger ladies were Goldsmiths and which were Poppery's.

Celeste did not know how long she enjoyed the evening through Bryn before a shout broke the spell.

"Who is there?" the voice demanded. When she attempted to shrink behind the plant, the voice became authoritative. "I suggest you come out now or I shall call the dogs."

With a deep sigh, Celeste stepped out of the shadows, just as the man covered the last steps onto the terrace and seized her arm. He was faster than she had thought he would be.

"I am coming out, have a little patience, sir. Do unhand me!" She yanked her arm out of his grip, then covered her mouth with her hand as she realized that her impertinence had escaped without consideration of the consequences. As a servant, she could be punished, even whipped for it. Real fear struck her in the moments after her astonished captor complied and released her arm.

"Miss Coombe?"

The voice was one that Celeste was both relieved and embarrassed to hear, and with no hint of his false accent. He really ought to give it up entirely. Then again, in her moment of surprise, she had also neglected hers.

"Mr. McKnell?" Her voice shook, and she tried to cover it by clearing her throat. He stepped further into the light.

"What are you doing out here in the middle of the night?" he asked, his brows raised.

Celeste had no intention of admitting to Mr. McKnell of all people that she had been watching the house party from behind a plant in the dark because she regretted not joining them when she had the chance, before embarking on a foolhardy sham, exchanging her title and privileges for voluntary drudgery that she was utterly useless at. And all of that so that she could avoid the prospect of a connection with the very family that employed him, who held his loyalty and respect.

She did not wish to say any of that.

"It is hardly the middle of the night," Celeste skirted instead. She cocked her head with a grin in an effort to appear more confident. She had been caught, and she knew it.

"Nice try, but I intend to have an answer from you." He tried to smother an amused smile of his own, but it deepened his existing laugh lines and distracted her with his attractiveness.

Celeste understood with very little effort that being truthful would be her only escape from this conversation.

"I do not wish to say." She raised her eyebrows and pursed her lips, hoping that the warmth she felt in her cheeks was not visible in the darkness.

"I think you should. I thought you were some bandit up to no good." His brow creased a little and he folded his arms across his chest as he waited.

"It is embarrassing." Celeste whispered, avoiding his eyes by looking at his shoulder. It shook in silent laughter.

"I could have set the dogs on you, or worse, without even realizing it was you, but you do not want to tell me what clandestine thing you're up to because it is *embarrassing*?"

At least the incredulity in Mr. McKnell's voice made it lighter. Celeste knew he was right, and the situation could have been far worse had someone less pleasant caught her. She took a deep breath and readied herself for the self-consciousness she knew would follow her explanation.

"It was nothing like that. I was just...watching." She indicated the window with a wave of her hand. It dawned on her that she was fortunate no one inside had heard Mr. McKnell's shout.

An audible chuckle escaped him this time.

"It is not as glamorous as it looks, you know." He sounded sympathetic. He did not seem to notice that he was standing closer to her than was proper as he leaned around her to see in the window. Considering that she was in his way, it was no fault of his own, and she ought to have stepped backward to allow him more room to see, but something about his closeness kept her from moving. It was not that he smelled particularly wonderful; he actually smelled like a horse, which was not surprising. She ought to have returned inside the moment he discovered her there, rather than risking her reputation by remaining alone with him. She simply did not wish to move away.

Before Celeste had time to evaluate her motives, Mr. McKnell turned back to her. In the glow from the window, she could see enough of his face to see the surprise in his brown eyes as he realized their proximity. She held her breath, her heart beating audibly.

Mr. McKnell did not move for several seconds, his eyes never leaving hers. As close as he was, she could make out his expression, and it was no longer jovial or concerned, but intense in a different way. It made her stomach feel as though she had swallowed a robin. She did not move until a gasp escaped her. She had forgotten to breathe.

Mr. McKnell stepped backward.

"Allow me to escort you back to the house," he offered, his voice deep and gentle. He half-raised his arm, but then let it drop, seeming uncertain. When her tired legs stumbled a little on the first step, he reached out a hand to assist her balance. Again, as soon as their hands touched, Celeste felt that sense of rightness, that her hand belonged in his.

The fact that neither of them was wearing gloves meant that she felt every tiny movement of his hand, turning her legs a little more unsteady than they already were. He responded by linking her hand through his arm, lending her his steadiness and the reassuring strength beneath his sleeve.

"Thank you, Mr. McKnell," she whispered as they reached the bottom. He walked her around to the kitchens' entrance but hesitated a moment.

Before anything could be said, Sally, the young kitchen maid, opened the door with a pail in her hand and gaped when she saw them there together.

"Miss Coombe was..." Mr. McKnell's hesitation seemed to support whatever assumption was making Sally blush. Celeste had not come up with a plausible excuse for being out so late to cover herself, not intending to be caught. It did not help matters that their arms were still linked.

As the silence stretched, Celeste began to worry. Mr. McKnell already had a reputation with Betsy, perhaps even from being of assistance as he was now. She was beginning to see how the servants' network of gossip was every bit as efficient as the tabbies of London. She had to do something, so she stepped away from him and felt immediately bereft.

"It is alright, Mr. McKnell, you need not cover for me," Celeste began. His eyes darted to hers, and she felt the same fluttering in her midsection that she had experienced on the terrace. It took great mental control to remember that she was trying to spare both of their reputations and continue to speak instead of focusing on that.

Celeste took a long blink and swallowed to break the spell, then turned to Sally.

"Mr. McKnell happened upon me as I was watching all the finery through the drawing room window and was kind enough to escort me back," she confessed. Then she added in a conspiratorial whisper, "They all look so beautiful in their fancy gowns."

Sally's smile brightened, appearing to understand the sentiment very well.

"Many a night I been tempted to do the same," she confided. Celeste turned to Mr. McKnell.

"Sally will not tell my embarrassing little secret, will you, Sally?" She turned her practiced dramatic gaze on the girl, the one she kept reserved for influencing her parents, hoping the slight shake in her voice would go unnoticed.

"No, Miss Elsie. After you helpin' me with my hand th' other ev'nin', I'll not tell a soul," she vowed, with the bandaged hand on her heart.

Without another word, Sally realized that she was still standing in the doorway and stepped aside to allow them entrance. Celeste clasped her good hand in gratitude, noting how callused it was for one so young, and felt a pang of something foreign in her heart.

With a quick bow, Mr. McKnell excused himself to resume whatever it was he had been doing when he passed by and found her.

Despite her little adventure, Celeste still had some time before she expected Bryn to return to her room, so she retrieved one of Bryn's plainer gowns and went to the servants' room she shared with Betsy to embroider some daisies into it. Bryn had mentioned before that she used to go searching for them with her sisters as a child, so Celeste set herself up with some thread and began her work.

The springs were noisy, but at least the bed was sprung. It could have been a slab with a thin mattress. Betsy had mentioned on more than one occasion that the Bellmoore's were generous with their servants. Perhaps that was one example of what she had meant. Celeste was very grateful when she sank down on the bed in exhaustion every night. It might not have been as soft as goose down, but it was far superior to what it could have been. It inspired her to inspect her own family's servant quarters upon her return home.

Half an hour and a few intricate daisies later, Betsy burst through the door backwards, trembling from head to toe.

"Betsy?" Celeste sat upright in alarm. Betsy turned her ashen face to Celeste, inspiring her to rush to her side.

"What is it, Betsy? What has happened?" she asked, wrapping an arm around her quivering shoulders while several terrifying speculations swirled in her mind.

Betsy reached a hand toward the door, so Celeste nudged it shut with her foot. As she led Betsy to sit on her bed, she turned wide, frightened eyes on Celeste.

"They's p—p—PIRATES!" She threw a hand over her mouth. Her eyes were like china plates.

Celeste froze. They were not close to any ports but were not far enough inland to discount the possibility. Still, the pirate threat had been for the most part eradicated. Hadn't it?

"What pirates?" Celeste asked in a hushed voice.

"I 'eard 'em." Betsy's speech grew worse with her fear. "They's pirates. That man, the dreadful one what makes any maid shudder."

"The valet? The brutish one?" Celeste asked about the one man she had met in the house party who fit that description.

"Yeah, 'im and 'is master. M—m—mort—" Betsy could not get the name out as tears streamed down her cheeks.

Celeste was unsure what to make of that. Reeves was not a nice man but a pirate?

She held Betsy's head to her chest and rocked back and forth in an attempt to be soothing. Being an only surviving child meant that she had very little experience being the one to calm anybody, so she tried to mimic what her father might do for her.

"There, there," she whispered, the way he would. "Slow down and start from the beginning."

Celeste rubbed Betsy's back until she was calm enough to sit up.

"Thank you kindly, Elsie," she said with an immediate improvement to her speech. Celeste had never noticed before the way Betsy's eyes crinkled in concentration every time she spoke. For someone who enjoyed talking as much as she did, that must have been quite an effort.

"That's alright," Celeste reassured her. "Now tell me, what is this all about?"

"Well, I were—was—on my way from her ladyship's suite and was walkin' in the shadows when I passed a door ajar. Inside was—were—the two men, that rotten one and his master. I thought I'd listen, and what do you think they were talkin' about?" She waited until Celeste shook her head. "They was talking about his ship what intercepted another one they didn't like, to fix themselves up with more gold or something." Her eyes widened further if that were possible.

Celeste was unsure what to make of it.

"Did they say anything else?" she asked. Betsy shook her head, but her eyes still rivaled carriage wheels. "It may be quite innocent, if we do not even have any context," Celeste suggested. It did sound suspicious to her too, but one could not assume anything on so little evidence, as she was learning. Besides, she was quite sure that the navy had put an end to the dreadful business of piracy long ago.

Betsy shook her head.

"No, I feel it, Elsie. I feel it in my bones. They's bad ones alright," she insisted.

"Did they catch you listening?" Celeste asked. Betsy's face paled further.

"I don't rightly know. I heard their footsteps and ran slapdash for the stairs and came 'ere, not lookin' behind me. Do you think they'll hurt me to protect their secrets?" She began to shake again.

"No, I do not think so," Celeste soothed, not at all as sure as she sounded. "They would have followed you all the way if they had seen you." She hoped her logic was sound.

No suspicious noises were forthcoming from beyond the door, even after some time had passed, so Celeste was able to reassure Betsy into falling asleep.

Chapter Fourteen

As Jacob woke for the day, he rubbed at the thickening stubble on his face. It took longer to grow than he preferred for his disguise, but he was surprised to find that he liked being unshaven. He was not one to spend a great deal of time over a looking glass, but he fancied it suited him. He wondered if anyone else thought so. In particular, he wondered if Miss Coombe thought so.

Jacob needed to have his head examined. Perhaps it was the pressure of the implied engagement cultivated by his mother that inspired his inconvenient reaction to Lady Celeste's maid. Even after finding out that her loyalties lay not with Lady Celeste, but with whomever was circulating gossip about the lady and himself. That still made him uneasy to think about. Though upon further reflection, Jacob could concede that he may have jumped to conclusions too soon. Since then, he had come up with a few possibilities for why she might wish to protect her informer. Most of them were innocent. Like, if Lady Celeste were trying to ascertain how far the rumor had spread and had asked her maid to find out what she could. That was fair enough, and something he also wished to know, but some of his ideas were not very flattering at all. Possibilities like Miss Coombe spreading an idle report for her own entertainment seemed a disservice to her character, especially after she had shown him such empathy. He did not wish to think so ill of her. Why he felt that way was something he was also hesitant to examine. It was inevitable that such reflections led Jacob to thoughts of the previous night.

He had come from the stables after a good long day of work when he had seen someone moving in the shadows near the house. Upon apprehending them, he was shocked to discover that his villain was the very non-threatening Miss Coombe. Despite any misgivings he may have felt about her, he was lightheaded when he considered the potential consequences for her had he sounded the alarm. Although he couldn't help but smile when he recalled her embarrassment at being caught daydreaming at the window. Not that he had seen that part, but he wished he had. His imagination had furnished him with a lovely image as soon as she had confessed her real purpose. In his version, he saw her gazing in, hands clasped to her chest, a wistful smile playing at her lips.

When Jacob had turned to find her standing so close to him, staring into his eyes, he had felt the insane urge to kiss her. Then her sudden intake of breath had reminded him yet again that he was indeed a gentleman, and so instead, he had seen her safely inside. It was by far the more sensible option, and now he was grateful he had taken it. Perhaps his charade would have to end sooner than he planned if he were entertaining ideas of kissing servants. Only then, his marriage to the lady who was sweet but stirred no such feelings would loom upon him like the impact after being thrown from a horse; a speedy inevitability that would appear to be in slow motion until the moment of inescapable impact. And she would bring her maid with her.

As it was, Jacob was struggling to maintain his false sickness in a convincing way for his mother. Though she had not shown any outward signs of suspicion, it had been almost a full week, and he lacked ideas on how to prolong his 'illness' after his apparent recovery when she had visited unannounced. He needed advice.

Without further postponement, Jacob climbed out of bed and rang for Giles, who startled him by appearing in an instant.

"Oh, Giles, where did you come from?" He calmed his breathing.

"Apologies, sir," Giles bowed. "I was in the room next door."

"Think nothing of it. Would you please summon Lord Blakely for me?" Jacob asked, then added, "With discretion."

"Right away, sir." Giles bowed again, then left the room, dignified as ever.

At first Jacob paced the room, but then stopped, wondering if his mother would accompany Zach for the visit. Muttering under his breath, he headed back to bed. He had just enough time to leap in before they both entered the room.

Upon seeing his increased breathing, Jacob's mother rushed to his side, worry etched on her brow. Jacob felt the guilt he had been contemplating expand further to include his mother. She placed the back of her hand on his forehead, followed by a hand on his heart.

"You are not fevered, but your heart is racing a little," she frowned. "I am surprised that you are still not feeling well, dear. You seemed so much improved. It must be worse than it appears. Giles, send for Doctor Fitzpatrick forthwith."

"Mother, I will be alright. There is no need for the doctor," Jacob protested in a panic, realizing that this was, as he feared, the beginning of the end. It had been naïve of him to think he could avoid the entire long party. He had been fortunate to get out of it for as long as he had.

"Nonsense, your eyes are positively wild." She may have been right about that. Giles' apprehensive glance in his direction showed the first sign of emotion Jacob had seen on the man before he left to carry out the countess' instructions.

Well, this was a fine pickle. How was he to fool a doctor? Should he even try? He could confess and have the whole thing over with, but there were still nine days of the house party left, and he was no more ready to face his future than when he had started on this course. He looked up to see Zach trying very hard not to laugh. He was doing a terrible job of concealing it though; his entire torso was trembling, and his forced frown looked as full of mirth as any smile. Jacob tried not to look at him.

"Mother, I am certain Doctor Fitzpatrick has many more pressing cases than mine at present. Babies being born, inert accident victims, elderly folk knocking at death's door…" he tried one last attempt at dissuading his mother from her course, but to no avail.

Doctor Fitzpatrick arrived all too soon, reassuring them that the day had been a quiet one for him, and it was no inconvenience at all. If Jacob had not known better, he would have thought the doctor was sabotaging his ruse. Zach made faces at his friend from behind the doctor, trying to elicit a laugh and force him to break character. He only managed to make Jacob scowl, which seemed to amuse Zach even more than achieving his goal would have.

After a thorough examination, and several hmms, the doctor stared at Jacob for a moment with his arms folded across his chest, one hand reaching up to scratch his jaw. He shifted his weight from foot to foot.

"Mr. Bellmoore, I am not certain how to tell you this..." The doctor glanced at the countess and Jacob frowned, his brow creasing in confusion.

"You cannot have anything dreadful to say," Jacob scoffed, glancing at each face in the room before settling back on the doctor.

"Mr. Bellmoore, I understand you have been under a good deal of stress of late?" he clarified.

"Well, yes, but nothing that is unusual for a gentleman of my circumstances. My mother is trying to force me into matrimony, nothing more." He looked at his mother, expecting to have to apologize for his words, but her face was impassive. Odd. She always had one emotion or another clearly readable in her expression.

Jacob looked back at the doctor. He had never been the most effervescent man, but he was not usually so uncertain and fidgety either. It was beginning to make Jacob nervous.

"Well, out with it, man." Zach's impatient tone came as a surprise to Jacob. There was nothing jovial in his bearing now. All the color had drained from his face, and Jacob realized he must be thinking of his late brother and his parents. He had lost so much.

"It seems that it may all be bringing you a bit low," the doctor stated after a pause.

"Whatever do you mean, Doctor?" Jacob's mother asked with a lacy handkerchief ready to wipe at threatening tears, a direct contrast to just seconds before. Doctor Fitzpatrick shifted his weight again.

"I am not a specialist in this area, but I do believe the stress has made you rather unwell. Your heart is quite fast, and it is most unusual for a young man such as yourself to react in such a manner at the onset of matrimonial news," he managed with several pauses between words. That brought both relief and confusion to Jacob.

"I can explain that—" Jacob began, ready to have this over with.

"Oh, my poor dear! Your heart!" His mother wailed, surprising Jacob. What had the doctor said about his heart? That it was a little fast? That could not be anything to be concerned over.

"What do you suggest?" Jacob asked.

"Plenty of rest, no great excitement. Perhaps some leisure or short walks might do you some good. I shall return tomorrow. Until then, you should stay in bed." Giving instructions seemed to bring the doctor's professional confidence back.

Jacob nodded, unsure of what had just happened. The doctor had not said anything of note, but Jacob's mother's tenuous fortitude lasted only until the doctor left. Then her tears came out with great sobs as she threw herself over her son.

"Mother, really. It is nothing serious. I am not even sick. My heart is just a little fast, which can be explained." Jacob tried to comfort her.

"My poor little angel!" his mother wailed. Jacob rolled his eyes. It was unusual for her to give in to theatrics, but he owned that he had caused her a great deal of worry of late.

"I am hardly that," he disagreed but stroked her hair as she drenched his shirt. He sighed. Doctor Fitzpatrick had just given him the perfect excuse to continue avoiding the house party, but he was feeling too guilty to take advantage of it. He could not have his mother believe he was in any real danger.

"Perhaps I should fetch your brother," Zach offered. Jacob could not tell by his expression if he put any stock into what the doctor had said or not.

"Oh, you are so thoughtful, Zachariah!" Jacob's mother turned her attention to him. "That is just the thing. We will discuss it and make a plan."

"Think nothing of it, ma'am, I am happy to be of service." He offered a quick bow, then left the room to fetch Whitbury.

"What a good friend Zachariah is. He has always been a considerate boy, even when you were children," Jacob's mother said, her sudden calm being an eerie contrast.

"Yes, he is quite the best of men. Mother, are you quite well?"

"Yes, dear." She sat beside him on the bed and patted his hand. "I was overcome for a moment, but I think you are right. Of course, it is nothing serious. You know how I can be."

"Yes, but you are not usually so erratic." He eyed her with concern. She laughed but said nothing more as she wiped away the last of her remaining tears. Not for the first time, Jacob wondered if he ought to be concerned about senility.

As Whitbury approached, his voice could be heard from down the hall.

"The entire family cannot be missing at once. I am the host and must see to the comfort of our guests. If Jacob does not wish to be one of them, then we should leave him be."

Jacob fought the urge to grin. His brother was being an ally without even knowing it.

"Our company will be well enough off for a few minutes," his mother said over her shoulder as Whitbury and Zach entered the room. "Lady Adelle is present, and she will relish the opportunity to play hostess in her future home."

"He does not appear any different from the last time I saw him," Whitbury asserted, whilst looking Jacob up and down like a stallion at Tattersall's. He leaned against the wall opposite the bed with his arms folded against his chest.

"His color is much better today, I must say. He appeared quite ghastly the other evening, you know," their mother added.

"*He* is lying right here!" Jacob piped in. "There is nothing the matter with my hearing."

Again, Whitbury peered at him with skepticism. Jacob had to remember that he did want his brother to believe that he was ill.

"And the doctor is certain that there is something the matter with him?" Again, Whitbury spoke as if Jacob were not present.

"Yes. You may ask him yourself when he returns tomorrow. He said there is something the matter with his heart." Their mother nodded.

Jacob had to bite his lip to stop himself from refuting the exaggeration.

"And he is required to remain abed?" Whitbury's right eyebrow raised.

"Yes, I am going to check on him every hour or so to be certain he is resting." She nodded again.

Jacob was confident that his heart might have stopped in reality for a moment or two. Having his mother check on him every hour meant that he could not leave the room. He could not attend the stables. He would be trapped. The large room was already beginning to feel more like a dungeon.

"How are you faring today, dear?" Jacob's mother finally spoke directly to him.

"I would feel better if not confined to this tiny room." He could not keep his legs still, already itching to go outside.

"This room is one of the largest in the house, next to the master suite, of course," Whitbury protested.

"It would not matter if it were the size of Hyde Park, I am still confined to the boundaries of this bed," Jacob retorted, looking at Zach for commiseration, but he was watching the scene with his brows drawn in worry.

"It is only until Doctor Fitzpatrick says otherwise. I am certain he will wish you to move about more soon enough. In the meantime, I shall send up a book with one of the maids. Any requests?" his mother offered.

"Miss Coombe if she is available," Jacob answered before properly considering the question.

Whitbury laughed out loud. "Taken a fancy to one of the maids, have you? Is she one of ours?"

"Charles! I mean Whitbury, I do apologize," she corrected. "That is not what he meant! Really!" Their mother blushed only a little less than Jacob himself, but her chagrin was also for a different reason. It was rare for her to forget to address her eldest son by his title instead of his given name, and Whitbury did appear annoyed.

"I only wished for someone who would have a passable taste in books if they are to fetch me one," Jacob fumbled out the excuse. It seemed to distract his brother well enough as his focus shifted back to Jacob, his mouth quirking upwards.

In truth, Jacob had no idea if Miss Coombe even read, only that she was protective of what Lady Celeste read. The memory of their unconventional meeting in the carriage house, and the fuss she made over the unknown book, made Jacob's face attempt to smile against his better judgment. It took physical effort to counter the urge. Not that it mattered, Whitbury did not believe the excuse any more than Jacob himself did if the laughter in his brother's eyes was anything to go on. At least he was no longer scowling at their mother.

"*I* will select a book for you, dear boy." There was something off about his mother's smile as she said that. Perhaps it would be best if Miss Coombe were not selected for the task after all.

Half an hour after they left, a soft knock on his door had Jacob's pulse racing. He hoped that was not an unhealthy sign. He shook his head. He knew full well that there was nothing at all the matter with him. Still, he had asked Giles to deliver a note to Tom explaining that he would not be tending the stables. At least not until he could work out how watchful his mother and brother would be, and for how long.

Jacob propped himself up and tried to appear as well as a man in his sickbed could.

"Come in," he called out. When the maid entered, he rather wished he had feigned sleep. It was the maid from Mrs. Thatcher's stairwell fiction, Betsy. He should have known that Miss Coombe would never be the one to bring him his book. She was a lady's maid, and not even a Whitbury servant. Although there was a part of him that was relieved. If she were the one to come, it would follow that she would find out his identity.

Betsy bobbed a curtsy as she handed Jacob a volume of Shakespeare.

"Mr. Bellmoore, your mother asked me to fetch this to you." She looked up at him for a brief moment.

"Thank you." He offered her an automatic smile as he took it. She gave a tiny gasp when their fingers touched.

"Are you alright?" He sat forward, concerned that she had hurt herself in some unseen manner. She looked up at him with eyes that reminded him of a small woodland creature he had seen in Italy.

"It's just that, I don't mean to speak out of turn, but—" she hesitated.

"Go on," he urged, feeling like her voice was triggering a memory. He tried to figure out if it was important.

"Well, I wondered why you asked for me, sir." She kept glancing down, then back up again, as if she were having trouble deciding where to rest her eyes.

"Oh, I didn't. That is, my mother offered to send a book." It was the oddest conversation he had ever had. For some reason, the answer embarrassed her.

"Oh, I thought, with Mrs. Thatcher and all. Or the pirates..." She began fidgeting with her apron.

"Pirates?" he asked, baffled.

"I don't want to be no trouble, I know they're his lordship's guests and all, and Elsie said they might be a context—" she rambled.

Jacob held up a hand at the mention of Miss Coombe.

"Sorry, what did Elsie say?" He asked, realizing too late that he had used her Christian name. He quite liked how it sounded, but he tried not to react.

The maid did not appear to notice, so it seemed he got away with it. She bit her lip.

"It is alright, you are not in any trouble from me." Jacob gave his best smile to inspire her to trust him, and she stumbled on the spot. He reached out a hand to catch her elbow on instinct, and when she looked at him agape with unmasked adoration, he remembered why her voice sounded familiar. She had been the one extolling his virtues to Elsie, *Miss Coombe*, in the kitchens a few days past. And Miss Coombe had agreed that she found him handsome.

His dual response of pleasure and dread as he froze with his mouth hanging open was interrupted by Betsy's breathless words. "Thank you, sir." She looked a little dazed. His discomfort increased.

Jacob removed his hand from Betsy's elbow as soon as he could and attempted to lead her back to the conversation.

"You are quite welcome. Now, what did Miss Coombe say about pirates?"

Chapter Fifteen

∽⌒∾⌒∾

When Betsy tore down the stairs to the kitchens, almost tripping on the last few, Celeste jumped. She looked around to see if someone was in pursuit, but the only people observable were those taking their lunch.

"Betsy, what is it?" she asked, worried that perhaps there was some trouble with Mr. Reeves, Lord Mortcastle's sinister valet.

Betsy leaned on the table and let out a sigh that would rival anyone on the stage. "He is so dashing, every girl's dream, he is!" She sat down with a vacant smile. It was clear that she was not speaking of Reeves.

"Have you had another—" Celeste lowered her voice. "Another moment with Mr. McKnell?" she asked, more interested than she ought to be.

"Oh, that's right, I forgot you don't know," Betsy giggled.

"Don't know what?" Celeste asked.

Mrs. Thatcher threw Betsy a sharp look from across the kitchen.

"Oh, that he is, uh, unwell," she stammered. "Oh, but he's still handsome, it's quite a feat to be handsome even when ill. Of course, nothing 'appened, and it won't, with him being the...um, decent sort and all, but oh..." And she was gone again. Celeste decided to drop the subject, knowing that she would hear more than she wished to later on when she would rather be sleeping.

Celeste could not smother the relief she felt at Betsy's admission that nothing had happened between her and Mr. McKnell, and she was concerned to hear that he was unwell. Even though Celeste's conversation with him about the marriage arrangement had gone awry, she had been impressed by his reaction to her withholding information regarding his master. She still wished to repair whatever ill he thought of her, but it was a mark in favor of his character that he was loyal. He had seemed his usual affable self when they had met by accident on the terrace the previous night, but that interaction strengthened her desire to resolve any misconceptions between them. She was not prepared to tell him the whole truth about herself yet, but she did not like the idea of him thinking poorly of her either.

Both Celeste and Betsy's daydreaming of Mr. McKnell was inter-rupted by the imposing figure of Reeves entering the kitchens. He was far bulkier than any other valet Celeste had ever seen, and his unruly black hair made him appear far too messy for the role. Another thing that seemed out of place about him was his American accent. Celeste was not an authority on the subject, but the few Americans she had met had come to England from wealth. Why anyone would come all this way just to be a valet was a mystery. The more often he spoke to her in his condescending manner, the more she was certain that he was one of the men she had overheard in the garden. The context of that conversation hadn't made a lot of sense either.

Betsy went rigid as he approached. Reeves looked at them with a sneer.

"Good afternoon, Mr. Reeves." Celeste greeted him with politeness, if only to draw his focus away from Betsy. He did not greet her back and for once refrained from asking how she managed to trip over herself to knock her head, but he looked her over with a grunt of appreciation that was quite indecent. She could not suppress the shudder that passed over her. Then, just as any other time he made an appearance, he collected his meal from Mrs. Cooper and left, not interacting with any of the other servants on his way. She did not see him again at all that day, which was a happy circumstance. She hoped it also meant that Betsy had not been discovered in her suspicions.

The following afternoon, Celeste had a welcome opportunity to leave the house, which had begun to feel oppressive. Lord Blakely invited Bryn to accompany him on a ride around the estate, and Bryn asked Celeste to come along as a chaperone. Celeste could not have been happier, not only to go outside, but to properly meet this Lord

Blakely who seemed to have captured Bryn's attention. She did not consider watching him carrying her, injured, from the stable house as a real introduction. Bryn had been no more forthcoming regarding any feelings for him, but it was obvious in her sweet smile and accompanying blush every time she mentioned the gentleman's name.

As they arrived at the stable yard, Celeste noticed, not for the first time, that the stable house with all its buildings and yards was the size of a manor on one of her father's smaller estates, and was very well kept. The Whitbury title must have been a prosperous one.

Drawing closer to the actual stable, Celeste heard arguing in low voices. At first, she worried that it may be the same men they had heard in the garden, but as they drew closer, she recognized the brogue of the stable master, Mr. McInnes, and she relaxed.

"I'll not have you droppin' dead in my care. You're like another son to me."

Celeste rounded the corner to see who he was arguing with, surprised to see Mr. McKnell's back. She recalled Betsy mentioning his illness but nothing so severe as that.

Celeste felt her heart drop into her shoes and stopped where she stood.

"Tom, you know as well as I do that there is nothing the matter with me! I am going mad locked up in that stuffy room with naught but Shakespeare for company." His voice was strained, but he insisted that he was well. Celeste hoped he was, and that it was not just a show of bravado.

"There's nocht wrong with Shakespeare, and you're lucky you have the education t'enjoy it," Mr. McInnes argued.

"My mother sent it up bookmarked at *As You Like It.* It has me worried," Mr. McKnell returned out of the side of his mouth.

Celeste searched her memory, trying to recall the details of that particular story. It was one she had found amusing, but she could not recall any of the prose, only the outline of Rosalind running around the forest trying to teach Orlando how to be in love with her. There was nothing she could think of that would be alarming about that.

"I've not read a great deal of Shakespeare maself. I dinnae ken which one that is lad."

Mr. McKnell may have been about to speak, but Bryn's approaching footfalls behind Celeste alerted the men to their presence, and they spun around. Celeste tried to appear as though she had heard nothing by looking around toward Bryn. She took the opportunity to regard Mr. McKnell through the corner of her eye while he was facing her. He did not appear unwell at all. In fact, he looked...strong. He had not shaved his face in a number of days as the beginnings of a beard were complementing his jaw, but that was the only thing different about him from the day she had arrived. Mr. McInnes's concern was incongruous with just how good he did look. Celeste's heart skipped a beat, and she swallowed, afraid that either of them might notice her scrutiny or the way her breathing had increased, just a little.

"Lady Celeste, Miss Coombe," Mr. McKnell greeted, glancing between them as if he had just been caught stealing treats from Mrs. Cooper's kitchen. Celeste did her best to school her own expression so that she would not appear similar.

"Mr. McKnell. How good that you are so recovered," she offered. She searched his face, hoping to discover a reason for his appearance of guilt.

"He's not recovered, and he's goin' back to bed!" Mr. McInnes commanded, turning back to Mr. McKnell. "If a doctor says you need to rest, then that's who I'll be listenin' to, regardless of anythin' else." Mr. McInnes sent him a meaningful glare.

Mr. McKnell smiled at the older man, even while he shook his head with a sigh.

"Alright, Tom. I'll return just as soon as I have exercised Thor."

"How is exercisin' a horse restful? Your bum's out the windae!" Mr. McInnes threw his hands in the air.

"My what is where?" Mr. McKnell asked with a mixture of incredulity and suppressed laughter, his eyes expressing his humor before his face ever had the chance. Celeste blushed at the vivid expression, looking away, but in the privacy of her own mind she also found it rather amusing.

"You're not makin' sense," Mr. McInnes translated in exasperation.

"You can come with us, Jack. We will keep to a walk," Lord Blakely offered as he approached from behind Bryn.

Celeste chastised herself for being a poor chaperone, having not paid the slightest attention to his arrival. Bryn did not seem at all unhappy though; she was smiling with her entire face. Lord Blakely appeared much the same, with an open countenance and a ready smile.

"Lord Blakely," Mr. McInnes turned his attention to the new arrivals. "Mr. ah, McKnell, has been informed by the doctor that he needs to rest his heart. Would you please keep an eye out for him?"

Mr. McKnell shot Mr. McInnes an annoyed glance, which was ignored. Celeste's mouth dropped open. A heart problem sounded dire indeed. She hoped it was something he could recover from.

"Of course I will, McInnes. Like he was my own brother," Lord Blakely nodded, his expression more serious than it had been a moment before. His voice even sounded thicker. It was curious that an earl should care so much for a stablehand, in someone else's employ no less, but Celeste liked him more for it.

"Thank you, My lord. *I'll* saddle Thor." Mr. McInnes shot Mr. McKnell a pointed look, who rolled his eyes as he paced a few steps away with grudging acquiescence.

The ride across the wide green landscape north of the manor was peaceful and warm, with the sun shining but not hot. Once they had crested a hill that hid civilization behind them, Celeste closed her eyes and basked in the feeling of warmth on her face and the steady movements of the horse beneath her. She stretched out her arms and splayed her fingers. She had missed the feeling of freedom a ride afforded her. It was just what she needed.

When she opened her eyes, Mr. McKnell was watching her. Celeste had forgotten for a moment that she was not alone. She lowered her arms, holding the reins loose, and looked ahead to see that Bryn and Lord Blakely were engaged in amiable conversation not too far away before speaking.

"Do not worry, I will not fall," she assured him.

Mr. McKnell smiled. "No, you appear quite comfortable on horseback."

"I have been riding all my life, but I did not consider what a fortunate circumstance I had until recently." She closed her eyes again but opened them when Mr. McKnell spoke.

"What made you see it?"

Celeste was surprised that he was interested. Perhaps manservants were not as shallow conversationalists as gentlemen. Though the thought seemed too generalized, even to Celeste.

"Being in the service of my lady," Celeste answered with sincerity, indicating Bryn with a nod. She was determined to be as honest as she could with him under the circumstances.

"Have you not been together long? You seem so well acquainted," Mr. McKnell asked.

"Well, we are—it is a long story. I have only been in this position for the duration of the house party, although we have known each other longer," she fumbled.

"I would like to hear that story sometime," he smiled.

"Are you so bored with your book?" she quipped with a grin.

He looked alarmed at first, his eyebrows shooting up before he recovered his expression. She was not sure what had inspired that and felt a strong desire to know.

"I apologize for overhearing a private conversation, but if you do not mind my asking, what is it you so object to in that play that would cause you such concern? I myself find it delightful."

Celeste's question seemed to unnerve him. Perhaps she should not have admitted to knowing Shakespeare. She was not certain if his works were something a servant would have ready access to.

"It is just that I..." He pursed his lips, thinking for a moment. "I played a little trick on my mother, and she is a very intelligent woman. I fear what her counterstrategy may entail if she finds me out. It has made me somewhat suspicious, I'm afraid. I believe the play is a clue."

Mr. McKnell smiled to himself, his expression brightening. Even though he was wearing a tattered, ancient-looking tricorn, the way the sun shone on his face highlighted his cheeks when they lifted.

Celeste could not be more surprised by his answer, but her interest in this aspect of Mr. McKnell's character overshadowed her curiosity about the jest itself and what *As You Like It* might have to do with it.

"You play tricks on each other? She plays them on you, and you do not mind?" The astonishment she felt was evident in her voice.

"Not at all. She is a rare one, my mother. If she has discovered my trick, I can guarantee she is already thinking of how to repay it." He laughed with open affection.

Celeste just stared at him for a long time, which was not at all difficult to do.

"I do not mean that as a slight on her character. It is something I admire about her," Mr. McKnell added when she did not respond.

"I apologize. I do not mean my silence to construe judgment. I am merely surprised. I thought most men despised a woman with intellect." She did not mean for the cynical words to tumble out like that, but he did not appear offended.

"It is far too common, I will admit," he nodded.

Celeste's brow creased in contemplation.

"You seem puzzled, Miss Coombe," Mr. McKnell remarked.

"It is just that my father is the only man I have ever met who has never required a lady to modify her conversation. He has never made me feel inferior or labeled me a bluestocking, but others certainly have."

Celeste searched Mr. McKnell's face again. His perspective made him more attractive. It was easy to see why Betsy swooned every time he gave her the slightest bit of attention. Or entered a room.

"Well, now you have met two," he replied, then rethought. "You had better make that three, as I believe Lord Blakely would be insulted not to make the tally."

Celeste smiled and nodded, pleased. Lord Blakely did seem to be very interested in everything Bryn was saying to him up ahead.

"How do you know him so well? If it is not prying to ask," Celeste thought aloud.

"We were at school together."

"I take it that was before your circumstances changed," she said with a small frown of sympathy. Mr. McKnell seemed startled, but after a moment he recovered his features.

"Yes, and his elder brother was also a good friend to mine."

"Was? Did they have a falling out?" Celeste wondered if that had anything to do with his current misfortunes.

"No. Lord Blakely's brother died of an accident just this year past." Mr. McKnell looked down.

"Oh, I see." Celeste berated herself. Now that he had said that, she did recall Bryn saying something to that effect.

They rode on in comfortable silence for a few minutes before Celeste built up the courage to approach the subject she had been wanting an opportunity to speak with him about.

"Mr. McKnell, I hope you will not think me too brazen, but I must address a misunderstanding between us," Celeste dove in.

"Oh?" His eyes widened, and his breathing seemed to still. Apart from the movement necessitated by the horse, he seemed to be frozen in place.

"There is no need to look so terrified." Celeste let out a laugh.

"I apologize. I have been a little on edge of late." He smiled, shaking his head. Some of his hair came loose from being tied back under his weathered hat, and it brushed his shoulder without him seeming to notice. She had not seen hair quite that long on other men of their generation, but it looked well on him. The loose strands drew attention to his well-defined jaw and neck, enhancing his attractiveness. She wanted to bring her horse closer so that she could reach out and touch the loose strands, brushing them aside, but that was ridiculous.

Celeste traced the curves of the pommel with her fingertips to help her focus on what she wanted to say.

"I refer to our conversation in the daisies regarding some gossip around our households." She could not look at him for fear of seeing his disapproval resurface. She heard him draw a deep breath.

"Please go on," he urged, his tone patient.

"It was not idle gossip I was referring to that day. I had heard directly from my lady—" or herself, "—that an arrangement may have been made between her parents and Lady Whitbury for a marriage to take place with the younger son, Mr. Bellmoore. As you can imagine, I was hesitant to share that information because I had no wish to add to any speculation on the subject. I apologize for not knowing what to say in the moment."

"You were avoiding gossip?" he clarified.

"Yes, exactly."

Celeste hazarded a glance in his direction. Mr. McKnell appeared to be studying his horse's mane. When he looked up and met her eyes, she was not prepared for the feeling that accompanied the softness of his gaze. She may have been imagining it, but she thought she could perceive respect there. It filled her from head to toe with a vibrant energy, very much like the feeling of sunshine.

To prevent herself from staring at Mr. McKnell indefinitely, Celeste decided to test his self-proclaimed humor.

"Why is a dog like a tree?" she asked without preamble. His eyebrows rose in surprise.

"They have a bark?"

"They both lose their bark when they die," she smiled. "I read that one in a periodical last year."

His returning smile did not tell her whether he found the joke funny or not, but she liked the gesture anyway.

After a few moments, Celeste was pleasantly surprised when Mr. McKnell began another. "Did you hear the one about the man who bought jewels for his wife every day?"

"No, tell me." She grinned wider.

"He called her *Dear*," he laughed. Celeste rolled her eyes but laughed anyway, enjoying his participation and the deep rumble of his laughter.

They passed the remainder of the ride that way, recalling every joke they could think of. Each one was more ridiculous than the last, and some should not have been funny at all, but by the time they returned to the stables their laughter had increased until they struggled to stay in their saddles.

Mr. McKnell dismounted first, then approached Celeste's horse to help her down. As she slipped into his hands, her heart beat faster, and she felt lightheaded, no doubt from laughing too hard. He held her waist to steady her for a few moments more.

"Are you alright?" he asked, his voice reduced to a whisper. He was standing close enough that the shade from his hat provided relief from the sun's heat to both of them, and seemed to enshroud them from the world, but the warmth she felt did not abate. It seemed to be coming from within her.

Celeste could do nothing but nod as her hands rested on Mr. McKnell's forearms. His eyes caressed her face and settled on her mouth. She held her breath, her lips tingling.

"Ahem." Lord Blakely's voice fractured the moment, and they leaped apart. Celeste went from hardly breathing at all to rapid inhalations within seconds. She looked at Bryn, whose eyes were wide, but her mouth was pulled up at the side in a knowing smile.

Celeste had been so caught up in the moment that she had altogether forgotten the other couple's existence. Her cheeks burned, and she looked to Mr. McKnell, but he was staring at the ground, his jaw flexing. It was such a drastic change to his countenance that it worried her.

"Mr. McKnell, are you well?" She reached out to him, but he stepped back.

"Yes, I am, thank you." He would not meet her eyes.

"Is it your heart?" she questioned further, not wishing it to be so, but also hoping she had not done or said something to upset him. Again. He looked up.

"Yes," he answered before swallowing hard. "I...I must return to the house." He touched his hat and strode away barely a moment after finishing his sentence. Celeste watched after him, worried for his health.

"I will inquire after him," Lord Blakely reassured her, then escorted Bryn back to the house.

Celeste followed at a respectful distance, reliving the moment when she was sure Mr. McKnell was about to kiss her, over and over in her mind.

Once alone in Bryn's room, both women turned to each other, watching for the other's reaction. Irrepressible smiles forced their light upon both of their faces. In unison, they clasped hands and squealed. When they managed to calm themselves, Celeste poured them each a glass of water from a pitcher, after which they flopped onto the bed like a couple of school misses.

"He is so..." Bryn could not find a word to adequately describe who Celeste assumed was Lord Blakely.

"Yes, he is," Celeste agreed, picturing a different man in her mind.

"If it isn't too bold to ask, does your inheritance specify *who* you need to marry?" Bryn asked after a pause, turning her head to look at Celeste. It was the last question she expected.

"I do not know, but I don't think so. That is my parents' idea," she shrugged. "I imagine they would have informed me after the ball that night if there were any more rules I needed to be aware of."

"He does not specifically have to be a gentleman, then?" Bryn surmised, glancing at Celeste sideways. "He could be anyone. Even a...stablehand?"

Celeste made no move to sit up, instead expending all of her effort in trying to stop the smile forcing its way onto her face. Whilst it was a little premature to contemplate such things, she could not dismiss the thought.

Chapter Sixteen

Jacob paced every open inch of his bedroom. He attempted to sit down more than once, but his agitation would launch him back onto his feet every time. He could not disregard the most enjoyable afternoon he had ever experienced. However, he also could not remove Zach's reproachful scrutiny, nor his own internal castigation. He had come dangerously close to kissing Miss Coombe this time as he had held her beside the horse after lifting her down. He should have led her to the perfectly serviceable mounting block rather than taking such a liberty.

During their ride, Miss Coombe had confided in him about Mr. Bellmoore's, *his*, situation, having no idea how much he already knew. Her trust should not have affected him as it did, but it made him feel things he could not yet articulate. They had laughed until it hurt, something he had never experienced with a lady before. Then, when he assisted her from her horse, she had seemed as loath to break the contact as he had been. She had looked up at him with her hopeful eyes and perfect face. How could he not want to kiss her?

Zach and Lady Celeste had reminded him that they were not alone, and Jacob realized the full force of what he had been about to do. A kiss was akin to a promise of affection. He could not promise what he was not free to give. Miss Coombe, in her kindness, had even asked him if his heart was the problem when he withdrew from her. He could not help a sardonic smile at the memory of purposefully misleading her. He had not hesitated to answer her in the affirmative. His heart was indeed the problem, just not in the manner she had meant it.

Jacob groaned and rubbed his face with his palms. He knew he would have to answer to Zach before the day was through. He never had ended up soliciting Zach's advice on his precarious situation, but he had a feeling he was about to receive it whether he liked it or not. Now what was he to say? He had seen the warning in his friend's eyes for what it was. Miss Coombe was a servant, and he was a gentleman. Jacob's views on social hierarchy were becoming more and more blurred the longer he spent pretending to be something he was not. Even if he threw expectation to the wind, he could not support a wife or even entertain ideas of a courtship until he established himself in a profession of some variety. And for that, he would need to consult his brother. With Jacob's recent behavior, a career in the church was looking less suitable. Not to mention that he was already trapped in this unfortunate betrothal to Miss Coombe's own mistress.

It would be cruel to allow the closeness that was beginning to grow between him and Miss Coombe to continue, only to disappoint both of their hopes. And if he did marry Lady Celeste, as was proper, it would be dreadful to live in a house where Miss Coombe would tend to his wife, and he would see her often, but to dismiss her from employment on those grounds would also be utterly unfair.

Jacob sat down on the edge of a wingback chair beside the unlit fireplace, finding no comfort or rest from the position. He held his head in his hands and groaned again. What a tangled mess he had created! He did not deserve either woman.

A knock at his door distracted Jacob from reprimanding himself. When he opened the door, Zach stepped through and looked him up and down, his eyebrows drawing together.

"And what has you in such a sorry state?" Despite his concern, Zach still sounded ready to laugh. To Jacob's surprise, it helped to calm him a little.

"I think you know," he replied, closing the door behind them and gesturing toward the chairs.

Zach sat down, leaning forward with his elbows resting on his knees. He tapped his splayed fingertips together, considering his words.

"You know you cannot have her. Other gentlemen may dally with servant girls, but not you, Jacob," he reproved gently.

Jacob's head snapped up.

"A dalliance? I was not contemplating anything of the kind." His words came out clipped. He knew it was common enough in society, but he valued his integrity. The thought that Zach doubted his morals stung as equally as his opinion was valued.

"Does she know that?" Zach knew the most uncomfortable questions and notwithstanding asked them anyway.

"Of course not. She does not even know who I am," Jacob retorted, but instead of rebutting Zach, it made his point stronger. Jacob had both lied about his identity and neglected to disclose his betrothal. He felt the discomfort of remorse squeezing his chest.

Zach raised a single eyebrow.

"She will be gone in a week." Jacob meant it to sound dismissive, to lighten the mood, but it came out like a lament.

"Have you forgotten that, as bothersome as the situation is, you are promised to Lady Celeste?" Again, Zach chose the worst question.

Jacob buried his head in his hands, grabbing fists full of his hair in the process.

"Why?" he groaned, knowing he deserved the reproach.

"Jacob, I need to discuss something with you, man to man." Zach's serious tone brought Jacob's attention back to his friend. His brow was knit and his eyes intense.

"What is it, Zach?" he asked, his relief that his friend had a problem they could focus on instead, only adding to the list of infractions his conscience held against him.

"I do not know where this will lead, but it seems time is not a luxury this circumstance can afford." Zach began fidgeting with his pocket watch.

Jacob waited for more, unsure where his friend was taking him.

"Your new heart problem could provide you with an opportunity to resolve the matter of your impending betrothal," Zach continued, surprising Jacob. This was not a different subject at all.

"You know as well as I do that my illness is nothing but a ruse. There is no heart problem." Jacob shook his head and stood, kicking at the edge of the rug that was uneven.

"That is not common knowledge, and in all likelihood it will not become so." Zach looked up at Jacob, and he stopped his fidgeting.

"You mean, she may not wish to be tied to someone who could have a health defect that might leave her a widow at any given moment?" Jacob asked, the morbidity of the question at odds with the hopeful tones in his voice.

"Essentially, yes. You may consider giving *her* the opportunity to cry off. To be fair."

"If we disregard that this is entirely based on a lie for a moment, there is still the unfortunate matter of her reputation. It would suffer, and her with it, you know that. A broken engagement would materially hurt her chances to wed anyone, no matter the reason. I could never do that to an innocent lady. That is why I am in this mess." Jacob shook his head.

"Uncomfortable with a lie, are we?" Zach laughed once and shook his head before continuing with his point. "To answer your concern, her reputation would recover if there were a gentleman of rank willing to overlook something so insignificant." His speech sped up. "I am not speaking of this just to cause you misery, Jacob."

"That is just a happy coincidence, I suppose." Jacob chuckled. Zach joined him, allowing them a moment of relief from the seriousness of the topic.

"No, I am honor-bound to inform you that I wish to court your affianced." Zach sat up straight and looked him square in the eyes. He was serious.

Jacob had to bite his lip to stop himself from accepting such a desirable solution straight away. This was a lady they were discussing after all, not a piece of property or a wager in a game of cards.

"Perhaps we ought to discuss it with the lady," he suggested, though his smile was wide and he felt like dancing.

"I hoped you would say that. However, it will mean coming out of your hiding place up here to do so." Zach grinned.

"Oh yes, I had not thought of that."

Jacob looked down at nothing in particular. He wanted more than anything for this mess to be over, but he did not look forward to having Miss Coombe find out that she had been lied to all week. He doubted she would accept his suit after that, despite his being a gentleman rather than a servant. She would probably never wish to set eyes on him again.

"Chin up." Zach stood up and slapped Jacob's shoulder. "I know you enjoyed your time in the stables, but I am certain McInnes would welcome you back any time you choose."

Jacob did like that thought, but it was not what had him worried. He took a deep breath.

"I will do it, Zach, but I shall need a little time. I have more than one lady to face with this turn of events, and my mother's reaction is not even the one I fear the most."

"I do not envy you that." Zach grimaced, but the grin he wore belied any sympathy he was trying to convey.

Yes, Jacob would come clean.

Tomorrow.

Jacob managed to avoid a visit from his mother until the following afternoon with a great deal of help from Giles, but by then he was almost ready to confess all just to escape his bedroom. He was leaning on the windowsill, staring out of his open window when she arrived.

"Contemplating escape?" she asked as she reached around him to feel his forehead with the back of her hand. Satisfied, she placed a chair before the door and sat in it to prevent his hypothetical breakout. He looked back at her and smiled, all but done with his pretense.

"I am so bored, Mother. Can you not send up something more exciting to read than this?" He pointed to the volume of Shakespeare, hoping to elicit more of an indication of whether she was onto him or not.

"There is nothing wrong with Shakespeare." She revealed nothing with the statement that was an echo of Tom's, but then she did seem to acquiesce a little. "What else would you like to read? *Gulliver's Travels*? *Robinson Crusoe*, perhaps? You liked those a great deal when you were at school."

"Yes, both of those! And anything else you can come up with. Do you have any Radcliffe?" he smirked, anticipating her reaction.

"Of course not! A good boy like you ought to know better than to read gothic novels. I'll bring you the family Bible." She nodded for emphasis, her face crimson.

"I am only teasing you. It was well worth it for your response," he chuckled.

It was a spot of luck that Jacob's mother did not have her fan, or he was certain he would have a new bruise from it.

"You are in possession of far too much cheek for someone your age," she reprimanded, but it lost any sting it may have possessed when she laughed.

"Mother, I would speak to you about something," Jacob began after a comfortable pause. She stood up with an abruptness that surprised him.

"Yes, I will send those books up posthaste. I shall visit again later, dear." She waved as she breezed from the room, leaving Jacob with his mouth hanging open, ready to speak. He had no idea what to make of that. His mother's behavior was becoming odder with every passing day.

Betsy, the maid, was sent yet again to deliver Jacob's pile of books, topped with a Bible as promised. Jacob smiled at that.

After placing news sheets and a periodical on top, Betsy shuffled on the spot, her eyes resting on him, then darting to the floor.

"Thank you, Betsy. Do you have any news?" Jacob invited. When she had informed him of Lord Mortcastle's conversation with his man, it had raised the hairs on the back of Jacob's neck. He had not had a great first impression of the man, but overhearing a portion of a conversation about ships and gold was not enough to act on. He had advised Betsy to stay away from them as much as possible to be safe, but to also keep him informed if she happened to hear anything further.

Betsy shook her head and bit back a small smile, staring at the floor.

"Are you certain? You appear to have something you wish to say."

"Oh, no, sir." Her eyes flew to his, wide and round, as though she had been caught misbehaving. "I was just thinkin' is all. I...erm, I've not heard much from the pir—er—them two men, except yesterday while I was just coming back from bringing Miss Adelle her tea in her room. I overheard something about his collar or, color all, I had a hard time making it out."

Jacob thought about it, trying to work out what she might have overheard.

"Collateral?" he ventured a guess. Her eyes lit up, and she waved a finger in his direction.

"Aye, that's it. T'wasn't much to overhear, but he said his collar—that word you just said, was needed to keep the captain happy."

"Did he say anything else?" Jacob asked.

If it were anyone else, he would likely dismiss it. Keeping a captain happy when one deals with merchant ships was not in and of itself an unusual thing to say, even the part about collateral. Although, for some reason he could not explain, Jacob had a niggling suspicion that there was more.

"No, sir, that was it. Then I scampered out of there afore I could get myself caught." She paled. Jacob made the mistake of smiling at her again. He did it to reassure her, but instead it triggered that expression that made him uncomfortable.

"Thank you, Betsy. I will look into it," he dismissed. Then, as an afterthought as she was leaving, he added, "Also, it will not be long before I am forced to join the house party as myself rather than Mr. McKnell, but I shall keep you informed of when that may be. Please be good enough to apprise Mrs. Thatcher."

Betsy nodded once and left. He hoped that her propensity to talk would not compromise his disguise before he was ready. To that end, he wondered if Miss Coombe already knew.

When evening came, Jacob could stand being in his bedroom no longer. He donned Tom's clothing and climbed out of his window once again under the cover of darkness using the rope. He walked around the outside of the house, knowing where he would end up and who he hoped to find there, ignoring his better judgment. He reasoned that, of course, he would need to speak with Miss Coombe in private if he were to reveal the truth to her.

Jacob was not disappointed. The smile that stole over his face was inevitable as he climbed the terrace stairs to see Miss Coombe, Elsie, admiring the party through the window. Why he found her curiosity so charming was anybody's guess, but it helped to settle the agitation that had been his constant companion this past week.

Jacob appeased himself with the thought that he would stay for but a short while to reveal his identity, then make a hasty retreat. He would do nothing worthy of censure or that would deepen their connection. Using her Christian name in the privacy of his own thoughts was a small indulgence he could allow himself. It would do no harm so long as he did not do so aloud.

Jacob leaned against the wide balustrade, unnoticed. Elsie was hovering near a sculpted box hedge, out of sight of the windows. She fidgeted with a loose thread on her dress, and when she chuckled to herself at something she saw, he had to restrain himself from laughing with her. Simply being near her made him feel lighter. He longed to know what she had found amusing, but he remained silent. He could ask her in a moment. In any case, his quiet observation had a regenerative effect that he was in sore need of with what he was about to face.

All too soon, Elsie let out a resigned sigh and turned to leave, halting as she saw him. Attractive pink swept across her cheeks before she turned her head to conceal the smile that was expanding there. She placed a delicate hand over her mouth while she struggled to school her features. It was the single most beautiful image he had ever seen, not that he was noticing. It spread warmth from somewhere deep within him through his entire body. He did not yet know if Lady Celeste was interested in Zach, but if she accepted him as an alternative, Jacob would be free to give his heart where he desired. And that desire was standing right in front of him.

Chapter Seventeen

~◦~◦~◦◦~◦~◦~

Celeste had come to her little hideout beside the terrace plant each evening since her initial visit on Wednesday. She had exercised more caution each subsequent time and thus far had not been apprehended by anybody else, much to her relief. She was very much enjoying her unobtrusive view of Bryn's experience, and this night was no different. Celeste had even confided the activity to her. It was always fascinating to hear Bryn's version of events afterwards, to fill in the gaps of conversation that Celeste was not privy to in the silence outside. Most of Celeste's assumptions were close to accurate, but sometimes she was comically incorrect. Like when she had seen a vigorous shake of Bryn's head at a gentleman, who Celeste now knew was Mr. Goldsmith, offering her his hand. She had assumed dancing was about to begin and worried about the slight of Bryn's refusal until it was explained later that he had been trying to coax her into singing, which she professed having less skill at than a goose.

Celeste laughed as she saw Mr. Goldsmith petitioning Bryn once again. Only this time Bryn managed to turn toward the window long enough to discreetly roll her eyes in secret communication with Celeste.

Celeste covered her mouth with her hand to smother the sound of her laughter.

Although the air was warm enough outside, Celeste never remained too long, the fear of someone other than Mr. McKnell finding her, ever present in her mind. She had not seen Mr. McKnell since they had spent the previous afternoon exchanging jokes on Bryn and Lord Blakely's ride. Celeste breathed a contented sigh as she relived those few delicious moments after Mr. McKnell had helped her dismount. She had been worried about him since then and wished that she could inquire after him without breaching etiquette. At least Lord Blakely had been good enough to inform Bryn that he was well, but Celeste hoped to see him herself soon to be sure.

As Celeste sighed and turned from the window, she was stunned to see the materialization of her thoughts leaning against the railing in front of her. The glow from the window illuminated his face enough to see that he was smiling, and his pallor appeared healthy. However, as the realization dawned on her that he had been watching her for who knew how long, she felt her cheeks flame, and she had to avert her face. She dearly wished to be angry with him, or at the very least indignant, but she was so relieved to see him whole and hearty that she could not manage a steely glare for anything. She raised a hand to cover the ridiculous smile that would not behave itself, knowing it was a futile effort.

Once she had some semblance of control over her countenance, Celeste worked to turn back to Mr. McKnell with as lofty an expression as she could affect. His smile did not diminish, and she felt her control slipping until a disobedient little snort of a laugh escaped her restraint. His answering laugh was soft but deep and happy.

In an effort to cover her mortification, Celeste snapped a twig off of the hedge beside her and tried to swat him with it, but he laughed more, struggling to keep the volume low. A hedge twig turned out to be a rather pathetic weapon and carried no impact whatsoever, breaking in half on the third swipe.

"Do you surrender?" he whispered, his voice thick with mirth.

"It seems I have no choice. I am at your mercy," Celeste shook her head at her poor excuse for a battle.

Mr. McKnell's brow creased for the briefest of moments before he stood straight and offered his arm.

"Since I have no need for a prisoner, shall I escort you back to the kitchens?" he offered, still smiling but different somehow. Celeste was not sure if she had said something wrong or if he was being polite. Either way, she took his arm, and they began a slow walk down the steps.

"Thank you. Are you feeling better?" she asked.

He shrugged. "Somewhat, but there is something I wished to speak to you about."

Mr. McKnell stopped halfway down the steps and looked into her eyes. As the air between them magnetized, Celeste panicked. Was he going to ask to court her? She had spoken to Bryn about her inheritance and the possibility of her being able to share it with him, but she had not yet asked her father if there were any stipulations to the contrary. She had not even begun to consider what she might do if that were the case. All of that aside, her real hesitation was that the truth about her identity needed to be shared with him before anything real could happen between them. She was not at all confident that he would want someone juvenile enough to pretend at being something she was not. She had been vacillating between whether she ought to trust him with such an enormous secret or not, but now that the moment was upon her, she lost her nerve.

Celeste intentionally committed the faux pas of taking the lead and tugged on Mr. McKnell's arm to indicate that she wished to continue walking. Every rule of decorum she had ever learned shouted at her for being alone with him in the dark in the first place, so it was a good excuse to keep moving. He followed without argument, resuming their descent.

Celeste searched her mind for a topic of conversation that was as far away from courting as possible. She had to change the subject before Mr. McKnell could begin to speak, or she might miss the opportunity to steer him away.

"Betsy mentioned that she spoke to you about the conversation she overheard. Is that what you wished to discuss?" She said the first thing she could think of but inwardly rolled her eyes at herself. She had no idea why Betsy had been speaking of pirates to a stablehand in the first place. Bringing it up now was so far out of place as to be about the most obvious topic change imaginable.

"About the ships?" he clarified, sounding surprised. His brow lowered, and he scrunched his eyes a little as he thought, but at least his response showed no signs of ridicule. Celeste nodded, relieved.

"Do you think there could really be pirates about?" she asked to retain control of the conversation.

Mr. McKnell took time to consider before replying. Celeste liked that he did not dismiss her out of hand, regardless of the subject.

"I do not think it terribly likely, but it would be wise to not behave contrary to how you have been. If they are guilty of some mischief, it might make them skittish if they suspect someone is onto them. If you see any odd behavior during one of your terrace vigils, it could be worth noting." His expression was thoughtful, but he smiled on the word vigil, and she had to smile too. Her nighttime excursions were a shared secret, and she was happy to have a reason to speak with him about anything she saw. The thought triggered a memory.

"I do not know if it is significant, but on one of my recent *vigils*, I saw Lord Mortcastle reading a note, then throwing it into the fire. It may have been nothing, of course, but he did not seem pleased with the missive."

"Hmm. If only there were some way to investigate if he is up to no good, any more or less than the next gentleman. Lord Blakely may have some ideas." He nodded.

Celeste reciprocated the gesture. It might all come to nothing, but the conversation had served her well to divert from the awkward truth for one more night.

Before anything more could be said, the kitchen door swung open, and Betsy flew out, stopping in her tracks as her eyes adjusted to the darkness outside.

"Betsy? Are you alright?" Celeste asked her.

Betsy blinked a few times, and when she recognized Mr. McKnell, her mouth dropped open.

"Betsy?" he asked with the same concern.

"Mr. B—Bc Knell!" The poor girl cringed as she stammered his name. "I—I just came to find Elsie," she stammered.

"What is it?" Celeste asked, reaching out a hand to Betsy. It must have been something significant for her to come flying out into the night like that.

"They was—were asking about you. The pirates," she mumbled, looking at the ground.

"Me? What would they want with me?" Celeste asked, not yet wishing to accept that they were actual pirates without any evidence but feeling the color drain from her face, nonetheless. They did not have to be pirates to be ne'er-do-wells. As far as they were concerned, though, Celeste, or Elsie Coombe as they knew her, was a nobody. Bryn had reported that Lord Mortcastle was hovering around her with increasing frequency, which had given her pause, but Celeste ought to be invisible to a man of his station. Unless the overheard conversation in the garden had been of more significance than she knew.

"I don't know. They just asked if you had much family hereabouts, and how you came to be in service and such." Betsy shrugged, her eyes flicking between Celeste and Mr. McKnell.

"What did you tell them?" Mr. McKnell's expression was fierce, and his arm tensed under Celeste's hand, still resting there. It made her heart beat harder. If he believed them to be a threat, that made the situation seem more real.

"I told them I never knew her 'till she came with Lady Celeste last week," Betsy answered, her words rushing out. "I thought I had best come warn her that they were snooping about after 'er." She looked up at Mr. McKnell like a frightened child.

"Did you say that both of them were asking about her?" Mr. McKnell queried.

"Oh, aye. First it was just that dreadful Mr. Reeves, but then 'is master came along and asked the same things." Betsy's gaze shifted to Celeste. "I could 'ardly talk for 'ow scared I was. They probably thought I was daft when I kept just starin' at 'em. You know how they give me the creeps."

Celeste gave Betsy's arm a brief squeeze as her eyes once again dropped to the ground. Mr. McKnell turned to Celeste.

"You mentioned yesterday that you have only had your position for a week or more. Have you ever met these men before, when you were in another position, perhaps?"

"No, never." She was able to answer that without hesitation since she had held no previous positions. Even after answering, she tried to remember if she had ever seen Lord Mortcastle in London whilst she was there as herself but could recall nothing. He either moved in different circles than her family, or she had not paid him any mind. She hoped he had not noticed her with her being ignorant of it. Did he know who she was? Fortune hunters were a breed of men she was always wary of wherever she went, being an heiress. They could be desperate enough to be unpredictable.

"Did he or they say anything else?" Celeste asked, but Betsy shook her head. It was far more likely, then, that Lord Mortcastle was the other man in the garden that day, but the conversation did not sound like that between a master and servant.

"I may have been caught eavesdropping on them myself a few days past," Celeste confessed.

Mr. McKnell chuckled once and shook his head, his half smile producing a dimple in his left cheek.

"For someone who claims not to gossip, you do a lot of spying. Working for the crown, are you?" he joked. Celeste laughed once before feigning indignation and swatting at him.

"In all seriousness, though, I do not think you should come out here alone of an evening, Miss Coombe, if you have captured the attention of the likes of Lord Mortcastle. Whatever his motivations are, I have my doubts that they are honorable."

Mr. McKnell's warning was valid, and yet Celeste wished to hold on to her secret outings on the terrace. They had become the part of her day she looked forward to the most; her tenuous connection to her real self. It was nonsensical, but she did not wish to give them up.

"Perhaps there is someone who can accompany me so that I may still observe Lord Mortcastle without his knowledge."

Celeste meant the comment innocently enough, but Betsy's expression had her reviewing her words. She glanced up at Mr. McKnell, whose expression was distressed. Her hand, lingering long in the crook of his elbow, suddenly felt heavy as she realized how she had been misunderstood. She dropped it to her side without delay.

"I do not mean—that is to say—I am not proposing..." Her face grew hotter with each attempt to rectify the misunderstanding that she was inviting Mr. McKnell for a secret rendezvous on the terrace each night. She struggled to figure a way around her blunder.

Mr. McKnell had the audacity to grin before smothering it.

"Tom, the stable master, might have someone who would be willing to lend a hand. I will speak to him," he paused. "But until you hear from me, I would suggest staying indoors after dark. I do not think you will gain much to make it worth it."

Celeste knew he was right. She nodded her head, still unable to speak through her mortification.

Betsy was silent for once, and Celeste was not at all certain that she liked it.

Chapter Eighteen

Once the maids were inside, Jacob returned to the stables, saddled Thor, and rode to Tom's cottage. Knowing that Elsie had caught the attention of the loathsome Mortcastle was changing his view on the matter. That Mortcastle had been asking after Elsie's family and circumstances sounded to Jacob like he wanted to know how protected she was. Jacob's betrothal and the headaches that went with it were nothing to the safety of his family's household and their visitors. Even if the questions turned out to have some reasonable explanation, they were worth investigating.

It took him a few minutes to reach the small dwelling where Tom lived with his wife and his eldest son's family, the same residence Jacob had begun to walk to with William the week before. Tom could have had a room in the stable house, but Jacob suspected that he was in a much more comfortable situation with his family.

As Jacob knocked on the front door, he realized that he had no idea of the time. He hoped it was not so late that they would be sleeping.

Tom's face went from irritation to alarm as he opened the door and saw Jacob standing there.

"Young Jack, are you well?" he asked, ushering him inside and showing him to a chair. Tom's wife fetched a pitcher of water while Jacob explained the situation to Tom.

"Aye lad, I'd be happy to stay behind and keep watch," he answered without hesitation. "I dunnae like that Lord Mortcastle. His poor beast has scars all over his flanks. 'Tis no way to treat a horse."

"I agree." Jacob paused. "Do you think there could be anything to what the maids overheard?" Jacob needed the older man's wisdom. He missed his father keenly, but in particular when a situation such as this arose, where everything was hunches with little evidence to go by.

Tom stroked his white shadow of whiskers as he considered.

"The nearest port is a long day or two's ride, more in a carriage..." He shrugged, knowing that could be an easy distance for someone with motivation.

"I don't even know why Mortcastle is here. I have never even met the man before. Do you know who he is?" Jacob asked.

"Well, he had some dealings with your father a while back, so I have seen him a time or two. 'Twas when you were away at school, if I recall. Your brother may have made his acquaintance that way. For all we know, he was added to the house party as a number, to keep things even."

Jacob thought about that. It was quite possible. He sighed. His time as Mr. McKnell was over. He could be far more useful ensuring Elsie's safety as a Bellmoore, even if she never spoke to him again. He had come so close to telling her the truth before she mistook his direction and asked if he wished to discuss pirates. He shook his head. How had he been steered so far off course?

"All will be well, young Jack." Tom patted Jacob's shoulder. "The Good Lord'll see to that."

Jacob smiled, grateful for his optimism, and rose to leave. "Thank you, Tom. I appreciate it."

"Aye. I'll have the boys keep an ear to the ground as well, just in case." He walked Jacob out and gave Thor an affectionate pat as Jacob untethered him.

Before mounting, Jacob turned back to Tom.

"I plan to tell Mother the truth in the morning. I do not know how it will be received, but by tomorrow, Mr. McKnell will be no more."

Tom nodded his acknowledgment, then gave a short laugh.

"You're a brave man, Jack, to take on a woman like that. Your mother is a rare breed." He chuckled again before repeating, "A brave man."

Jacob laughed in agreement, knowing he was about to get his come-uppance. He did not push Thor on the ride back. Instead, he just enjoyed the quiet of the night and the sway of the horse's calming rhythm supporting him. When he reached the kitchens after leaving Thor in the stables, he was fortunate to see only Mrs. Thatcher there, speaking to one of the scullery maids about a more efficient way to scrub a stove.

When Mrs. Thatcher saw him, he beckoned for her to follow him to a quiet corner and explained his concerns surrounding Mortcastle and his man. At first, she was skeptical because the source was Betsy, but when she heard that the men were poking around for information about one of the visiting maids, she sighed.

"I've known that type before, who pay too pointed attention to the female staff, I'll keep an eye out." She nodded.

"Mrs. Thatcher, you should know that you can come to me if you feel any of those under your care are in trouble at any time. I wish you all safe," Jacob offered.

Mrs. Thatcher looked down at her hands for a long moment, then blinked a few times and nodded.

"Aye, you're a good lad, like your father. You always were. We will all miss you when you're wed."

"Ah, speaking of that." Jacob inclined his own head and folded his arms across his chest. "I plan to inform my mother in the morning of my charade as Mr. McKnell."

Jacob almost laughed when Mrs. Thatcher's expression matched what Tom's had been.

In the morning when Jacob's mother came to visit, he was already up and dressed. Giles had managed a smile when Jacob told him it was time to come clean, and he had taken extra pains to make him presentable. The valet seemed genuinely to enjoy giving him a well-overdue shave. Jacob even caught him humming as he trimmed his hair. It was still a little longer than was fashionable, falling just below his ears rather than his shoulders, but it would aid in keeping him less recognizable.

"Sweetheart, are you feeling ready to greet your guests?" Jacob's mother asked when she entered, surprise evident in her voice.

Jacob turned from the window he had been gazing out of.

"Not quite, I need one more day."

"Whatever for?"

They sat down in the wingback chairs before the unlit fireplace, and Jacob took his mother's aging hands in his.

"Mother, I need to make a confession." He drew a deep breath.

"We are not Catholic," his mother joked, and attempted to retrieve her hands and stand in a single motion, but he held tight so that she could not escape the conversation again.

"Why do you keep avoiding speaking with me?" he asked, suspicious of something he could not quite place. She sighed and settled back.

"What is it, dear?" she acquiesced.

Jacob ignored her avoidance of the question and steeled himself against her possible reactions to his admission.

"Well, when I first was ill, I...wasn't," he began. Her expression did not change, which in some ways was more frightening. His voice cracked before he cleared his throat to continue. "I used a warming pan to elevate my temperature, and whilst you thought I was in bed, I was really—"

"In the stables, I know." She spoke as if he had merely visited a neighbor. Jacob's brow creased.

"I—What? You knew? For how long?"

She laughed at his expression. "Do you really believe I am so easy to fool?"

"I..." Jacob was at a complete loss for words. "But... how?"

His mother gave him a shrewd look.

"I will admit that for the first day or two I believed you," she began, "but then I grew suspicious when you volunteered to keep to your room. You. Volunteered." She raised an eyebrow to indicate what a poor performance that had been.

Jacob exhaled. She was right. He had never been one to be confined, as evidenced by his more recent resistance.

"Were you truly sick, you would have been trying to convince me otherwise so that you could go and play." She nodded, her brows raised in a smug expression.

"Play, Mother? I am not a child."

"Oh, really?" she asked in mock surprise, a hand at her chest. "What would you call gallivanting about the countryside play-acting that you were a servant? Or pretending at being ill to be excused from a perfectly civilized activity that your dear mama had prepared for you? Hmm?"

Jacob squirmed.

"Alright, Mother, you have made your point." He held up a hand in surrender. She wore a very satisfied, half-lidded expression with a triumphant smile.

"Why go to the trouble of having Doctor Fitzpatrick examine me and parading me before Whitbury, if you knew it was a ruse?" Jacob squinted as if he could see her thoughts better by doing so. When there was no reply, he noticed his mother shifting her weight in her chair. Her mouth opened and closed several times as she glanced at the door. He had found the subject she had been avoiding. He clasped her hands again to prevent her escape.

"You have been very brave in your honesty, and I have been very forgiving. Now I must require of you to do the same for mine." She paused, casting a fleeting glance up at his face and took a deep breath. "You do not have any heart condition."

"I know." Jacob rolled his eyes. That was nothing new. "My pulse was racing because I leaped back into bed every time someone was coming. Also, it was blasted hot in there."

Jacob's mother rushed on as if he hadn't spoken, seeming to miss his acknowledgement.

"When Doctor Fitzpatrick came, I told him that you were pretending, but that I needed him to say something convincing that I could use to keep you up here. It was a fiction created by me..." She trailed off, her eyes widening. "Wait a moment, did you just say that you already knew? And then I said..." Her cheeks broke out in flames as she seemed to comprehend that she had admitted to far more than she had to. She closed her mouth abruptly.

There was a long pause as Jacob digested all he had just heard, in particular the parts she would not have owned to at all if she had initially heard him say that he already knew.

"Do you mean to tell me that you invented an illness? That you wanted me to think it was something serious?"

"No, I wanted your brother to think that so he would not send you away!" she almost shouted.

Jacob found that he did not have a single word come to mind for more than a minute. He just sat there, understanding dawning. Everything she had done, all of her interference, had been for this same objective. It also explained her strange behavior of late. It had all come back to her wanting to prevent him from being shipped off to the army by his brother. Had she already given up on her own plan to marry him off, then? Or had Whitbury seen through it?

"See now, that is what I mean. You must be forgiving of me as I am of you." She misinterpreted his silence. "You lied, I lied. We shall both need to appeal to God."

Jacob lost his composure and broke into a laugh.

"Oh, Mother. We are the same, you and I, with our clever plans. How did you convince Doctor Fitzpatrick to go along with you anyway?" He struggled to stop laughing once he had started. He was beginning to see Zach's point of view.

"Well, dear, that was the easy part." She joined him in his mirth, the tension in the room abating. "Robert Fitzpatrick has never been able to say no to me. Besides, he did not have to say anything untrue or exaggerate in the slightest. I took care of all the theatrics if you recall." She waggled her eyebrows. He wiped some moisture from his eyes from the laughter.

"I remember well, but what other underhanded deeds has he accomplished for you?"

"Nothing so dastardly as all that. This was the biggest favor I have asked of him, certainly, in terms of consequence. When we were young, and he wanted to be sweethearts, well, my father would never have allowed that, but we were good friends. And he could always be relied upon to assist me with any request." She bit her cheeks to refrain from grinning, though she still looked smug.

"And how many courtesies do you owe him in return?" Jacob asked. She affected a shocked expression.

"It would be unconscionable to hold a tally against assistance to a lady." She sniffed as if the very idea smelled bad. At that, Jacob laughed again, very much hoping she was in jest and did not have the poor man running around doing her favors all the time.

After a long silence, lost in their own thoughts, Jacob's mother spoke again.

"You have decided to join the house party now and face Lady Celeste. Are you sure?"

"I am," Jacob inhaled a deep breath. "I have learned from her maid that she is aware of the arrangement concocted by you and Lady Kingstone, so I really ought to discuss it with her in person. Besides, Lord Blakely has expressed an interest in her, so I may be free to—" Jacob cut himself off, clamping his jaw shut to prevent himself from speaking further.

"Free to what?" His mother sat up straighter with keen interest in what he was trying not to say. "What are your plans, Jacob?"

"I have no more plans, Mother. I merely wish to untangle myself from a lady for whom I have no affection," he sighed.

"Is it so you can court someone who has caught your eye? Is that it?" she perceived with far too much clarity. Jacob wondered if she was clairvoyant.

"How do you do that?" he asked, shaking his head.

"I am your mother. Do you think I cannot tell when you are lovesick?"

"I am not lovesick," he protested.

"Ha-hah." She pointed at him as though he had just proved her point rather than refuting it. He looked himself over for whatever clue she had discovered on his person.

"What?"

"Who is she? She cannot be a guest at the party—you have not been in attendance." She tapped her chin, then looked up. "She is not a servant, is she? Jacob!" Her tone turned to one of chastisement.

"I have already had this conversation with Lord Blakely. I am not dallying with servants. My interest in Miss Coombe is genuine," he blurted.

"And does this Miss Coombe share your feelings?" she asked, her eyes extracting more from him than he wanted to share.

Jacob was distracted for a moment as he reflected on the moments he had allowed himself to draw too close to Elsie Coombe. They had misunderstood each other in the beginning, but when those things were resolved—indeed when he had been seconds away from kissing her—she had shown no signs of being opposed to the situation. Only the previous night, she had held onto his arm until it had become an embarrassment for her.

Something in Jacob's face must have given away his thoughts because his mother gave a delighted little squeal, snapping him out of his memories.

"You have fallen in love, Jacob! How has this happened? She is not one of the Whitbury servants, so *when* did this happen? Whose servant is she?"

Jacob held up a hand to stall the barrage of questions.

"Alright, I surrender. I will tell you, but in return I would ask for your help. One of the guests, Lord Mortcastle and his valet, have been asking about her, her personal history and family, and so forth. It makes me uneasy. One of our maids has also overheard them speaking of what sounds like privateering."

"Jacob, you do not really think that Lord Mortcastle is a pirate, do you? His uncle is the Earl of Essex." She reared back.

"Perhaps not, but I would like to be certain. That is why I require a little more time before I join the party. I would like to be satisfied that there is nothing to be concerned over. I can accomplish that while the guests are at dinner," Jacob proposed.

"Alright, I will go along with you. It will serve my purposes anyway to consider how I might delay your brother's plans for you if you will not be marrying an heiress," she sighed.

"Perhaps the Marquess of Kingstone has a position in his stables," Jacob quipped, thinking of his conversation with Elsie, and only half joking.

Jacob's mother turned her face, agape, toward him.

"She is not Lady Celeste's maid?!" Her tone begged for contradiction. Jacob felt his cheeks move into an expression that had always given him away as a child. He tried to prevent it, but it seemed he had lost control of his face. His mother pinched the bridge of her nose, squeezing her eyes shut.

"Oh, my dear boy. You finally fall in love with a girl, and it has to be the servant of the Lady you are betrothed to. Does she know who you are?" She shook her head, and reached a hand out to rest on his shoulder.

"No, she thinks I am Mr. McKnell, gentleman turned stablehand. I plan to tell her tonight on the terrace."

"The terrace?" She pulled back with a creased brow.

"Yes, she likes to go there to enjoy the glamor." He smiled, remembering the way she laughed and how it highlighted the curves of her face.

"Hmm." His mother's noncommittal sound made alarm bells ring in his ears. He could not remember what he had just said. He searched his recent thoughts, and with horror, Jacob realized that he may have just caused a lot of trouble for Miss Coombe by divulging her unconventional pastime.

"Mother, I have spoken out of turn, I—" He tried to speak, but his mother stood.

"Well, I think this has been a most productive conversation, dear. I look forward to meeting this maid."

Before Jacob could do more than step forward with a grunt of protest, his mother was out the door. He could follow her, but if his brother saw him out of his sickbed, he would have to join the party early, sending his plans awry. All he could do was hope that his mother did not disapprove of Elsie's little pastime, and that she would see it for the innocent diversion that it was.

Chapter Nineteen

Celeste had been uneasy all day and into the evening. Mr. Reeves had approached her twice, asking her things like how someone so pretty came to be in service, and then asking her if she was quite recovered from her head injury. His apparent show of concern was confusing. She paced in the kitchens, waiting for the arrival of Mr. McInnes, having been informed by Mrs. Thatcher that he wished to speak with her after her meal. She assumed he would be her escort onto the terrace.

The previous evening, Bryn had been spooked by the possibility of Lord Mortcastle's awareness of their situation and suggested that they switch back, but that was impossible without scandal and significant consequences for her. Celeste would not risk that after all Bryn had done for her, but they had come up with a plan. Bryn would try to find out anything she could about Lord Mortcastle through innocuous conversation. As it was, he did his best to converse with her at every opportunity, so she would not need to do more than feign a greater interest in encouraging him to talk about himself. She would also gather what she could from any other sources, including Lady Adelle. Celeste smothered a pang of guilt that the tightness in her chest eased just a little at Bryn being saddled with that task.

After Bryn was tucked away in bed, Celeste had retired as well in the hope that she could speak more with Betsy, but Betsy was tired and grumpy, saying very little, which was odd. Celeste began to worry when she did not speak much again all day. Without Betsy, she had no idea how to make use of the servants' gossip network without sounding suspicious. Beyond that, something could be very wrong if Betsy had become rendered speechless.

Celeste's fretting was interrupted by Mr. McInnes entering the kitchens through the outer door. He smiled at her before Mrs. Thatcher pulled him to the side for a private word. Celeste was not reassured by the regular glances in her direction.

"Are you ready, lass?" He offered his elbow as he approached.

As Celeste walked with Mr. McInnes outside, she took the chance to ask him a few questions about Lord Mortcastle. If she slipped in the odd one about Mr. McKnell, she hoped it was not obvious. Celeste had asked Bryn to have a letter franked by Lord Whitbury and mailed to her father after breakfast, not explaining herself, but requesting further information regarding the stipulations of her inheritance. She hoped he would be forthcoming without her needing to ask in a more straightforward manner if she were at liberty to marry a man of significantly lower social standing.

"Thank you for accompanying me, Mr. McInnes," she began.

"'Tis no trouble at all, Miss Coombe. You must call me Tom." He patted the hand she had rested through the crook of his arm.

"Alright. Then you must call me Elsie. How long have you been the stable master here?"

"Och. Many, many years. I cannae recall how many. I started as an apprentice when we first came down from Scotland when I was a lad, back when the late Lord Whitbury was the age of his sons," he answered with a thoughtful nod.

"I suppose you know all the guests. All of Lord Whitbury's friends." She tried to make it sound like a casual statement rather than a question.

"Is it Lord Mortcastle that you'd like to know about?" His directness surprised her. Celeste blushed before nodding. He patted her hand again. "'Tis alright, dearie. I know he has you worried. Unfortunately, I know very little. He was only here a time or two before in years past."

Celeste digested that.

"What about Mr. Reeves, his valet? Did he always come with him?" she asked.

"No, this is the first time I've ever laid eyes on that one. I'd steer clear of him though, he seems to be the sort who answers to no one," he warned.

"Thank you, I do try to avoid him." She suppressed a shudder.

"My grandson, William, will keep an eye out as well." Tom inclined his head toward a shadowy area of the terrace as they arrived, but Celeste could see nothing. He grinned. "Alright lad, we know you're a canny wraith, now show yourself."

As instructed, a boy of about eleven or twelve years old materialized out of the shadows and waved with a mischievous grin before disappearing again. She could not be certain, but she thought he might be the same one who had been walking with Mr. McKnell a few days ago.

"How does he do that?" Celeste asked, amazed at his stealth.

"He has a future in espionage ahead of him if he has a mind to." The warmth in Tom's praise was obvious.

"Will it just be the two, er, three of us then?" Celeste asked, unable to help herself. Tom gave her a knowing smile.

"Aye, Mr. McKnell is indisposed tonight."

"Is he well?" she asked a little too quickly. "That is, is his heart bothering him?"

"No, I believe his heart is well, if a little conflicted," he answered.

"Whatever do you mean?" Celeste forgot all about watching guests or rooting out potential pirates as she waited for his answer.

"You'll need to be askin' him that yourself, lass, but be kind. He's not so canny as he likes to think he is," he replied cryptically.

"Does he expect me to be unkind?" she asked, not liking that thought at all. Tom blew out his breath slowly.

"That's not what I meant at all. His business is not mine to tell, so I cannae explain. I only ask that you listen to all he has to say when he has a chance to say it." He held up his hands to indicate that that was all he would divulge.

Celeste turned to her task of observing through the glass. She was even more confused than she had been before asking but a little excited as well that Mr. McKnell might at least be considering trusting her with his secrets. Perhaps he had already tried. She thought back to the previous evening, and her panic at the thought of him requesting a courtship. She shook her head in her vanity. That may well have been his attempt at sharing a confidence, and she had not listened. Instead, she had gone on about pirates. She would not be such a poor friend again. The next time he attempted to speak, she would control her wild mouth and imagination to listen.

Just then Bryn looked directly at the window, grabbing Celeste's attention. She turned and engaged Lady Adelle and her sister Charlotte in conversation soon after, the set of her shoulders rigid, reminding Celeste of a soldier attending to an unpleasant duty with stoicism. Celeste sighed in sympathy but looked around the rest of the drawing room to find out whatever Bryn wanted her to know. The other gentlemen had joined the ladies, but Lord Mortcastle was nowhere to be seen. She wondered if he had been absent for dinner as well or if he had wandered off somewhere.

Celeste watched and waited, entertained in the meantime by Lord Blakely's attempts to gain Bryn's attention. And her attempts to feign avid interest in whatever thing the woman she had described as Lady Adelle was discussing. It was quite amusing to watch Bryn's untrained body turn a little toward Lord Blakely, while her face remained fixed in the direction of Lady Adelle.

Eventually Lord Mortcastle entered, along with Lord Whitbury, or so she assumed by the way he had greeted Lady Whitbury with a kiss every evening as she watched. He did also look familiar from when they had been introduced last season. His hair was a similar color to Celeste's, but perhaps a little darker. She could not see his eye color from her situation on the terrace, but she thought she remembered them being blue. He had a face that always appeared deep in thought, with a prominent upper lip, but he was passably handsome for a serious person.

Celeste wondered if she would be granted a glance at Mr. Bellmoore, Lord Whitbury's younger brother and her own intended husband, before the house party would be over in a few more days. She still did not even know what he looked like. At this point, she was beginning to wonder if he even existed.

Just then, she caught sight of Lord Mortcastle, who was receiving a missive from a footman. His eyebrows rose as he read it, then he approached Bryn with purposeful strides. Celeste's heart sped up as he went through the polite motions of any gentleman, but even then, somehow they were off. Bryn appeared uncomfortable with whatever he was saying. Celeste tried for all she was worth to watch the movements of their mouths to determine their words, but the few she may have caught could not be verified until later.

Before long, Lord Blakely stepped into the conversation and commandeered it, but Bryn patted down the front of her dress several times, a clear sign to Celeste that she was feeling distressed.

"Tom," Celeste called in a whisper. Within a moment, Tom was beside her.

"Aye, lass? Have you seen somethin'?" He peered through the glass from behind her shoulder.

"Bryn—I mean Lady Celeste—well, she knows I am out here, and she has been facing this way to show her distress. I do not know what to do."

"Bryn?" He stepped back, standing straight, his right eyebrow raised in question.

Celeste blushed furiously, trying to think fast, but came up with nothing. She had no choice but to confide in him now. At least Tom was a good man, she was confident of that.

Celeste drew a fortifying breath, hoping she had not misjudged him.

"Bryn is the woman you see there." She waved a hand in Bryn's direction. "The true Lady Celeste is...me." She dropped the accent she had been maintaining for the house party and held her breath as she awaited his reaction. He only shook his head and muttered something indiscernible.

"Sir?"

Celeste had hoped for more of an indication of his willingness, or not, to keep her secret. She would never forgive herself if something happened to Bryn because of her. She could be whipped or sent away. In truth, Celeste knew little about the disciplining of servants, but her imagination was vivid.

"You're off your head! The both of you!" Tom folded his arms across his chest following his outburst.

"I am sorry for deceiving you, Tom, it was unforgivable." She squirmed under his intense scrutiny. "Right now though, I am very concerned that Bryn, who is in fact my maid, may be in very real danger from that Lord Mortcastle."

Tom closed his eyes and exhaled.

"You mustn't fret. We'll not allow that snake to harm you. Either of you," he emphasized. Celeste reached out to him and placed a hand on his arm in gratitude.

"You are a good man, Tom. I thank you." She smiled, remembering what Mr. McKnell had said about the effect it may have had on Tom before. He softened, then stiffened again as he looked inside.

"I've no idea what signals you've decided on between yourselves, but I cannae imagine that to be a good one." He inclined his head toward Bryn, who was sneezing repeatedly. They had not thought to discuss things like signals, but Tom could be correct.

"I think it is time to go." Celeste turned and hastened down the steps and around the side of the house, Tom close behind her.

"What is it you plan on doin'?" he asked, not even a little out of breath, as she was. She stopped at the outer door of the kitchens.

"I will go and wait in Bryn's bedchamber, so I am there if she needs me. Thank you again." She smiled at him again before flying inside.

Chapter Twenty

❧᠆᠊᠊᠊ᜒᜒᜒ᠆᠊᠊᠊᠊᠊᠊᠊᠊᠊᠊᠊᠊᠊᠊᠊᠊᠊᠊᠊᠊᠊᠊᠊᠊᠊᠊᠊᠊᠊᠊᠊

Jacob made his way down to the study whilst the house party dined. He lost a little time in nostalgia, remembering being in the room with his father sitting at the desk while Jacob tried to mimic what he was doing. Jacob's brother Charles had become the new Lord Whitbury upon their father's death, and in the years since had changed just about everything, with the exception of the study. Jacob hoped that would make old records and correspondence to do with Lord Mortcastle easier to find.

Jacob had barely begun his search when he thought he heard footsteps approaching. He had not realized he would be required to hide so soon. He did not waste time looking for a suitable hiding place, opting instead to climb into a window bench he had sometimes played in as a child. It was a tighter fit as a fully grown adult, but he managed to pull the hinged seat down just as he heard the door open. He almost climbed back out in relief when he heard his brother's voice, but then his blood turned cold as Whitbury spoke to the person with him. He held himself as still as he could.

"Brandy, Mortcastle?"

Jacob did not hear the answer, but the clink of glasses followed.

The next snippets of conversation were impossible to discern with the seat lid closed, so Jacob opened it, just a crack, relying on the dimness of the light to keep him concealed. The rush of cool air that flooded in was a welcome relief.

The gentlemen did not appear to notice his presence as their conversation continued.

"...have not found them yet. Are you quite certain he signed them?"

Whitbury asked.

"Yes, Whitbury. You were in this very room with us when he did," Lord Mortcastle assured him in a pleasant voice that was surprising. "Even if you do not find them, it is a small matter. I had another copy of them drawn up. Here. After all, you are Lord Whitbury now."

"I remember the discussion, but I do not recall his decision," Whitbury hesitated. Whatever it was they were discussing, Jacob wished he were privy to it so he could support his brother in his caution.

"Well, that is to be understood, you were only nineteen at that time." Lord Mortcastle's voice was unrecognizable when he was friendly.

"You are but one year older than I," Whitbury answered.

"True. If I recall, you were rather distracted by that maid. What was her name?" Mortcastle answered with a short laugh.

Whitbury laughed at the reference. "Yes. I do not recall her name. Florence, or Flossy. Something that sounded floral."

Indignation expelled the air from Jacob's lungs, and he fought to keep his reaction silent. Flora had been a maid in their home who was quite suddenly dismissed some years before. The pieces of the puzzle were forming a tasteless picture. Not that he could judge, since he was distracted by a maid himself. Perhaps there was more to the situation. Jacob remembered Zach's warning to him not to dally with the servants, and it struck him that he may well have known something about Flora, since his elder brother had been friends with Charles at the time.

"Quite right too, she was a pretty thing," Lord Mortcastle continued, making Jacob grimace.

"Well, I shall look these over in the next day or so. Let's rejoin the others, shall we?" Whitbury returned to the subject of their business with a sigh. Jacob willed his brother not to commit to anything, whilst also wishing him to hurry up so he could break free of his sweltering prison. Breathing was becoming much more of an effort than was healthy.

"Certainly. I plan on returning to London in a couple of days anyway, so I shall have my man see to any arrangements," Lord Mortcastle agreed.

"You are not staying until the end of the party?" Whitbury asked.

"No. I have some business that needs urgent attention." His voice rang with false lightness, laced with tension.

"Nothing to do with this, I hope." Whitbury laughed with unease.

"No, no," Lord Mortcastle reassured him before lowering his voice so that Jacob had to strain to hear him. "It is a difficulty involving my sister, but I know I can trust your discretion."

"Of course," Whitbury assured him, sounding relieved.

Another pause, then another mumbled comment followed, after which they both left the room together. On their way out, Jacob heard Lord Mortcastle asking after Lord Tardington, who had been missing since luncheon, as well as enquiring after Jacob's health and when he might be expected to join the party.

When Jacob considered it to have been a long enough wait to be safe, he burst out of the stifling window seat, gasping for air and covered in sweat. Even if he had wished to join the party now, he was in no state to do so. He stretched and drew several deep breaths before he could continue his search. At least the papers Whitbury and Lord Mortcastle had been speaking of had been left there, right atop the desk. Jacob stood over them and began to read. It was a business contract for shares in a shipping company.

Jacob paused when he felt the unaccountable sensation of being watched, and spun around to spot a movement in the shadows near the second window of the room. He drew closer, his heart beating harder in his chest, but when he arrived at the darkened corner, there was nothing there. Chiding himself for being paranoid, he surmised that the drapes must have shifted in the night breeze. It was perhaps a little negligent of the servants to leave a window open so late, but it was a small matter, and anyone could have made such a mistake.

Taking a deep breath to chase away the adrenaline from his imaginary monsters, Jacob parted the drapes to close the window himself. He found that not only was it already closed tight, but he had indeed exposed a dark figure crouching atop that window seat.

Jacob jumped backwards as the man stepped down and the candlelight in the room caught the side of his face.

"Lord Tardington?" Jacob blurted, although it came out sounding somewhat like an accusation. He was grateful that his heart condition had been a fiction, or he may have expired on the spot. The man was known for being mysterious, yet his brother saw some reason to invite him. Jacob wondered how Whitbury would react to being spied on. Not that Jacob could say anything without giving himself away.

"Mr. Bellmoore. Do try to keep your voice down or we shall both be exposed," Lord Tardington greeted with cool detachment. His voice was at such a low timbre that it seemed to melt into the shadows, giving him an even greater aura of mystery than the man was already known for. He wore all black except what little could be seen of his shirt, including a black cravat and gloves. One noticeable light feature was his pale grey eyes, which were a stark contrast to his raven black hair. A scar that ran from behind his ear and down his neck into his collar caught the light and made Jacob wonder if he were quite safe.

"Very well, but I demand to know what you are doing in here," Jacob whispered, his fear making him sound harsh. Lord Tardington raised an eyebrow, challenging Jacob's hypocrisy.

"*I* live here," Jacob defended lamely. "Spying on one's brother is a time-honored tradition. What is your excuse?"

Lord Tardington's expression did not change in any obvious manner, but Jacob was certain the man's eyes were laughing. He looked at Jacob directly for several long moments before responding.

"Everyone is hiding something. Before I make political alliances, I have a duty to determine whether a man's secrets are nefarious or benign." He made it sound so reasonable that Jacob almost dropped the subject.

"Are you suspicious of my brother?" Jacob again saw that eyebrow raise at his hypocrisy. He had just admitted to spying on Whitbury himself. "I am more concerned over Lord Mortcastle," Jacob offered.

Lord Tardington gave an infinitesimal nod as if Jacob had given him more information than he intended. Then, the perplexing man moved to step around Jacob as if the matter were closed.

"Am I expected simply to allow you to leave without any further explanation?" Jacob asked as Lord Tardington reached for the door.

He paused, his hand still outstretched for his escape, and turned only his head back in Jacob's direction.

"I have told you my motives. And Mr. Bellmoore." He waited for Jacob's acknowledgement before continuing. "Since we have both been missed, it would be wise for us to express at breakfast how much we enjoyed our conversation tonight in the library about the corn laws."

"Corn laws?!" Jacob answered, astonished. Lord Tardington tilted his head upwards, and though Jacob could not see his eyes, he had the distinct impression they were rolling.

"Yes, the corn laws. I presume you know enough about them to make it convincing?" he snapped.

"I suppose so..."

"Good. Then I look forward to our *brief* conversation tomorrow before I leave for my estate."

"You are not staying for the ball?" Jacob asked further. Lord Tardington did not answer but shook his head as he exited, as if lamenting Jacob's lack of intelligence. Jacob just stood there staring, questioning his own intellect and what had just happened for several minutes before remembering what he was there for in the first place.

After turning the study inside out and tidying it up again, Jacob had gained nothing but a throbbing headache. His mother found him there, slumped in a chair, exhausted.

"You ought to sleep, my boy," she encouraged, kissing the top of his head.

"Yes," he agreed as he rose and stretched.

"Did you find anything?"

"Not much. Just one lousy shipping contract that is as boring as it sounds." He waved a hand in the direction of the desk. He decided not to mention Lord Tardington.

His mother looked at him with concern.

"Perhaps you ought to check the old steward's office," she suggested. Jacob slapped himself. In his tired state, it stung more than he had intended.

"Of course. Why did I not think of it?" he asked rhetorically, but his mother answered anyway.

"Well, your brother had Mr. Morris retire not long after your father's passing, and he was never replaced. I have often wondered why your brother does not hire another one on, but he does not care for my interference. Perhaps he has a man of business in town." She shook her head.

"Where is Mr. Morris now?" Jacob asked, hoping he did not live far.

"I believe he is still living in the hamlet over the hill. But do get some rest for now."

Jacob smiled at her. He would see to it in the morning after his mandatory cover story with Lord Tardington was established. With any luck, he might also get to have the conversation with Elsie he had been both desiring and avoiding all day.

At breakfast, Jacob was surprised by how smooth an actor Lord Tardington was. His manner in recapping their imaginary conversation from 'the library' about the effects of the corn laws on the poor was so natural that Jacob had to concentrate to remember what had really happened. Then, as promised, Lord Tardington left the house party for his estate without a backward glance or any sign of concern for their subterfuge. It was equal parts baffling and masterful.

Afterward, Jacob headed to the stables to saddle Thor. Zach happened upon him there and offered to ride over to the hamlet with him. For some reason that Jacob could not account for, Tom had a case of the chuckles every time he looked at him. It was unsettling.

Once they were on their way, Jacob did his best to outline where he was going and why. He could not do that without speaking of Miss Coombe and expressing his concerns for her. After a pause, Zach broke the silence.

"Miss Coombe will at least be returning to Herefordshire with Lady Celeste in a few days, so that will be some relief for her safety. As for Lord Mortcastle and his valet, perhaps you ought to speak with

Whitbury. He is your brother." he offered with a slight shrug.

"Perhaps. Although I do not think he would welcome my interference in the household. He has been discussing my future with Mother but never directly with me. I fear I do not know him as I thought." Jacob did not take his eyes off of the road ahead of them.

The truth of the distance between his brother and himself created a heavy knot in Jacob's chest. He did not know when or how they had grown apart. He had not even noticed it happening. Since Jacob's return from the continent, his brother had appeared happy enough to interact with him, laugh with him even, but it seemed that he desired ultimately to be rid of him.

When they reached the old steward's home, Jacob was surprised to see how comfortable Mr. Morris was in his retirement. His home was not large but far nicer than Jacob had expected. It had two stories and a large flower garden that appeared to travel all the way around the abode. A stone half-wall ran around the perimeter of the property. His father would have been pleased that Whitbury was keeping up the, no doubt, generous pension stipulated for him. Their father was like that, always eager to reward a job well done and had included all such matters in his rather lengthy will.

"Would you like some tea?" old Mr. Morris offered as he welcomed the two much taller men inside. Despite the warm weather outside, the high ceiling kept the sitting room cool and comfortable. It had whitewashed walls accentuated with decorative timber balustrades. In the center of the room, surrounding a generous fireplace, were two green velvet settees with overstuffed chairs to match.

"No, thank you, Mr. Morris. We shan't keep you," Jacob waved off the offer. "I only wish to know if you might remember a certain gentleman that my father had some business dealings with. A Lord Mortcastle."

At the mention of the man's name, Mr. Morris became agitated, turning his head in disgust as if he had just eaten something rotten and almost dislodging his round spectacles.

"Are you asking for yourself or that lazy, pompous brother of yours?" Morris asked as they took their seats. Jacob had never seen him so cantankerous before. All his life, Mr. Morris had been a model of civility. Jacob wondered what Whitbury had done to earn such severe disapproval. It did not sit well to have someone commenting on his family without intervention. Still, he needed to remain in favor with the man to gain information, so he bit his tongue and allowed the slight on his brother to pass.

"Whitbury does not know I am here. My mother suggested the visit," Jacob explained, hoping that would calm the man.

"She always was an intelligent woman." He gave a brief smile. "It is strange to hear the Whitbury title, but not in reference to your father or grandfather."

"Yes, I do not remember my grandfather, but I miss my father a great deal," Jacob agreed.

"So, Lord Mortcastle." Mr. Morris slapped the arm of the chair he was seated in.

"Yes. I overheard Lord Mortcastle and my brother last night. They were discussing a matter of business and referred to something that Father agreed to some years ago, perhaps around 1805. I brought with me copies of the papers that needed signing. I realize that it may all be perfectly innocent, but—" Saying it out loud made Jacob feel ridiculous.

Mr. Morris cut him off with a scoff. "Nothing involving that Mortcastle family is innocent. With the gambling debts run up by his grandfather, the entire family and his father's title have been lucky to survive. You were right to be concerned." Mr. Morris's words were both alarming and a relief.

"I confess I am not as well-versed in these things as my brother, so I cannot tell if there is anything untoward in the document." Jacob handed the papers he had pilfered from the desk in the study to Mr. Morris, who adjusted his spectacles to sit on the very edge of his nose.

After reading for some time and grunting to himself with some interesting eyebrow dancing, Mr. Morris handed the sheets of paper back to Jacob.

"It appears to be similar to others of its kind. It does have the mark of one of Lord Mortcastle's little schemes on it."

"Little schemes?" Jacob asked.

"Yes. When your father was alive, he only ever did one business deal with Lord Mortcastle. He learned quicker than most gentlemen that, whilst there was nothing strictly illegal, Lord Mortcastle would always somehow come out far wealthier from these investments than anybody else. Your father made a little money, but he was uncomfortable with it all, as well as the history of the family, *but*, he never did any investing with this Hughes Shipping Company. This must be new." Mr. Morris leaned back in his chair.

Jacob thought about that for a moment.

"Do you have any idea of what became of the old contract or any correspondence they might have had?" he asked, losing hope that he was going to find anything useful at all.

"Everything I worked with I kept in my office at the Manor, if it still exists." He shrugged with an exaggerated frown.

"Thank you, you have been most helpful, sir." Jacob stood and extended his hand. Mr. Morris took it with a smile.

"Mr. Bellmoore, I do wish you all the best. Please give my regards to your mother."

Jacob nodded, donned his hat, and followed Zach toward the door but paused halfway out. He turned back toward Mr. Morris with a hand on the frame.

"Mr. Morris, do you happen to know, is it a common practice for one shipping company to intercept another in competition for, say, gold or other?" Jacob asked, thinking about what Betsy had overheard. Mr. Morris scoffed.

"In these recent wars, perhaps privateers might. It is all legitimate if you have a letter from the Crown. In the old days, we'd call it piracy."

Chapter Twenty-One

"If your lady does not require you at present, Lady Whitbury would like a word with you in her sitting room." Mrs. Thatcher could not have any idea of the terror those words instilled in Celeste.

Lady Whitbury was Jacob Bellmoore's mother, a man Celeste was yet to meet and marry if it could not be prevented. And more than ever, she wished to prevent it. To complicate everything, she had growing feelings for one of the Whitbury stable staff.

"Did she indicate why?" Celeste knew it was an impertinent question by Mrs. Thatcher's expression. Her next words left no doubt.

"You do not ask why, you obey. That is if you value your position. Do you ask Lady Celeste so many questions? Off with you."

Celeste did not argue further but made her way to Lady Whitbury's sitting room.

Celeste's timid knock was answered with a call to enter. With a large gulp, she stepped into the room. It was feminine, decorated with ornate white furniture and pink floral wall papers. Fresh flowers were in vases situated atop white tables in perfect symmetry on either side of the plush white sofa in the center of the room, where Lady Whitbury was seated.

Celeste noted with relief that she did not appear to be cross about anything. In fact, she smiled as she patted the cushion beside her, indicating for Celeste to sit. She obeyed, hoping this was not some kind of test. Perhaps she should have shown more humility and sat on one of the chairs opposite since she was playing a part, but it was too late by the time she thought of that.

"There is no need to appear so terrified my girl. I do not intend to eat you." Lady Whitbury smiled in a mixture of reassurance and amusement at her shocking comment.

Celeste took a fortifying breath, wishing she were not so nervous so she could enjoy it more.

"You wished to see me, My lady?" Celeste tried to imitate Bryn's natural way of speaking.

"Yes. I have it on good authority that one of the other visiting servants has shown an interest in you. Are you aware of this?" she asked.

Celeste was quite unsure how to answer. She wished to be honest about Mr. Reeves, but did not want to be seen as a tattle teller either. What was the protocol for this? Celeste considered from Lady Whitbury's point of view. There was no protocol. Anything of this nature would be handled by the housekeeper or the butler, since it involved a manservant. Being a valet though, Mr. Reeves would answer to Lord Mortcastle himself. That was an ominous thought.

"Do you intend to keep me waiting for an answer indefinitely? I am an old woman and would appreciate a response before I expire." Lady Whitbury's soft spoken question snapped Celeste out of her confusion. The words were not a reprimand, her eyes were twinkling with humor.

"I am sorry, My lady," Celeste began. "I find myself at a loss. Have I done something wrong?"

"Oh no, no, my dear. I am concerned for you. Has Lord Mortcastle's valet been making unwanted advances toward you?" Lady Whitbury patted her hand.

Celeste sat straighter in surprise.

"Not precisely," she answered.

Lady Whitbury continued to hold her hand and watch her face. "That is, he has rarely spoken to me. I have it from one of the other maids that he has been making somewhat personal inquiries."

"Does that trouble you?" Lady Whitbury asked with her brows knit together.

"I do not wish to appear theatrical," Celeste skirted.

"Never mind that," she waved off. "It is clear you do not welcome these attentions. Do you have any previous acquaintance with the man?"

"Not at all. I have never laid eyes on him, or his master, before this house party. I cannot imagine what has motivated his interest."

"You are quite a pretty thing. I imagine that has something to do with it." Lady Whitbury said frankly. Then she pulled out her fan and switched between fanning herself and fidgeting with it several times before speaking again, reminding Celeste of her mother. "One of the other servants—oh what was his name again? A man from the stables..." It was unusual that she was so flustered about forgetting his name.

"Mr. McKnell?" Celeste offered the only name she knew other than Tom or his grandson.

"That is it!" The countess clasped her hands before muttering something that sounded like "Preposterous" under her breath. "This Mr. McKnell mentioned that you are fond of spying on my guests."

Until that moment, Celeste had not realized that she had allowed herself to relax somewhat. Her chest constricted, and she found herself unable to draw a breath, knowing how her mother would react to the same scenario. Innocent intentions would bear no relevance.

"Do not fret, you are not being reprimanded. No, he disclosed this in the strictest confidence."

That did not explain why Mr. McKnell would implicate her. Surely, he did not wish for her to be in trouble. For all he knew, she would be sent from the house.

"He also has expressed an interest in you, my dear. Does he inspire the same discomfort as the valet?" Lady Whitbury peered at her as she waited for the answer.

"Hardly," Celeste blurted without thinking. She clamped a hand over her mouth to stop anything else from flying out and was certain her face was turning crimson.

Lady Whitbury laughed. "You welcome *his* attentions, then?"

"Well, I...he has not paid me any special attentions." Celeste tried not to think of the moment in the stables where he had almost kissed her, lest her face give her away. He had not stated any direct intentions toward her, which she assumed was what Lady Whitbury was getting at. Her denial was ignored in any case.

"He does not have a lot of money, and there has been talk of joining the army. Does that bother you?" Lady Whitbury seemed bothered by the prospect herself, the way her brow puckered, and she looked away. Was it because Mr. McKnell was so invaluable to Tom that he could not be spared? Or perhaps she was acquainted with his family and had taken him on to do them a favor, which would explain her worry. Celeste had no idea why he would need to change profession at all, but knew she was thinking too long when the countess raised an eyebrow, waiting for a reply.

"I hope it will not come to that." Celeste also hoped the answer would satisfy her, but it did not.

"Would you be content to be the wife of a soldier if it does?" Her directness startled Celeste into an honest reply.

"He has given no indication that he would even wish for me to be his wife."

"And if he did?" she probed further.

Mr. McKnell's wife? Celeste had to exert significant effort to halt the smile that was trying to force its way onto her blazing face.

"Would you be content for him to throw himself into the fray to support you?" Lady Whitbury pushed. When phrased that way, it was an awful thought. Celeste felt the smile drop as she reared back.

"Certainly not." She shuddered. "But he would not need to with my inher—erm—" Celeste cut herself off, coughing into her hand.

An eerie silence filled the room. Celeste searched frantically for a way to cover her mistake. She found her eyes roaming the room as if salvation could be found in some corner or painting. Her mother had often warned her that her mouth would be her downfall.

"I shall need you to forego your activities on the terrace this evening," Lady Whitbury instructed with unflappable calm. The abrupt change of subject made Celeste's head spin. Was she to be let off so easily? Had the countess somehow missed Celeste's blunder? It had felt so loud and obvious to Celeste. She dared a look into Lady Whitbury's eyes and saw satisfaction in them. Did she suspect Celeste's identity? Either way, Celeste was at the countess's mercy, and she felt the unspoken reality that she knew it.

"Is there something you would have me do?" Celeste asked, hoping her willingness was clear. It did seem to please Lady Whitbury, judging by the soft smile at the edge of her mouth.

"I would like you to remain indoors and contemplate the things we have discussed regarding Mr....McKnell. The house party is almost over, and it would be best to know your heart beforehand," Lady Whitbury instructed.

"Yes, My lady," Celeste agreed, perplexed.

"Do you love him?" Lady Whitbury asked with unexpected softness. She could have begun an Irish jig, and it would have surprised Celeste less. Did she love him? Her heart began to beat a furious rhythm at the mere thought, but love was more than that.

"I have only known him a short time My lady, and I am quite put out with him for sharing my evening pastime. However, I believe I am halfway there." For some unknown reason, Celeste told her the complete truth.

"Splendid!" Lady Whitbury clasped her hands in front of her. She dismissed Celeste with a smile and a pat on the hand.

For several minutes, Celeste wandered the halls in a daze, repeating the baffling conversation over and over in her mind until she had quite given herself a headache. The one thing she kept asking herself was why Lady Whitbury had involved herself in the first place. It was not unreasonable to suspect that Celeste had exposed her secret, but then they had not spoken of her position or identity. If the lady of the house was aware of Celeste's subterfuge, then why did she not address it? There was something peculiar in the whole thing.

Then there was Lady Whitbury's knowledge of Celeste's nighttime activities on the terrace. She knew she ought to be chastised or punished for that, but it had been disregarded. And Mr. McKnell! She could scarcely believe he had divulged such a thing. He had mentioned being unsure of his position, which made her worry that he may have revealed it under some kind of duress. It would make sense with all that talk of joining the army when he already had work at Whitbury

Manor. He could not be so very desperate that he would betray her confidence in such a way that would risk her position, could he? She would be happy to find him work somewhere, even if he had no desire to be with her. She had imagined that they were at least becoming friends. Was she mistaken?

Celeste burned with humiliation as she wondered how much detail Mr. McKnell had shared with Lady Whitbury. Did the countess know that they had spent time together unchaperoned? With that came the alarming question of the lady's opinion of Celeste. If she indeed knew or suspected that Celeste was her own son's intended, what did she think of Celeste being 'halfway in love' with one of their servants?

Awareness dawned on Celeste with sudden devastating clarity that she really could be ruined by her own admissions. The worst part of it all was that she would not know Lady Whitbury's intentions until she decided to act, nor what would become of Bryn. Celeste expected little warning before the whole thing crumbled around their heads.

With panic-fueling anger, Celeste marched toward the stable house where she found Tom in the stock box.

"Where is Mr. McKnell?" she demanded upon seeing his startled face.

"Uh..." He blinked several times before continuing. "He has not returned to the stables."

It was obvious the statement was true, but it told her nothing.

"I need to know where to find him." She knew she sounded impudent, but she struggled to maintain control of her mouth at the best of times, and this situation was not the best of times. She was embarrassed and terrified, so her mouth had free reign. Besides, Tom already knew she was a titled lady, so there was no point in expending the energy to pretend otherwise.

"Has somethin' happened? Have those blackguards done somethin'?" He dropped what he was doing in an instant, which ebbed Celeste's wrath a little.

"No, it is nothing like that," she answered in a softer tone and took a deep breath. "I have not even seen Mr. Reeves, or Lord Mortcastle. It is—I am very angry with Mr. McKnell." She felt tears burning her eyes and blinked to stop them from forming. Tom relaxed somewhat, hearing that there was no danger.

"What's he done to get you up to high doh?" he asked with a little amusement.

"He has—I do not wish to own to it." Celeste paused. "Oh dear, that sounds bad. Now I shall have to explain." She looked heavenward as it for assistance, willing the dreaded tears to stop forming. "He has told the countess about our being on the terrace in the evenings together. Oh dear, that sounds worse." She creased her brow in frustration. "Is there not a way in all of the English language to phrase this so I do not sound like some sort of light skirt?"

"There probably is, but it would not be nearly so entertainin'." Tom's amusement raised her indignity to a new level.

"I am going to find him. If you happen to see him before I do, would you please tell him I wish to speak with him?" she ground out between clenched teeth.

"Aye, but I may get your message mixed up with a warnin' to run for his life," he laughed, bringing a portion of her dudgeon back to himself.

"Mr. McInnes, I hope you will not be laughing when my reputation is ruined by this madness, or when my maid is whipped and cast out into the streets to starve. Lady Whitbury has indicated to me that she may be aware of who I am. If that is the case, I need to know what Mr. McKnell has told her so that I may know how dire the circumstances truly are." Her speech removed the levity from Tom's eyes, which was replaced with concern.

"I dunnae think she'd ruin you, and she has never in all her years whipped anybody. She's a strong woman, but not unkind."

"Tom, I am supposed to be engaged to her son. If she knows who I am and believes me to be cavorting with her servants—no lady would allow such a scandal to taint her home," Celeste explained. The anxious tears escaped to the edges of her lashes and were thick in her voice, making her throat feel like it had its own corset.

With the reality of the situation spoken aloud, and the prospect of Bryn's fears becoming a reality, all of the fight went out of Celeste. It was over. Both her carefree charade, and the possibility of her reputation and marriageability, and with that her ability to protect Bryn. She could also bid her inheritance a fond farewell.

What had she done? She began to tremble all over her body.

"Och, now dunnae cry," Tom wrapped her in a fatherly embrace. "It's not as bad as you think."

Celeste pulled away and wiped her face with her apron.

"I am afraid Tom," she admitted, her voice shaking and small. "Why would he do this to me? I thought..." Her voice sounded far away. She was certain there were no major rivers nearby, but she could hear one growing louder. She covered and uncovered her ears with her palms to test them.

"Lass, I can assure you that her ladyship will not misuse..." Tom's sentence faded out in Celeste's ears; the river was too loud. There was no blackness for relief, but she did stumble as the world spun around her.

Tom's seasoned arms stopped her fall, but she could not understand anything that was being said to her outside of his call for help. Then the blackness came, but not in a pleasant way. It was like being lost in a headache with fleeting moments of confused consciousness.

It was interesting that, as angry as Celeste was with him, it was Mr. McKnell she dreamed was carrying her. In her dreams, he smelled better too.

Chapter Twenty-Two

∾⌇⧓⧓⌇∾

Jacob felt mixed emotions as he carried the very woman he had been seeking out when he arrived at the stable house. Unconscious was not how he had hoped to find her. He had heard of her whereabouts in the stable house from some other servants who had seen her walking in that direction and then had followed Tom's shout of alarm to the stock box. She appeared so serene as she rocked back and forth in Jacob's arms as he walked. He had fought the desire to hold her on several occasions, but this was not what he had in mind. She was not in his arms of her own fancy but had fainted.

The undefined floral smell emanating from her hair was subtle, and he had no notion of which flower the perfume resembled, but he liked it. He resisted the urge to kiss the top of her head.

As Jacob walked down the hallway slowly, he contemplated the revelations his mother had just thrust upon him when he had been in her sitting room a few minutes before. In truth, he must have missed the lady now in his arms by mere moments.

Jacob's mother had confessed to him that she had been puzzled by the difference in Lady Celeste's appearance compared to her portrait in Honeychurch House in London, but having only seen it the once, she could not be sure she was remembering it with enough clarity to be any kind of judge. After seeing Lady Celeste's maid Elsie, however, she recognized her as the subject of the painting. Not only was Miss Elsie Coombe, in reality, the woman Jacob was supposed to marry, the real Lady Celeste Honeychurch, but she had also confessed to being head over heels in love with him. Though he suspected that part may have been embellished by his mother. He doubted very much that she had elicited that level of confidence in so short a time, but whatever Celeste had divulged, it was good news.

Jacob had smiled like a fool as he left his mother. The idea that he no longer had to fight his feelings made his steps light. She wasn't a maid at all. All of his thoughts were focused on Celeste, the times he had wanted to kiss her, telling jokes as they rode across the estate. All along she had been the very lady he was hiding from. He had startled a footman by laughing as he considered that they had both dreamed up the same solution to their mutual problem of being pushed into a marriage by their parents. He was curious about the process of how the idea had occurred in her mind. He had wanted to find her, his confession seeming far less significant now that he knew she was guilty of the same deception.

When Jacob had entered the kitchens, he took the time to steal one of Mrs. Cooper's strawberry tartlets before addressing Sally to ask if she had seen Miss Coombe, but before he began to speak, she had indicated that he had crumbs on his chin.

"You'll not want Mrs. Cooper catching you, or she'll have your hide," she warned. Jacob would admit to being a little afraid of the cook, so he made himself presentable before asking after Celeste and being directed outside with a warning that she had appeared to have her own personal storm cloud overhead as she left the house. That had him a little worried.

As Jacob had found Celeste unconscious in Tom's arms, his heart stammered.

"What happened, Tom?" he had asked in near panic.

"She had some distressin' news and fainted dead away," he began, worry thick in his voice.

"My mother?" Jacob asked, already knowing the answer. She had used the information he had shared with her to cause trouble, as he had feared. Why she felt the need to inspire his untimely demise, he did not know. Celeste was sure to be furious with him for betraying her trust.

"Aye, she was in high doh about scandal and having her reputation destroyed. I tried to tell her that your mother would ne'er wish her harm, but she didnae listen. 'Tis my fault," he lamented.

"How could it possibly be your fault?"

"She was all riled up at you, and I thought it was sort of adorable, and I laughed. It made her cry, and then she fainted. She came to me with her troubles, Jack, and I was a clipe."

"You—what was that word you used?" Jacob asked, momentarily distracted.

"I said I was a clipe, you scunner. Stop askin' daft questions and get the poor lass inside." His terse words did not disguise how miserable he felt.

"I am certain she will be well, and Tom." Jacob looked back as he had lifted her into his arms. "This was not your fault. It was mine."

The heaviness of the statement weighed on Jacob as he carried Celeste the rest of the way inside.

Celeste's head moved several times during the walk, sometimes with a mumbled threat to Jacob's person, but it never lasted for more than a few moments. It was obvious he would have some explaining to do when she was coherent, but at least he was in her thoughts, if that could be any consolation.

Rather than taking Celeste to the servants' quarters, Jacob went directly to the guest bedroom assigned to Lady Celeste, now that he knew she was the lady in question. That fact alone buoyed him up as William, Tom's grandson, followed him and fetched Betsy to help.

Betsy was silent and agape when she saw Elsie unconscious in Jacob's arms and rushed ahead of him to turn down the bed and fetch a nightgown.

"William, run and get your cousin Sally from the kitchens to come up here and help. I know she is not an upper maid, but she can be trusted to keep mum." Jacob instructed quietly.

William did not hesitate but bounded out the door.

"You'd best be off, Mr. Bellmoore. I need to have her changed and send word to her mistress." Betsy indicated the door. "Do you think

Lady Celeste'll mind her maid being in here? I know she's chums with her and all, but won't Elsie be in trouble if she's in the Lady's chamber? In her bed?"

"Thank you, Betsy, but I am certain all will be well. Lady Celeste will not mind at all. And do not trouble yourself with alerting her. I believe I know where she is, so I shall inform her of the situation myself."

"I hope you're right." She wiped a loose strand of hair from Celeste's forehead and removed her mob cap. Jacob paused at the door. He had never seen Celeste without the fabric covering her head, save those brief moments after her tumble with the other Lady Celeste. Now that he was free to pay attention, her golden hair added to her beauty.

Jacob noticed Betsy staring at him and cleared his throat.

"It will be alright, Betsy. You need not worry. I will tread carefully and take full responsibility should she challenge Miss Elsie to a duel," he reassured her, making Betsy laugh.

Jacob headed straight back to his mother's sitting room. He suspected that her next guest for the day would be the woman pretending to be Lady Celeste.

His suspicions were confirmed as he entered the room to see the poor creature sitting across from his mother, looking as though she were facing judgment in the assizes. What was surprising was Zach's presence beside her. Jacob wondered how much had been revealed and how Zach might feel about the situation since he had developed a regard for the lady.

"What is it, dear?" His mother looked at him with wide, innocent eyes.

"I have just come to join in a spot of conversation," he said, taking a seat in a separate chair between his mother and the others. "What are we discussing?"

"Well, before you burst in, we were just learning of Lady Celeste's hesitancy to marry a mercenary lunatic. I was quite enjoying the story. If you do not mind, I would very much like to get back to it." Zach grinned.

The lady who was not Lady Celeste gave Zach a shy smile that looked to Jacob like the feelings Zach had expressed a few days previously were mutual. She could be a gently bred lady who was doing Celeste a favor, or perhaps a hired actress from Drury Lane. More probable was that they were looking at the real lady's maid. Zach reciprocated the affectionate glance; either he did not yet know which, or did not care either way.

A small intentional cough from Jacob's mother brought their attention back to the room at large.

"Have you been treated well?" Jacob directed the question to the girl he had thought was Lady Celeste. She glanced at his mother before nodding. "Good. My mother can be quite the tyrant, so you just say the word if we need to assemble the hordes in your defense." He winked at her for added reassurance. She smiled but remained cautious.

"Tyrant, indeed. You certainly have a flair for the dramatic." His mother scoffed and rolled her eyes.

"Then it must be an inherited trait. Because in Lady Celeste's bedchamber, lying unconscious, is the real Lady Celeste." Jacob did not mean to snap.

The imitation lady stood at once, a hand flying to her mouth. "Is she alright, Mr. McKnell?" She sounded on the brink of tears.

"I am certain she will be," he replied, deciding to address his own identity when emotions had settled somewhat. He returned to less gentle tones with his mother. "She fainted after you frightened her."

"Frightened her? I did nothing of the sort! Our discussion was quite civil, I assure you." To her credit, her brow creased, and she did sound concerned.

"Yes, as I am sure your current discussion has been quite civil also, yet the poor lady is shaking in her slippers." He turned to the poor woman, whom he could not continue thinking of as Celeste's imposter. "I am sorry to be a part of this, but will you please tell me your name?"

"B—Bryn Owens." Her eyes kept flitting between everyone else in the room as though she did not know where to look.

"Thank you, Miss Owens. Now, Mother, what have you to say for yourself?"

"First of all, young man, I will ask you to cease addressing me in this hostile manner. You know I have no ill intentions toward the girl, either of them in fact," she began, quite on her dignity. "And second of all, I have every right to know what is transpiring in my own household."

"If I may interject," Zach spoke up for the first time. "I believe we ought to give Miss Owens an opportunity to speak."

"I would very much like to see Lady Celeste," Miss Owens took the opportunity to request. She looked at each of them, seeming unsure whom she ought to ask.

Jacob's mother gave her hand a maternal pat. "Yes, quite right. We shall visit her directly. I just have one more question for you, then something of great importance that should only take a moment."

"Yes, My lady?" she asked.

"My question, and I expect a direct and truthful answer." She looked Miss Owens in the eyes.

Jacob cleared his throat to warn his mother that she was being intimidating again. She glanced at him with a slight blush.

"Right, yes. Well, of course you will be honest, my dear. My question is, who are you?" She gave a small smile to soften the question.

Jacob had never seen his mother back down from her side of an argument unless she believed that she had been wrong. It pleased Jacob that she was bothered by the idea of frightening these women.

"I have been lady's maid to Lady Celeste Honeychurch these three years. Her parents do not know that we have switched places." Miss Owens' voice shook, making her words warble.

Jacob looked at Zach to gauge his reaction, but there was none. He already knew! Jacob made a mental note to gloat over him for chastising Jacob about his interest in a maid, then falling for one himself.

"Well then, that puts me in mind of the other matter of importance I wished to suggest. That is, we continue on as if nothing has changed and speak of this to no one else. I believe we may all come through this with our respectability intact if we continue on through the final few days of the house party. Can you agree to that, Lord Blakely?" Jacob's mother nodded with resolve. Zach did not hesitate to nod his assent. "Jacob?" She asked. He cocked his head with a raised eyebrow as if the answer should be obvious. "And you, my dear? How do you feel about it? Do you think Lady Celeste will be amenable to that?"

Miss Owens hesitated.

"We will all look after you," Zach reassured.

"We are all sympathetic to those in your position," Jacob added. "I should confess to you that I, too, am guilty of parading as someone else. My name is not McKnell, it is Bellmoore. I am your mistress' intended."

As understanding dawned, Miss Owens allowed herself a half smile in return, followed by a quiet laugh. Then she agreed to remain Lady Celeste a little longer for the sake of all their reputations.

Chapter Twenty-Three

Celeste stepped out of the fog around her mind with caution. Before opening her eyes, she became aware of several hushed voices around her. She decided to listen while they were yet unaware of her alertness.

"Has she been eating well?" a male voice she did not know asked.

"I believe so. The cook or the housekeeper might have a better idea." She recognized Bryn's voice as the one replying. Mrs. Thatcher was sent for by somebody before the unknown man asked another question.

"Has she been unconscious the entire time?"

"For the most part." That voice she knew. Mr. McKnell was there. "She did have brief moments of consciousness, but aside from mumbling about my demise, she was incoherent."

Celeste did not remember that, but she thought he sounded ready to laugh. That meant that it must really have been him carrying her, not a dream. As she pictured herself being held by him, all the way from the stables, her heart rate increased, and she felt her cheeks warm. When considering what he may have heard as she bounced back and forth from reality, she had to force her facial muscles to relax so that she would not smile to herself and let on that she was awake. It served him right.

"Her color is returning!" Bryn's excited voice pronounced.

She felt someone's hand on her forehead and then light pressure at her wrist. The unknown touch must have been from a doctor or apothecary.

"Miss Honeychurch, can you hear me?" his kind voice asked. She was surprised that he was privy to her true identity. Not enough to know her title, it seemed, but he knew her name.

For believability, Celeste waited until the doctor repeated the question a third time before groaning.

"She is coming around." Mr. McKnell sounded pleased. She decided to throw in a little something for him.

"I'll put manure in his boots...putrid boots..." she mumbled, then went limp. She was certain that a career on the stage was a real possibility for her if she did lose her inheritance.

"Come back now, there's a good girl." Was that Lady Whitbury? Celeste felt a hand patting her cheek, so she fluttered her eyelashes until she was focusing her eyes in the bright room. It was still daylight and quite warm too, but a gentle breeze blew from somewhere. She was disoriented at first. At least she did not have to pretend that part. She could not tell where she was until realization dawned that she was lying atop Bryn's bed.

"Miss Honeychurch, do you know where you are?" The physician asked her. Celeste was not sure how best to answer that. She could not claim to be in Lady Celeste's room, since the doctor was referring to her as Miss Honeychurch. It may not have been the correct form of address, but it meant that everyone in the room knew who she was now. Lady Whitbury *had* caught her after all. She felt her heart go into her throat at that but did not have time to focus on it since the doctor was waiting for an answer. Not knowing how well informed they were about Bryn, she could not risk her security by answering with too much information.

The doctor frowned, taking her hesitation as confusion. She had to say something.

"I am at Whitbury Manor." She answered in the vaguest way she could think of.

"Do you remember what happened?" the doctor asked.

"I spoke to her ladyship, and then I went to the stables." Celeste looked directly at Mr. McKnell for the first time since opening her eyes. To her surprise, he was clean-shaven and rather finely attired, and someone had cut his hair. He looked like a gentleman. That added to her confusion and made her wonder how long she had been unconscious. Had his circumstances been reversed in so short a time? Or had he benefited financially from sharing information about her? Her chest tightened. Celeste made a conscious decision to stop her thoughts. She was not going to allow speculation to swallow her whole without verification.

Ignoring her initial reaction to his magnified handsomeness as well as his much-improved aroma, Celeste announced with indignation, "I was looking for him!" She glared at Mr. McKnell, who at least looked a little regretful. Or was it frightened?

Just then, Mrs. Thatcher entered.

"I think we ought to give her a little space to breathe. Let us all adjourn to my sitting room while Doctor Fitzpatrick examines her. Except of course, you, Mrs. Thatcher." Lady Whitbury suggested, ushering everyone out the door.

Mr. McKnell gave Celeste a brief, lingering look that she could not quite discern before following the others into the hall, an odd sort of tension passing between him and the doctor on their way out.

Part of Celeste wanted to run after Mr. McKnell and strike his handsome face, whilst yet another yearned to make everything right between them. She chided herself for being foolish enough to believe he cared in any way. Had he not proven himself disloyal?

"You seem troubled, Miss Honeychurch," Doctor Fitzpatrick observed. Mrs. Thatcher appeared surprised at her name. At least one person had not to known every dark corner of her life. She knew that was an exaggeration but did not care. In her own thoughts, she would allow herself to be as dramatic as she wished. She closed her eyes and breathed a long sigh.

"I received some...startling news. I was a little overwhelmed. I believe you will find that I am in excellent health otherwise."

The doctor smiled at Celeste and put his tools away into a black bag.

"I hoped as much. Your heart and lungs seem strong and clear, and there is no sign of fever or illness. I would suggest a good long rest and a hearty supper," he concluded. "Mrs. Thatcher, I have a few questions I would ask you, but may I rely on you to see to those instructions?"

"Of course, Doctor," she agreed.

When the doctor took his leave, Mrs. Thatcher continued to peer at Celeste for a long moment. Celeste inhaled, bracing herself against the oncoming confession. She did not want to bring yet another person into her confidence, but the doctor had left her with little choice. She hoped the housekeeper was trustworthy.

"Mrs. Thatcher, please do not be offended, but you have been victim of a deception," Celeste began.

"Go on." Mrs. Thatcher's expression did not change. That was not encouraging. Bracing herself, Celeste pressed on.

"I am not a lady's maid. I am Lady Celeste Honeychurch, the reluctant intended fiancée of Mr. Jacob Bellmoore. I was surrendering to my cowardice by pretending to be a servant."

To Celeste's great astonishment, Mrs. Thatcher laughed. She had almost never seen the woman even smile before. Once Celeste recovered from the shock, she asked, "Are you truly amused? You do not think me silly?"

"It is not my place to say," Mrs. Thatcher struggled to contain her mirth. "I do apologize. Please forgive my outburst, My lady." She brought herself back under control.

"Not at all, laughter suits you. You have a lovely smile." Celeste watched her expression change from suspicious to gracious as she seemed to note Celeste's sincerity.

"Thank you. I shall leave you to your recovery." She bobbed a curtsy.

"Oh, Mrs. Thatcher?" Celeste called out. The housekeeper paused in the doorway. "I am uncertain who knows of this, so your discretion would be appreciated."

"Of course, My lady," she answered, but smothered another smile as she left the room.

$\wp\cdots\bullet\cdots\wp$

When it was time for Bryn to make ready for dinner, Celeste insisted that she be allowed to assist.

"I am feeling much better," she reassured when Bryn hesitated. In the end, Bryn still did all she could, only allowing Celeste to do the bare minimum.

"Do you still wish for me to call you Elsie?" Bryn asked as they worked on her hair together.

"I should like that. We ought to enjoy these last days of our characters while we may," Celeste answered after a moment's consideration. She gave Bryn's shoulders an affectionate squeeze.

"Thank you. It has been marvelous." Bryn's wistful expression had not dimmed with her experience of society. Celeste could learn much from her about appreciation.

"Bryn, I have been thinking. How would you feel about being my companion when this is over? I cannot bear the thought of you returning to the duties of a maid, and this way you would still enjoy society to some extent." She looked into Bryn's eyes through the mirror.

"I am not gently bred," Bryn protested, but the wistfulness was still there in her eyes.

"No one need know that. We shall just have to make up some noble Welsh bloodline." Celeste argued.

Bryn laughed. "You could never have married a vicar like Mr. March. You tell too many falsehoods." Her eyes grew wide, shocked by her own words, but Celeste was far from offended and laughed along with her.

"I believe you are right," she agreed, determined to have Bryn happy, no matter how the situation turned out. She kept to herself her worries over whether she would be able to afford her after the brewing scandal; a lady shunned by society had little need for a paid companion after all.

Chapter Twenty-Four

Jacob put a valiant effort into keeping his focus on the dinner conversations around him, but his mind kept wandering upstairs. Despite Lady Celeste's anger toward him, he felt light and hopeful, knowing that she was the one his mother had engaged him to. He no longer wished to fight it. Indeed, he hoped she would become amenable after learning his identity too. His mother had advised him to allow Celeste to rest for the evening and seek her out the following day when there would be plenty of time for discussion. He had an idea for that. On the basis of his mother owing him for landing him in hot water with the lady, he had enlisted her aid in how he would reveal the truth.

The following evening, Whitbury planned to have a bit of a dance. Not a grand ball, that would be on the final day of the house party in four days' time. There had already been a few evenings of dancing, and the morrow would bring about another one of them. Jacob hoped to use the setting for his revelation. He would send a note on to Celeste, begging her forgiveness and inviting her to meet him as near the terrace as practical, considering the doors may be open. He would then slip out himself and have his mother accompany him in order to facilitate proper introductions. He hoped that even if she were not ready to accept him as a suitor, she would at the very least dance with him.

Until then, Jacob had asked Miss Owens to keep his confidence now that she knew who he was. She had acquiesced, but he could not tell if she were happy about it or not, so he could only hope for her cooperation.

In the meantime, Jacob had joined the house party for dinner. He turned to Miss Goldsmith on his right as she addressed him, something about the weather. He responded with something equally generic. He ought to have made more of an effort, but every moment of inane conversation served to strengthen his justification of hiding out for the majority of it.

After dinner, when the ladies removed to the drawing room, Jacob was introduced to Lord Mortcastle and Mr. Goldsmith, whom he had not formally met before. He knew Lady Adelle's father, Lord Waverley, already. He received hearty congratulations from all three gentlemen on his betrothal, as well as his recovery from illness, all of them referring to him as Whitbury's little brother. That at least told him what he had wondered—that the news of his arranged engagement had spread amongst their acquaintances. Not that he minded anymore.

One gentleman who surprised Jacob was Lord Mortcastle. He approached as others had and was so affable that Jacob almost forgot his opinion of him. His manner was so different from during their first encounter, when he had mistaken Jacob for a servant, that it left no doubt that Mortcastle did not recognize him. That was amusing in its own way.

"So good that you are recovered. Your brother was beside himself with worry." Mortcastle gave him a pat on the back. Jacob doubted that.

"Is it true, Lord Whitbury? Were you quite despairing of your little brother ever recovering? Or hoping you would not have to pay his allowance anymore?" Lord Waverley guffawed as if his comment were the wittiest thing he had ever said. In Jacob's estimation of his intelligence, it may have been. Whitbury simply lifted his port glass with a polite smile from across the room. Jacob had been in company with these men for one evening, and already he was bored to tears. Could his brother not acquire any decent friends? The lack-wit rogue and the silken-tongued villain were not promising, although the lack-wit was technically Whitbury's future father-in-law rather than a friend.

Mr. Goldsmith had not been arrogant thus far like the others, but neither had he been as verbose. Jacob appreciated that quality in him. Nathaniel Carringham, the late Earl of Blakely, had been an excellent friend. The world needed more like him, and Zach, his brother.

When they finally re-joined the ladies in the drawing room, Jacob and his brother sought out their mother together, each taking a turn at kissing her cheek. When Jacob leaned close, he whispered, "Are you certain I cannot become a groom in the stables?"

She smiled and patted his cheek, then whispered through barely moving lips, "The only groom's work I will allow will be in the presence of a vicar."

"Thank you." He smiled at her.

"For what, dearest?" She reared back in surprise.

"For the banter, and your crazy schemes," he returned with a grin.

She chuckled and patted his cheek once more, then sighed.

"I suppose we ought to put Lady Celeste in a proper bedroom now. It is not decent for her to be staying with the servants."

"Except that then everyone will become aware of the truth," Jacob answered. His mother sighed again and shook her head, furrowing her brow before clearing her expression as she left his side to go speak with someone else.

Jacob kept discreet track of Mortcastle as he circled the room, not that he expected the man to do anything suspicious in company. Thus far, he had done nothing but flatter everyone in sight. At first his practiced manners appeared genuine, but after seeing them rehearsed to all and sundry, the air of falseness became evident. He was Machiavellian in his approach to whatever it was he wanted.

As Jacob continued to gaze around, he noticed Miss Owens appearing uncomfortable in the company of Lady Adelle. Considering Miss Owens' humble circumstances, a conversation with the insipid lady would be a difficult thing to endure. He sometimes struggled with her effusiveness himself. Zach was also with them, which gave Jacob a reason to approach.

"Lord Blakely, well met." He extended his hand as he approached.

"Mr. Bellmoore. May I introduce you to the Lady Celeste? Or have you met?" He winked at his friend.

"I do not believe I have had the pleasure. Lady Celeste. Lady Adelle." He gave a bow to each lady, enjoying Miss Owens' expression becoming more amused than troubled, as it had been.

"Mr. Bellmoore. How lovely it is to finally meet you. I have heard good things." She bobbed a curtsy.

"All terribly inflated, I am sure." He hoped his imitation of the pompousness of some of the guests was obvious. Zach's eyes were creased around the edges in amusement, at least.

"Oh, come now, there is no need to be modest," Zach played along. "I am certain that the story of you rescuing the village children from a wild beast cannot possibly be exaggerated."

Jacob struggled to maintain a polite exterior rather than laugh. In truth, Zach referred to the day of their visit to Mr. Morris. As they rode home, they had heard a scream from a garden further along the road and investigated to find two young girls huddled atop a rock because they were afraid of a mouse near the front door. Jacob had evicted the 'beast' amid tearful thanks from the girls, whose ages could not have exceeded ten years old.

"Did you truly save those children, Mr. Bellmoore? For that is noble indeed, and you ought not be ashamed of it," Lady Adelle asked with wide eyes.

"I thank you, Lady Adelle. Out of curiosity, why do you believe I would be ashamed of it?" Jacob inclined his head.

"Well, some would not burden themselves with the welfare of the poor. I myself am always kind to those beneath me. I have it on good authority that the staff were so happy that I shall be mistress here that they had a little dance in my honor. Of course, I could not attend. After all, they are servants, but I did send word through my maid that I would not punish them for neglecting their duties in my honor. They must all be very excited that they will soon be able to serve me when I become the new Lady Whitbury, but it is still worrisome that they would abandon their work for such a diversion."

Jacob was not at all certain that Lady Adelle had drawn breath. Miss Owens appeared to be exercising self-control with difficulty. She attempted to speak, but Lady Adelle continued, "Still, I shall let it pass this once. It is my duty, after all, as a lady of great importance and standing, to be kind to those who are not so."

"Not so important?" Miss Owens asked agape.

"Well, of course. What impact do their lives have in society when each of them is replaceable? Despite this, I do believe we ought to be a little generous in our dealings with the poor souls."

"You are magnanimous." The veiled sarcasm in Miss Owens' comment, uttered through teeth that were not quite clenched, was lost on Lady Adelle, who reached out an affectionate hand and smiled at her.

"Thank you, Lady Celeste. I knew as soon as I made your acquaintance that you were a lady of great goodness, like myself. Is she not, gentlemen?" That was not difficult to agree with, but the conversation in general had Jacob concerned for the welfare of the Whitbury servants upon his brother's marriage. He very much doubted that they had held any festivities in honor of Lady Adelle's future position in the household if Miss Owens' agape glare was anything to go on.

"Lady Celeste, you look a little flushed. The terrace doors are open this evening. Would you care for some air?" Zach offered. She accepted his arm, and his rescue as they walked toward the doors.

Whitbury approached from behind him. "Jacob. I see you have met your future bride."

Jacob was confused for a moment until he remembered that his brother did not know that Miss Owens was not the real Lady Celeste.

"Whitbury, how do you fare this evening?" he changed the subject.

"Very well. Lady Adelle, I hoped to persuade you to sing for us," Whitbury asked his fiancée. She accepted the invitation as if it were the greatest compliment she had ever received.

In thanks for Whitbury's invitation, Jacob was able to remove himself from the conversation. He wandered in the general direction of Lord Mortcastle in the hopes of overhearing something, but he could not discern what it was Mortcastle was saying to Mr. Goldsmith. It was not long however, before Mortcastle approached Jacob himself.

"Mr. Bellmoore. It is a happy event, is it not? Your brother's engagement."

"Yes. And how about yourself? Do you have any plans in the near future?" Jacob hoped his approach was not so direct as to cause suspicion.

"Unfortunately, no. I confess I did hope to find a suitable match by attending this house party, but all the pleasing women are spoken for," he replied, shaking his head in exaggerated remorse. He looked around the room over each lady in turn. It took conscious effort for Jacob not to scowl.

"A pity. What will you do now?" Jacob asked, aware that Miss Owens and Lady Adelle were amongst the women Mortcastle had labeled as pleasing but unavailable. Having either woman being noticed by the likes of him was worrying.

"I shall be returning to London first thing in the morning, following the ball. We shall see what will happen from there." Mortcastle shrugged.

The conversation came to a natural conclusion as the men ran out of small talk. Jacob should have put in more of an effort, but it was not like he could come out and ask the man if he were involved with privateers or acts of piracy of any kind, or if he had any ill intentions toward any of the visiting servants. Neither could he ask about the shipping contract or the company because he was not supposed to know. He sighed. Perhaps his only recourse was to speak with his brother after all. He just had a feeling deep in the pit of his stomach that such a conversation would not go well.

Chapter Twenty-Five

❦

Bryn burst into the bedroom and paced angrily. Her behavior was so unusual that it made Celeste jump to her feet from her chair, the mending she had been doing falling to the floor, forgotten.

"Bryn, whatever is the matter?" she asked.

Bryn startled, seeming to have forgotten that she was not alone. After a moment, she resumed her pacing, though without quite so much intensity.

"I cannot stand that conceited, pompous, arrogant woman!" It was the most unfavorable thing Bryn had ever said in Celeste's presence.

"Of whom are we speaking?" Celeste asked.

"The future Lady Whitbury, who shall grace these grateful halls with her saintly presence." Bryn held her hands up and danced from side to side as she gave the sarcastic tirade in a sing-song voice. Then she stopped and was so rough tugging at the pins in her hair that several strands came with the fixtures. Celeste jumped in to intervene before Bryn rendered herself bald in her frustration.

"Do you know what she told Mr. Bellmoore this evening?" Bryn continued, looking at Celeste. "She declared that the servants are so ecstatic to have her as their new mistress that they have organized some sort of below-stairs party. Then she went on to speak as if they ought to be punished, though she was too great in her own eyes to dish it out. Insufferable!" Bryn muttered another word or two Celeste had never heard in her life. She was not sure she wished to know their meanings.

"Is that not the kind of thing she always says?" Celeste asked, trying to remember what other things Bryn had said about her.

"Yes, but tonight she added that the serving class are disposable!" Bryn spat, shoving her fists into her eyes to stop angry tears and plonking herself down on the side of the bed. "Can you imagine? Human beings, disposable? What utter rot!"

Celeste could do nothing but gape for a good long moment. She had never seen Bryn so passionate about anything before.

"What a dreadful prospect," Celeste agreed, thinking of Betsy and Mrs. Thatcher. People like Mrs. Cooper, and Sally, and Tom. She knew she had never been as snobbish as Lady Adelle, but her experience had taught her the value of those who toiled to keep a household running well. She would never look at a servant the same again, and had even considered marrying one.

Bryn snapped Celeste out of her thoughts, startling her. "Are you thinking of Mr. McKnell?"

"I—how did you know?" There was no point in denying it.

"Just the way you were smiling to yourself."

"I was not smiling. I am very angry with him," Celeste protested.

"Yes, I can see that." Bryn's smile turned mischievous, and her eyes twinkled.

"What do you think of him? After all that has happened, and the consequences that may yet arise from his exposure of us, do you still believe that Mr. McKnell is a good man?" Celeste asked, sitting beside her.

Bryn thought for a minute before answering, then nodded.

"I do. I am certain he had sufficient reasons, which he will no doubt explain when he feels you have rested adequately. I mean, he must have heard what happened to you..."

"What if he does not care for me at all?" Celeste asked, feeling vulnerable. "He has betrayed my confidence, Bryn. I did not think there was anyone who could have such humor and kindness and—" She dared not finish aloud.

"Someone you could love?" Bryn finished for her, looking up.

Celeste wanted to argue that she had not known the man long enough to feel such a thing, but what was the point in denying what Bryn already knew? She nodded, feeling the burning in her chest mirrored in the backs of her eyes.

Bryn surprised Celeste by embracing her. It was something she never would have been bold enough to do before their little adventure. It brought back Celeste's smile. When Bryn pulled back, she yawned, reminding Celeste that she ought to vacate the room so that Bryn could sleep. She had planned to ask her more about Mr. Bellmoore before the conversation turned, but that could wait until morning.

Celeste helped Bryn make ready for bed before donning a dressing gown and lighting a candle. Before leaving the room, she took Bryn's hand.

"I am so happy that we have become friends." She gave the hand a little squeeze. Bryn blinked rapidly, sending tiny droplets of moisture bouncing off of her lashes.

"As am I," she reciprocated, squeezing back.

As Celeste made her way through the dark house, she began to feel as if she were being watched. She spun around several times to find all still and as it should be and chided herself for behaving like a skittish little girl. By the time she reached the room she shared with Betsy, she was almost running. When she turned to push the door open, she thought she saw movement out of the corner of her eye, but as she held up her candle, again the hallway was empty. Still, she dove into the room and closed the door with more force than she intended, her heart in her throat and beating wildly.

Betsy sat up with a start. She looked around in confusion until her eyes settled on Celeste.

"I am sorry, Betsy. I did not mean to wake you," she apologized, expecting the cool reception she had received from her of late, but it did not come.

"You look like you've seen a ghost, Elsie. You haven't seen a real ghost, have you?" she asked, eyes wide.

"No, no ghosts, although my mind was playing tricks on me just now," Celeste admitted as she climbed into bed.

"I'm not surprised with you creeping through the 'ouse at this hour." Betsy looked worried. "You weren't with a gentleman, were you?"

Celeste did her best to suppress her offense at such a question.

"Of course not! I was helping my lady."

"I was only askin', since you've been so friendly with Mr. B—McKnell." Her face fell, and Celeste understood.

"Is that why you have not been speaking to me, Betsy? Because you think I have stolen your beau?"

At first, Betsy seemed surprised that Celeste had reached that conclusion, but eventually she nodded.

"Well, you knew how I like him. It's not fair that you're so much prettier than me." She looked so sad that Celeste wanted to reach out to her, but she did not know how Betsy would react.

"That is not true, I am not prettier than you." She could see that Betsy did not believe a word of it and she felt terrible. "Oh, Betsy, I am so sorry. For whatever it may be worth to you, nothing has happened between us."

"You want it to. I can see it every time you look at 'im. Not that I blame you; he is so handsome and wonderful," she sighed.

"You are right. I do like him very much," Celeste had to admit.

"It's alright," Betsy said without conviction.

"Perhaps we ought to allow him to decide his own heart. Besides, I am leaving in a few days, then you shall have him all to yourself again." Celeste suggested, hoping she was not making things worse. Betsy smiled a small, wistful thing.

"When you say it like that, I feel better."

Both women laughed at that.

"Truly, Betsy, you have been such a friend to me. I am not much of a lady's maid, and without you, I fear I would have been an utter failure. I would so like it if we could remain friends, no matter what Mr. McKnell decides, or does not decide."

Gradually, Betsy's expression lifted, seeming to change from doubtful to accepting.

"I'd like that too, Elsie," she decided. "And you're right. Y'are a bit of a dismal lady's maid." She laughed, and Celeste had no qualms laughing with her, thoughts of potential ghosts and frightening shadows quite forgotten.

Chapter Twenty-Six

Jacob awoke feeling both nervous and excited. He had never been disinclined to dance, but neither had he relished the opportunity either. His hopes for beginning the process of winning over Lady Celeste—the real Lady Celeste—were his primary inspiration for looking forward to the one being held that evening.

There was an entire day between waking and dancing. He could use a ride to work off some of his energy. He bounced out of bed and rang for Giles.

After making ready, Jacob left for the breakfast room. It was crowded and noisy with conversation, but he found himself equal to the greetings and polite conversation as he piled his plate with a sampling of everything on the sideboard. Zach and Miss Owens were present, but he seated himself beside his brother.

"Good morning, Jacob," Whitbury greeted, raising his eyebrows in surprise.

"Good morning, Whitbury." Jacob smiled.

"It has been some time since you joined me for breakfast," Whitbury commented as Jacob sat down to eat.

"Yes, I do not know why that is," Jacob admitted, "but since you will be married soon, and so will I, I felt that time was running out to enjoy simple brotherly companionship."

Several people were vying for Whitbury's attention, but he was fixed on Jacob.

"You intend to go through with it then?" Whitbury cocked his head slightly to the side, seeming to forget the half-eaten piece of toast in his hand.

"With what?" Jacob asked, filling his cheeks with eggs.

"This farce of a marriage that Mother has arranged for you." The conversations in the room reduced immediately, and several sets of eyes avoided them. It seemed that Jacob was still fodder for gossip.

"I do not know what you mean, Whitbury. I am delighted with my bride to be." Jacob indicated the prying ears with a movement of his head. Whitbury nodded and let it drop, but it was clear that would not be the end of the matter.

The rest of the breakfast consisted of appropriate and shallow conversation until Jacob left for his ride. As he neared the stables, he became aware of footsteps running behind him.

"Jacob!"

He turned to see Zach jogging after him.

"What is it?" he asked, waiting for his friend to catch up.

"Nothing, old boy, I just wanted to ride with you." He slapped Jacob on the shoulder as he approached.

When they arrived at the stables, Tom called their attention.

"Good morning, Tom. Is there something I can help you with?" Jacob greeted.

"No, but I have something here that may be of interest to you." He pulled a sheet of paper from his pocket.

"It looks like a letter." Jacob frowned, wondering what it was about.

"Aye, 'tis. It's a letter from my son, young William's father. He's away in the Navy. He writes mostly to say that he'll be home for a spell in a day or so, but this passage here..." Tom pointed to a couple of lines in poor handwriting halfway down the page.

Jacob took the paper and read where Tom had indicated.

"This says that there are some privateers who have been giving them pause, and that—what is this word?" Jacob could not make out the handwriting in places.

"Sorry, lad," Tom leaned over. "Oh, that says 'suggest.' He wants me to warn Lord Whitbury to stay away from Hughes Shipping."

Jacob's head snapped up.

"That is the name of the company Mortcastle wants Whitbury to invest in. Does he say why?" Jacob's mind was razor focused, scanning the page for any more information.

"Nay, lad. He just put it in there for caution. He has no knowledge of what's been going on here of late, but you can ask him yourself when he comes."

"I will, and I think it is time I had a talk with my brother."

"Aye, but go for your ride. He's surrounded by guests at the moment. Wait until he's alone," Tom advised.

"Good advice, thank you, Tom." Jacob extended a hand toward Tom, who shook it with a smile.

Jacob and Zach set out on their ride but did not get far before the weather turned bad, and they were obliged to turn back. Impending rain was as good an excuse as any to allow the horses their heads. Without words, it somehow became a race, even as the rain began in earnest. It did not take long for the sudden unexpected downpour to soak them through, and somewhere along the way, Jacob managed to lose his hat.

Knowing that Thor was afraid of lightning, Jacob ought to have kept tighter control. They had not yet seen any, but as they neared the stables, great fingers of light flashed above the house in the distance, startling Thor, and he reared. Jacob attempted to hold the reins tighter as his wet hair whipped into his eyes, but when Thor reared a second time, he lost purchase and landed in the muddy grass.

"Are you alright?" Zach asked as Thor bolted for the safety of the stables. When Jacob stood, in good order but covered in mud, Zach could not contain his amusement and chortled. To that, Jacob made a mud pie from the clumps sticking to his knees and threw it up at him, landing it across his chest. In response, Zach gave his horse a nudge. As the beast leaped forward, it kicked up more mud.

Jacob held his coat above his head as he walked the remainder of the way, but it did little good, leaving him the very picture of a mud monster from some penny dreadful. When he neared the gate to the stable house, the rain died down as suddenly as it had come. He left his coat hanging over the yard railing and made use of the wet mud and a little dry dirt along the outer wall of the stable to create as big a cannonball of mud as he could. He knew Zach was close by, from the sound of his laughter, and rounded the corner into the covered stable itself, where Zach had just handed his horse to William, then turned to walk away past the line of stalls. Jacob waited until Zach was clear of other people and obstructions and then launched his weapon. His aim was true, and Zach soon had mud exploding across the back of his head and neck. As he stopped in his tracks, his hands reaching toward his head, Jacob pointed and laughed like a schoolboy, only stopping when a small feminine gasp pulled him up short.

Poking her head out of one of the stalls was Lady Celeste. *His* Celeste. When he had begun to think of her as his, he did not know. He stopped short at the sight of her. He snapped out of his temporary trance only when Zach started laughing. Celeste smiled. It was beautiful.

"Please do not call a ceasefire on my account," she said, looking between them and tapping her lip thoughtfully. "Based on overall battle wounds, I believe Lord Blakely is the winner." That fed Zach's enjoyment of the situation, and he began pointing and laughing at Jacob, mimicking his action of a moment before.

Lady Celeste moved further into the stall, Thor's stall, and spoke to the jittery animal. Jacob shook hands and slapped shoulders with Zach as they passed each other. He was no doubt returning to the house and a hot bath, which was a splendid idea. Jacob shivered but chose to approach Thor instead of following.

Celeste had already removed the saddle and blanket and was doing her best to soothe him, so Jacob moved past her to remove the bridle. Thor seemed to be much calmer under Celeste's gentle ministrations. Once Thor was content, munching on some hay, Jacob picked up a brush and stood beside Celeste.

"Are you cold?" she asked, giving him an assessing look. Most of the mud he was aware of had washed off of him during his walk in the rain, but it had left him soaked. She did not look as though she might faint from worry, and she did not appear as angry with him, which he took as an improvement from their last encounter.

"A little, but poor Thor here is spooked by lightning, so I ought to finish tending him before concerning myself with my own vanity." He smiled.

"That is very selfless of you. Here, at least clean your face before the mud dries." She retrieved a rag from a hook in the stall wall.

He took the rag and did his best, but without a mirror, he could not ascertain his success. Celeste looked at him and laughed, then took the rag and reached up to a spot on his cheek just under his eye.

"There, much better." She examined him, leaning in, making his pulse quicken. Noticing another offending spot, she reached up and cleaned just under his ear. In that moment, he forgot about his horse, his appearance, his name. All he was aware of was the lady standing before him, too close to be considered proper, her delicate fingers brushing his jaw as she wiped. He was no longer aware of the cold.

Celeste smiled in satisfaction as she completed her task, her hand stilling an inch from his jaw as she noticed the intensity of Jacob's gaze. The blush stealing across her cheeks let Jacob know she felt the intimacy of the situation. Her hand was still poised in the air as her gaze flitted to his.

"Why are you looking at me like that?" she asked, sounding breathless. Jacob did not answer in words but lightly stroked her jaw under her ear in a similar manner. Her eyelids fluttered, and her breath caught. He felt the grin stretch across his face.

"That's why," he whispered, stepping closer when he ought to have been stepping away. She did not protest but bit her lip. He stroked her cheek again and leaned his face down toward hers, ignoring the voice in his head reminding him that he had not explained everything to her yet.

As Jacob's face neared Celeste's, he was surprised when she moved up on her toes to meet him and rested her hands on his chest. Her fingers were warm, as were her lips. He wanted to wrap his arms around her, but conscious of his cold wet shirt, he opted instead to cradle her face with his hands, moving slowly toward her hair.

The kiss was like Celeste herself, surprising and irresistible, their mouths moving in perfect synchronization. Even when they stumbled back, bumping into Thor's side, causing the horse to step away from them, they both laughed mid-kiss. Then, without even opening their eyes, they resumed as if there had been no interruption. It was the most glorious feeling Jacob had ever experienced. When they parted, their foreheads rested against one another, and Jacob did not drop his hands. His breathing was rapid, as was hers, and he could not resist planting a series of short kisses on her cheeks and nose and lips as they caught their breath.

Chapter Twenty-Seven

Celeste was in trouble. She had come to the stables with the sole intention of asking for an explanation from Mr. McKnell about the information he had shared with Lady Whitbury but had ended up kissing him instead. Her heart was still beating wildly even as she willed it to settle as they stood forehead to forehead in his horse's stall after the most incredible moment of her life. She felt as though her legs no longer existed, and she were being held up solely by the strength of his large, gentle hands wrapped through her hair. He continued to kiss her softly on one cheek, then the other, then the tip of her nose, then her lips. Oh, how she wanted him to linger there a little longer.

He had sent her a gift through Bryn: a miniature volume comprised entirely of jokes with an apologetic note asking for her to meet him at their spot on the terrace that evening. The risk he took in approaching her 'mistress' that way and sending the note through her was enough to soften her ire. The gift itself had also made her smile, recalling their ride together.

Celeste was not one to wait and had made her way to the stables only to find his poor horse bolting in without him. She was good with animals and immediately set about calming the beast, who went straight to his stall looking for food. She had happily obliged him, patting his neck and reassuring him that he was safe, and all was well. Then Lord Blakely had arrived and had just stepped past her when a large clump of muck flew into the back of his head. She had peered around the horse to catch Mr. McKnell cackling and dancing around like an overgrown child, gloating over his successful strike. Alarmed, she looked to Lord Blakely. Did Mr. McKnell have no concept of what could happen to him for treating a lord thus? She looked at Lord Blakely, who seemed to be enjoying the game. Indeed, he had laughed and smiled and had even shaken hands with Mr. McKnell. It was baffling. 'Though, she did recall Mr. McKnell saying that they were friends.

Mr. McKnell had been surprised to see her, that much was clear. The problem was that as soon as she had seen him animated with laughter, she could not remember anything she was supposed to be worried about. When he entered the stable, rain-soaked, muddy and with his hair hanging damp down in his face, it made him more handsome than she had ever seen him and did strange things to her internal organs. Her heart quickened, her stomach fluttered, and her lungs forgot how to do anything much. Then he had approached.

Mr. McKnell was not shivering, but she had asked if he were cold. At least she told herself that was all she was concerned with. It had nothing to do with how warm she in fact felt or how much smaller the stall seemed with him standing so close beside her.

She had been trying to help. Her offer to wipe the spots he missed on his face was innocent, but her awareness of him increased with every touch of the cloth on his strong jaw until she realized that she had leaned in far closer than she had intended. His eyes had been afire, drawing her in, the air between them magnetic, just as it had been the last evening he had joined her on their terrace. She had hoped he did not notice her brief glance at his lips and tried to cover the moment with a silly question. His answer had been to stroke her jaw in return, sending waves of warm shivers through her middle. She never knew a shiver could be warm before that moment.

When Mr. McKnell stepped closer, she should have been the sensible one and stepped back. It would have been the perfect moment to demand her answers of him. She had spent the past day and a half so concerned that he did not care for her at all, but the spark she could see in his face lit the fire of hope inside her. Then he leaned down, and she could not wait. His lips were gentle and soft, and they had moved with hers like a poetic dance. She could have kissed him all day.

Celeste realized with mortification that she had just relived the entire encounter, smiling like an empty-headed fool. When her eyes snapped to Mr. McKnell, he was doing the same. She smothered a giggle.

"What is it?" he asked, his half smile making her stomach do acrobatics.

"Just that we both seem to be in the same sort of daze."

Mr. McKnell kissed her forehead again and stepped back, looking as though it required great effort to do so.

"I cannot disagree with that." His eyes were still alight.

Celeste looked around to make sure no one else was nearby. "I need to ask you something," she began, wondering if she was about to ruin everything.

"Of course," he nodded, but his smile lost its joviality. Celeste took a deep breath.

"Do you know who I am?" she asked. He had been in the room when the doctor referred to her as 'Miss Honeychurch.'

Mr. McKnell looked down at the ground for a moment, then back up at Celeste, cocking his head to the side.

"I do," he nodded once. "You are Lady Celeste Honeychurch, daughter of the Marquess of Kingstone."

Despite the accuracy of his answer, Celeste was surprised. She did not know he would have that much awareness of who she was. She took a moment to gather her courage before speaking again.

"What I am about to tell you may change your opinion of me. Would you hear me out anyway?"

"Of course," he answered, brow creased. She had a feeling she may have just insulted him.

"Right." She drew another deep breath. "You may have heard a rumor that I am engaged or promised to your master, Mr. Jacob Bellmoore. That rumor is true in part, but it is a situation of our parents making, and I have had no hand in it." She looked at him to gauge his reaction thus far, but he was unreadable. She cleared her throat. "Since being here, I have—that is—my feelings..."

"Are you—" Mr. McKnell tried to spare her, but she held up a hand. She had to get this out.

"This may be unconventional, Mr. McKnell, but I do not care that you are a stablehand. I am hoping that kiss meant that you will not allow my identity or my standing to stop you from—if it is your intention to..." Celeste felt her face betray how self-conscious she was. She had not even managed to finish a single sentence.

"Are you trying to declare yourself?" he asked, the light in his eyes and lift in his cheeks making his face smile rather than his mouth, which was slightly open in an expression that warmed her.

Celeste looked away, unable to meet Mr. McKnell's gaze, but his gentle fingers lifted her chin to look at him.

"Celeste." His whispered use of her name sent ripples through her. "Do you mean to tell me that you would take me like this, as a servant?" He stared into her eyes, his fingers still on her chin. All she could do was nod. He surprised her by pulling her close into a tight embrace. She melted into him, her fears draining away into the dust at her feet.

When he pulled back, Mr. McKnell did not release Celeste entirely, but kept his hands on her shoulders.

"I have something I need to tell you. It will explain a great deal, but please try not to be angry with me," he pleaded.

Celeste went instantly rigid. "What?"

"I understand why you would pretend to be a servant so that you might avoid a marriage arranged by your parents, as I am guilty of the same," he began.

"Do you have a hidden fiancée somewhere?" Celeste gasped, striking his chest with her fist.

"Ouch, no, that is—" He grasped her hand in his. "*You* are my hidden fiancée, Celeste. I am Jacob Bellmoore."

Celeste could not react for an embarrassing period of time. She just stood there uncomprehending with her fist in Mr. McKnell, no, Mr. Bellmoore's, hand. As she slowly came to her senses, her first awareness was how large and warm his hand was around hers. Also, that she had ceased trying to hit him and yet he was still holding it.

The second thing she realized, as she thought of his name, was that he had begun calling her Celeste, which she rather liked the sound of. And he wanted her. That simple fact made her heart expand in a most pleasant way. However, on the heels of these feelings followed the full implications of his revelation.

Mr. McKnell was Mr. Bellmoore.

"You are a telltale!" Celeste declared. He had the good sense to scrunch his face a little in remorse, and he dropped her hand. She did her best not to focus on feeling disappointed at that.

"You speak of my mother. I can explain." He held up his hands in surrender.

"You had better! It helps a little that you are her son and not a groveling servant, but it still does not excuse your betraying me to her in such a way that could compromise my position, my maid and my reputation. So, do. Explain yourself." Celeste folded her arms across her chest. This was what she had come to the stables for in the first place before becoming distracted.

"I had no intention of saying anything at all, but my mother discovered that I had an interest in you, and—"

"How?" Celeste interrupted.

"I'm sorry?"

"How did she discover it? Were you writing sonnets about me? How?" Celeste narrowed her eyes.

"Not exactly." He laughed in an awkward staccato and rubbed the back of his neck with his hand. "I believe it was what you might call mother's intuition. When she asked me if you knew who I was, I told her that I planned to speak to you on the terrace. It just sort of came out that way. I was not trying to harm or compromise anyone."

"Do you understand that you have, though? Your loose tongue could have devastating consequences." Celeste felt her eyes welling up again as her worry rose.

"I am truly sorry, Celeste. For whatever it is worth, my mother has no intention of revealing anything of what she knows. She has even spoken with your maid and asked that she continue the ruse so that it will not be discovered." He reached his arm out as an invitation. Celeste stepped into his embrace, grateful for the comfort, relief making her tremble.

"I have not given you leave to use my Christian name," she said weakly.

"Do you wish for me to address you as Lady Celeste?" he asked, his voice serious.

"No," she laughed. "I was merely hen-pecking. Lady Whitbury intends to help us?" she asked, hesitating to believe.

"Yes. She has some sympathy for your situation. It turns out she has a mutton-brained son, you know. He decided to pretend to be a servant himself." Mr. Bellmoore smiled.

Celeste felt much of her anxiety slipping away again with the knowledge that she and Bryn would be safe, and that Mr. McKnell, or Mr. Bellmoore, was not a fortune hunter as she had feared, but there was a little of her ire remaining. She checked again that they were still alone.

"There is one more thing, Mr. Bellmoore." Celeste stepped away, bumping into Thor once more and narrowing her eyes.

"I very much enjoy hearing my real surname from your lips, but you may call me Jacob if you wish," he invited.

"You kissed me!" Celeste accused, storing her delight at his offer to call him Jacob away for later. He only grinned in that handsome way.

"Yes, I did. Would you like me to do it again?" He stepped closer, making Celeste's heart rate increase, and she almost forgot what she wanted to say. Again.

"No. Yes. That is—wait." She held up the forefinger of her free hand and tried her best to give him a stern look. "You kissed me without telling me who you really were. I thought you were someone else."

"I wouldn't say that. I have been as honest as I could be about who I am. It was only my station and my surname you were deceived in."

Celeste was about to protest, but he spoke again.

"And just to be clear, you kissed me back, quite enthusiastically I might add, before being sure I knew who you were." He raised an eyebrow to emphasize his point. Celeste's brow creased. He was right. She had suspected he knew her identity, but she had not checked.

"I did not know you were going to kiss me," she reasoned.

"You could have stopped me," he argued, his voice turning soft. He looked at her mouth. She lost all coherent thought and just shook her head. No, she could not. Or rather, would not. And just like that, he was kissing her again. For several blissful moments, this second kiss was even more beautiful than the first, with the heady freedom of both of them knowing who the other really was. She was Lady Celeste Honeychurch, and he was Jacob Bellmoore.

With a start, Celeste pulled back.

The man Celeste was falling in love with was the same one her parents had chosen for her. Her face fell. She thought back on the night her mother had told her of the arrangement she had made with Lady Whitbury, and she felt the indignity afresh.

Celeste looked up at him. Drat it all, she really was in love with him. And that meant that her parents were right. Not only that, but her mother in particular was right. Celeste had gone to all of this trouble, had put Bryn to all of this trouble to avoid becoming entangled with Mr. Bellmoore in defiance of her parents, and here she was in love with that very man. And worse still, she would have to admit it. Even if she eloped with him, her mother would know eventually. Unless he did become a stablehand and changed his name to McKnell. Celeste shook her head. Her thoughts were absurd.

Just then, she heard the sounds of men's voices entering the stable. She had to leave before she was compromised.

"What is it?" Jacob asked, his brow pulled in worry, then seemed to hear, leaning out a little.

"Why could you not have remained a servant?" Celeste muttered, rubbing her forehead.

His eyes snapped back to her with his brows drawn together in confusion. "I do not follow."

Celeste did not know how to explain, and the men were growing closer. She turned to leave.

"Please," Jacob's worried whisper gave her pause. "I know that neither of us is who we said we were, but I believe we can be happy together. Could we not begin again? Give me a chance to know you, and you me. As ourselves." He reached out a hand.

"Jacob, you do not understand. I am not upset with *you*," she forced out through her constricting throat. She opened and closed her mouth again, then shook her head and swept passed him out of the stall, fleeing from the other grooms in the stable, her feelings, and the inevitable awkward conversation that had to come.

Chapter Twenty-Eight

Jacob was at a loss. He stood in the stable for a long while and found himself brushing down Thor without ever making a conscious decision to do so. He had no idea what had just happened. One moment he was kissing Celeste, the next, she was running away amid declarations of wishing him to stay a servant. Try as he may, he could not make sense of how such a complication could be favorable. She did need to leave before being spotted by the approaching stable staff, but the rest left him bewildered.

Jacob continued working in the stable in an attempt to unravel what Celeste might have meant. At least until Tom happened upon him and sent him back to the house, claiming he looked like a vagabond.

Once he was bathed and feeling human again, Jacob went looking for his brother. He really wanted to find Celeste, but could not be obvious about looking for her since she was still posing as a maid. Stealing frequent glances down corridors, he walked the entire length of the house before finding Whitbury in the study. It was disappointing not to have seen any sign of Celeste, but he still had hopes that she might meet him on the terrace later, where they could talk without being interrupted. She had finally called him Jacob, but he would like to hear her use his name under more favorable circumstances.

Jacob sighed and approached the desk where his brother sat looking over some papers. Light filtered in through the window between the open green drapes.

"Charles, might I have a word?" Jacob began. His brother looked up, his brow creased in something like consternation. It took Jacob a moment to understand why. He had slipped back into old habits and forgotten to address him with the proper respect. "I am sorry, Whitbury, I should have used your title. I have a lot on my mind." Jacob pinched the bridge of his nose and sighed again. It was like there was no room in his head for anything but Celeste until he could know that she was alright.

Whitbury's expression softened with a small smile. He stood and walked over to Jacob, then sat on the edge of his desk.

"It is of no consequence." He waved it off, then took a deep breath. "Well, Jacob, I have to admit that I am surprised at your willingness to do Mother's bidding. I was certain you would stop at allowing her to decide who you would be leg-shackled with."

"I will admit that I did not wish it at first, but then I met the lady." Jacob smiled as he thought of Celeste and the ridiculous way they had ended up meeting by trying to avoid each other.

Whitbury shrugged. "She looks well enough, I suppose, and she certainly has enough money."

"She is more than that." Jacob did not like her being dismissed in such a manner. It was not lost on Jacob that they were speaking of two different ladies, but Miss Owens did not deserve Whitbury's dismissal any more than the real Lady Celeste did.

"Well, I am certain you will be comfortable, and it solves the problem of having you here when Lady Adelle becomes Lady Whitbury."

Jacob could not begin to fathom the reasoning behind that statement. It was not as if Jacob would be in their way; it was a very large house.

"Is it true that you would have packed me off to the army without even speaking to me about it?" He tried to keep his voice neutral so as not to reveal the sting he felt every time he thought about this particular revelation. He had avoided asking for so long because he was afraid of it being confirmed. Whitbury rolled his eyes.

"The old lady has a big mouth." He poured himself a glass of brandy. Jacob barely restrained himself from landing him a facer.

"Have some respect!" he demanded. Whitbury looked up with his eyebrows raised in surprise but only laughed.

"Don't call me out, old boy, it was merely a turn of phrase."

Jacob just stood with his arms folded across his chest, wondering what had happened to his brother. He barely knew the man standing in front of him. Much had changed since Jacob had gone to Europe two years before.

"Alright, Jacob, I concede." Whitbury closed his eyes as he swirled the glass in his hand. He opened them after a low sigh. "You are right, of course. I ought not speak of Mother that way."

Jacob peered at his brother to ascertain his sincerity. Whitbury seemed to notice and gave him a small smile that was almost a frown as he walked back and stood beside him.

"I did think of purchasing a commission for you, and I asked Mother for the name of that admiral who was a friend of our uncle, the previous Lord Whitbury before Father, so that I might write to him and set you up well. We do not have a war on anymore, so I thought it nice and tidy. I do not bear you any ill will, brother." Whitbury admitted, looking down at his glass, then raising his eyes for the last part, his lips pursed in emphasis.

"I am relieved about that. You had me quite worried." Jacob smiled.

"I am sorry for it." The sincerity in Whitbury's eyes and tone was unmistakable. "Although now you have the option to marry an heiress and live off of her money for the rest of your days." He clapped Jacob on the shoulder, changing the mood.

Jacob did not comment on his brother's assertion, but it bothered him. He was interested in the lady herself, not her money. Yet he was not sure Whitbury would understand or believe him. Perhaps that was a conversation for another day. Instead, he decided to redirect it back to where he had intended it to go.

"Whitbury, something has been brought to my attention that could be quite serious," he blurted, in for a penny, in for a pound.

"What is that?" Whitbury asked, his head tilting to the side.

"I am aware that Lord Mortcastle has some dealings with a Hughes Shipping Company, and—"

Whitbury's reaction was a complete turn in countenance. He put his glass down onto the desk with more force than required, causing a loud thunk.

"What do you know of this?" he demanded, narrowing his eyes. He glanced at the window box as if suspecting where Jacob had found his information. It was no secret that he used to hide in there as a child. In fact, if Jacob thought back on it, it may have been Charles who had shown him that hiding place.

Jacob's thoughts were interrupted by Whitbury clearing his throat.

"I am concerned because Tom received a letter from his son, who is in the navy as you may recall. He knows nothing of this but wanted to warn you against having any dealings with Hughes Shipping Company. It appears their privateering activities are causing some concern." Jacob explained.

"Privateering?" Whitbury reared his head back, then scratched his chin. "Mortcastle never mentioned that."

"I know I am only your younger brother, and I know nothing of managing estates, but I could not be silent, Whitbury. Not when Lord Mortcastle is known for questionable dealings, and with Lady Celeste—"

"What?" Whitbury's eyes flew to Jacob's in alarm. "What about Lady Celeste? Did he take money from a lady?"

"No, I meant that he has been approaching her maid and asking personal questions. It has the lady worried."

"Well, I can believe that. He is not known for being a rake exactly, but he does have a reputation for being a bit of a silver-tongued rogue. That was why Mother invited him, you know. She was confident he would be available to even out the numbers when she invited Lady Celeste at the last minute, due to the family's unpopularity."

Jacob nodded. Everything Whitbury said confirmed what Jacob had been wondering, and although having even numbers to go into dinner was important in society, it did not seem worth it to have Lord Mortcastle there.

Whitbury opened his mouth to speak again, but was interrupted by Mr. Norman announcing the unexpected arrival of Lord and Lady

Kingstone.

Celeste's parents had just arrived at Whitbury Manor.

Both of the brothers joined their mother in the main hall to greet the new arrivals, smoothing their features into neutral expressions. It took great effort on Jacob's part to hide his panic. He leaned over and whispered to his mother that Whitbury did not yet know about Elsie the maid. Whitbury raised an eyebrow at their obvious exclusion of him from the conversation but said nothing. Their mother looked between them, some of her well-concealed worry seeping out through her eyes. Jacob hated to vex her, but she had always been a strong woman, not easily shaken, who preferred truth to gilded lies.

Just then, the marquess and marchioness were shown in by Mr. Norman. Jacob's mother greeted them with no hint of her worry showing.

"Lord Kingstone, Lady Kingstone, may I welcome you most warmly. Allow me to introduce you to my sons, Lord Whitbury and Mr. Jacob Bellmoore."

"Lady Whitbury, please forgive my interruption, but I am eager to make the acquaintance of your new guests," Zach said, appearing from nowhere. Jacob must have been very distracted not to have even noticed him entering the large hall. The polished floor was not quiet to walk upon.

"Not at all, Lord Blakely." His mother was ever gracious and introduced them.

"Would you care to rest before we visit?"

Jacob managed not to laugh at his mother's wording. The awkward discussion awaiting them hardly qualified as mere visiting. His admiration of her fortitude increased.

Lord Kingstone bowed his head. "No, I thank you. I would appreciate being directed to the whereabouts of my daughter. I imagine she must be either resting or due back from some activity at this hour." Lord Kingstone was direct, but despite his austere appearance, the hint of a smile twinkled in his eyes, rendering him less intimidating.

"Certainly, Lord Kingstone. I shall have your things removed to your room and some tea sent to the drawing room." She waved Mr. Norman over.

Once the butler had led Celeste's parents a sufficient distance up the grand staircase, Jacob's mother leaned in close to his right side.

"Do you know where Lady Celeste is at present? The real one?" she whispered, her increased breathing the only outward sign that anything was amiss.

"No, I was speaking with her earlier, but she became distressed. I do not know where she went," he shrugged, his chest tightening.

"I will ask Miss Owens," Zach whispered from Jacob's left side, bracing his shoulder with his hand. The reassurance was greater than he would be aware of. Of course, Miss Owens would know where Celeste was.

Whitbury leaned in from beside Zach. "What do you mean, the real one?"

Chapter Twenty-Nine

After leaving Jacob in the stables, Celeste had found herself in the scullery scrubbing clothing. It was not laundry day, she was told by one of the other maids. Besides, such things were accomplished out-of-doors en masse rather than in the scullery, but she could not have her hands idle with her thoughts in such a whirl. After she had worn holes in a few of the more delicate underthings from scrubbing them too hard, she gave up the endeavor.

Once in Bryn's bedchamber, Celeste began to pace around the room, looking for something to fill the time until Bryn would return and they could talk. She knew that Bryn would have some wise perspective that Celeste had not thought about yet.

She stopped in her tracks.

Bryn had been introduced to Mr. Bellmoore. That meant that she had known that Mr. McKnell was Mr. Bellmoore for almost a full day, yet she had said nothing. She had even championed him the night before, the turncoat.

With a flash of irritation, Celeste picked up two pillows from the bed and threw them. They did not go far. One landed back on the bed, and another tumbled over the bed and fell down the other side. It was not very satisfying.

"You are ridiculous!" she chastised them, then stood there scowling with her arms folded across her middle, unsure what to do next.

That was how Bryn found Celeste a few minutes later.

"Elsie, are you quite well?" she asked, concern etched into her brow. Celeste looked up at her, not bothering to mask her feelings.

"How long have you known that Mr. McKnell is Mr. Bellmoore?"

Bryn's face paled, and her mouth hung open.

"I—they—" she stammered.

"Were you ever going to tell me?" Celeste demanded, ignoring the little voice in her head that reminded her of the loyal friend and servant Bryn had been.

"Tonight. It was supposed to be tonight that he would tell you everything." Bryn blurted, raising a hand and stepping forward as if she were trying to calm a wild horse.

Celeste did not relax her stance, but she felt the scowl melt away. She had to admit that it made sense. The note she had received from *Mr. McKnell* had requested that she meet him on the terrace that evening. Had he bound Bryn to keep his confidence until then?

Celeste looked at Bryn. She had moisture filling her lower eyelids, ready to spill over at any moment. Her chin was not yet quivering, but it was all wrinkled under her frown and could start at any time. Sighing, Celeste approached her and reached out a hand. Bryn reciprocated, though her expression did not change.

Celeste shook her head, more at herself. Her temper tended to burn hot but short. "I am sorry, Bryn. I should not have been angry, but why did you not tell me?" she implored, still feeling the sting enough to want an explanation. Now it was Bryn's turn to sigh before placing a hand over her forehead and swaying slightly. Celeste was instantly beside her, bracing her shoulders.

"Bryn? Are you going to swoon?" She planted her feet wide so that she would be in a position to catch her if the need arose.

"I am quite well," Bryn nodded, her eyes closed.

"I do not believe you. Tell me what it is," Celeste insisted.

"You would not wish to hear it," Bryn insisted with a touch of irritation. This was new. Celeste did not think she had ever seen Bryn annoyed before, except at Lady Adelle.

"I am very concerned. Tell me what is wrong."

Bryn took a few deep breaths before answering. She opened her eyes and glanced at Celeste before looking down at the floor. "Very well, if you must know, I am recovering from the fright of finding you out of humor with me." She took another deep breath, and a couple of silent tears slipped out.

"Is that all? Surely, I am not that frightening." Celeste reared back, relief mixing with confusion. It was not a comfortable feeling to quarrel with someone, but to swoon over it was a little overdone.

Bryn's sudden hard stare in her direction disagreed with Celeste's thoughts.

"All? Do you have any idea what *all* even is?" she snapped. Celeste just stood there agape as Bryn continued. "You all wield so much power over the lives of others and give no thought to the impact it might have. If my mistress is displeased with me, it can mean dismissal without references and possibly starvation for me and anyone I am responsible for, and it can happen on a whim!"

"Bryn, I hope you would know by now that I would never dismiss you like that. I am not Lady Adelle!" Celeste defended, the very idea insulting.

"No, I confess I do know that—now," she conceded. "But between you and Mr. Bellmoore demanding that I keep this secret and that, I am forced to disappoint one of you when your demands conflict with one another and I inevitably fail. Yet you take no responsibility for crafting the deceptions in the first place. Honestly, the two of you deserve each other!" She threw up her hands and stepped away, her breathing heavy as she finished her tirade. Celeste was stunned and could do no more than stare. Her hands that had been at Bryn's shoulders just hung in mid-air. No one had ever spoken to her like that, but she did not resent it as she might have before switching places.

Slowly, Bryn turned back toward Celeste, a hand at her mouth. "Lady Celeste, I..." The passion on her face bled out into horror as she realized how free she had been with her opinion.

Despite the set down, pride swelled in Celeste's chest at how far Bryn had come. She would not have her lose her forthrightness for anything, even if it forced Celeste to eat a little humble pie. As she recovered from her shock, Celeste began to applaud. Her smile grew as Bryn's brow creased in confusion.

"Bryn, I am so pleased to see how much steel you have in you!" she explained, feeling a lump in her throat. She had wanted Bryn as a real friend all along, and this finally felt like they were crossing that impenetrable gap. Bryn's disbelief gave way to a hesitant smile and then the floodgates burst on the emotions she had been holding back. Celeste pulled her into a tight embrace and let her cry out the tension that had no doubt been building for the entire party.

"There, there," Celeste crooned. "I would not change you for the world, and you must remember to give me a good set-down whenever I deserve it." At that, Bryn pulled away.

"Do you mean that?" she asked, her voice laden with skepticism.

"I do," Celeste affirmed with a nod.

"I shall remind you of that." Bryn began to laugh and wiped at her eyes, and Celeste could not resist joining her.

It was not long before their lovely moment was interrupted by a tap on the door. Both ladies hastened to wipe their eyes and adjust their appearances, assisting each other before Celeste resumed her Elsie persona and opened the door. On the other side was the last person she expected to see. He was someone Celeste would always welcome, but this time his presence left her standing agape. Her father.

"Well, this is a surprise," Celeste stated after staring at him for a long moment.

Celeste's next instinct was to look around him to see if her mother were there too. She could not stop the butterflies from taking flight from her abdomen into her throat at the prospect of her mother seeing her in one of her old gowns, stained with laundry suds, and wearing a mob cap.

"She is waiting in the drawing room, Celeste. She expects to see her daughter, not Miss Owens greeting her there presently." He nodded toward Bryn, who gave a deep bow. Her cheeks were a deep red, and she could not meet his eyes.

Celeste turned back to her father after staring at Bryn in a panic for more than a few seconds.

"Father, what happened? I thought you were not coming to the house party?" she asked. Not that it mattered now. They were here.

"Well, we did not say we would not come, only that we would be delayed in town, but since you wrote to us asking about your inheritance and whether it stipulated the social standing of the man you had to marry, your mother and I began to worry. We felt that perhaps it was time for us to join you after all." He raised an expectant eyebrow.

"I did not write to you both, I wrote to you! Did you have to share it with her?" Celeste protested.

"Celeste, believe it or not, I am your mother's husband. And as much as I like to think that you and I are good chums, I am still your father, and I will admit to being more than a little concerned by your missive. I can see now that we were right," he answered with an exasperated exhale.

Celeste looked back at Bryn again. She was no longer bowing, but she was still staring at the floor. Celeste turned back to her father.

"It is not so dire as you believe, sir," she mumbled, knowing the moment for confession had come. It was not as painful to admit to her father that she had fallen in love with Jacob Bellmoore as it would be to her mother, but she would not relish it.

"Oh? Do enlighten me." He clasped his hands behind his back and waited.

"Perhaps you ought to come in," Celeste suggested.

"Very well, but I do not think we should keep your mother waiting too long or she may come searching." He grimaced a little at the thought, which she quite understood, considering her state of dress. He followed her into the room, closing the door behind him.

Celeste offered her father a floral embroidered chair in front of the unlit fireplace, which he took, and she sat in the one across from him. Bryn melted backwards against the wall like the servant she was, automatically becoming invisible.

Celeste cleared her throat at least three times before she began, unsure of where to start, but the threat of her mother making an unexpected entrance loosened her tongue somewhat.

"You see, Father, the gentleman I have developed feelings for is, well, I thought he was one of the stablehands, you see—"

His hands grasped the arms of the chair as he leaned forward on the edge. "What? Celeste, you cannot marry a stablehand! Even if it is not stipulated, it is simply not done for the daughter of a marquess to—"

"Calm down, Father. Do not have an apoplexy. I am not going to marry a stablehand." Celeste waved a hand. She almost laughed at his expression. Perhaps it would be a little fun to tell her mother after all, if she told it right.

"Well then, why did you say...?"

"I said I *thought* he was a stablehand. That is, he turned out to be J-b-b-B-mmm." She mumbled Jacob's name.

"What was that?" Her father squinted and leaned closer to hear better. "I am sorry, Celeste, I did not—"

"Jacob Bellmoore!" she blurted, feeling her face heat up.

Celeste's father just stared at her for several long moments, and she could see his mind working as his eyes blinked and squinted.

"Did you just say that the stablehand turned out to be Jacob Bellmoore? And you fell for him whilst you were dressed up as a maid, I take it? And he was, what? Also pretending to be a servant or something?" he clarified.

Celeste nodded. Her father nodded in turn as he processed that information, then he held a fist up to his mouth and coughed. Then coughed again. It took Celeste a moment or two, peering more at the dimples in his cheek and the crinkles around his eyes, to notice that as he continued, he was not indeed coughing, but trying very hard not to laugh. Then the sound burst through, and his laughter filled the room.

"You...fell...for the...oh my giddy aunt!" He hardly drew breath as he laughed so hard that he had to clutch his belly.

Celeste could not keep a straight face. She glanced back at Bryn and saw her smothering a smile as well. It was rather funny, really.

"Well, Celeste, it seems we chose well," he commented as he calmed himself.

Celeste sobered. Those were the exact words she was afraid of. If her parents congratulated themselves on this, there would be no end to their interference in her life.

Celeste's father waited in the hall for her to change into a gown befitting her station. She chose one of her older gowns that was still in good order and would not garner questions from anyone but her mother. She also kept her hair simple but removed the mobcap and tidied it up a little with Bryn's help. Bryn also changed, swapping back to her position as lady's maid with one of Celeste's old gowns but without the mobcap so that either of them could pass for the lady or the maid. Celeste could not begin to imagine how to answer the questions of the Whitbury servants if they went about it in any other way. She had much rather tackle her mother's disapproval. That was a known battlefield.

When they emerged, Celeste's father smiled and kissed the top of Celeste's head before they all moved toward the drawing room together. By the time they arrived, there was quite a gathering that included Lady Whitbury, Lord Whitbury, Jacob, Celeste's mother, and Lord Blakely.

Lady Whitbury and Celeste's mother were seated beside one another on the sofa in the center of the room, the waning light from the windows showing their faces to advantage with a softening glow. Celeste reached for Bryn's hand and gave it a reassuring squeeze before sitting on the other side of her mother. Bryn stayed standing, facing the ladies. The gentlemen were all seated on individual chairs that had been moved closer to the sofa for the sake of the conversation. Lord Whitbury and Jacob sat beside each other, perpendicular to their mother's side of the sofa, while Celeste's father and Lord Blakely sat at the same angle to her.

"I thank you for attending our little party here, Ellen, Lord Kingstone. It is a delight to have you here," Lady Whitbury began, patting Celeste's mother's hand.

"It is wonderful to see you again, Mabel," Celeste's mother reciprocated the gesture. It surprised Celeste that they were on a first-name basis with each other. She had only ever heard her mother's Christian name from her father or her grandparents. She had not even considered that Lady Whitbury had one. Well, of course, she had one, but it was not something Celeste had thought about. She looked up at Jacob to see an equal measure of surprise on his face.

"We have had a few adventures though, some of which we need to speak of for the sake of discretion," Lady Whitbury continued.

"Oh?" Celeste's mother sat with a rigid spine, all informality forgotten. She glanced at Celeste with something like trepidation before turning her attention back to Lady Whitbury.

"Jacob, dear, would you care to continue?" The countess turned her head and smiled sweetly at her youngest son, who was looking as though a specter had just appeared before him. His eyes were wide, and Celeste could not tell if he was breathing.

Jacob cleared his throat with a fist in front of his mouth, which seemed to have drained of all color.

"Yes, well..." He tugged at his cravat.

"Would you like to borrow my fan, dear?" Lady Whitbury winked. Celeste employed her father's tactic and hid her laugh with a cough into her hand, but Jacob appeared too busy narrowing his eyes at his mother to notice.

"No, I thank you." He turned his attention to Celeste's parents. "I must be honest with you. I was hesitant to have my future dictated to me in terms of marriage to a lady I did not know. When my mother suggested it, I resisted by way of—" He paused, considering.

"What? What did you do?" Lord Whitbury leaned toward his brother on the edge of his seat. Jacob turned to his brother and spoke.

"Well, I pretended to be ill and went and worked in the stables," he explained. Lord Whitbury looked confused.

"Why would you want to work in the stables?" he asked, a frown forming.

"I enjoyed working with my hands. It took my mind off my situation. And I thought it would give me a chance to observe Lady Celeste from a distance, only—" Jacob stopped himself short and looked Celeste in the eyes. She had railed at him only that morning for being a telltale.

Lady Whitbury interjected. "To be clear, my son was not simply assisting in the stables. He was pretending to be a servant."

Celeste noted that the reactions around the room were as varied as the people. Her father had just learned of this and schooled his features well, although his eyes twinkled with amusement. Lord

Blakely had a large grin but did not appear surprised. Her mother was gaping in what appeared to be something between disgust and horror, and Celeste could see the moment the confusion cleared for Lord Whitbury. His brow smoothed and a slow smile spread until it lit up his whole face. Then he suddenly laughed out loud, surprising her. Jacob's head whipped around to his brother, who then threw his head back so hard that his chair tipped. Even as he crashed to the floor, he continued chuckling as he righted himself. The room was frozen in shock for several moments before Jacob and Lord Blakely leaped into action and were by his side, offering assistance. Lord Whitbury waved them off but clapped Jacob on the shoulder.

"I knew there was nothing wrong with you! But a servant? Oh, Jacob, why did you not tell me? What a lark!"

Jacob sat staring at his brother without blinking. Celeste could not tell whether he was worried or pleased by the reaction. Perhaps both.

"Are you quite alright, Lord Whitbury?" Celeste's father asked.

"Yes, My lord. Please excuse me. It is not every day one discovers that their little brother is so entertaining," he answered, shaking his head. He emphasized the point by scruffing Jacob's hair until Jacob ducked out of it, making his brother laugh again.

"I have not seen you so happy in years, my boy." Lady Whitbury wiped at the corners of her eyes as she watched her sons. Lord Whitbury gave her a full smile.

"Yes, well as entertaining as all of this is," Celeste's mother interjected, not sounding the least bit amused. "I would like to know how this will affect my daughter. Who knows of it? I do not wish any harm to come to her reputation. I am certain you understand." She looked at Lady Whitbury, and something serious passed between them.

"Yes, of course. Lady Celeste, would you care to address your mother's concerns?" Lady Whitbury looked over, and Celeste could feel rather than see Jacob grinning. It appeared to be her turn.

Just then, Celeste's father reached out and clasped her hand in his. It gave her more comfort and strength than she would care to admit at her age.

"Yes, My lady. You see, Mother, I also pretended to be a servant."

She waited for some kind of reaction, but her mother just stared at her for the longest time.

"Is this a joke?" she eventually asked.

"No, Mama. It is not. Lady Whitbury only discovered it yesterday," Celeste admitted.

"How has it been explained to the guests? Who did they think you were? What did they think happened to you when you did not come? What of your reputation?" Her voice became more shrill with each question.

"Mama, please. I will answer all of that, but please be still." Celeste raised her hands up and down to calm her mother. Her mother did not appear calm in the slightest, but she ceased asking so many questions for the time being.

Celeste began her explanation. "I convinced Owens to stand in as me, while I took her place as lady's maid. It was a simple swap, and only the people in this room know of it, so it has had no effect on my reputation at all. I even changed my name to Miss Elsie Coombe." She forgot to mention that Tom also knew, but thought that might be better to remain unsaid.

"You have allowed this to continue?" Celeste's mother turned to Lady Whitbury.

"Mother, I have presented myself to the guests and staff as a lady's maid. It would be an unforgivable embarrassment to this household if I were to suddenly change places now," Celeste reasoned, eliciting a grunt from her mother.

"Ah, you are concerned with embarrassment. How thoughtful." Her voice dripped with sarcasm. "And what of you?" She turned her sights on Bryn.

"Mother, Bryn only did as she was told and under duress, I might add. I refuse to allow her to be punished in any way." Celeste stood, creating a protective barrier between her mother and Bryn.

Just then, Lord Blakely interjected. "Lord Kingstone, Lady Kingstone, may I reassure you that Miss Owens has behaved with the utmost decorum for the entire house party and has been a credit rather than a disadvantage to your family name."

"Thank you, Lord Blakely, that is indeed comforting," Celeste's father responded.

"And you, Mother? Have you nothing to say?" Celeste prompted.

"Do calm yourself. I never had any intention of punishing the girl," Celeste's mother dismissed, not making eye contact. Then she added in an aside, "Anyone would know you dragged the poor thing into it."

Celeste breathed a sigh of relief and looked behind her to see Bryn offering her a tremulous smile and a nod but looking shaken.

"There are only a few days left of the house party," Celeste declared. "I can continue on as a lady's maid for three more days and no one will be the wiser. The question is, can you pretend that Bryn is me?"

Celeste's mother's eyes widened to the size of teacups.

"I think I shall simply keep to my room. No one knows we are here."

"Very well. We shall carry on, then, and if it becomes too difficult, we can always depart early." Celeste's father agreed, looking at his wife.

Celeste glanced at Jacob, not liking that idea at all. She mouthed the word terrace, and he gave a subtle nod. She wanted to meet him there so that she might explain her earlier outburst and make certain he knew how she felt, especially with the threat of her parents whisking her away. She needed to ensure they had a future.

Chapter Thirty

The drawing room had certainly been interesting. Jacob watched Celeste scurry up the stairs with Miss Owens, looking around herself as if afraid of being caught. Anyone would think Celeste was the imposter with the way she was behaving. He laughed to himself in silence. What a situation they had found themselves in. He had not expected Whitbury's reaction. Had he known his brother would be such a good sport about it all, he could have included him in the plan. It may have made things easier to have an ally in the party to distract his mother.

A hand on Jacob's shoulder made him jump. He turned his head to see his brother materializing out of his thoughts beside him.

"You know, Jacob, you could have come to me," Whitbury said, a small smile on his face. His eyes seemed to tilt downward with a hint of sadness, despite the contradiction of his mouth. Before Jacob could answer, Whitbury patted his shoulder again and continued past him, leaving Jacob to wonder at his brother's thoughts. One moment, Whitbury seemed intent on being rid of him, the next, he wanted to engage in a lark like they might have when they were young with Zach and his brother, Nathaniel, or sister, Esther. Jacob could not reconcile the contrasts.

Jacob did not have a long time to consider the state of his brother's mind before he was approached again, this time by the marquess.

"Mr. Bellmoore, we still have an hour or so before dinner. Would you honor me with a moment of your time?" he greeted with a bow, which Jacob returned.

"Certainly, sir." Jacob gestured back toward the drawing room since it had just been vacated. He did not know why Celeste's father had requested a private conversation with him, but it was very likely to do with the state of their relationship. On that note, there was something he would like to ask in return.

Jacob sat across from Lord Kingstone and tried to hide the nervous energy that was making its way through his limbs and manifesting as annoying tapping of foot and fingers. He planted his hands on his knees to stop them from bouncing.

"Is your chair in want of repair?" Lord Kingstone asked as he made himself comfortable on one of the single chairs. Jacob looked up, startled out of his reverie.

"Ah, no, sir. It is adequate," he answered. He thought the marquess had a twitch of humor at the edge of his lip, but it was so subtle that Jacob could easily have been mistaken.

"You are bouncing about like a rabbit. Do explain yourself if you please." Lord Kingstone's amusement was more obvious this time. It was clear that he was well-practiced at confining it to his eyes, but they danced despite his face giving nothing away.

"You must know," Jacob took a chance. There was no way Lord Kingstone could be oblivious to Jacob's reason for being nervous around the man who could become his father-in-law.

Lord Kingstone raised an eyebrow.

"Oh, must I? Were I not so fond of you after today's little circus, Belmoore, I should think you impertinent."

"Ah, but you are fond of me, by your own admission." Jacob grinned, coaxing a strong twitch in the man's cheek, which Jacob found satisfying. "Alas, I shall satisfy your curiosity." He took a deep breath.

"I am gratified to hear it," Lord Kingstone said.

"Lord Kingstone, I am aware that dishonesty is not an ideal foundation for courtship. Indeed, although it is something both your daughter and I share in common, I do believe our situation to be unique." Jacob hoped that his words would not be misunderstood as placing any blame on the lady. He had not noticed how rude his words sounded until they were out of his mouth.

"Your situation is that," Lord Kingstone agreed. He did not seem offended.

Jacob breathed a sigh of relief.

"I believe that posing as servants the way we did gave us opportunities to become acquainted in ways we would not have under normal circumstances—"

"What precisely do you mean by that?" Lord Kingstone interrupted.

"Nothing untoward, I assure you," Jacob replied with haste, waving his hands in the air in front of him. "I only meant that as we were both against the union as arranged by our parents, we would have been predisposed to prejudice against one another. Which did not occur when we met as staff."

Jacob resisted the urge to wipe his sweating palms on his trousers, not at all certain if he was being clear, but Lord Kingstone seemed to relax somewhat.

"I see," was his only response. It was not reassuring.

"Sir, what I am trying to say, is that, with your permission, I am now amenable to the match and have no objections to courting, and if she will accept me, wedding, Lady Celeste," Jacob persevered, holding his breath without conscious thought to do so.

Lord Kingstone steepled and un-steepled his fingers before answering.

"You know you already have my blessing, since I had a hand in arranging this with her mother and yours."

"Yes, sir."

"Then why do you require it again?" Lord Kingstone scrutinized Jacob, making him squirm a little.

"Well, sir, because this time *I* am asking you, as my own man, for Lady Celeste's hand, not my mother. I am also aware that you may disapprove of a son-in-law who pretended to be a stablehand for the sole purpose of avoiding your daughter."

With difficulty, Jacob looked Lord Kingstone in the eyes to show his sincerity, although he wished he could un-say his last sentence. However, a statement, having left one's mouth, was no longer accessible for editing.

Slowly, the restraint on Lord Kingstone's smile retracted until it spread across his face. He even let out a short laugh, allowing Jacob to draw breath.

"I do believe, Mr. Bellmoore, that you and Celeste are quite compatible. I am confident that should she accept you, you will be very happy, and it pleases me that you would ask for yourself. A word of caution though, if you will indulge me?"

"Of course," Jacob agreed without hesitation.

"Her heart, once given, will be yours forever. She will not give it lightly, and I urge you to take seriously your responsibility to cherish it." Lord Kingstone blinked a time or two in succession, but that was the only sign of his emotion.

"I know it has been a short acquaintance, but it has been an intense one. What I am trying to say, sir, is that her happiness is of the utmost importance to me," Jacob assured him.

"That is good. I respect you, Bellmoore, and I thank you for your candor." Lord Kingstone smiled.

"A pleasure, sir," Jacob reciprocated. He laughed at Lord Kingstone's questioning brow. "A frightening one certainly, but a pleasure all the same."

Dinner that evening seemed to go on forever. All Jacob could think about was seeing Celeste. She had tried to communicate something to him, and he thought it looked like she was mouthing the word terrace. If so, it meant that he would be able to speak with her alone and find out if all was well. Also, why she had fled the stables in such a state earlier. His anxiety for her had not abated since that moment. It was beginning to give him indigestion.

As promised, Celeste's parents kept to their rooms, and the other guests were none the wiser as to their presence.

After dinner, the guests gathered together in the drawing room, along with some of the local neighbors who had joined them for the socializing and dancing. All Jacob could think about was getting outside onto the terrace. When they entered the room though, the terrace doors were all wide open, light spilling out onto the stone landing outside. He considered that he may have to wander down the outdoor staircase off to the side to find her, if she had ventured there at all with all these people present.

Jacob danced a set with Miss Owens and one with Lady Adelle before it was the time he expected Celeste might be waiting for him. As he made his way out the doors, it felt as if a host of bees swarmed inside of him.

At first there seemed to be no sign of Celeste, but he soon spied her peeking out from behind some foliage at the base of the stairs. He almost tripped forward on a step when she made eye contact with him, and he was about to head toward her when he heard his name being called from inside. He looked back to see one of the guests, Mr. Goldsmith, looking around with large eyes.

Jacob glanced back toward the bottom of the terrace stairs where Celeste had been, but she was gone. He closed his eyes for the duration of a deep breath. He would have to see to Mr. Goldsmith and then return. He hurried inside, not wanting to lead anyone out toward Celeste.

"Mr. Bellmoore, it is your brother. He is in need of a physician!" Mr. Goldsmith said as he approached. His own sister, Miss Hannah, gasped from where she stood nearby.

"A physician? What has happened?"

"He is in his study. Please come quickly."

Jacob lost no time in following Mr. Goldsmith down the main staircase toward his brother's study. Once there, he found Whitbury indeed in distress, on his hands and knees as he cast up his accounts onto the floor. Their mother rushed past Jacob from behind, having followed them. She was by Whitbury's side within moments, brushing his hair away from his face and loosening his cravat, then turning to Mr. Goldsmith and requesting both his discretion and that he do her the service of sending for the housekeeper. She then turned to Jacob.

"Jacob, would you please send for the doctor?"

"Of course." Jacob nodded and immediately turned and left the room in search of Mr. Norman. His mother's calm and practical reaction to Whitbury being genuinely ill was the opposite of the theatrics she had employed over Jacob when she had known he was acting. He really should have seen that she was onto him.

Jacob found Mr. Norman in the main hall, welcoming a neighbor. with as much politeness as he could bring himself to present, Jacob approached and asked Mr. Norman in hushed tones to send for Doctor Fitzpatrick once the guest had been seen to. He stopped in his tracks when he turned from the butler at what he saw just beyond the main doors. Lord Mortcastle's carriage hurtled past and down the drive at a reckless speed.

"How is your brother? I heard Mr. Goldsmith say he is ill." Jacob leaped out of his skin as Mortcastle himself appeared at his shoulder.

"Lord Mortcastle! Your carriage..." Jacob exclaimed to the man beside him. He waved his hand at the dark shape growing more distant by the minute.

"What?" Mortcastle leaped forward out of the double doors and down the front steps in alarm. He kicked at the graveled ground with an expletive. Jacob could only stare as Lord Mortcastle expressed his duress, his styled hair flying in various directions before he re-joined Jacob by the doors, red-faced and breathing heavily.

Jacob stood watching in stunned silence as Lord Mortcastle complained to no one in particular, whilst pacing back and forth in the vestibule, his eyes not leaving the ever-shrinking carriage.

"Mr. Bellmoore, sir, your mother is asking for you," Mr. Norman informed him. He had not realized he had been standing there gaping long enough for the butler to show the guests to the drawing room, speak to his mother, and then return.

"Certainly, I will go to her." Jacob turned, but then paused. "Oh, Norman? I know Whitbury handles county matters, but do we have a part-time constable in the area?" Jacob asked. Mr. Norman's eyes grew wide, but he nodded.

"Yes, sir. Mr. Brown, the candlemaker," he replied.

"That is a relief. Would you please send someone for him?" Jacob instructed. Norman nodded, still looking a little stunned.

"Make haste, man! Someone has just made off with my carriage."

Lord Mortcastle demanded. He stomped right up to the doorway but then turned his dissatisfaction on Jacob. "If your incompetent staff are responsible for allowing the theft, I shall expect full compensation and the position of whomever was negligent."

Jacob blinked slowly several times but did not bother giving Lord Mortcastle an answer. Mortcastle knew full well that any financial decisions on the Whitbury estate required the authority of the earl.

"They have probably run off by now anyway," Mortcastle grumbled as he pushed past Jacob back into the house.

By the time Jacob arrived at the door to the study, some of the guests had noticed the absence of all of their hosts. Half a dozen people had wandered out onto the small balconies on either side of the grand staircase in the center of the great hall to satisfy their curiosity. The two Miss Goldsmiths, as well as Lady Waverley, and at least three of the local neighbors, had found their way there. They all began to call questions down to Jacob at once, Lady Waverley descending the staircase as she did so. That seemed to inspire the others to follow suit, and he became surrounded.

Jacob felt torn between his duty to protect the image of his family and his duty to the family itself. After a moment of indecision, he asked Mr. Norman to inform his mother that he would be along as soon as he had seen to their guests. He had often been told that he could charm his way out of any sort of trouble. That was mostly by elderly ladies he had flattered in London ballrooms, but that did not signify. It was time to put it to the test.

With a deep breath, Jacob plastered on his best smile and began corralling the curious few back toward the drawing room, insisting that nothing was amiss. Lady Waverley did not look at all convinced, but she did not protest, and Jacob had the uneasy feeling he would be required to explain things to her at some point.

Miss Harriet Goldsmith was the elder of the two sisters and also the most verbose, so Jacob focused on making the girl laugh. That, in turn, seemed to put the rest of the company at ease. It was by no means a difficult task, and by the time they returned to the rest of the party, they seemed to have forgotten that there might have been anything worth gossiping about downstairs at all. Unfortunately, Miss Goldsmith was also quite hesitant to release Jacob into the company of anyone else. The look she gave him resembled one he had seen recently on the face of Betsy, the maid, when she had brought him reading material. He resisted the urge to sigh.

The voice of Lady Adelle coming toward him caused such a contradiction of feeling as to render Jacob speechless for a moment. He did not usually look forward to her company, as shallow as the lady was, but at that moment, he could have sung at her presence. She was the precise person he needed to speak with.

"Mr. Bellmoore, there you are!" She held out both of her hands to clasp his, as she approached with a perfect smile.

"Do excuse me, Miss Goldsmith. I must speak with my future sister-in-law a moment. Please forgive me." He nodded toward the lady at his side in apology.

"Of course, Mr. Bellmoore. I shall just be over there with my sister." She offered him a curtsy and a giggle and made her way to the other side of the room where she began to whisper animatedly to the younger Miss Hannah. He did not know if she was aware of his engagement to Lady Celeste, but he did not have time to worry over it at present.

Jacob turned his attention to his brother's fiancée.

"Lady Adelle, I am relieved to see you." He spoke in low tones as he returned her handshake.

"Oh dear, Mr. Bellmoore, your manner does not bode well. Do tell me there has not been some terrible disaster." She looked at him with wide, pale eyes under slightly pulled eyebrows, but her practiced smile stayed in place.

Jacob copied Lady Adelle's tactic of smiling as though they were speaking of inconsequential pleasantries.

"Of that I am not yet certain. You see, my brother is ill in the library, and a carriage appears to have been stolen. The countess is with Lord Whitbury, but she has sent for me to assist her. And so, although I am reluctant to place such a burden upon your shoulders before you are the official Lady of the house, I find myself obliged to ask you if you would please take on the role of hostess. Just until my mother is at liberty to return."

Jacob switched between watching Lady Adelle's subtle reaction and the crowd around them to be certain he was not overheard.

"My poor Whitbury!" she responded with a thickness to her voice, a delicate gloved hand at her mouth before she corrected herself by pretending to laugh behind it. "Of course, Mr. Bellmoore, you may depend upon me to secure the honor of our family. It will soon be my role when I am the countess to see to such things, so I am only too happy to help. You go now, dear brother, and see to it that my love may be well."

She dipped a curtsy before turning with a flourish, her hands clasped in front of her as if in excitement. Before Jacob had even drawn a breath, she was calling for a game of bullet pudding.

Jacob stood blinking for a moment but then made a hasty escape before any attention could be drawn in his direction. He smiled to himself, confident in Lady Adelle's abilities as a hostess. She would take care of things.

As Jacob made his way back to Whitbury's study, he was once more interrupted before entering, this time by Lord Kingstone as he approached the main staircase to descend.

"Mr. Bellmoore, might I have a word?" he asked, his tone short. Jacob inferred that it was not really a request.

"Certainly, My lord," he answered, hoping he would not be delayed long.

"I cannot find my daughter. I went to the chamber where Miss Owens has been staying, but no one is there, so I sought out the housekeeper, who sent a maid for her, but no one seems able to find her."

Jacob opened his mouth to reply but then closed it again, having no satisfactory answer. If Mrs. Thatcher could not find Celeste, then she may yet be out-of-doors. He could not say that she might be waiting in the bushes outside for a private tête-à-tête with him, especially to her father.

Just as the silence was stretching long enough to cause both men to fidget, Mrs. Thatcher herself appeared on the staircase carrying a small stack of folded cloths, with Whitbury's valet carrying a basin of water in tow.

"Mrs. Thatcher," Jacob called out. She paused as she reached the base of the stairs, and Jacob caught up with little effort. "When you have assisted my brother, could you please send for Betsy? I have an errand for her." Far better to have her find Celeste on the terrace than someone else.

"Certainly, Mr. Bellmoore." She bobbed a quick curtsy and continued toward the study, but Jacob did not miss the slight squint to her eyes before she did so.

Lord Kingstone approached from behind. Jacob turned and gave what he hoped was a reassuring smile.

"We shall get to the bottom of this before too long, My lord."

"It makes me uneasy not knowing where to find her." Lord Kingstone looked away into the distance before bringing his attention back to Jacob. "I had hoped to speak with her on the subject you and I discussed earlier." Jacob looked around. His mother was still waiting for him in the study, and Lord Mortcastle was still pacing with heavy footfalls across the hall stones, making an echo. It was the worst time for a conversation of this nature, and Jacob felt his cravat beginning to strangle him.

"I do hope Betsy will be able to locate her swiftly for you, My lord," Jacob nodded, then lowered his voice. "If you will forgive me, my brother has taken ill, and I must be of assistance."

"Of course, I will not detain you." Lord Kingstone held out a hand in a gesture for Jacob to proceed, his expressive brow moving from being raised in surprise to being pulled together in compassion within moments.

"Thank you, sir." Jacob nodded before turning back toward the study, noting that Mortcastle had not interrupted his pacing and muttering, seeming oblivious to everyone else's troubles.

Jacob entered the study just in time to see Doctor Fitzpatrick giving his mother a heavy look. He must have arrived while Jacob was in the drawing room. Jacob rushed over to his mother's side, apologizing for his delay as she curled into his side, holding a lacy handkerchief under her nose. He had never seen her so distraught. In Jacob's absence, Whitbury had been laid on the sofa with a pail placed on the floor by his head, and his valet had already managed to adorn him with a dressing gown. He did not appear to be conscious, and his breathing was barely discernible.

Before Doctor Fitzpatrick could say a word, a knock at the door preceded Mr. Norman announcing the constable. Jacob did not leave his mother but nodded that the man should be shown in.

Mr. Brown, a part-time man for hire who worked as a candlemaker by day, appeared to be about to speak. He stopped short at the sight before him and surveyed the scene with a practiced eye.

"Has Lord Whitbury taken ill?" he asked.

Doctor Fitzpatrick looked at Jacob's mother before responding. She nodded her consent for him to speak.

"I fear that this illness is not brought on by nature," he began.

"Do you think he was poisoned?" Jacob almost jumped forward, dragging his mother with him and almost making her trip. He stepped back immediately and patted her arm in apology, but she waved him off.

"Now, now, let's not jump to any conclusions; that isn't what Doctor Fitzpatrick said. Mr. Brown interjected.

"Well, his symptoms may have a number of causes, but I do believe he is displaying signs of excessive opium consumption," Doctor Fitzpatrick continued.

"There, you see?" Jacob said tersely.

"He could easily have ingested that himself," the constable argued.

Mr. Norman again knocked on the door. "If you will pardon the interruption, sir, the Marquess of Kingstone is begging entrance."

"Show him in," Jacob sighed, feeling a throbbing pain in his head. He pinched the bridge of his nose for whatever small relief it could afford.

Immediately upon his admittance, Lord Kingstone strode straight toward Jacob, his face hard.

"Mr. Bellmoore, Celeste has been abducted. The housekeeper has just informed me that the stable master's grandson reported seeing her being carried off. I intend to go after her. Will you assist me?"

Chapter Thirty-One

Celeste rubbed her forehead where it had hit the side of the carriage as she had been forced inside. She had not gone without a fight, but she paid for it now. She tried to make sense of what had happened, but her head seemed to be fleeing from all sense and equilibrium.

She had gone to the terrace to meet Jacob, hoping to explain her earlier erratic behavior. Then someone had called to him from inside, and she had slipped back into the shadows, intending to remain close by in case he had an opportunity to reemerge later.

As it turned out, someone else was occupying those same shadows. As Celeste stepped backwards toward the outer wall of the house, she had been seized and dragged from behind.

"If you scream, you're dead," a familiar accented voice had whispered beside her ear. The point of a dagger against her side persuaded her to listen.

Her mind had blurred, racing faster than it ever had before, trying to find some way to save herself.

"What WILL they TELL GRANDFATHER?" Celeste had called out as loud as she dared in the hope that William would be lurking somewhere, invisible, and understand the message to fetch Tom. A strong hand had covered her mouth so tightly that no more sound she attempted could push through the barrier. The hand was so large that it covered her nose as well, preventing her from even breathing. She regretted not screaming when she had the chance, blade notwithstanding.

"Don't give me any trouble," her captor commanded beside her ear. She had attempted to nod but could not even move that much as he used his entire body to restrain her against him. She suspected him of being Mr. Reeves, Lord Mortcastle's slimy valet. She had never been close enough to smell him before, but his sweaty aroma hit her like a wave until she lost the ability to inhale when he clasped her mouth.

He had not relinquished his grip as she had hoped, and she had begun to feel light-headed. She tried to indicate with her hand that she could not breathe without appearing to fight, supposing that to be her best chance at receiving air. She intended to make him think she would be cooperative and then seek a strategic means of escape, but he did not budge and only snickered.

"You'll get air just as soon as I'm good and ready." His total lack of regard, coupled with her instinct to survive, made her plan to be still and calm impossible. Her body twisted and struggled without any intellectual command. She even tried to bite him, but his grip on her jaw was too tight. Then she was being hauled into a carriage.

As Celeste began to feel herself going limp and the black tendrils of unconsciousness conquered her will, she was aware enough to suppose that the movement she felt was physical. It could have been due to the deprivation of air, but at least she was no longer being restricted in that regard. Despite that, her head felt weighted, her body lethargic, and she could not long resist the pull of sleep.

Chapter Thirty-Two

Jacob's heart fell into his shoes. Celeste. Abducted.

He could have taken Thor and followed directly if he had not been distracted. By now they could be long gone in any direction. His first guess would have been to suspect Lord Mortcastle, but he was still blowing off steam in the main hall.

"What about Betsy? I sent her looking for Celeste," Jacob thought aloud, turning to Lord Kingstone.

"I am sorry. It appears that she is also missing. Mrs. Thatcher could not find her." Lord Kingstone's features softened a little from what they had been.

"My apologies, your Lordship, but might I be of assistance?" Constable Brown spoke up.

"And you are?" Lord Kingstone asked with restrained impatience. His face had not changed expression, but one eyebrow flinched upwards. Anyone paying attention could see that the man did not wish to waste time.

"This is Mr. Brown, Whitbury village's part-time constable," Jacob introduced, speaking fast.

"If you have any suggestions in the next five minutes, I will be happy to hear them, but I only intend to stay long enough for Mr. Bellmoore to make himself ready to ride," he stated, then looked at Jacob. "I did not bring any weapons with me."

"Do you have any idea who might have done this?" Mr. Brown asked, scratching his head, deep lines forming across his forehead.

"Lord Mortcastle's carriage was stolen not long ago, I do not know by whom." Jacob answered.

"What about his valet? There have been several complaints from my female staff about the man, and he could easily procure the carriage without raising suspicion. Could he not have been the one to carry her off? He would also have been in a position to slip something into Lord Whitbury's drink to keep us all occupied for him to do the deed." Jacob's mother suggested, clinging to Jacob for comfort.

"Your Ladyship, I really don't think—" Constable Brown began, shaking his head at her as though she were a child. He was cut off by Lord Kingstone.

"And I really do not know why we are standing about arguing whilst my daughter is being removed further away." He glared at the much shorter man. "It is as sound a supposition as we are going to get with so little to go by. Now, a carriage traveling at high speed will have drawn attention, and we may ask questions along the way. Bellmoore, are you with me?" he asserted rather than asked before striding out the door.

The marquess was more than halfway to the stable house when Jacob caught up with him. He had stopped to retrieve a pair of swords and Whitbury's dueling pistols. Lord Kingstone acknowledged Jacob's presence with a nod. He had no difficulty matching strides with the marquess, as anxious as he was to have Celeste returned safely. He did not allow himself to think about what might befall the lady if they were too slow.

When they entered the stable yard, Jacob called out to Tom at the top of his lungs. He appeared almost instantly, calling instructions over his shoulder to someone so that he could give them his full attention.

"There y'are, Mr. Bellmoore." He used the honorific in front of the other men. "I suppose you heard what has occurred by now?"

"Yes, Mr. McInnes, I have. This is Lord Kingstone, Lady Celeste's father."

Tom's eyes softened, and he struggled not to frown.

"I am sorry to meet you under such circumstances, Your Lordship."

Lord Kingstone acknowledged the gesture with a bow of his head. "I am told your grandson saw my daughter being carried off?"

"Aye. 'Twas dark, but he saw it all right. I have no doubt it was Reeves. That's Lord Mortcastle's valet, Your Lordship. Lady Celeste was still dressed as a maid though, so he may not know who he has."

Jacob looked at the marquess for his reaction, but his eyes were squeezed shut.

"Who is that?" Lord Mortcastle demanded. Jacob looked toward the sound to see him marching up the incline toward the stable house with Constable Brown.

"It is the Marquess of Kingstone." The abruptness of Mr. Brown's answer gave the clear impression that such questions were a waste of his time.

Lord Kingstone ignored their entrance.

"I thank you for your assistance, Mr. McInnes. Is there anything else your grandson can contribute that may assist us in Lady Celeste's recovery?"

"Lady Celeste? Do not tell me something has befallen her?" Lord Mortcastle shoved his way forward.

"As if ye dinnae ken that your own valet carried her off this verra night!" Tom's anger was barely held in check as he addressed Mortcastle without looking at him.

"What? That is preposterous! What would my valet want with a lady of rank? She would not be worth the consequences. No offense intended, My lord." He bowed toward Lord Kingstone, who still had neither moved nor blinked.

"Well, he was the one who made off with your carriage with the lass inside, so what else would you make of it?" Tom enunciated each word, implying insult.

"And we are assuming all of this is true based on shadows a child saw moving in the dark?" Mortcastle retorted.

"What have you done with her, you scabby pirate?" Tom demanded. Mortcastle had no time to respond as the angry Scotsman lunged at him. Tom was bigger in every respect, and the fear in Lord Mortcastle's widening eyes reflected that in the split second before Constable Brown intervened, pulling Tom roughly aside.

Just as Jacob was about to intercede, Lord Mortcastle stepped up close to him, his face red and only inches away, speaking through clenched teeth, "I expect to see that servant flogged and would be

happy to carry out the chastisement myself if you will defer to me."
He stepped toward Tom, having no notion of anyone refusing him.

Jacob seized Lord Mortcastle's arm and looked him in the eyes.
They were the same height.

"You have no authority here, Mortcastle. Kindly remember that."

"You would allow your *staff* to insult a peer?" Lord Mortcastle again
stepped too close to Jacob, his top lip curled back.

Jacob did not respond with words but did his best to insinuate as
much resoluteness as he could with his eyes by not flinching. Holding
fast to Mortcastle's arm, he felt an immense satisfaction at the slight
twitch under Mortcastle's eye as he attempted to pull away. Jacob did
not blink as he released his arm and allowed him to step backwards.
A strong hand on his shoulder from behind preceded a whispered
reassurance from the marquess.

"You go assist McInnes. I will speak with this gentleman."

Jacob nodded, relieved. Lord Mortcastle far outranked Jacob, but
Lord Kingstone outranked Mortcastle.

Jacob caught up with the Constable and Tom just as Tom was spout-
ing some very creative insults about someone's mother. Jacob could
not tell if they were aimed at Constable Brown or Lord Mortcastle.

Jacob called out to them just as Tom was about to be struck by
Mr. Brown. The man continued to glower at Tom but was willing to
forbear, probably in favor of garnering information.

"Is there anything else you can tell us, Tom?" Jacob asked as the men
took a tense, but less combative stance with their arms folded across
their chests.

"Aye. I thought it odd that Mortcastle's man wished to prepare his
carriage at night, seein' as he does not live locally. Then William came
tearin' through my stables to tell me that the lady had been dragged off
by Reeves himself."

"This is nothin' new. You already said all that before," Constable
Brown accused, a snide edge to his tone.

Tom clenched his jaw, and Constable Brown reciprocated by standing at the ready, with his fists twitching at his sides, and looked as
though he would welcome the challenge implied by the Constable's

posture. Jacob began to question the wisdom of his position between them. He had never seen Tom behave in a like manner, but liked this protective side of him that would not be cowed.

After a silent battle of glares, Constable Brown sighed and stepped back.

"Can your grandson be relied upon to identify the man?" he asked, abandoning their private little war.

After another moment of tense silence, Tom returned the gesture in kind.

"Aye, he works in the stables with me and could identify any one of the guests and their servants. There's no doubt in my mind that all that pirate talk Betsy overheard was true, which probably means they're headed to a port."

"Betsy is also missing," Jacob sighed, closing his eyes against the dread building inside of him. They needed to leave.

Tom grew several shades paler, and muttered something that Jacob could only guess at.

Lord Kingstone soon joined Jacob, Tom, and Mr. Brown.

"Lord Mortcastle is keen to go after his carriage, just as we are, but for different reasons." Lord Kingstone shook his head. "I have suggested that we travel together. Are you ready, Mr. Bellmoore?"

"Yes." Jacob nodded and joined the marquess, feeling as though his boots were on fire. "Lord Blakely may accompany us if you are amenable. I believe he would be an asset," Jacob suggested.

"Very good," Lord Kingstone agreed, and Jacob sent one of the stablehands to find him.

A short time later, they were all assembled, while Mr. Brown introduced two new arrivals of his own, whom he had sent for in the village. Mr. Jones was in his forties at least and was short and stocky with brown hair and thick fluffy chops on the sides of his face. Mr. Stevenson was the opposite, with pale blonde hair, bright blue eyes, and no sideburns of note. He stood at least a foot taller than the other two men and could only be in his twenties at most. Mr. Brown was just touting their credentials when a horse whinnied and then galloped out past them, kicking up dirt behind it. It took them a moment to gather their wits as it sank in that Mortcastle had just broken ranks and taken off without them. They packed the last of their provisions and mounted, following behind.

Chapter Thirty-Three

⌒⌒⌒⌒⌒

Somewhere in the English Countryside

Celeste awoke with a pounding headache. As her awareness increased, she could tell that she was still in a carriage from the sounds and the uncomfortable rocking. She opened her eyes and rolled onto the solid floor. She was no longer in a normal carriage. A single tiny, barred window at the top of the door at the rear of the conveyance allowed very little light through, but it was daytime. She sat bolt upright, feeling every tight and bruised muscle in her body. There were no seats to speak of, and with alarm, she recognized that it was the kind of locked carriage she had seen used to transport criminals in London.

Celeste's moment of realization was interrupted by a muffled sound behind her. She spun around to see another person huddled in the corner, her face buried in her knees, whimpering. She was basically a dress with feet.

"Where are we?" Celeste asked gently, so as not to further frighten her inmate. The face looked up, a glimmer of hope in those familiar eyes. Betsy. Without another word, she threw herself at Celeste, embracing her as great sobs wracked her body. Celeste did her best not to fall backward, and held Betsy as much to comfort herself as her fellow maid.

Once the crying had settled into occasional hiccups, Celeste tried again.

"Betsy, do you have any idea where we are, or where we might be going?"

"I don't rightly know. I only woke up when that odious, hateful, disgusting, good for nothin'..." Celeste's look stemmed the outpouring of adjectives.

Betsy cleared her throat and began again. "I woke up in the wee hours when Reeves were takin' us from the fancy carriage and throwin' us into this one."

"I have a frightful headache. I am not certain that I was conscious for that part. What else do you remember?" Celeste asked, searching her own memory for anything else that might be useful. It was devoid of anything beyond falling asleep. The headache she now sported made it difficult to concentrate on a single thought. She rested her palm on her forehead, feeling rather ill.

"I were in the scullery, tryin' to help with that mess you left in there, so you wouldn't get the sack. Then that Mr. Reeves came in sayin' that you had gone for a walk and taken another fall but that you wouldn't let him near you, so would I come out to help. I did, knowin' well why you should refuse help from the likes of 'im. When we got outside, o' course, you weren't there. Then he started pretendin' we was all cozy, and I said to him 'I ain't nobody's conquest'. And I said it, not like that, but like a *real* lady, but he didn't pay me no never mind and tried to kiss me. Then I bit him, and he hit me with somethin' I can't recall.

"Next thing I knew I was wakin' up in the arms of that—well, he put us in here. I tried screamin', but he laughed, sayin' that we's in the middle of nowhere and that I could scream all I like 'cause no one's ever goin' to find us. Then I thought I should save my voice in case we do see somebody on the road." It was a long speech, even by Betsy's standards.

Celeste was touched that Betsy had cared enough to attempt to protect her. She had forgotten all about the abandoned laundry. When Betsy had seen her scrubbing away earlier, she had produced a tin of salve made by the cook to help with the irritation of her hands. Celeste had treasured it for the tingling relief to her skin, as well as the kindness of her roommate. The memory had her stomach knotted up in guilt. If not for Celeste, Betsy would be safe at home dreaming of

Mr. Bellmoore.

Jacob. That was another point of guilt. He probably still thought her to be upset with him.

Celeste tucked her knees up in front of her and hugged them. She had to make it through this to tell Jacob that she loved him. With a sudden thud to her chest that felt like a physical impact, she realized he would be out of his wits to still accept her after a successful kidnapping. She would be considered compromised, regardless of whatever did or did not happen to her. Even her miraculous good fortune of having her reputation survive switching places with a servant could not hold out against that. It was romantic to think about, but not at all realistic. She had no real hope for marriage now at all. She had finally found a man who had depth of character, good humor and kindness in his soul. Someone for whom she had asked herself if she would make a good wife, rather than only considering whether he would be worthy to be her husband. She groaned out loud. Risking her own happiness to defy her mother seemed so juvenile now.

Celeste turned her face and rested her cheek on her knees, trying not to allow despair to claw its ugly fingers around her heart. She reached a hand to the front of her gown, where a small discrete pocket housed the miniature volume Jacob had gifted her. She did not dare take it out, but found comfort in knowing that small piece of him was there with her.

"Are you thinking about Mr. McKnell?" Betsy asked, once again, focusing on her diction. Celeste gave a humorless laugh.

"It is alright, Betsy, I know now that he is Mr. Bellmoore."

"You aren't angry, are you? About me keepin' his secret and all?" Betsy asked, biting her fingernails. Celeste shook her head as best she could without changing her position.

"No, I am not angry. You could not be expected to disobey your employer." She thought of Bryn and all that she had said. That added yet another person to her list of worries.

"When did you find out?" Betsy pushed for more information.

"Yesterday," Celeste answered simply, the memory of Jacob's kiss causing an ache in her chest.

The carriage stopped.

Celeste leaped to the window at the rear to see that they were in a yard. She could see the side of a building to her left and several people milling about or walking along the road they had just come from. She could hear horses, but they could be the ones pulling this conveyance. Squeezing her face right up against the bars gave her a slightly wider field of vision, and she was able to note a sign hanging from an awning. They were at an inn, maybe to change horses.

The rumble of voices could be heard from around the carriage, but Celeste could not make them out, other than the general baritone and accent that sounded like Reeves.

"What's happenin'?" Betsy whispered loudly from behind her.

"Shh, I am trying to hear." Celeste waved her off. She pressed her ear against the little barred window where her face had been a moment before, but it achieved nothing more. They must have been around the front of the carriage. Unwilling to lose another opportunity, Celeste filled her lungs and screamed the word 'help' as loud as she could. She jumped back in surprise, tumbling over Betsy, when a melon hit the window, spraying her with juice and pulp. Then she heard Reeves' distinctive voice say the one word that explained it as he drew closer.

"...lunatics..."

Celeste could kick herself. Her scream had played into Reeves' story. She did not need to hear the rest to know the basic content. More fruit came flying toward them, making Betsy squeal in fright. Celeste again ventured toward the rear window and tried another approach.

"Please, we are not lunatics—he is carrying us off. Please help us! I am a titled heiress. I will pay five hundred pounds to anyone who will help us escape," Celeste called, using all those elocution lessons she had always considered a waste of time to prove her point. When she heard nothing, she increased the sum. "A thousand—"

An apple hit the bars, the part that did not disintegrate becoming stuck. Celeste had not eaten since the previous night, so she extracted the fruit, assuming its integrity meant that it had not spoiled. Not that she cared one way or the other if it had, as hungry as she was. She handed a piece to Betsy, who took it with thanks.

"Do you have any bread or cheese to throw at us? We are quite hungry," she called out in frustration. She could see several people gathered, but all kept a distance, as if she and Betsy could burst out at any moment.

"As I said," Reeves could be heard better the closer he came. "The poor orphan believes she is a duchess or some such. It's so very sad."

"I am no duchess, you swine!" Celeste spoke with calm forcefulness. "My father, the Marquess of Kingstone, who is quite alive, will pay handsomely to anyone who assists in my release. What is your name, sir?"

The man with Reeves did not answer her but spoke to him. "You are quite right, Mr. Smith. She does sound quite convincing."

Celeste scoffed. "Smith? Is that the best your imagination has to offer, *Reeves*? For a pirate, you are astonishingly boring!" She did not care if Betsy were mistaken in her assertion of his being a pirate or not; she needed that word and all the generational memories that went with it to assist them in that moment. It had the intended effect; a ripple of sound moved through the growing crowd. Celeste did not miss the warning in Reeves' eyes this time just before he left the other man, whom she presumed to be the innkeeper, to head back around to the front of the carriage. Although Reeves frightened her enough that her whole body trembled, she felt bone-deep satisfaction to know that she had ruffled him.

If she achieved nothing else, the other man was looking at Celeste now. She made calm eye contact with him to prove she was of a steady mind. A look of alarm entered his eyes just as the carriage began to roll away.

"Please, sir, do not leave a lady in distress! When my father comes looking, tell him which way we have gone. The Marquess of King-stone!" she called out, feeling more panicked with every inch of ground that extended between her and anyone that may offer assistance.

Celeste breathed against the bars she clutched as the carriage turned and she lost sight of her only hope of rescue, but not before seeing the man stop one of the other onlookers from throwing more food.

Chapter Thirty-Four

Basingstoke, England

It had been a long night of riding. The party had lost track of Lord Mortcastle sometime in the wee hours. He must have suspected that they were not far behind him, because he had become adept at evading them, rendering him more suspicious.

Constable Brown had stayed behind in case he was needed in Whitbury, but Jones and Stevenson were well-trained, and Jacob suspected they may have had military backgrounds. All in the party agreed that they ought to lead the group. Zach had been in the army but seemed content to allow the others to lead.

Sometime during the night, the group had stopped to rest in Basingstoke at an inn, then later in the day they stopped to eat and change horses in Petersfield. In the morning, when Stevenson joined them, he announced that he had just had a most enlightening conversation with the innkeeper.

"He has a very interesting story to tell regarding a carriage that passed through here earlier today carrying a couple of lunatics." He made eye contact with each man at the table. "One of them claimed to be the daughter of a marquess."

Lord Kingstone was on his feet, his chair clattering to the floor behind him, before Stevenson finished speaking. He lost no time in striding toward the yard where Stevenson had just come from. Jacob rose and followed after him. The story gave him hope that they would hear something more useful than idle gossip.

When they found the innkeeper shoveling manure from the public pathways, he was all too happy to tell what he saw. Jacob suspected the part about being afraid for his life might have been an embellishment, but the rest of the story about the lunatic with a ready wit and steady gaze who claimed to be an heiress, sounded so like Celeste that Jacob had difficulty retaining an aloof expression. Finally, Lord Kingstone spoke up, and Jacob hoped he would ask the questions burning on his own tongue.

"I am the Marquess of Kingstone and my daughter, Lady Celeste Honeychurch, has been kidnapped along with a maid. Did the girl you spoke of give any indication of knowing where they might be going?" he asked to the point.

The man's eyes lit up.

"Kingstone! That was the name she said. I remembered on account of it sounding so noble! That's when I began to suspect that they weren't lunatics after all. You can't slip one past ol' Joe." He puffed his chest out. Jacob resisted the urge to roll his eyes. Reeves had done precisely that.

"Did you hear anything about where they were going?" Jacob repeated Lord Kingstone's question, unable to keep the impatience out of his voice. He was grateful for the confirmation, but the man seemed to have difficulty retaining the original strand of conversation.

"I can't rightly say, but they headed down that road." He pointed to a road that seemed to curve south.

"Where does it lead?" Lord Kingstone inquired, his calm façade more intact than Jacob's.

"It runs south through a few counties, but if you follow it long enough, it takes you all the way to Portsmouth." The man scratched at his chin, then stopped, his eyes wide. "You don't suppose…?"

"Thank you. You have been most helpful." Lord Kingstone did not give the man the opportunity to finish saying what they were all thinking. Portsmouth was a hub for shipping companies and the like. It would be precisely the kind of place they would be headed.

"We need to leave," Jacob thought aloud. Lord Kingstone bobbed one brisk nod, his calm expression replaced with a frown. He gave the innkeeper several coins for his trouble, enough to make the man's eyes pop out of his head.

Despite being so far behind, it seemed they were on the right trail. And now they had a chance to catch them up.

The party stopped for information and fresh horses several times, but they still covered a lot of ground in good time. Doing so often also meant that they could ride hard. Not much conversation could be had between them at such a pace, but there was not much to be said.

Jones and Stevenson rode on ahead, and by dusk, Jones returned with a report.

"We caught up with Lord Mortcastle. He turned off the road about a mile from here and seemed to be headed for a small hamlet to the west, perhaps a meeting place," he announced, breathing hard, his horse doing the same.

"If that is the case, there may be others," Lord Kingstone added.

"Yes. We will need to approach with caution. I suggest we seek out the local constable here, if there is one, and apply for his aid," Jones agreed, looking to Lord Kingstone.

Jacob could see the wisdom in that, but he did not wish to wait. He had no idea if any of the counties they had passed through were large enough to warrant a constable, part time or otherwise. And a squire was just as likely to send them along as offer any real assistance. They might have more luck in whichever hamlet they were heading toward.

"I would be happy to continue on ahead to keep watch, in case they move on," Jacob volunteered, trying not to sound as impatient as he felt.

"I will join you. One of us can run a message if need be," Zach joined him. Lord Kingstone said nothing but nodded. Jacob held back the urge to gallop off on the errand and instead waited for a consensus.

Jones pulled up one side of his cheek, making a clicking sound, and pursed his lips, shaking his head.

"Stevenson has tied off his horse and is following on foot. It would be best if I catch up with him myself in Furzeley Corner while the marquess rallies some local support nearby. Then we may have better numbers for a strategic approach. I will return as soon as I have a definite location. Clanfeld parish is not far from here. We can stop there for the night and meet in the public house."

Jacob let out a frustrated breath. If Jones and Stevenson were going to Furzeley Corner, then they should as well. There was only an hour or two of daylight left, and it ought not be wasted sitting on their backsides in the local public house waiting for Jones. Jacob was on the edge of madness as it was. He could feel his foot beginning to tap and willed it to stop lest his horse get the wrong idea. Or the right idea. He very much wanted to continue riding in the direction Lord Mortcastle had gone. He had very little doubt they would find his valet there with Lady Celeste and Betsy.

Jacob suppressed a shudder and shut the door on the direction his thoughts were heading. If he allowed his imagination to run away with him, no power on earth would be able to stop him from taking off immediately. Only, he could very well jeopardize their safety further by rushing headlong into a scenario he knew too little about. No, the situation required information and strategy. Jacob ground his teeth together as he was forced to admit that Jones was right.

Chapter Thirty-Five

Somewhere in the English Countryside

When the carriage stopped, Celeste jolted awake. She had no way to orient herself with the passing of time and could not say with any certainty what day it was. Betsy had fallen asleep with her head resting on Celeste's shoulder, so Celeste moved out from underneath, taking care not to jostle her. She looked out of the small, barred window. It took her eyes a moment to adjust to the blinding afternoon sunshine, but when they did, she was surprised to see that they were not at another inn, but a farmhouse in the middle of nowhere. Then again, what sort of abduction would it be if they were treated to a cozy room and a warm bed with an opportunity to elicit help?

Before long, Mr. Reeves and another burly man came to the door. Celeste scurried backwards and bumped into Betsy. She had no opportunity to apologize for waking her, though, as once unlocked, Reeves pulled Celeste and Betsy out of the carriage by their wrists. They stumbled, bumping into each other before righting themselves. Reeves smirked, then tied an old scratchy rope around their wrists, linking them to each other by their hands. As they were shoved together toward the farmhouse, Celeste was determined not to stumble again or show any other signs of weakness. She would bring that man no more amusement if she could help it.

They were shoved into a sparse room at the top of a basic, narrow wooden staircase, and the door was locked behind them, leaving them alone. There was one small high window at the top of the opposite wall, a little square no larger than a handkerchief with no opening mechanism, beneath a peaked timber ceiling. The room contained a straw mattress on the floor and a pail, presumably for use as a chamber pot, but was otherwise empty. Celeste was grateful for the mattress after being on the hard wooden floor of the carriage for so long, even if it did not look fresh.

Working together, Betsy and Celeste lowered themselves, toppling in the end, and laid down. Neither spoke aloud of the difficulty in dealing with the itchiness the mattress would produce later. Celeste would never have believed that a straw mattress on the floor could feel so heavenly. Both women breathed a sigh of relief.

"It won't be long 'till we're rescued." Betsy surprised Celeste with her optimism.

"I like the sound of that, but what makes you so certain?" Celeste asked.

"Because the Bellmoore's are not like other gentlefolk. They care about people, even their servants. Mr. Bellmoore will come for us, you'll see." Betsy's voice was full of confidence. "Perhaps he will be so happy when he finds us that we will each get a kiss," she added as an afterthought with a giggle.

Celeste gave a sad little laugh, wishing it were likely. With her reputation destroyed, she held out very little hope of that.

"I very much doubt he will want to kiss us. For one thing, we smell atrocious." Celeste tried to laugh, but she did not like the watery edge in her own voice.

"Perhaps not, but that is what I'm goin' to dream about," Betsy sighed.

As images of Jacob with mud on his face swirled through Celeste's mind, she could not argue with that.

Chapter Thirty-Six

❦

Clanfeld, Hampshire

Jones was boring. It could have been that Jacob was liable to break out of his skin at any given moment if his body did not move, but it was easier to blame Jones and his plan.

Clanfeld was not a large parish, and so the public house they waited in was like being in a poor man's sitting room. There were only three basic wooden chairs around a single table that wobbled when they touched it. The hamlet was too small to have any kind of law enforcement except for an elderly squire, who was not a great deal of use in such situations.

A rider had been sent to Portsmouth with a message from Lord Kingstone to an admiral of his acquaintance, apprising him of their current circumstances and to appeal for his aid should their journey take them there as anticipated. However, there was no expectation of a formal reply in so short a time. All they had left to them was to await the return of Stevenson and Jones from their scouting expedition. Lord Kingstone had retired for the evening, and neither Jacob nor Zach were big drinkers, so they mostly sat in silence, eating a meagre meal, as interminable time stretched on. They also paced the room a good deal, but that was nothing but a delusion of productivity.

Finally, just as Jacob was slouching in a chair and considering how bad it could really be to storm the farmhouse on his own, Stevenson and Jones stepped in under the low doorframe from outside. Jacob could have embraced them simply for showing up. He found himself on his feet, and Stevenson raised an eyebrow, but otherwise did not acknowledge the eager response to their entry.

"Won't you join us?" The invitation from Zach was polite and unnecessary. Still, the gentlemen accepted and dove straight into their news in low tones.

"They are being held in a farmhouse in Furzeley Corner, not far from here, Mortcastle's horse is tethered outside," Stevenson said.

"There are a few men keeping watch in various locations. It was difficult to draw close enough to see anything," Jones added, ever one to cite caution.

"We ought to forget cover, round up as many sympathetic men as we can find in the village, and rescue Lady Celeste." Jacob leaned in closer, pressing his forefinger into the wood of the table for emphasis.

"We do not want to rush their hand. It may inspire drastic action." Jones advised.

Jacob sat up straight in alarm. Jones was right about that, but they could not do nothing.

"We must rescue them, somehow. We cannot simply sit here in this pub until our dotage!" He did not mean to demand or plead, but somehow he accomplished both without raising his voice very high.

"Yes, I agree." Stevenson leaned in toward Jacob, the muscles in his neck tight and his face hard. "I think we ought to follow them when they make their move and await our best opportunity, but Jones believes we should wait here for a reply to Lord Kingstone from the Royal Navy." Stevenson shrugged and sat back. "There could be merit in it."

"That is unacceptable." Jacob shook his head. There were no guarantees that the message would be answered at all, let alone in a timely manner.

"I agree," Zach chimed in. "Even if we could rely on naval support, which we cannot, consider how the officers would act. If we are discussing apprehending pirates, they are an embarrassment to England in their very existence and are not likely to surrender their ship." He raised an eyebrow to accentuate his point.

Jacob's face drained and his mouth hung open as realization dawned. "They may fire on her."

"That is a possibility. The navy will never forbear the capture of a pirate vessel for the sake of two women, especially if they believe them to be of little consequence. We must get to them before they make it to Mortcastle's ship." Stevenson nodded.

Jacob's heart was racing in his throat, making it difficult to breathe and impossible to speak. It took him at least a full minute to realize that he had discarded his chair and was standing, muscles taught and ready for confrontation.

"Are we certain they are even planning to board a ship?" Zach asked, glancing from Jacob to the two men across the table.

Jones and Stevenson sat back in consideration, looking at each other every few moments.

"No, but why else come this far south?" Jones answered after a small pause.

"And Lord Kingstone seemed to believe that the admiralty would handle the situation, so it is a fair assumption," Stevenson added.

"What now?" Jacob asked, no less tense. There were still too many unknowns.

"Lord Blakely, I believe you have some military experience?" Stevenson asked.

"Yes," Zach seemed surprised he knew that. "I was fighting Napoleon not long before my brother died, but I have very little expertise. I was not in the army long."

"Nevertheless, it may be useful if we do indeed encounter the Royal Navy. We do not wish to be underfoot, so if that should happen, your experience will best be used as liaison."

"Very well," Zach agreed.

"Good man." Stevenson sat up straight and drew a deep breath. "I believe it is time to act. We all need a little rest, so we shall meet back here in half an hour." He looked each man in the eyes until he received a nod from them all in turn, lingering longer on Jacob. After the relentless riding they had done, Jacob could not deny Stevenson a solitary hour of respite, so reluctant as he was, he nodded and headed upstairs where he knew he could not be still. Praying, yes. Pacing, probably, but repose was not something he thought himself capable of.

Chapter Thirty-Seven

Furzeley Corner, Hampshire

A shuffling sound near the door alerted Celeste to the presence of one of their captors. She looked up to see a cross-looking, sun-tanned woman with black hair and matching eyes entering the room. Celeste jerked back, almost sitting on Betsy.

"Oh, you're a woman! How lovely!" Betsy exclaimed. The woman glared at her.

"There ain't nothin' lovely abou' me. If not for my orders, I'd make you regret that." She scowled, implying that she took umbrage to the word.

"A lady must want in her heart to help other ladies," Betsy went on. She seemed determined not to see what was right in front of her. The woman's eyes widened as her brows descended in a steely glare.

"I 'ave no 'eart, and I ain't no lady!" She dared Betsy to contradict her.

"But—"

Before Betsy could say anymore, the woman cut her off in a low growl.

"If you say one more word, I'll cut out your tongue and feed it to the dogs."

As Betsy's mouth opened, Celeste elbowed her in the ribs. She was all for irritating their hosts, but there was something about this woman that was dangerous. Some instinct told her that she was in the presence of a predatory animal, and she did not dare ask who this angry woman was and for what purpose she had come. Seeming to read her mind, the woman spoke again.

"I'm 'ere to change your clothes, them dresses are ridiculous, but to do tha' I 'ave to cut the rope. Before you git any delusions o' grandeur, jis remember tha' I'm the one 'oldin' the knife." She made no move to step forward but eyed Celeste and Betsy with a slight upturn of her mouth. She pulled the promised blade from her black masculine boot with a malevolent grin, then pointed it back toward the door. "Tha' there door is locked, so it's jis you an' me," she chuckled.

Celeste and Betsy looked at each other but said nothing and allowed the woman to cut the rope that both bound and tethered them together. They both rubbed their sore, welted wrists before following instructions to assist each other in undressing and redressing into men's clothing. Celeste's skin itched from the rough fabric and the clothing was too big but not by much. It must have been intended for boys rather than men. She wanted to ask why they needed to change, but she did not dare.

When they were done, their captor replaced her dagger into her boot and crossed her arms across her chest. Something as feminine as a pout shaped her chapped lips as she huffed.

"Thought you'd a' leas' put up a figh'." She sounded disappointed. When neither Celeste nor Betsy responded, she curled her lip and left the room, locking it behind her and grumbling under her breath as she went. At least she had not re-tied their hands.

"I don't say this about many folks," Betsy began, "but she is worse than Lady Adelle!"

Celeste laughed before covering her mouth with her hands.

"You hold on to that thought when we return home and Lady Adelle becomes the new Lady Whitbury," Celeste counseled.

"I do think I'll prefer even her to that piratess." Betsy's eyes grew wide. "Do you think that's it, then? Do you think that woman was a pirate too? I never thought a woman could be a pirate, but then I read this story in a periodical. One of them serials..."

Celeste allowed Betsy to tell her all about the story, enjoying her non-stop chatter. It was familiar and normal, and that was exactly what she needed.

Once the light faded from the small window at the end of the room, Celeste began to worry. Without light, the frightening woman they had dubbed Captain Blackboots could return without them even noticing if they did not hear the door. The thought sent a shiver down her spine.

There was not much to do except lie down on the straw mattress. Both Celeste and Betsy were beginning to feel lightheaded from the lack of food and water and had little else to occupy them even with light.

Celeste froze as she heard the door mechanism. Betsy gasped, and both women clasped each other's hands. A single candle preceded its owner, but it was not Captain Blackboots. Their visitor was too tall. As he drew closer, his face became clearer.

It was Lord Mortcastle.

A wave of dizziness prevented Celeste from leaping up and either begging for his help, pounding him with her fists, or pitching the chamber pail at him. When he held the light closer to them, his eyebrows shot up, and his mouth dropped open. Celeste wondered if he was expecting someone else. His nose scrunched in revulsion. That was hardly necessary. She felt her embarrassment and indignation warring with one another, achieving nothing but heated cheeks and burning eyes.

"Have you had something to eat?" Lord Mortcastle asked the last question Celeste expected, and in a gentle tone that surprised her. She shook her head once.

Just then, Mr. Reeves came into the room, holding a lantern just behind Lord Mortcastle's shoulder.

"I just got word to bring them aboard," he announced.

"Give them something to eat!" Mortcastle hissed, turning only his head toward Reeves. His breath came out in short puffs.

"What for?" Reeves answered with contempt.

"Do you have no concept of how to treat a lady?" Mortcastle surprised Celeste further, and she looked at Betsy to confirm that she had heard correctly. Betsy just stared with her mouth in the shape of the letter O, her eyes matching perfectly.

The painful burn of thirst in Celeste's throat was the only thing reassuring her that what she was experiencing was indeed reality. If she were delirious, her imagination ought to have been merciful enough to remove that.

"They're no ladies. They're just maids."

Celeste's doubts that Reeves had ever been a valet at all, increased every time he opened his mouth. The way he spoke to Lord Mortcastle held little if any respect at all. It reminded her of the conversation in the garden maze.

Lord Mortcastle turned his whole body to face Reeves.

"She is Lady Celeste Honeychurch, you imbecile!"

Even in the low light, Celeste could see that the muscles in his neck were taught and his jaw was flexing. His fist clenched at his side. Celeste hoped Reeves would continue his belligerence, if for no other reason than to facilitate an opportunity. If the two men began to fight, she could grab Betsy's wrist and drag her out of there.

"The captain will not wish to risk keeping her; an inquiry has already begun. Her father is a marquess and is looking for her. I had to ride hard and keep off the roads to avoid him," he spat out through clenched teeth.

Celeste had not registered the implications of Lord Mortcastle's words until that moment, but the mention of her father grasped her attention. She had to use her hand to pull her cheeks down from the smile forming on her face. Her father would not stop until she was recovered, she was sure of it.

"She tried that one on me too, but we met Lady Celeste back at Whitbury Manor." Reeves rolled his eyes.

"No, she is just a cousin or some such, and a decoy. This is the real Lady Celeste. Her father showed up and revealed the whole thing after you took off with my carriage." Lord Mortcastle gestured toward Celeste with an outstretched hand, and almost hit Reeves on the nose with his nose as his face jutted forward in emphasis.

For the first time, Celeste saw Reeves hesitate. His expression did not change much, but he glanced several times between Celeste and

Lord Mortcastle.

"Whitbury's nosy little brother already seems suspicious of me. You will be implicated as well if anything happens to her," Lord Mortcastle explained further.

Reeves peered at Celeste, and she could no longer resist a smug grin and a raised eyebrow. The high of seeing him squirm made her giddy—or that could have been the lack of sustenance. She felt great satisfaction though, at seeing his mouth open and close a few times before he turned and stomped out of the room, grumbling about the captain being displeased.

Celeste hoped that Lord Mortcastle might be persuaded to release them. There appeared to be something of a gentleman inside him.

"What is going to happen to us?" Celeste asked, wishing her voice sounded stronger.

Lord Mortcastle smiled, but it was not a joyful expression. He sighed and rubbed his forehead.

"You are to be taken to the ship Victory's Glory. There, Captain Hughes will decide your fate. It is likely the maid will remain aboard to be sold in the Orient somewhere, but you, Lady Celeste, are too well connected. He will want to be rid of you as soon as possible. I will have him marry us before then so that your reputation may recover. You may still have some work to do to regain your footing in society, but an elopement is far easier to overcome than a kidnapping."

If Celeste was supposed to find the words comforting, she failed. At first, she could not even form a response. Her face was twisted in open-mouthed staring, while her mind stood still in horror. Then Betsy whimpered on the bed behind her. That was enough to snap Celeste out of her stupor. She forced herself to swallow the bile rising up her throat and attempted to reason with Lord Mortcastle.

"You must see that you have found yourself in a perilous situation. This captain will not be happy with you for bringing a titled lady and all of the attention that comes along with me. And as you said, my father is on his way to defend my honor. This cannot end well for any of you. You would be much better off letting us go."

"I am afraid it is too late for that, Lady Celeste. Arrangements have been made. And I am bound by—that is—I cannot—" He shook his head, his eyebrows tilted in sadness and looked down with a deep frown that seemed to be reflected by his entire body. His shoulders slumped, and his height appeared diminished.

"Please—" Celeste began, her voice thick, but she was cut off.

"I will do what I can to see to your comfort," he said, his eyes pleading. If only comfort were her concern. Perhaps he sought forgiveness or understanding.

Betsy's whimpering turned into sad hiccups.

"I can help you with your debts. You could take us to my father, and I will tell him that you rescued us. He will reward you. No one ever need know that you were involved at all." Celeste blurted out, becoming desperate.

"Do you think me a complete fool?" His eyes narrowed, and the strength in his voice returned. "What motivation could you possibly have to fulfill such an agreement once you are freed? And to put my entire future into your hands after all that has happened, when all I have to do is marry you and both of our problems go away?" He scoffed a short laugh and shook his head.

"I am already promised to someone else and cannot marry you, so you might as well take my offer," Celeste bluffed. No one would expect Jacob to honor any arrangement now, but she hoped that it would give Lord Mortcastle pause anyway. Something in his eyes hardened.

"I very much doubt that, or you would not have had your cousin acting in your place and attaching herself to other gentlemen in your name. No, we will marry, and I will gain your fortune, after which, I do not care what you do."

Celeste's jaw dropped, and she leaped off of the bed, fueled by desperation. She threw herself at Mortcastle, but her attack was ineffective owing to her weakened state. He held her arms easily and laughed.

"What happened to your notions of how to treat a lady?" she spat.

"That, I will not compromise. You will be treated well. Even the captain will not harm you since he will not wish to end up swinging on a short noose at Execution Dock. I cannot say the same for your little friend, but she is not a lady. She will be fed though; a weak slave will not fetch much." He loosened his hold but did not release her.

Betsy's cry behind Celeste prompted her action. She could not break free of Mortcastle's grip, but she drew on every remaining drop of moisture in her mouth to spit in his face.

"I will never marry you!"

Lord Mortcastle wiped away the uninspiring dribble with his shoulder and chuckled.

"You forget, Lady Celeste, that a sea captain has authority to marry. He has the Letter of Marque and operates somewhat within the law, but I very much doubt he will ask you for permission."

"That is against the law," Celeste argued. Lord Mortcastle laughed again, shaking his head.

"And how do you intend to prove that you did not give consent? It will be easy to drum up witnesses. No one will listen to you. You are a woman, and a disgraced one at that."

"My father—" she began before Mortcastle cut off her words.

"Your father will be forced to support the match to salvage your reputation. Not that he will know where to find you. I would not hold out hope of rescue from him." He pulled her close to him. "Let me be clear, Lady Celeste. I will be good to you, but I will have your money and your charms, and no one will question my use of either."

Lord Mortcastle leaned close, his eyes raking over her face before resting on her mouth. Celeste's entire body went rigid, and he hesitated. His eyes flickered before he pulled back a little, still holding her. Celeste did her best to fight him, then kicked and clawed at him like the lunatic she had been paraded as. She achieved little more than leaving a nasty scratch across Lord Mortcastle's cheek before she became too dizzy and stumbled, still trying to fight but without any accuracy or direction. He caught her before she fell and walked her back to the mattress, placing her gently down beside Betsy. Captain Blackboots entered behind him with some bread and goblets of what she hoped was water.

Before leaving Celeste's side, Lord Mortcastle leaned close enough that she could feel his breath on her ear, and whispered, "I think I shall enjoy being married to you. I had been looking for a wife, but did not expect someone so entertaining." Then he quit the room, followed by a scowling Captain Blackboots.

Celeste could barely move but managed to wipe her mouth with her sleeve where Lord Mortcastle had stared at it, the thought making her shudder.

"You're a brave one, My lady. Here." Betsy lifted her head with one hand and dripped some water into her mouth. The cool streams of hydration spread through her and moistened her lips.

When Celeste had drunk enough water to stop her head from spinning, she sat up slowly and shared the bread with Betsy. She had not missed Betsy's switch to calling her 'My lady.'

"Betsy, I am sorry that I lied to you about being a servant."

"Begging your pardon, My lady, but why did you want to be one?" she asked, her nose scrunched. Celeste laughed.

"Actually, you may find this amusing, but before I tell you, would you please stop calling me 'My lady'? I consider us friends."

Betsy thought about it.

"I suppose, but may I still call you Elsie? It can be our little joke." Celeste nodded.

"I would like that. The reason I pretended to be a lady's maid is that my parents arranged what they hoped would be a match for me, then sent me off to this house party to meet him. I knew nobody in attendance, and so I switched places with my maid to avoid him."

"Who'd they want to fix you up with? It weren't Mortcastle, was it?" she asked, her eyes wide with interest.

"This is the part that will make you laugh. The man I was encouraged to marry was Mr. Bellmoore." Celeste laughed herself, around a mouthful of bread.

Betsy did laugh. "And you were trying to hide from him? I'd wager you wouldn't avoid him now that you've seen him." She laughed again, but it gave way to a sad sigh that made Celeste want to cry without reason.

"What is it, Betsy?" Celeste reached out a hand in the dark.

"I was just wishin' I was you. You'll have to tell me what it's like to kiss him." She sighed again and then giggled.

"Well..." Celeste hesitated, blushing. Betsy gasped.

"Has he kissed you already? You have to tell me everything! Don't leave nothin' out! Oh, what was it like?"

Before Celeste could say a word, Mr. Reeves entered the room with Captain Blackboots. It seemed the time Lord Mortcastle had bought them for eating was over.

"Time to go. Get up," Captain Blackboots barked. They did not dare disobey her and rose, still somewhat unsteady and a little nauseated, although much improved. She bound their hands together again and tied gags so tight around their mouths they were painful before herding them outside. It may have been Celeste's imagination, but Captain Blackboots seemed to dislike them even more than she had in the beginning.

Once they were outside, and Celeste stared toward the empty blackness of the carriage, she did everything she could not to allow herself to be confined in it again.

Captain Blackboots was not as tough as she looked. When Celeste pushed backwards against her, using her feet against the dreaded carriage to propel herself, Captain Blackboots stumbled. Celeste did her best to headbutt the woman, but she reared back. For some reason, she was not retaliating as expected. Celeste did not know whether Mortcastle or her own status were protecting her, but whatever her shield was, she made use of the advantage by kicking and struggling as much as possible. Poor Betsy was pulled and thrown about a bit, but she did not complain.

In a lightning move, Captain Blackboots pulled out her dagger and held it to Betsy's throat. "He said I can't 'urt you, but 'e ain't said nothin' abou' 'er."

It was the only thing that could inspire Celeste to cease her campaign, and they once again found themselves inside the prison carriage. Celeste was gasping, perspiring, and shaking. Her stomach heaved. Betsy was eerily silent, which added to Celeste's trepidation as they huddled together for the uncomfortable journey to meet their loathsome fate.

It was less than an hour later that they halted. Celeste could see nothing, but she could smell the distinctive mixture of salt, fish, and rotting wood that made up the aroma of the seaside. Lord Mortcastle himself came for Celeste this time and pulled her and Betsy, still tied, from the carriage. She still thought of him as a fortune-hunting rogue, but he was gentler than Captain Blackboots had been.

As Celeste looked at the gangplank ahead of them, she stopped in her tracks. Once they were on that ship, their lives were as good as over. They might end up wishing they were. She would do everything in her power to not board that ship, even if it meant drowning.

Again, Captain Blackboots appeared to read her mind. In an instant, she and Betsy were being lifted off their feet. They were still tied together, but Mortcastle and Reeves held them under the arms while Captain Blackboots held their legs in a solid grip, her arms locked around them. Escape may not have been possible, but she would not make it easy. To think that she had once run from a marriage to Jacob Bellmoore. Thinking of him inspired her to struggle with all her might so that she at least might see him again. It did not achieve much more than a few bruises for Captain Blackboots, but that was satisfying in its own way.

Chapter Thirty-Eight

Furzeley Corner, Hampshire

As Jacob and the rest of the rescue party approached the farmhouse it became evident that they were too late. The place was already deserted. Stevenson alighted and examined the wheel ruts, then remounted and led the men.

Lord Kingstone placed a paternal hand on Jacob's shoulder and gave it a squeeze. It had been a long time since he had felt the comfort of a father's protection. He would do all he could to be worthy of Lord Kingstone's trust.

Jones had been right about Portsmouth. The party caught sight of the much slower carriage just as it approached the shipping yards and pulled around the side of a warehouse toward the docks.

Jacob had spent as little time as possible considering the conditions Celeste and Betsy might be enduring for fear of losing his ability to be rational, but seeing the prison-style carriage created an unexpected urge deep inside him to rise up. It spread through every muscle in his body, including his jaw, and sharpened his senses. Every part of him was tensed and heightened. He was ready to fight for his lady.

At a silent wave of the hand from Stevenson, the group moved between two warehouses. They tied off their horses and huddled together.

"I did not think it wise to move too close on horseback. I suggest we use these warehouses for cover and move closer on foot. Remember, we may not receive any aid, so do not take unnecessary risks. We are here to rescue the ladies, first and foremost," he explained in an urgent whisper.

The men all nodded and crept around toward where they had seen the carriage. They approached the area nearby, spreading out and taking cover behind carts and crates and other objects around the dock.

Lord Mortcastle and Reeves could be seen under the moonlight, accompanied by a few others, pulling Celeste and Betsy from the carriage and carrying them toward a gangway. Jacob's heart ached with both pain and pride as he saw them thrashing about to free themselves.

Taking as careful aim as was possible in the dark, Jacob leveled his weapon at one of the abductors, but he hesitated. He could not see well and worried about who he might hit. Still, he could not allow them onto the ship. Their chances of success were far greater if the women remained on land and not inside a floating fortress.

Without further indecision, Jacob pulled the trigger, exploding the night with sound. He could not see the results of his aim, but he hoped that the uproar that followed meant he had been close to accurate. Shots fired toward his general direction, but none of Mortcastle's men were certain where their target was. Amid shouts and smoke, Jacob crept around some large crates to get closer to the gangplank. He would still need to cross several yards of open space to reach it, so he regretted alerting the men to his presence by opening fire on them, but it was a little late to rethink that.

Then, as suddenly as the shots began, they ceased, all manpower being focused on boarding the ship. Jacob looked to where Celeste and Betsy were being carried, flanked by their captors. Both women put up a fight, writhing and struggling. He hoped the feminine shouts he was hearing from their direction indicated that neither had been hit by a bullet. With their attention elsewhere, Jacob made his move and began to cross the open space in a wide arc. A shot fired from the direction of Lord Kingstone's hiding place, on the opposite side of the walkway. Jacob was grateful for the misdirection that drew both fire and attention away from his approach.

Jacob knew he could not simply walk up and board. He was not certain how he planned to proceed when a movement from the corner of his eye caught his attention. Stevenson had found a ladder in the darkness leading down to the water and beckoned Jacob to follow. He did not hesitate. He had done his fair share of swimming when he was in Italy and was confident enough in his abilities.

As soon as they reached the water, Stevenson removed his coat and dropped it onto the dock. Jacob had not thought of that and followed suit before they slipped in. Stevenson wet his hair in an attempt to darken it, decreasing their visibility, but making him shiver. Swimming in England was a different matter from swimming in the Mediterranean. The water chilled Jacob all the way through, making him grateful they had moved into the summer months.

However unfavorable lowering himself into the water had been, pulling himself out of it to climb the side of the ship was much harder. It was not something Jacob had ever thought he would do and was far more difficult than he would have anticipated. His hands slipped several times, but it was obvious that Stevenson, climbing ahead of him, had done this before. His movements were smooth and sure, so Jacob focused on mimicking them. His hands and arms burned with the unfamiliar demand of the ascent, and his fingers cramped with the cold. As they reached the quarterdeck, adrenaline took over, numbing his fatigue. They peeked over the railing and were happy to see that all attention was on making ready for an immediate departure rather than on a lone couple of madmen attempting to mount a rescue by themselves. Using the stairs for cover, they kept to the shadows and waited for an opportune moment. Blood pulsed through Jacob's veins in anticipation.

Chapter Thirty-Nine

Portsmouth, England

When a shot rang out, Celeste's heart had jumped with the hope of rescue.

Reeves had grunted and stumbled but righted himself with the speed of someone accustomed to battle. Lord Mortcastle was not so calm, and Celeste's terrified heart took delight in his panic when they hastened to board and retract the gangway.

Celeste and Betsy were dumped onto the deck, and the men took up defensive positions. Lord Mortcastle scurried toward what Celeste assumed to be the captain's quarters. His lack of courage was as pathetic as it was heartening. She hoped they could find a way to use that cowardice to their advantage.

Without further delay, Celeste began focusing her attention on the rope binding her hands to Betsy's. She had no previous experience with being restrained, but she had tied a halter rope or two for a horse in her time, so she hoped the knots were similar enough to give her an advantage in untying them.

"What are you doing? We should jump off the boat while they ain't lookin'." Betsy whispered. Her slipping language was a clear sign of her distress.

"I am attempting to loosen or untie these ropes, but it is very difficult to get at them," Celeste responded, growing frustrated as her efforts were slippery at best. It turned out that tying a horse and a human were very different endeavors.

"My mother always said she would rather die than be a slave. We should jump now." Betsy implored, her voice thick.

Celeste paused and looked up at her. Betsy's panic was increasing; after all, it was she who had the most to fear. Celeste glanced around. Reeves, *Reeves*, shouted orders at everybody in preparation to set sail. He really was a pirate after all. And one important enough to bark orders whilst he bled from the bullet wound in his right arm. Nobody seemed to be paying any attention to the captives at all. Celeste nodded to Betsy, and they worked together to move with slow caution toward the side of the ship where they had boarded. At least overboard they had a hope of being rescued by whomever had done the shooting at their captors. Preferably before they drowned.

When they reached the railing, they cast a glance at each other before throwing themselves toward it. Their flight was interrupted by several pairs of strong, calloused hands pulling them back, and they were dragged toward the assumed captain's quarters, while a voice behind them laughed.

Celeste looked around and felt rather than saw someone observing them from the shadows. It was not the disconcerting feeling she had experienced from Reeves and the others. Rather, it was more like the tingling sensation of hope. Perhaps she was going mad under the circumstances.

Once inside the cabin, they overheard the end of an argument between Lord Mortcastle and a man whose air of authority had to come from command.

"We are casting off. You were stupid enough to bring them aboard, and I do not accept your terms." His accent, unlike Reeves', was not foreign, but it was chilling in a different way. This was an Englishman willing to turn his back on his own. He ceased his tirade as the room filled and watched as Celeste and Betsy were escorted to stand in front of him.

"It seems these two are fond of swimming," the man who dragged them in chuckled.

Even though their wrists were forced together by rope, the two women clung to each other's hands for comfort. Both of them shuddered as the grey-haired captain raked his eyes over them with a grin.

"There has been a terrible misunderstanding here, My lady. I was not informed that we would be having such delightful company, and I am afraid we are ill-equipped for the pleasure of entertaining fine ladies. I offer my sincerest apologies, but as soon as we reach Calais, I will have Lord Mortcastle escort you from the ship," he offered with a slight bow. His words were pretty, but sounded hollow and rehearsed, like he only took out his good manners and dusted them off on occasion when required.

Celeste bobbed a curtsy, reciprocating anyway. She would take the civility as far as it could go. "Thank you, sir. However, there is no need to provide us free passage all the way to France. We may disembark now and save you the expense and the inconvenience of entertaining unexpected guests."

The presumed captain hesitated a moment, weighing his next words as he tapped on his lip as if in deep thought.

"My men, good honest sailors, have been fired upon. My first officer is wounded. We need to pull out of port if there are villainous types on the docks. We wouldn't want you in any danger now, would we?"

His triumphant smile with a hidden layer of sneer was the kind that inspired revulsion and terror. He circled them like a vulture with his hands clasped behind his back, assessing and leering at the same time.

"Undoubtably, you refer to us *both* disembarking in Calais?" Celeste changed tack. It was not the worst place to end up.

he sighed. "I think not. You, I have no need for. Your maid..." He shrugged once as if in defeat, letting the sentence hang without conclusion. He was probably aware of how much worse one's imagination could be in filling in the gaps of the unknown.

"I will not leave without her," Celeste declared. Betsy clung tighter to her, and Celeste tried not to let her gaze break from the captain's.

"That is unfortunate." He shook his head and turned his back, returning to Mortcastle.

That seemed to signal the end of the negotiation, if it had ever really been one in the first place. Celeste wondered if she should have taken the opportunity to be dropped off in Calais, even on her own, when it was offered, but she dismissed the thought immediately. She was not prepared to leave Betsy to a fate worse than death. She was distracted for a moment by the sympathetic-looking frown on Lord Mortcastle's face. It surprised and confused her, like it had when they were in the farmhouse attic.

Celeste pulled her attention back to the matter at hand, of hers and Betsy's freedom and she tried one more time.

"I thank you for your kindness, sir," she began, controlling her voice to sound polite. "Perhaps we could simply find out who the men outside are. After all, I do believe my father is looking for me, and I would not wish him to gain the wrong impression of your good, honest sailors. He is a peer of the realm after all, with a great deal of influence." She hoped her meaning was clear.

The captain turned around and narrowed his eyes, but the worst of his glare turned toward Lord Mortcastle. Before anything else could be said, the ship began to move slowly beneath them. All chances of bargaining escape were all but lost. The captain seemed to realize this at the same moment. Before he could speak and ruin all her hopes of the situation ending in any way other than disaster, Celeste tried to milk a little more out of his charade of civility.

"May we be shown to a cabin now? We are dreadfully tired and wish to rest until we reach the next port, if you please." She did her best to sound as if she expected such treatment, though she would be astonished if they were accommodated anywhere but a barred cell in the hold.

The captain laughed, but then the rest of his pretense melted away, and Celeste's stomach fell into her shoes.

"*You* may be shown to a cabin. She will be placed below decks."

"No!" Celeste cried out, pulling Betsy around behind her as best she could with their hands still tied. "What do you intend to do with her?" she demanded, glaring into his eyes. She hoped her pretended confidence would be an asset and not land them in more trouble. She further hoped that the movement of the ship would hide the way her legs shook.

"As I said, we are not equipped for feminine company, so we will have to make do. You cannot stay in the brig. There is too much risk with you being a lady and your father being a man of influence. Therefore, you also cannot stay with me unchaperoned without unfavorable consequences to me at his hands. A pity, since you are the prettier of the two." He raised an eyebrow.

Celeste turned her head away in revulsion. She was grateful for the safety her position had afforded her in his precarious game, but he still had not answered her question. She did not believe he had any intention of doing so either. She could only guess at Betsy's fate, and it terrified her. The poor girl started to cry in little hiccups into Celeste's shoulder.

Without needing instructions, Captain Blackboots stepped up and untethered them, then took Betsy out of the cabin, her wide brown eyes staring back at Celeste in an image certain to haunt her. Celeste stepped toward them to follow but was restrained by the man who had thought himself funny with his allusion to swimming. His grip on her upper arms allowed no arguments, and she was forced to turn back and again face Lord Mortcastle and the captain.

"Good evening, My lady," the captain dismissed, and just like that, Celeste was hauled toward the doorway.

"And what of Isabelle?" She heard Lord Mortcastle ask.

"She will disembark with you in Calais. She too is not worthy of my time, though she is not as well protected as this one."

"She is here?" Lord Mortcastle sounded alarmed. The captain only sighed in response.

Celeste had no idea who Isabelle was, or her significance to Lord Mortcastle, or why she was there, but she saw an opportunity. Perhaps she could vex her host into wanting to be rid of her sooner, since he was apparently unwilling to harm her.

"You ought to challenge him!" she suggested to Lord Mortcastle over her shoulder as she was pulled along. A duel between them could very well aid her fate. She did not have great hopes that it would work, but it was worth a try.

The man hauling Celeste along paused. Celeste assumed it was out of curiosity. It was long enough to give Celeste delusions of grandeur in any case. She shoved against him and ran about two feet before he caught her again around the shoulders and yanked her back into the cabin.

"Bring her here!" the captain barked.

At the same time, Lord Mortcastle stepped forward with a hand stretched out. "Steady on there," he creased his brow in her captor's direction.

"I have quite had enough of this little game," the captain announced, the hardness in his voice more than convincing. "You have nowhere to run to, yet you seem determined to try. Very well," he nodded, stepping forward and grabbing Celeste by the wrist. He pulled her toward him, but she ended up closer to Lord Mortcastle. Being yanked about in every direction was disorienting, and she was quite frightened but did her best not to allow it to show.

"I am prepared to be civil. This is a merchant vessel after all, in the service of His Majesty, but I cannot have you running about the place taking my men away from their duties to restrain you. I shall have to place you in the care of Lord Mortcastle. You should know he has asked me to perform a marriage between you." The captain paused, watching.

"I will not marry him! And I will not cooperate, so you might as well leave my maid and I right here and be on your merry way while you still have the chance." Celeste bluffed, her lips in a snarl. In truth, she did not know with any certainty if the men outside the ship were any friendlier than the ones on board, but she was willing to take her chances.

The captain half smiled. "You know, I almost admire your spunk. But it is a nuisance. Mortcastle." He turned his attention to Lord Mortcastle, who looked as though he had not slept in days. The dark shadows on his face showed where a beard would grow if he did not employ a *real* valet soon. Had he been a kind of hostage to Mr. Reeves all this time?

"Yes, Captain Hughes?" he answered.

The captain squeezed his eyes shut and drew a deep breath as if to force himself to be patient. Lord Mortcastle had just revealed his identity. Celeste had not known his name before then but would store that in her mind for later.

"If I return your sister to you when we reach Calais, will you, in exchange, take this woman out of my sight and keep her out of mischief?" He did not open his eyes until the end of the question, then they seemed to bore a hole into Lord Mortcastle's face. "I, of course, mean that indefinitely."

"Yes, Captain. Should you return my sister and perform the favor I asked, I will see to it that she is no trouble. Do I take this to mean that my debt is repaid?"

Captain Hughes laughed, a short staccato sound that made Celeste jump. It was like hearing a dog bark before knowing one was there. He narrowed his eyes.

"Do not get ahead of yourself, Mortcastle. Do well tonight, and I may be willing to take another look at your brother's contract."

Celeste became aware that her mouth was hanging open as she listened to the conversation that made very little sense. She wondered what this captain held over Lord Mortcastle and his family, though she stayed silent to allow them to say as much as possible before remembering her presence. Something about his brother and his sister. She knew his family had debts. Celeste wondered if that was why Lord Mortcastle had been involved in all of this. Then why not seek assistance from the Admiralty?

Just then, Captain Hughes turned his vulture eyes back on her, and he shoved her hand into Lord Mortcastle's, holding it there when she tried to withdraw.

"I trust that you will plague this man to no end, repaying him on my behalf for all the trouble he's caused by bringing you aboard?" The question seemed rhetorical, but Celeste was too lost in the implication to answer anyway.

He was really going to marry them. Bone-deep dread filled Celeste. She did not know if his words were legally binding, but who would believe her that she was an unwilling participant? If word got out of her current situation, Lord Mortcastle would come off as a hero who saved her from ruination, and she would just sound to all the world like an ingrate. And if no one ever found out, it would look like an elopement, just as he had said at the farm. Celeste felt as if her lungs were frozen in giant blocks of ice, yet she could hear her rapid breaths louder in her ears with each passing moment.

"I see no need for the flowery words of the marriage ceremony. *Lord Mortcastle,* do you want her?" He sneered.

"I do." The dreadful man smiled.

Celeste shook her head violently. "No, no, no, no, no."

Captain Hughes gave a dark chuckle. "I do not intend to ask you. I suppose I will now pronounce you—"

He was cut off by a loud thud as the door crashed open. Without thinking, Celeste threw her hands protectively around her head, her elbows covering her eyes.

"Bellmoore!" Lord Mortcastle blurted out in surprise.

Celeste peeked, and sure enough, standing in the doorway to the cabin, dripping water from head to toe, was Jacob Bellmoore. The warmth flooding her heart at the sight of him thawed every piece of ice that had been suffocating her a moment before, and her arms dropped to her sides. Had he glanced in her direction, she would have run to him, but she suspected this was not the time or place. His gaze was fixed on Captain Hughes, who had drawn a pistol from somewhere and held it aimed at Jacob's heart.

"No!" She did not mean to shout the word and, had she given it any thought, would not have shown how much Jacob meant to her, so it could not be used as leverage, but it was too late, and the word was free.

Captain Hughes cast a quick glance with only his eyes in her direction before returning his intense gaze toward Jacob.

"It is the height of bad manners to interrupt a wedding," he sneered.

"Ah, but I am the groomsman and did not wish to miss the festivities," Jacob quipped with half a grin. Celeste shook her head. His humor was ill-timed indeed, but she lost a little more of her heart to him.

"State your business," Captain Hughes demanded, not amused.

"Is it not obvious? I am here for Lady Celeste," Jacob stated, shaking his head as if the captain lacked intelligence.

"But—" Lord Mortcastle's protest was cut short by a look so serious

from Jacob that it belonged on another face. Celeste would not recognize him on the street looking so severe. Lord Mortcastle did not
seem to know how to respond and just stood there agape.

Jacob turned his attention back to Captain Hughes. "Sir, may I
request—"

"This is Captain Hughes," Celeste interjected.

"Thank you." Jacob looked at her then, only briefly, but he gave her
a bow of the head and a half smile that made her stomach flip over
several times. It took all of her restraint not to run into his arms on the
spot.

The captain rolled his eyes. "Now that we are introduced properly...Reeves!" He shouted, but Reeves did not come.

An eerie silence filled the ship. For an immeasurable pause, it
seemed to be felt by all as a tingling silence swept up the arms of
everyone present.

Then came an announcement that allowed Celeste finally breathe
again, "Royal Navy!"

Chapter Forty

Aboard the Ship Victory's Glory, Portsmouth

Jacob could not contain the smug smile stealing across his face as the battle outside the captain's rooms began.

Before Jacob had burst into the cabin, Stevenson had climbed back down the side of the ship to negotiate with, and assist the officers so that no mistakes would be made with regard to their little rescue party. Then Betsy had been taken below decks. Jacob had done his best to see where she had gone before returning to overhear a marriage being performed between Lord Mortcastle and Celeste. He did not hesitate to stop that from continuing.

When Jacob had first entered the cabin, he felt his shoulders relax as he noted the healthy color in Celeste's face and how she did not appear the worse for wear. She was dressed in men's clothing, so loose it was comical. There was no way anyone would mistake her for a man. She almost looked like a child playing dress-up. He was unsure where her feelings lay since her ambiguous exit from the stable house after their kiss, but he would still marry her without hesitation. Even if she wanted nothing from him but to preserve her reputation. Though, she had given him a very encouraging smile just now. Perhaps there was still hope after all.

All heads snapped up at the sounds of battle erupting just outside the door.

Jacob turned back in time to see Lord Mortcastle draw a pistol and aim it at Captain Hughes, who lowered his brow.

"What are you doing, you quivering pile of rodents' entrails?" Captain Hughes' face was mottled red, though his voice sounded calm as ever.

"Did you not hear? It is the navy, which means you are headed for the gallows, and my brother's debt to you is void," Mortcastle exalted through gritted teeth, his nostrils flaring.

"No, lackwit, I am a merchant. I have a letter of marque," Captain Hughes retorted, rolling his eyes. "We simply need to comply with the investigation and clear up the misunderstanding as we always have. I have nothing to fear from the navy."

Lord Mortcastle did not immediately shift his position, but his right eye twitched and his gun hand wavered. Jacob worried about his resolve. He had intense curiosity about Mortcastle's reasons for involvement with Captain Hughes, but that could wait. The man was too easily swayed.

"The navy knows you are a pirate, Hughes." Jacob grinned.

The look of loathing that was turned his way was the most frightening thing he had ever seen in his life, but it was also a little thrilling. He felt sure he did not mistake the glimmer of fear he saw in the captain's shifty eyes as they darted around the room, whether for escapes, hidden treasures, or fighting advantages. Perhaps it was a combination of all three. There was a great deal of cunning in those eyes, and Jacob did not want Celeste in the presence of such a man any longer.

"In any case, we shall be leaving now," Jacob announced with a theatrical bow and reached a hand out toward Celeste as if they were doing nothing more than attending a dance set. "Lady Celeste?"

She not only took his hand but curled into his side, and the warmth that radiated from her was more than a physical comfort. Her presence beside him filled him with such relief he scarcely remembered the existence of anything else. He could feel her steady breathing and see the pink in her cheeks as she looked at him with trust and hope as he held her. He neglected to consider the contrast of how cold he must feel to her, and when she shivered, he wished he had a coat to offer her. He moved to step away, but Celeste pursed her lips and clutched him tighter, making him chuckle under his breath.

Without warning, Captain Hughes drew a sword and slashed at Jacob, but Jacob's reflexes were quick, and he thrust Celeste behind him as he drew his own weapon, stepping mostly out of the way as he spun. He felt the sting across his shoulder as the blow glanced off, but he did not think it had struck him hard. When he turned back to counter, he noticed that Lord Mortcastle was standing uselessly to the side with his pistol halfway up, seeming unsure of what to do with himself. By the time Jacob had rolled his eyes and stepped forward to engage the captain once again, the doors burst open behind them and several naval officers filled the room. Lord Mortcastle lowered the gun.

"See, my friends, I was on your side the entire time. Played my part well, don't you think?" He did not sound at all sure that he even believed himself.

"Captain Hughes, you are under arrest for piracy, smuggling, withholding goods from the crown, and kidnapping. Your letter of marque is revoked," a naval officer declared as he approached. He snapped his fingers and pointed, indicating his officers toward the captain, ignoring the beginnings of a protest as Hughes was dragged away.

Behind the officer, Lord Kingstone rushed in, his eyes frantic, with Lord Blakely and Mr. Stevenson close on his heels.

"Celeste!" Lord Kingstone rushed forward as soon as he saw his daughter. Jacob relinquished her to him but missed her presence immediately.

"Papa!" Celeste cried, her eyes filling as she threw herself into his embrace. Her father's face scrunched as he seemed to notice that half of her was damp. He removed his coat and wrapped it around her, filling Jacob with both relief and envy. He looked Jacob up and down, no doubt noticing where the water had originated. Jacob frowned an apology, and Lord Kingstone nodded, but his face did not relax.

"Captain, Lord Mortcastle played a role in these events," Lord Kingstone said, addressing the naval officer.

"No, no, I played along to set things up nicely for your men, I—" he defended.

"Rubbish!" the officer barked. "No one knew of tonight's operation."

Lord Mortcastle froze. His face lost all color, and his jaw lay open, looking as though all life had gone from him.

"Take him with the others," the officer ordered, standing there long enough to watch his men detain him, before turning and leaving without ceremony himself.

"Please." Lord Mortcastle did not address anyone in particular as he looked around wildly. "My sister is being held aboard this ship somewhere! Please, you must rescue her!" As his dark eyes met Jacob's, something passed between them. Perhaps it was the desperation Jacob recognized, but it was the sincerest expression he had seen on the man's face. He nodded and thought he saw Lord Mortcastle's struggles reduce as he was escorted from the room. The moment was so fleeting that Jacob could not be certain his nod had been seen, and it bothered him.

"Well, I cannot say that was the strangest thing that has happened today, but it is close." Zach shook his head with a grin. Jacob appreciated the light-hearted moment that allowed him to draw a breath.

"Where is Miss Small?" Mr. Stevenson asked, looking around.

"Who?" Celeste and her father intoned together.

"Betsy," both Jacob and Mr. Stevenson answered in unison. The four of them looked at each other and smiled.

"Betsy was taken by Captain Blackboots. I can only assume they went below..." Celeste trailed off, seeming to notice the scrunched faces, and heads cocked to the side, around her.

"My dear, is that an alias?" Lord Kingstone asked, absently rubbing her shoulder to warm her.

"Pardon? Oh! Yes, there is a female pirate aboard this ship, though she does not look it, and Betsy and I do not know her name, so we gave her one of our own."

Jacob smothered a laugh.

"We ought to check below then." Mr. Stevenson nodded and turned, not willing to waste any more time.

"I would like to search for Lord Mortcastle's sister," Jacob announced, raising the eyebrows of the other gentlemen. "Seeing as there was some kind of arrangement between him and the captain, she is not likely below decks. She may have already been found by the officers, but I would like to be sure."

"I will accompany you." Zach stepped toward him, ever the faithful friend. There was something in his eyes that spoke of sadness and determination, and Jacob had the feeling he was being more than just helpful. Nathaniel's loss had hit him extraordinarily hard, and Jacob suspected he struggled with it still, so he did not argue.

"I will return when Lady Celeste is safely off the ship," Lord Kingstone reassured the men, guiding his daughter toward the door.

"Wait." She placed a hand on his shoulder and stood firm. "I will not leave without Betsy."

"Mr. Stevenson has the matter in hand. He will see to her safety," he pushed, but his frown deepened.

"Father," she said gently but pursed her lips into a firm line. "I have learned many things about myself over this past fortnight, and not all of them have been complimentary. I wish to mend my ways, and so I will not leave without her."

Jacob could not look away from her, feeling his heart grow as she refused to let go of her compassion.

Lord Kingstone pinched the bridge of his nose. "Where did you say they went?" he acquiesced through gritted teeth, a heavy sigh accompanying his words.

"Below decks, this way," she declared and marched out onto the deck amidst the battle, as if she knew where she was going.

Jacob could only shake his head and smile.

Chapter Forty-One

Aboard Ship Victory's Glory, Portsmouth

Celeste did not think before launching herself into the middle of the battle, and the sight brought her to an abrupt halt. She squeezed her eyes shut and just stood there for a moment, unprepared for the shock of it. She felt her father step in front of her to shield her, pulling her close.

"Please allow me to take you away from here," he pleaded.

Celeste hated herself for a moment, as she was tempted by the offer of protection and solace, but she knew that wherever Betsy was, she would not just disappear when Celeste left this all behind. She would still be living and breathing this nightmare. Celeste shook her head.

"No, I will not abandon her," she declared, tears squeezing out of her closed eyes.

"There are others who can save her. It does not have to be you, Celeste," he reasoned, his voice strained.

"She was terrified. She will need the comfort of another woman." She opened her eyes, and her next words were gentle but firm. "Could you leave someone you care for behind? My conscience will not allow it."

When her father's eyes turned skyward, Celeste knew she had his support. It was not as if he went gallivanting about the countryside rescuing people, but she knew her father, and her words struck a chord within him. She gave him a squeeze around his middle, then drew a deep breath and sent a wordless prayer heavenward as she stepped forward.

Celeste skirted around the edge of the fray as much as was possible, but the deck was full of swords and men wearing various expressions along a spectrum of determination, desperation and death. The threat of slow execution by short noose that awaited all pirates who were caught, kept them fighting. Suddenly, she was yanked by the arm of her shirt from somewhere on her right. Thinking fast, she pulled her arm back into the loose fabric of the shirt, leaving only the end of the sleeve in the man's grasp. She could not have done that in a gown. He looked confused for a moment, which gave the nearest naval officer time to gain the advantage and her father the opportunity to maneuver himself between her and any other potential threats until they reached the other side of the deck. He had done an admirable job of protecting her from the battle itself, as well as the sight of it, but she felt a great deal of relief when they climbed below decks and found the area abandoned.

The Victory's Glory was a large ship, and so it took some time for them to search for the cells where prisoners might be held. She did not notice at first that another man, who was also dripping wet like Jacob, had followed behind them, and she startled when she saw him.

"This is Mr. Stevenson." Her father introduced the stranger as they hurried through the ship.

"A pleasure." Mr. Stevenson nodded. Celeste reciprocated and had to shake away the strangeness of exchanging pleasantries in such a situation.

A voice rang out, filling Celeste with hope.

"Louis Stevenson?" Betsy's surprise led them straight to her. She was in a barred cell with half a dozen other women, shocking Celeste into a gaping silence. Her father was not hindered in such a way and shook the door, then began looking about for a key.

"I have a pistol—stand back," Mr. Stevenson instructed. All the women scurried away from the door, but when he tried to shoot the lock, nothing happened.

"You swam to the ship with Mr. Bellmoore. Your gunpowder is wet," Celeste's father reminded him. Celeste felt her eyebrows fly upwards. Jacob swam to the ship? She ought not to have been surprised, considering how wet he had been, but she had been so happy to see him that her mind had not processed any of that. It was not the moment to indulge in romantic fancy, but the idea of him scaling a ship to come save her made her heart flip.

"Louis, what are you doing here?" Betsy's eyes were wider than usual, if that were possible.

"Do you two know each other?" Celeste asked the obvious, looking between Betsy and Mr. Stevenson.

"I live in Whitbury hamlet," he explained.

"We were friends, but then—" Betsy stopped, her blush so deep that Celeste almost forgot their situation.

"Cover your ears, ladies," Celeste's father interrupted, instructing those around him before turning his own pistol on the lock and successfully firing.

The women all came out of the cell, most not saying a word, but there was one who was better dressed than the others. She looked like she must not have been there long. She could have just wandered in from a ball or a musicale. She looked Celeste's father in the eyes and curtsied.

"To whom do I owe this debt?" she asked.

"I am Lord Kingstone. Is there someone we can send for to assist you?" he reciprocated with a bow. Again, the manners seemed so out of place, and yet Celeste was grateful for the reminder that they were civilized.

"I am Lady Isabelle Mortcastle. My father is the Earl of Braintree. I have two brothers, but I do not know either of their current whereabouts." Celeste and her companions stood staring at her for longer than would be polite anywhere.

A cold ripple ran through Celeste when she heard a shot ring out from the deck above them, and a feeling of dread swept through her. Nothing indicated that Jacob was the intended recipient, but somehow, she *knew*.

Chapter Forty-Two

❧

Aboard Ship Victory's Glory, Portsmouth

Jacob and Zach had searched through all the above-deck cabins and potential hiding places they could find in case Lady Isabelle Mortcastle had escaped and was waiting for the fighting to cease before coming out. They had been thorough but had found no trace of her anywhere.

Eventually, they had found their way back onto the deck. The fighting had died down with most of the crew arrested or dead, but there was no sign of Celeste. Jacob scanned the area, trying to see through the darkness if her outline was somewhere on the deck, hoping not to see her among the wounded. She was still dressed as a boy and could have been mistaken for one in the confusion. Zach found the naval officer who had arrested Lord Mortcastle and made some inquiries.

Jacob knew that he ought to have been more aware of his surroundings. He was on a pirate ship after all, not the place to grow complacent. He had contemplated more than once what it might be like to stare death in the face when Nathaniel had passed away. He wondered what had gone through his mind in that silent moment, and if it had been as the poets wrote in prose, as though time stood still.

When the shock of the bullet pierced his skin, he did feel a slowing of time. He was able to see the barrel of the musket being aimed at him with strange clarity, as well as the focused stillness of the man firing it, who stared at Jacob with menacing intent. He had not known that a body could twist and flip backwards so fast that it made an audible snapping sound. He didn't know if it was his bones being flung about or the impact of him hitting the solid railing behind him. He felt a profound sadness that he had failed to find Lord Mortcastle's sister, but before the intense pain took away his consciousness, Jacob was sure he had heard Celeste's voice calling out his name, and he was content.

Chapter Forty-Three

Ignoring her father's attempt at restraint, Celeste bolted back up toward the deck in time to see Lord Blakely frozen in place, his wide-eyed gaze fixed on an empty space by the railing. His mouth hung open in horror just before his scream of Jacob's name mingled with hers, confirming what she most feared. Within seconds that moved in slow motion, he shed his coat and ran for the railing, diving off the side of the ship.

Celeste ran over to the space Lord Blakely leaped from, gripping the side as she leaned over, staring into the black water below. She could no longer feel her heartbeat. She was barely aware of Reeves being apprehended and disarmed. In the darkness she could see nothing. Not the waves, nor the men who had been on the solid deck moments before. Only darkness. Her ribs shrank and began to strangle her lungs.

Celeste hoisted her leg up to climb over the edge in pursuit, desperate to follow Lord Blakely and rescue Jacob from the bottomless abyss below, but a solid arm around her waist pulled her back. She kicked and writhed to free herself, desperate to reach Jacob before the watery darkness could consume him and steal him from her forever.

"Celeste," her father spoke in her ear, his urgency not calming at all.

"Jacob!" she screamed into the open air, continuing to fight her father's grip. He held her with both of his arms, seeming to gain a better hold of her the more she struggled.

"Celeste, stop, please," he pleaded. The plaintive quality in his voice confused her and weakened her by distraction. He continued in an urgent whisper. "Celeste, I have seen what happens to a lady's reputation when she throws caution to the wind. Even with the best intentions. You must stop!"

"Hang my reputation!" she threw back, struggling harder. She managed to pull them both against the railing, though she had not yet freed herself.

"It is more than words!" he shot back, anger or something like it, strong in his voice. It was so unusual in his tone that it shocked Celeste into momentary stillness. "Unjust as it may be, a lady's life can be determined by it."

Celeste looked up into her father's face and saw his jaw flexing and his eyes ablaze. She could not tell if it was anger or sadness or a mixture of both, but it did not matter. Only Jacob's life mattered. She threw all of her weight toward the barrier, but he anticipated her and used her momentum to swing her in an arc, placing himself between her and the side of the ship. He glanced over his shoulder.

"Look, Celeste. Blakely has him!" He said the three words that could make a difference to her. His eyesight must have been better than hers because, even squinting to adjust her vision, she could just make out a shadow against the more fluid darkness below. Then she heard Lord Blakely call out and other men respond. She could make out the rough shape of a small boat moving over the water, and she let out a breath she did not know she had been holding.

"Shh, it is alright. All will be well now." Her father's deep voice was soothing as his grip on her loosened, and it took on the quality of an embrace rather than a restraint.

Celeste's legs seemed to exhale as much as her breath did, and they began to shake, threatening to collapse beneath her, but her father held her upright. She did not realize that she was crying until his wet cravat moved against her eyelids. Under normal circumstances, she would have been ashamed to use a man's neckcloth as a handkerchief, but she needed to clear her eyes so she could see.

"Father, I need to go to him." It was a statement of intention rather than a request for permission. She would proceed with or without his cooperation but knew this night had asked much of him already, and she would spare him where she could.

He frowned. "Are you sure? What if—?"

Celeste did not wait for him to finish. The sting his words inflicted was like the crack of a whip to a horse and motivated her to hasten off the ship and toward the docks to intercept wherever Lord Blakely might land with Jacob, in whatever state he might be in. She did not turn to check but could feel that her father followed. He loved her; he always would. She had not appreciated what a beautiful thing that certainty was before this misadventure.

Despite being on foot, Celeste still arrived before the boat did. She was left to pace as the small craft was rowed toward her at an excruciatingly slow speed. It was too dark to make out any expression on Lord Blakely's face as they approached, but the slumped form of Jacob seemed awfully still.

As a sailor hopped out and tied the boat to the dock, Celeste reached down herself to assist in hauling Jacob out of the craft. Between her and her father, they managed to get him out of the boat quicker than if they had waited for its occupants to climb out and see to the task themselves.

"He is cold," Celeste said to her father, who draped his coat around Jacob. Celeste's hands shook as she brushed the wet hair away from his face. He lay too still on the dock. There were no wounds on his head, so she began a frantic search, first on his chest, then abdomen.

"It is his shoulder," Lord Blakely spared her. "He should recover if we can get him warm and to a surgeon."

"I will see to it right away." Celeste's father gave her shoulder a quick squeeze and stood. "Lord Blakely, might I leave my daughter in your care while I make arrangements?"

"Of course." Lord Blakely nodded. He traded out his usual smile for a small one, shivering and looking as though his eyes may close of their own volition at any moment. He rocked on his heels, hugging his knees.

"Perhaps fetch some blankets, Father."

"I shall."

Celeste breathed some warm air onto her hands and then rubbed Jacob's. She was not confident it would do much, but she could not do nothing. He was alive, and he had to stay that way. One of the sailors approached with some blankets for both Jacob and Lord Blakely. Celeste wrapped one around Jacob's head, and by the time the sailor had wrapped his body, a carriage had arrived to take them to an inn. Celeste climbed in after the men, determined that nothing would pry her from his side until he was well.

Chapter Forty-Four

Portsmouth, England

Jacob awoke with a start. He gasped for breath, fighting to sit up, some instinct dictating his actions for him. He regretted it as the pain stabbed through his shoulder, making his stomach heave and his head spin. He did his best to right himself and gain his bearings, but as his eyes adjusted to the darkness, he could tell that he was alone in unfamiliar surroundings. Or he was dead, and his recent habit of deceitfulness had relinquished his place in Heaven. He shook his head; even he did not believe that scenario. He was in a man-made room with basic furnishings. He'd been in enough inns of late to make an educated guess that he was in one, though he did not know where.

Jacob felt the explosion of pain in his shoulder all over again as he relived the memory of being shot by Lord Mortcastle's valet. He did not know how much time had passed since then, but someone had bandaged him. His shoulder was bound so tight that he could not move his right arm at all. It was difficult to breathe with the bandages anchored around his chest.

Feeling around with his left arm for a candle turned out to be a fool's errand. He achieved nothing beyond making a lot of noise by knocking items to the floor. He rolled to the side until he half climbed, and half fell out of the bed, then began attempting to tidy the mess he had made in the dark.

Before too long, Jacob heard the door behind the bed opening, and he poked his head up in time to see the ghostly glow of Zach's face behind a candle entering the room. Seeing Jacob sitting on the floor, Zach hurried over to place his candle on the nightstand and bent down to assist him.

"It is a blessed relief to see you awake, Jack, but what on earth are you doing?"

"I was looking for a candle. Zach, where am I?" he asked as Zach helped him to stand.

"We are still in Portsmouth, at an inn. Are you hungry?"

Jacob had not considered food, but the question was answered by his stomach rumbling.

"Where is Lady Celeste?" he asked, ignoring the emptiness in his belly and the throbbing in his shoulder.

"Her father took her home. You had a fever, Jacob. It has been several days."

Jacob was unsure how he felt about that. He remembered nothing of having been unwell. He was relieved that Celeste had not seen him in that state but also a little disappointed that she had not stayed.

"She simply left?" he asked before considering his words. Zach chuckled.

"Hardly. Mr. Goldsmith has come to be of assistance and brought a concerning letter from Lady Kingstone."

"It is not Mr. Goldsmith I wish to see." Jacob shook his head, not meaning to sound so terse. He closed his eyes and inhaled through his nose and out through his mouth. "Please, Zach, tell me what happened."

"Very well. While you suffered the worst of the fever, Lady Celeste did not leave your side. It was as though she had slipped back into the role of Miss Owens quite naturally, though she did make a command here and there where necessary." Zach smiled. Jacob would have paid a handsome sum to see what he was remembering. "She read to you as well. Do you remember any of that?"

"No, nothing. What did she read?" Jacob searched his mind but found nothing after falling into the water.

"It was strange. One would have expected something sensible like philosophy or poetry, but she had a tiny volume wholly comprised of jokes. She must have read you the entire thing." He shook his head.

Jacob could not respond. Celeste had carried his little gift all this way, despite being dragged across the countryside by pirates, and it meant enough to her to read from at such a time. His throat felt thick for reasons he could not explain. It was a joke book, for pity's sake. It was supposed to make one laugh, not get emotional over. Especially in front of a friend. He cleared his throat, hoping his feelings were not obvious.

"Mr. Goldsmith came from Whitbury?" He changed the subject. Zach took it up without question.

"Oh. Yes. He came to offer assistance and was carrying with him a missive or two. One was from Lady Kingstone to the marquess, informing him of her intentions to quit the manor and return to their country estate in Herefordshire." He paused, his jaw flexing.

"What is it?" Jacob asked. Zach looked down at his hands.

"The letter—it indicated some disciplinary action toward Miss Owens. Protecting her was the only thing that had any power to distract Lady Celeste from her vigil by your side. She remained torn, but the danger had passed, and you were on the mend, so I insisted that she go. And it would not do for her and I to trade places, with me storming the marquess's estate, and her staying alone here with you." He laughed with one side of his mouth turned up.

Jacob found himself smiling at the absurd picture Zach painted. Though he could not dislike the idea.

"As amusing as that is, you seemed to be forming an attachment to Miss Owens. I cannot imagine it is easy for you to be tethered to my sickbed like this," Jacob said, watching for his friend's reaction. He was both pained and grateful for the sacrifice.

Zach did not speak straightaway. He examined his hands again, his lips pursed, as he tilted his head to one side, then back to the other.

"You know I have no one to answer to, which gives me the freedom to place my heart where I choose. And I do not give a fig for society's opinion."

The silence stretched on. Jacob did his best to be patient as he waited for his friend to say more, but eventually his stamina wore out.

"Well, man? What have you decided? Are you just going to leave me waiting for an announcement in the Gazette?" He threw up his hands, realizing too late the multidirectional pain that would shoot through him as a result. He gasped and clutched his shoulder. Zach was to his side in a moment.

"Settle down, old boy. I cannot have you bleeding out on me." Zach fussed over him until he shooed him away. "Alright, alright," Zach acquiesced.

"Do you intend to try for Miss Owens?" Jacob asked once he was as comfortable as he could be.

"Yes. I cannot like the thought of her and her family suffering because she did as she was told."

"It is more than that," Jacob observed.

"Yes, I care for her a great deal," Zach admitted, looking down with a smile."Then what are we waiting for?" Jacob demanded, again attempting to launch out of bed. Zach prevented him by giving him a gentle push against his good shoulder.

"After you are done healing." He nodded, his mouth in a firm line.

"Very well," Jacob grunted. "We shall return to Whitbury, but the moment I am able to ride without flinching, we will head to Hereford-shire, agreed?"

Zach smiled then, the tension seeming to leave him.

"Agreed."

Chapter Forty-Five

Willoworth Estate, Herefordshire

Celeste arrived at Willoworth ready for battle.

As the carriage traveled down the long, graveled drive, the familiar sights of home were not enough to release the tension in every muscle of her body. She sat rigid and straight, waiting for the confrontation with her mother. The letter that had arrived with Mr. Goldsmith from Whitbury Manor, informing her father that 'the situation with Miss Owens has been dealt with' still sent chills down Celeste's spine each time she thought of it. That phrasing could mean anything, but in all probability, Bryn had been disciplined or dismissed. What was worse was that Celeste had not been there to protect her as she had promised. She would do all in her power to rectify that now.

A small sigh caught Celeste's attention from across the carriage.

"My dear, I know you are concerned for Miss Owens, but do try to keep your good sense about you." He leaned forward as he spoke, resting his elbows on his knees so that his hands extended beyond. Relaxed, but ready to offer support.

"As I am certain you did when you were concerned for me, Father." She felt the side of her mouth rise a little. She knew he would have outwardly remained every bit the gentleman whilst coming to her rescue, but he could not pretend that he would have been calm and sensible in every thought.

"Of course." He raised his eyebrows and pouted a little in a look of mock piety, making her laugh. She reached out a hand and squeezed one of his.

"You are an excellent father. Thank you," she said, her throat feeling thick. He always managed to give her strength, even in humor. He did not have time to respond as the carriage stopped outside the entrance to the main house.

As soon as Celeste and her father alighted, they were stunned into stillness by a rush of skirts coming toward them.

"Mama?" Celeste asked, uncertain if she were seeing an apparition that merely resembled her mother. She had never seen the woman move faster than a hurried walk, and only then on the rarest of occasions. At this moment, however, her mother could be described as running toward her. She embraced Celeste hard in a flood of tears. Tears!

In her bewilderment, it took Celeste a few moments to gather her wits enough to return the embrace. She was not certain what else she ought to do and glanced at her father over her mother's shoulder, but all he did was wink before abandoning her for the house. The scallywag.

"Oh, Celeste, my dear, dear girl. I have been beside myself with worry for you. It is so good to have you returned to us!" she gushed as she stood back. Celeste had not thought her mother capable of gushing; indeed, that was one word no one had likely ever used to describe Lady Kingstone before. She still held Celeste's shoulders, her eyes sweeping over her as if to inspect her for possible damage.

"Mother, you are crying," Celeste stated the obvious, unable to construct anything better.

"Nonsense," she denied, then her face lost the battle for her by crumpling. "My little girl has been through a terrible ordeal. I am allowed to cry."

The words sounded much more like her old self, but her eyes shone as she patted Celeste's cheek. "Now come along inside before you catch your death." She wrapped an arm around Celeste.

"It is summer," Celeste pointed out. She would not grow ill from being outside in the warm evening. In fact, it was quite a relief after being cooped up in a carriage for so long. Or a barred carriage. She suppressed an involuntary shudder.

"Do let me dote on you a little, there's a good girl." her mother implored. Celeste was shocked into silence. Her mother patted her cheek once again, making Celeste wonder if the whole affair had left her in leave of her faculties.

Once inside Willoworth, around all that was familiar and comforting, Celeste's thoughts began to resume a more normal pace. As they climbed the main staircase, she decided to broach the subject she had been fretting over, albeit in a more subtle manner than she had planned, due to her mother's strange behavior.

"It is good to be home. I do love Willoworth far better than Honeychurch House," she began.

"Yes, you have made no secret of that these past few seasons," her mother agreed, shaking her head with a smile. Celeste had to blink a few times. Her mother did not practice indulgent smiles.

"Will you please have Bryn draw me a bath? I think I shall take a tray in my room tonight after such lengthy travel," Celeste sighed, rubbing her neck for emphasis, but keeping her eyes on her mother for her reaction.

"Certainly, dear," she agreed without breaking stride.

Celeste felt her foot hover above the step for a moment longer than necessary in her surprise, but she quickly recovered herself. The relief she felt was a physical thing. Where her chest had been tight, it released and allowed her to breathe once again.

More than one of the upper maids assisted Celeste with her bath and then dressing afterwards. She wondered when Bryn was going to join them. After she settled into her bedroom, she was greeted by a lady's maid, but it was not Bryn. A stone of dread dropped into the bottom of Celeste's stomach.

"Where is Miss Owens?" she asked. The girl did not make eye contact, only bobbing a curtsy before answering.

"I am Kate Frances, My lady. I'll be looking after you from now on."

Celeste did not bother responding before striding out of the room toward the drawing room. No one was there yet, and according to the clock, her parents would be at dinner. Celeste headed toward the dining room, startling them both as their soup was cleared away.

"Will you be joining us after all, dearest?" Her mother's whole face lit up, weakening Celeste's armor a little. She drew a fortifying breath.

"Mother, where is Bryn?" she demanded.

"There will be time enough to discuss all that tomorrow when you are well rested. Come sit down and have something to eat. Simpson, fetch another plate for Lady Celeste, please," her mother dismissed. Before she knew it, there was a plate on the candle-lit dining table in front of her, and her mother had begun the next course as if Celeste weren't still standing there agape. Celeste looked up with resolve.

"No, Mother. If you wish to put off such a simple thing as telling me her whereabouts, then she cannot be on these grounds."

The servants in the room did not react except to throw surreptitious glances at each other when they thought no one was looking. They were subtle enough that Celeste would never have noticed before, but these were real people to her now, with thoughts and opinions and lives.

Her mother did not answer.

"Fine. I am certain she would have told Lord Blakely where she is from. I shall start there." Celeste spun on her heel to leave the room.

"You cannot write to a gentleman to whom you are not related or engaged," her mother admonished. "Your reputation—"

"Do you think I still have one?" Celeste turned again. "I was carried off, Mother! My reputation is as good as ruined."

"You do not know that. Many a young lady has come back from worse if she is swift enough. Mr. Tullford will be dining with us to-morrow evening and knows nothing of these events. The news of it has not yet reached Herefordshire, so there is still time to secure you a good match," she countered.

Celeste felt all the blood drain from her face and limbs.

"Mr. Tullford? What? What about Mr. Bellmoore? I was finally happy to cooperate with you," she choked. She had to force her voice out, and yet it still sounded small. She placed a hand on the base of her throat, wondering why she could not speak all of a sudden.

"My dear, sit down. This is why I wanted to discuss all this tomorrow. You are not ready for it all without some proper rest." Her mother sighed and rubbed her forehead.

"I will never be ready for this conversation; it is absurd," Celeste argued, but she did sit.

As the silence stretched on, it became clear that Celeste's mother had no intention of answering her questions.

"Mother, I ask you again, why do you not wish for me to marry Mr. Bellmoore anymore, after all of this?" She waved a hand as though everything she had been through were on display above them.

"Because it will take too long. I am sorry to seem unfeeling, but Mr. Bellmoore may take too long to recover from his injury, or he may not recover at all. We need to act now, before news of the incident reaches all of society. While you still have some way of salvaging your dignity." Her mother exhaled, putting her fork down with more force than necessary.

Celeste could not move, speak, or even breathe for several heart-beats. When she did, she was gasping, and her eyes filled with angry tears.

"Listen to me carefully, Mother, for I will not be misunderstood. I will not marry Mr. Tullford, or anyone else you place before me. Against my own wishes, I have done as you intended and fallen in love with Mr. Bellmoore. Not only that, but the man has risked his life for me!" Celeste said, forcing her voice through a throat trying to convulse in small hiccups. She reached out her hands as if she held his offering before her as a physical object.

"What if he does not recover? Then what is to become of you? Your father will not live forever to protect you, and society can be cruel and unforgiving. You must see that in order for you to live a decent life, you must marry posthaste," her mother objected, pleading.Celeste stood. Her heart was racing, and she feared she would soon lose control of her tongue.

"I care nothing for such a fickle mistress. I do not need the good opinion of society. I have seen what it is to live as a servant, and I could do so again if I must, but I will not abandon Mr. Bellmoore!" she declared, and with that, she turned and stormed out of the room before she would be tempted to say anything worse.

Chapter Forty-Six

Whitbury Manor, Berkshire

Whitbury Manor had been strangely quiet for the entire two days that Jacob had been home. Other than the preliminary welcome, almost no-one had said a word to him. His mother had visited him in his room but had not spoken above a whisper. He had not even seen his brother yet, and the household staff were skulking about as if afraid to speak. It was most peculiar. Perhaps if he had not indulged in that penny dreadful on the journey home, he would not be finding it so eerie. He'd had to have some distraction from the shards of pain induced by every sway and bump in the road, and reading of vampires had helped with that at least a little.

Zach had departed for his Tidenham estate as soon as he was satisfied that Jacob was settled, and who could blame him? However, it had left Jacob to face this strange new version of his home by himself, and there was only so much of his bedroom that Jacob could take. He had already endured more sitting still than he ever thought he could handle. The muscles in his legs were twitching with the very thought of visiting the stables, though he knew he was a long way off of riding yet. His shoulder was healing well, but holding reins would be weeks away. Still, he found himself walking in that direction. Just for a visit.

Tom spotted Jacob as soon as he passed through the gates of the stable house and ran out to greet him, William following close behind. They fired questions in a cacophony that the most talented linguist could not decipher until Jacob waved his good hand in surrender.

"Please, one at a time." He smiled, happier than normal to have a loud conversation.

"Right, then I'll go ahead," Tom began. "You're not intendin' to attempt a ride with that arm, are you?"

"No, Tom, rest assured. I have come to see you all, and I have brought an apple for Thor." He smiled, then let out a laugh at Tom's dubious expression. "Really, I intend to behave."

"I'll look after him," William reassured his grandfather. "After all, Miss Elsie..." He trailed off, looking at his feet.

"Let us have none of that. You could not have fought off Reeves on your own, and alerting us all aided in saving her. The slower path can be the wisest. Especially when the other fellow is bigger." Jacob reassured.

"And uglier," Tom added out of the side of his mouth, making them all laugh.

After spending half an hour in the fresh air and the good company of the stable yard, where he reassured Thor that he was alive and well, Jacob headed back to the house. It was irritating how soon the fatigue set in. The doctor in Portsmouth had told him it was all part of healing and to be patient with himself, but he was not enjoying it.

As he drew closer to the house, Jacob saw his brother reclined in a chair on the terrace. He altered his course to join him and was surprised to see a smile follow the initial look of surprise on his face. Whitbury stood and clapped him on his good shoulder before offering him an empty chair and retaking his own.

"Jacob! It is good to see you up and about! Mother has the entire house tiptoeing about as though you are on death's door."

"I could say the same for you. The last time I saw you, you were straddling the remains of your lunch." Jacob reciprocated.

"Thank you for that reminder." Whitbury scrunched his face and waved a hand to stop Jacob's description, his other hand resting on his belly.

"What are brothers for but to help you recount your humiliations?"

Jacob joked.

"Yes, I appreciate you taking your duty so seriously, but you needn't go to so much trouble." Whitbury laughed once through a grimace.

"It is my pleasure." Jacob placed a hand over his heart and bowed.

Whitbury did his best not to laugh, but his grin deepened the lines in his cheeks and gave his eyes depth, making his affection evident even without much audible sound. After a few moments though, his expression began to change, with his eyebrows pushing upwards together and the corners of his mouth tightening down. He struggled to maintain his cheerful expression but was losing to whatever feeling was overpowering his face and making his breathing more rapid. He soon pulled at his cheeks with his hand to reassert control, while spinning away from Jacob, then turning back again as if he could not make up his mind whether or not he could face him.

"What is it, Whitbury?" Jacob asked, his own brow knit in concern.

"Jacob, I am sorry. I am so sorry." He began, then faced away again, gripping his jaw with one hand, the other resting on his hip.

"For what? You have not wronged me." Jacob reached out a hand but had barely touched his brother's arm before he whirled back around to face him again.

"For everything!" Whitbury spat. He pursed his lips as he fought for control, his eyes becoming glassy.

"Charles—" Jacob reached out again, worry for his brother overriding all other thoughts.

"I have failed you." He turned his head, pulling his lips back from his teeth as if the words hurt to say, then looking Jacob in the eyes with such intensity he almost stepped back.

"No, of course you have not. After Father died—" Jacob protested.

"When Father died, I grieved heavily, I did," Whitbury acknowledged. "But it was not unexpected. It was not like Natha—" A wheezing sound replaced the end of the name that he could not seem to finish. He doubled over.

Again, Jacob reached out to support his brother, but Whitbury threw out a hand as a barrier and forced himself upright, tears spilling down his cheeks.

"I must say this, I must—" he forced out through clenched teeth before taking a deep breath. "When Nathaniel died, it was not like Father. It was not the natural order of things. And I should have learned!" He was shouting by the end of the sentence. "I should have learned what it meant to be a brother! Instead, I—I tried to send you away, to—to throw you on the mercy of the world—worse! At the mercy of Bonaparte! My own brother!"

"Whitbury, please, I was in no danger of Napoleon. He was defeated this very year!" Jacob tried to reassure, though his mind was whirling.

"He has come back before," Whitbury shook his head. "No, Jacob. I should never have betrayed you like that. Please allow me to beg your forgiveness. When you went after Lady Celeste, and I found out that you had been shot by *pirates*, I—" He could not finish his sentence. Instead, his mouth clamped shut, and his eyes turned haunted. "I have been worried about the stupidest things, like making sure you call me by my title." He shook his head.

"That is not so bad. You are an earl, and I respect you," Jacob reassured.

"But I am, first of all, your brother. Charles."

Jacob reached out for his brother then. This time he reciprocated and pulled Jacob in tight, almost aggressively, toward him, repeating over and over that he was sorry. When he pulled away, he reassured Jacob that he had no need to ever worry about being sent away and could choose any profession he wished.

"Why did you want to send me away?" Jacob asked, regretting it the moment the question was asked. His brother had given him so much already, and he was afraid of the answer.

As it was, Charles did not speak right away.

"I think I am yet too great a coward to answer that question now. Would it be unforgivable of me to request that you ask me again another time?" he whispered, looking into Jacob's eyes.

"I cannot pretend to understand, but you have already been more than forthcoming with me," Jacob acquiesced, wishing the refusal did not sting.

"Just believe me when I say that I bear no animosity toward you,

Brother. It is not you."

"Then please come to me if I can be of help. You need not struggle alone."

"I am just beginning to learn that." Charles managed a small smile, making Jacob wonder what had happened to change his brother. "On that note, *you* managed to fight off pirates with the Marquess of Kingstone. They are being held in the Marshalsea, you know. You seemed to have made an impression there."

"What do you mean?" Jacob asked, wondering what Charles knew of the matter.

"I received a letter from the marquess yesterday, thanking us for our hospitality in inviting Lady Celeste to my Engagement House Party, and by way of reciprocation, inviting our family and Lady Adelle's to stay at Willoworth. As soon as we are both sufficiently recovered, that is."

Jacob could have leapt in the air. He forgot to ask further about the Marshalsea and Lord Mortcastle.

"I am recovered enough. We could leave tomorrow," he answered before thinking. His brother's smirk told him he should have downplayed his enthusiasm at least a little.

"Has something happened between you and Lady Celeste then?" Charles asked, all traces of his former emotion gone from his face and posture except for a slight slump in his shoulders.

"Well, it did when we were both pretending to be servants, but things became a little muddled, and we did not have the chance to mend things because she was carried off, and I was shot. Blakely said that she read to me during the fever, though, so she cannot be indifferent."

"Ah, she was the servant you asked for in your sickbed? That makes sense," Charles mused. "Well, we had best get you to Herefordshire."

"How are you faring? Are you recovered yourself?" Jacob asked.

"Yes. I am feeling a little fatigued, among other things, but I shall be up to snuff. We will need to go to London first to acquire a special license." He rested a hand on Jacob's good shoulder, and they began walking inside.

"A special license? How? Why?" Jacob stopped, shocked. He had no idea how he was supposed to convince the Archbishop of Canterbury to see him in the first place, let alone approve a special license for him.

"Jacob, word of Lady Celeste's kidnapping can only be contained for so long. Of course, we will protect her as best we can, but the damage to her reputation cannot be helped. If you do intend to marry her, I would suggest you do it as soon as arrangements can be made. Then society will be left to wonder if it were already done before your daring rescue," Charles reasoned.

Jacob considered that. He had no issue with any of it, but did not want Celeste to think his intention was only to protect her. He would have to be careful how he worded things, or she may become angry with him again. He should definitely kiss her, though. He looked up to see his brother smiling at him, and he began to pay attention to his face, telling himself to remove the silly grin he could feel there.

"Do not worry, I will assist you," Charles laughed. It made Jacob so happy that he did not even care if it was at his expense.

Chapter Forty-Seven

Willoworth Estate, Herefordshire

Celeste had become adept at avoiding her parents.

When she refused to attend the dinner with Mr. Tullford, her mother had tried to persuade her by reminding her of her inheritance. That subject had diminished in priority for her since Jacob's kiss, and she had not even thought about it since being abducted. The primary worries on her mind now were Jacob and Bryn.

Since then, she had spent days finding nooks and spaces that she had not taken advantage of on the grounds before. She tried to assist the servants, but she was still an abysmal maid and was getting underfoot. She wished she knew where she might send a letter to Bryn, but the housekeeper would not divulge her address. She would not give up though.

As was inevitable, Celeste did bump into her parents whilst looking for a quiet place to read in the evening. She had thought the conservatory would be the last place her mother would go, but as she approached the wire-framed bench amid some unknown greenery, it was occupied by both of her parents.

At first, Celeste turned to leave, but her father spoke, asking her to stay. There was another bench across the way, so she nodded and sat down, her throat feeling tight. She made a conscious effort not to fidget. She would not show how nervous she felt.

Her father began. "Celeste, we have always desired your happiness.

Despite mistakes we have made, we have tried to do what is best. We do not wish to go against you."

"I know that. And you do not always get it wrong," Celeste acknowledged without letting her guard down all the way.

"That is a relief. We do worry over you though, as is natural," he smiled.

"Yes, Father, and I can see what you are going to say. It is yet another road to an argument that none of us wish to have, so let us not tonight. Please?" Celeste anticipated with a heavy sigh. She leaned on her toes, ready to stand, but hesitated when her mother spoke.

"You do not know everything, Celeste. For instance, how to be a maid. You claim that you can support yourself, but I have it on good authority that you are not as gifted at being a servant as you may think."

"No, I am well aware. I just hoped you would not be." Celeste shook her head. Her parents exchanged heavy looks.

"Ellen, I think it is time we told Celeste the reasons for our continued interference," her father broke the silence. Her mother stilled. Everything about her was motionless except her blinking, which had increased significantly. Then she gave a single resolute nod and turned her body to face Celeste.

Celeste had never seen her mother afraid until now. She had seen her in the presence of a mouse or something that may have given her a temporary fright, but the fear in her mother's wide blue eyes as she sat braced across from her was unquestionable. After several swallows and attempts to find her voice, Celeste's mother shook her head with her eyes squeezed shut and stood.

"My dear." Celeste's father stepped toward her mother.

"I cannot speak of it, Phillip, you know I cannot."

The pleading, tear-filled sound in her throat was so vulnerable and unexpected that Celeste was unable to form a thought. All she could do was sit there, clutching the edge of the bench and watch the scene play out in front of her.

Celeste's father was quickly beside his wife, stroking her shoulders.

"Ellen, I know, but you are safe here to open your heart. Celeste is our daughter. She loves you. All will be well." He pulled her into his chest and held her. She astonished Celeste by wrapping her arms around his waist and burying her face in his cravat. It was such an intimate moment that Celeste felt like she ought to turn away, but her eyes were riveted to the scene. She had never seen her parents like this. She became aware of her gaping mouth when her mother turned her face back toward Celeste.

Without being asked, her father offered his handkerchief. Her mother had to let go of him in order to use it to dab at her eyes and nose, but she stayed tucked into his side. It was such a sweet image that Celeste felt her defensiveness melting away. She wished she were a talented painter and could capture the moment.

Celeste's mother blinked away her tears and drew a deep breath, pulling herself up to stand with her usual posture, but stayed half beside, half in front of her husband, still in physical contact with him.

"Very well," she spoke, her voice not quite steady. She had Celeste's full attention. "When I was a girl of sixteen, I—" She cut herself off and squeezed her eyes shut again. Her mouth pulled down into a grimace. Her father reached for his wife's hand, and even though her eyes were still closed, she reached for his in the same moment and squeezed it, the handkerchief trapped in between.

"Mama, please be at ease." Celeste spoke softly. She stepped forward in and kissed her cheek. Her mother's eyes opened and filled again, but this time, she had a tremulous smile. She reached up and placed a gentle hand on Celeste's cheek, and Celeste thought she saw pride in her mother's eyes. Or perhaps it was affection. Either way, it filled Celeste with warmth from her toes all the way up to her face.

"Alright, dearest, I suppose it is time you knew. I have never spoken of this to anyone who did not already know of it. It is very difficult for me," her mother began, her voice shaking again. "When I was a girl of sixteen, I almost—well, that is, I...eloped."

Celeste's eyebrows shot up so high she wondered if they had left her face entirely.

She questioned what she had just heard. If the situation were any different, Celeste would have thought that someone was playing some kind of joke. *Her* mother? Her perfect, always-behave-like-a-lady mother had done something as scandalous as elope?

"With whom? Not with Father?" she blurted. "Sorry, I am only surprised." she added afterwards.

"Yes, that is why I never speak of it. It is my greatest shame and an utter embarrassment to myself and my entire family and will be forever." Celeste's mother closed her eyes again.

"Mama, it is a shock, I will not lie to you, but I do not think less of you for it. Please do not be afraid. It was brave of you to tell me." Celeste gave her mother's arm a light squeeze where her hand still rested. Her mother opened her eyes, and her head tilted.

"How could you possibly not think less of me? I eloped. And to answer you, no, it was not your father. Thankfully, he and the late Lord Whitbury arrived before we reached Scotland, or it would have been much worse—"

"What? The *late* Lord Whitbury? Jacob's father?" Celeste interrupted without thinking.

"'Jacob' is it?" Her father raised an eyebrow with a half-grin that said she would need to explain that familiarity later.

"Yes. Mr. Bellmoore's father rode with yours when he came for me." She took both of Celeste's hands and squeezed them. "When I speak of how unkind society can be, it is because I know from experience. You cannot even support yourself without a reputation, Celeste—it is everything. And society has a long memory. I am not afraid because I care for the opinions of others. I am afraid because I know what poor opinions can cost."

Celeste took a moment to digest everything she had just learned. She had so many questions, not all of which she was confident would receive an answer, or should even be asked.

"Everything seems fine now. I have never heard a bad rumor about you, ever. And you were still able to marry a title." Celeste shrugged, not seeing the disaster her mother was trying to paint.

"I was very fortunate, yes. Your father and I were already engaged. It was a match orchestrated by my parents, but I was swept up in the excitement of what I thought was first love and a French accent."

"He was French?" Celeste exclaimed, shocked again.

"That is beside the point," her mother stated with a blush. "The real point is, that if not for your father being valiant, and some very heavy personal sacrifices, I would have been at the mercy of my parents. They *did* care for society's opinion and wanted nothing more than to throw me out and wash their hands of me."

"What sacrifices?"

"There were many, but the hardest was losing my dearest friend. She tried to warn me, and was even brave enough to break my confidence for my own good. Then, after everything, she did not turn against me, but my parents needed someone to blame." She stopped speaking, her voice too thick to continue.

"Lady Whitbury?" Celeste asked. Her mother nodded. "Do you not see? That makes this all the sweeter. I fell in love with her son! I tried not to, but it happened anyway. Why would you give up now?" Celeste turned her hands over and squeezed her mother's in return.

"I am just so afraid that if something happens, and he does not make it, that you will be left without protection, Celeste. That is all. I want you to be able to marry him. I cannot think of anything happier, but what if it cannot happen and you wait too long?"

Celeste considered, for the first time, her mother's perspective. She had no intention of giving up on Jacob, but she would find a way to ease her mother's worries if she could.

"Mother, I understand now, as I did not before. And when I left Mr. Bellmoore, he still had a fever, but the doctor assured us that he was out of danger. Otherwise, Lord Blakely could never have convinced me to leave his side. And before you ask, I was chaperoned," she added for good measure.

Her mother did not argue or dismiss her words but nodded, seeming to accept that.

Celeste's father chirped in. "You should know that I have sent an invitation to Whitbury Manor for the Bellmoore family to join us here at their earliest convenience. I have not yet heard back from them, so I do not know how young Bellmoore fares, but after your dining room declaration, I could not do nothing."

Celeste jumped up and wrapped her arms around her father's neck.

She had every faith that a message would soon come, putting everyone's minds at ease.

"Why did you not say so before?" She could not help bouncing up and down on her toes.

"Do not rest all your hopes on this letter. You need to be able to recover if this yet does not go well," her father warned.

"Yes, Father." Celeste did try to take in the wisdom he offered, but sometimes hope grew wings of its own without asking for permission.

Celeste's father had sent James as a courier, rather than using the post, which was much faster, and a letter returned with him the following day. As her father stood motionless by the window in his study, Celeste did her best to exercise patience while she waited for him to share the news it contained. If she did not know better, she would believe he was just staring at the paper he held rather than actually reading it. She had tried to bribe James for the missive upon his arrival but had quit that course of action when he had laughingly asked her if she were trying to have him sacked. After what had happened to Bryn, she would take no chances.

As it turned out, Celeste was about as good at pretending patience as she was at pressing gowns. She watched the late afternoon sunbeams dance around them from between the heavy drapes for about as long as she could stand as she shifted her weight from foot to foot. Her father's eyebrow began to twitch, along with the corner of his mouth as she tried to be subtle about peeking over his tall shoulder.

"Curious, are we?" he grinned.

At that, Celeste gave up her lost cause at subtlety and attempted to snatch the letter out of his hand, but he bent his fingers, having the effect of folding the page deftly out of her reach.

"That was bad manners." He made a tsk sound.

"As is making me wait so long when you know it is excruciating," she retorted.

"Very well, I will show you mercy," he laughed. "Though I have not had time to read the full correspondence yet, due to someone's impatience, the gist of it seems to be that Lord Whitbury is recovering quite well from the Laudanum."

"I am relieved to hear that, Father, but you know that is not what I am waiting for." Celeste began tugging on his arm as she had as a child to get at something he was holding. "Your good humor does give me cause to hope that the correspondence does not contain bad news, however."

He nodded with a smile. "Very astute, my dear. Alright. He also writes that his brother has returned home well and whole and is fit to travel. They will be here by Friday." He had to step back then to avoid being struck by Celeste's arms flying up in the air as she leapt in her exuberance with a squeal. It was not behavior her mother would condone, but she was not present. Not that it would have deterred Celeste. Her happiness in that moment could not be contained.

Celeste's father continued reading while Celeste did a celebratory twirl or two until he spoke again.

"Celeste, there is news here of Miss Owens." He recaptured her attention in an instant. She rushed to his side and grasped his forearm.

"What does it say?" she practically begged.

"Lord Whitbury writes that Mr. Bellmoore received a letter from Lord Blakely on the same day that James arrived at Whitbury Manor. He reports that Miss Owens is well, and that she wanted to convey her continued affection for you and wishes you the very best. She is at home with her family, and they will be detained there for some time due to some pressing business related to her father. They send their regrets that they will miss the inevitable nuptials between Mr. Bellmoore and yourself."

To that last part of the letter, her father raised an eyebrow, and Celeste felt herself blush. There was not yet an official understanding between her and Jacob, though she did like the sound of 'inevitable.' Her self-consciousness did not remain dominant for long with so many happy feelings coursing through her. To hear such good tidings from both Jacob and Bryn! Celeste felt as though her heart were being replaced from the inside with pure sunshine. Friday could not come soon enough.

By the time Friday evening made its tardy appearance, Celeste was no longer able to form coherent sentences. All day she had made diligent attempts to do something other than wander about aimlessly, but she was far too distracted to be fit for any useful occupation. Her mother had managed to pull together a neighborhood dinner party, though Celeste thought it would be kinder to allow the gentlemen a restful evening without social expectation while they were still healing.

When Lord Whitbury's carriage arrived, Celeste's mother forced her to stand politely in the appropriate greeting line with her parents inside the vestibule, instead of rushing outside as she wished to. Her mother elbowed her in the ribs for not standing still at least three times as they waited. Perhaps her mother was not eating well enough, for her elbow was quite sharp, and Celeste was certain she would gain a bruise.

Celeste cast her eyes along the greeting line. Her heart grew in her chest as she saw Jacob, and she was certain she could hear music playing. Another nudge from her mother, this one more subtle, reminded her to focus on each person as they stood before her. Though she did cast sneaky glances in Jacob's direction at every opportunity.

The first to greet Celeste was Lord Whitbury. His eyes were perhaps not as bright as when she had seen him last, hinting at his fatigue, but it was such a relief to see him up and about after what had occurred at Whitbury Manor. She curtsied to him as he bowed, and he smiled at her with more warmth than she remembered. After all the trouble she had caused his household, it was quite a surprise. Lady Adelle was beside him, her sister and parents, Lord and Lady Waverley, close by, with Lady Whitbury and Jacob behind them.

"It is so good to have you safely returned to us," Lady Adelle offered as she curtseyed, her eyes never quite settling on Celeste. Given what

Bryn had said about interactions with her, she seemed uncharacteristically reserved. Lady Waverley, however, did not suffer from the same affliction. The large feathers in her headpiece waved as she spoke.

"Yes, you are so fortunate to have found your way out of such a compromising position. A talent that runs in the family, no doubt." She smiled without a shred of sincerity.

"Mother!" The shocked gasp came from Lady Adelle's sister, while Celeste just gaped, her surprise rendering her speechless.

"All I am saying is that not all ladies would be able to walk through society so easily after allowing themselves to be caught out like that. It was a compliment. Do not worry, I will not cut you." Lady Waverley shrugged. With that, she gave the smallest of curtsies and proceeded to the drawing room, walking with her chin unnecessarily high in the air, her family scurrying behind her.

Celeste wished they could uninvite her, but her association with Lord Whitbury made that impossible, especially with him and Lady Adelle still unmarried. She looked at her mother, who was doing an admirable job of holding her emotions in check. It was clear she had been practicing this for many years, but it was only Celeste's first experience with the unkindness her mother had warned her about. She did not even notice that Lord Whitbury had not followed his fiancée until he spoke.

"I beg your forgiveness. I hope you know that the Bellmoore family does not share her opinion. We hold your family in the highest regard." He bowed then, and after shaking hands with Celeste's father, stepped aside.

Lady Whitbury stepped forward and grasped Celeste's hands and kissed her cheek. Celeste realized that she had forgotten to breathe, not knowing what to expect from this woman who had figured her out, but she was smiling at Celeste with genuine affection. A dizzying contrast after what had just transpired.

"It is so wonderful to have you home. I was terrified for you." She smiled. Celeste could not help but reciprocate. Lady Whitbury rested a gentle hand on her cheek before turning to her mother and clasping both of her hands. The rest of their greeting was lost on Celeste.

Jacob.

Finally.

He was last in seniority and had to wait for the back of the line. While Celeste had been glancing at him, she had avoided his eyes for fear that she might never look away. He wore a deep blue jacket that did not sit quite right, probably concealing bandages underneath. He looked so different to how she had first met him in the carriage house with long hair tied back, wearing a coarse work shirt and however many days' worth of stubble on his face to conceal his identity. She smiled and shook her head at the memory. He stood in front of her, clean-shaven with a perfect cravat, his expression soft as he gazed down at her.

"Ja—Mr. Bellmoore."

She curtsied, he bowed, and their eyes met somewhere in the middle.

"Lady Celeste." His voice cracked a little as he greeted her. She did not even notice that she had offered her hand until he placed a light kiss on her knuckles. She was wearing silken gloves, but the warmth of his lips sent electricity up her arm as if they did not exist. As he lingered a little longer than was proper, the force of his gaze boring up into hers was similar to that of his kiss. She fought a gasp.

With a clearing of his throat, Celeste's father stole Jacob's focus, and he stood and greeted her parents, but she was certain the smile he wore was still meant for her. As he walked away toward the drawing room and the next guest approached, Celeste could not resist a surreptitious glance under her lashes at Jacob. He was achingly magnificent. Without warning, he looked back in her direction and caught her. She looked away quickly but had to bite back a smile.

Mr. March was going to ask Celeste to perform, she just knew it. She could sing passably well but did not wish to do so for the likes of Lady Waverley, not knowing what unkind gossip would be spread about the countryside regarding her performance. Nevertheless, Mr. March always asked her to sing.

Celeste's mother had set up the drawing room with small groupings of chairs and tables throughout, not unlike a card party. She did not want to encourage suggestions of dancing, knowing that both Jacob and Lord Whitbury would find such an activity difficult in their current state of recovery. Celeste appreciated her thoughtfulness in that.

It was a large room, and they had a good selection of neighbors, so Celeste had been able to avoid Lady Adelle and her family for most of the evening. All she wished for now was to converse with Jacob. And avoid drawing undue attention to herself.

"Good evening, Lady Celeste," Jacob greeted as he approached her, then looked at Mr. March. "I do not believe I have had the pleasure."

"This is our vicar, Mr. March," she introduced. "May I present Mr. Bellmoore of Whitbury Manor in Berkshire."

"Ah, I hear you are quite the hero." Mr. March's face lit up as he slapped Jacob on his injured shoulder. Celeste almost fainted on his behalf, but he managed barely a flinch. His jaw clenched and flexed though, and Celeste could only imagine how much it must have hurt.

"Thank you, sir, but I believe the real heroes are the ones helping people every day, without any fanfare." Jacob bowed.

"Quite right, my boy." Mr. March gave a wide smile, his wrinkles almost completely covering his eyes. He soon saw someone else of interest and excused himself, leaving Celeste and Jacob together.

"Are you alright?" she asked. He looked at her, his smile natural and laced with some of the pain he had concealed.

"I am relieved he did not strike again, or I may have had to feign a swoon," he laughed.

"Are you certain you would have been only counterfeiting to swoon?" Celeste asked, half serious but also referencing *As You Like It*. She had re-read the play, and now understood why a Shakespearean story about disguise had caused Jacob distress when she had overheard the conversation between him and Tom in the stables that time, just before their ride together.

"I knew you understood that reference far too well. I was so worried that day," he admitted.

"I wondered about that. We had the most marvelous conversation, and then your behavior changed so abruptly. What happened? Were you really unwell?" she asked, relieved and grateful that she could.

"First, will you answer a question for me?" He leaned in close.

"Of course," she agreed, her heart rate increasing in direct relation to his proximity.

"Do you have a terrace?"

Chapter Forty-Eight

Willoworth Estate, Herefordshire

The terrace was right outside the drawing room and well lit; it was only a matter of opening the doors. Jacob noted that it was much larger and closer to the garden than his terrace, with a wide staircase leading down to a manicured lawn. It did not quite have the same feeling of privacy they had found at Whitbury Manor, but walking to the stone balustrade still afforded them a little more space than they had inside.

"You were about to tell me what was wrong on the day of our ride," Celeste prompted.

"In truth, I was never unwell. I made that up so that I could work in the stables during the house party. My real struggle that day was not physical."

"Oh?"

"I thought you were a maid! I felt horribly guilty because I was—" He stopped mid-sentence.

"Please go on." She looked up at him with her large multifaceted blue eyes, and the same urge to kiss her he had felt that day came back in an instant, this time without the weight of deception or self-reproach.

"I could not be a gentleman and take advantage of what I thought was your position, but neither could I deny, at least to myself, that I had feelings for you. If it were not for Lord Blakely's arrival..." He trailed off, staring at every inch of her face. He was not unaware of the way she looked at him.

"What?" she asked, a little breathless. "What would have happened?"

Jacob laughed then. He had come so close to kissing her that day. He had held her too long and too near, and she was asking him for details of that moment for a reason. He stepped closer to her and saw the small smile light her face as the pink in her cheeks increased. The obviousness of her desire to be kissed by him drew him in, and he leaned in slowly, drawing out the moment, enjoying the way her eyelids fluttered, and she leaned up toward him.

The kiss was sweet and lingering, making Jacob forget the pain in his shoulder, the travel fatigue, and every other concern he had ever had. Nevertheless, he pulled away before he could entirely forget where he was and that other people could happen upon them at any moment. Celeste could ill afford more gossip to spread about her.

He leaned in beside her ear. "Should I take this to hope that you are no longer angry with me?" he asked in a low whisper before stepping back.

At first, Celeste looked confused, then realization dawned, and she chuckled. "Oh, yes, that. I meant to explain that to you. You see, and I am not very proud of this, but I was upset because I realized that my parents were right."

Jacob did nothing but stare at Celeste without comprehension for several seconds. "Pardon?"

"That's it." She shrugged. "My parents were the ones who wanted me to marry you, and when you told me who you were, I realized that they had chosen well and that they were right. I could not stand it. I told you I am not proud of it. It was very childish."

Jacob blinked several times, understanding filtering through.

"So, what you are saying is that you would like to marry me?" He very much enjoyed the play of emotions across Celeste's face as her eyes went first wide, then narrow, then darted away as an attractive blush stole across her cheeks. Then they came back as she opened and closed her mouth several times before speaking.

"It is ungentlemanly to ask me to declare myself first." She sniffed, turning her nose in the air.

Jacob bit back a smile and did not remind Celeste that she had already declared herself first, back in Thor's stall just before their first kiss. Sincerity was what she seemed to be asking of him, and he was happy to give it. He could feel it flowing through him like a fountain.

"Celeste." He stepped closer again, reaching up to stroke her cheek and smiled.

She looked into his eyes, her lips parted slightly.

"Celeste, I know I have already caused you a good deal of vexation. I am very much hoping that you are able to forgive my stupidity with the knowledge that, although it is likely to be a lifelong ailment, I will do my utmost to cure myself of it."

Celeste smiled then, a full smile that lit her eyes and face and the entire terrace. It made his whole body feel as light as a feather. Then, as quickly as her smile had come, she reduced it, biting her lower lip. He missed it instantly.

"Bryn once said that a smile could be misconstrued as laughing, but I am not laughing at you," she explained.

"That is very thoughtful," he nodded. "Though I do love your smile and would not have you hide it." He stroked her cheek again, enjoying the warmth of her blush under his thumb as her smile once again spread across her face. She closed her eyes and leaned into his hand.

Jacob lost the ability to think. Everything he thought he wanted to say as he had traveled in the carriage fled his mind, and all that was left was a feeling he was not certain he could express.

"Celeste, you have taken over every thought in my head, every feeling in my heart." He struggled to explain what had been building inside of him since he had met her. "My very soul no longer lingers in my body but is interwoven with yours. I love you."

Chapter Forty-Nine

~⟨⟨∞⟩⟩~

Willoworth Estate, Herefordshire

Celeste could not breathe. She could not move. Jacob had just said the very words she had been aching to hear. She was no longer aware of the sounds of the garden or the hubbub of voices from inside the doors behind them. It was as if the entire world slowed down to enjoy the moment with her, and nothing existed but the terrace and the two of them.

"We have had so many misunderstandings since that first moment in the carriage house." Jacob shook his head. "I cannot risk another by being less than frank with you. Please say that you will have me, Celeste. Not because our parents want it and not to prevent hardship or poverty. I wish that we may laugh at terrible jokes on our daily ride and to plant you a garden of those roses you like. And watch the light from every sunrise kiss your cheeks." He ran his thumb over the line of her cheekbone, sending a pleasant shiver through her, and she closed her eyes.

"Jacob..." she whispered his name. Her heart thudded in her chest as if it were trying to take a running leap to lift her into the stars. She opened her eyes again to look into his.

There was not a great deal of distance between Jacob and Celeste, and she had felt that he had been holding what little space there was. However, as she said his name, his eyes softened, and he smiled, then closed the distance between them, leaning down to give her lips a gentle caress with his. When he raised his head, she teetered slightly, blinking at him several times before she was able to form a coherent thought again.

"Do you know that is the first time you have called me by my name without being angry with me?" He smiled at her in a way that made her very much want to kiss him again.

"Jacob," she repeated, then threw both hands over her mouth in shock as she realized that she had said it aloud to him, practically requesting another kiss. Heat filled her face, but he laughed and planted a soft kiss on the back of her knuckles where they covered her mouth. She felt her eyes go wide, and she could not look away from him.

"I apologize, Celeste," Jacob said with a grin that did not look the least bit apologetic. "I interrupted you. I believe you were about to answer my proposal."

Celeste's eyebrows shot up, and her hands slipped down so that only her fingertips were touching her mouth, which was hanging slightly open. He was right; she indeed had not yet given him an answer. Not that it was her fault. Jacob and his kisses were clearly to blame for her distraction, though she could easily forgive him such infractions.

"You are right." She nodded. She was tempted to make a joke but changed her mind when she saw the hopeful way his eyes changed and how his grin froze, and his breathing stopped. "Jacob, I would have accepted you as Mr. McKnell, the stablehand. Of course, I will accept you as yourself."

Jacob's smile lit his entire face, and he wrapped his arms around her, lifting her before dropping her back on her feet with a grunt of pain.

"Please be careful, my love. You have taken the time to travel all this way when you ought to be resting at home." She reached out to caress his injured shoulder, her fingertips barely touching the fabric of his coat.

"Time is one thing I can offer you in abundance," he said, his voice low, his eyes happy. "I may not have a lot to offer you, but everything I do have is yours."

The truth of Jacob's words expanded in Celeste's chest. She knew it from everything he had already done. He had risked everything to free her, was willing to endure a lifetime of gossip from the likes of people like Lady Waverley to marry her. He had shown kindness to Bryn, not to mention the esteem he was held in by the servants of Whitbury

Manor. Even the small gift of a book of jokes was a thoughtful reminder of one of their happiest days. Which led to the memory of his almost kiss and, of course, their actual kisses. She could endure anything if kissing Jacob were at the end of it.

Celeste knew that Jacob would be able to see the direction her thoughts had turned by her overly expressive face, but she did not try to hide it this time. She wanted him to know how she loved him, and she would do everything in her power to see him happy. The contented smile he wore as he looked at her with eyes full of warmth and a sparkle of something else, let her know she was well on her way to achieving that.

Epilogue

Honeychurch House, London, 1816

Celeste had done it! She had survived her first ball of the Season with all its whispers. There were not as many as she had feared, at least not within earshot of her. And she had felt a delightful stomach flip whenever she had been announced as 'Lady Celeste Bellmoore.' She would never tire of hearing her married name. She had danced and socialized and worried, but all of it with Jacob at her side.

They had entertained callers on at-home days after that, and Celeste was surprised that so many came. That number doubled after the Admiralty sent Captain Hughes and many of his crew to execution dock, and Celeste found herself alluded to in the news sheets. Her father had sufficient influence to keep her name from appearing, but the gossip had preceded the trial, so she could not be spared entirely from speculation.

Lord Mortcastle, it seemed, also benefited from the good fortune of his relations. He did lose his honorary title and incurred a fine his family could scarcely afford, but he was released. According to the latest periodicals, he had wasted no time in disappearing into obscurity.

Jacob was discussing just such an article with Celeste's father when she entered the breakfast room, three weeks into the Season. It was a much smaller room than the one at Whitbury Manor; the walls were papered in a pale yellow with white swirly patterns throughout. The room was flooded with natural light, with the large, windowed doors leading out to a small balcony beyond.

Celeste's mother was picking at the dishes along the sideboard, while her father sat at the small round table in front of an emptied plate, with Jacob standing behind his shoulder as they discussed the paper in his hand. Her father moved to stand as she entered the room, but she waved him off. Jacob approached her with a smile.

"Elsie, so good to see you," he greeted in a low voice, taking her hand. Celeste felt warmed at his reference, as well as his touch. They had been married a few months now, but the effect had not diminished.

"And you, Mr. McKnell, is it? You seem a little familiar to me. Have we met before?"

Jacob's eyes gleamed with mirth.

"My lady, I am wounded! To think you have forgotten me so soon!" He sighed dramatically, with a hand to his heart.

Celeste tried to force a contemplative expression.

"No, I am afraid I cannot account for it."

"Masquerading as a servant? A daring rescue from pirates? No?" he prompted. Celeste tapped her lip.

"I am very sorry to disappoint you, but I have no recollection of any events of which you speak," she sighed. "You do have a delightful imagination though—have you considered penning a novel?"

Jacob attempted to appear shocked, but his face would not allow it, his wide smile and a coughing laugh pushing past its restraints.

"Goodness, are you still saying hello?" Celeste's mother exclaimed. "Mr. Bellmoore, dear, do allow Celeste to break her fast before she starves to death."

"Indeed. Do forgive me!" Jacob did not appear at all repentant, but he at least escorted her toward the sideboard and passed her a plate, his grin never fading in the slightest.

As they moved along the sideboard, Celeste bumped into Jacob by accident, but enjoying the humor in his eyes, she did it again. This time, he looked at her a little differently, the air changing between them. The flicker of his brow and the way he swayed a little, back toward her, built that magnetic draw she had first felt on the terrace at Whitbury Manor. He reached for something on the sideboard that she did not pay the slightest attention to, her full focus on her husband as his hand grazed hers, sending aching fire up her arm. She looked up into his eyes, and all thoughts of food or other people in the room vanished. She was mildly aware of a throat clearing, but the sound did not have a great enough impact to pull her out of the enchantment of Jacob's gaze. Time ceased to exist as they engaged in silent conversation, the subject of which was beyond the capacity of words. Every nuance of expression connected them, deeper and sweeter.

"It looks like we are alone," he mumbled.

Celeste glanced around the room to see that Jacob was correct. She had not even noticed. She felt her cheeks heating a little at how lost she had been in front of her parents and servants, but that was immediately forgotten as Jacob used two fingers to turn her face back in his direction. Her breath caught as he moved those fingers along her jaw and up her cheek to place a stray curl back into place. His hand lingered behind her ear as he stepped closer to her. It did not matter how many times he had kissed her; it could never be enough.

Celeste did not wait for Jacob to lean down but stood on her toes to meet him, impatient for the sweetness and warmth that always melted through her like hot chocolate in the morning, only better. Jacob laughed against her mouth but was soon moving in sync with her, his fingers weaving into her hair and his free hand wrapping around her waist. She placed a hand on his chest, thrilling at the way his heart raced with hers as she melted into a blissful oblivion of nothing but the two of them.

During a moment of pause between them, a throat cleared in the doorway, drawing their unwilling attention to the butler.

"Yes, Graves?" Jacob answered without his gaze moving from Celeste's. She did not dare move even a fraction, for her desire to retain the moment as long as possible.

"A visitor for Lady Celeste in the receiving room," he announced.

"We are not at home." Jacob grinned.

"You may wish to take her card," Mr. Graves insisted.

Celeste felt their delicious moment slipping away. Jacob squeezed his eyes shut before heaving a sigh. When he opened them, he stepped back and planted a kiss on her knuckles before walking over to the door where Mr. Graves held out the small calling card. Celeste stayed where she was but watched as he read the card, his eyebrows lifting in surprise.

No guests were expected at Honeychurch House until later in the evening when they would be hosting a small family dinner with their parents and Charles, accompanied by Lady Adelle, but without Lady Adelle's dreadful parents.

Jacob's expression cleared as he looked back up at Celeste, tapping the card on his palm.

"I do think we ought to see to our guest. It would be poor form to ignore a Lady who has come to call on you after all," Jacob suggested, extending a hand in invitation for Celeste to join him.

Mr. Graves bit back a smile, which was very unlike the stoic older man. It was most singular.

"And who is this mystery caller?" Celeste asked, walking toward the door.

"Lady Blakely, My lady," Mr. Graves answered with a bow.

"Lord Blakely's mother has come to call on me? Whatever for?" Celeste asked, perplexed.

"Well, it is high time you met her. After all, you did introduce her son to the servant he fell for," Jacob said as they walked. Celeste hesitated before continuing.

"Do you think she is angry with me?" she asked. Jacob merely shrugged and continued walking. He was no help at all. Celeste's heart was racing for a very different reason than it had been in the breakfast room. This was far less pleasant, but she would face the woman. She hoped Lord Blakely's mother would be a cheerful sort if she were anything like her son.

When they entered the receiving room, Celeste saw the figure of a well-dressed woman facing away from her, silhouetted by the window to the street, looking out.

"Mr. Bellmore and Lady Celeste Bellmoore," Mr. Graves announced, then left the room.

The woman turned, and Celeste's breath caught in her throat. Everything she had been afraid of melted away in a single moment, and her eyes filled with tears of relief as she ran toward her guest.

"Bryn!" she exclaimed as she wrapped her arms around her.

"Oof." Bryn's sound of surprise was followed by a pleasant laugh as she reciprocated Celeste's embrace.

After a moment, Celeste pulled away but held Bryn at arm's length.

"Bryn! I am so happy to see you! I have worried after you these many months. Where have you been?" Celeste asked. "Jacob said..."

Suddenly, Celeste realized that it was Jacob who had allowed her to worry over Bryn being Lord Blakely's mother. One look in his direction confirmed that he had known all along. He had that infuriating handsome grin on his face.

"McKnell!" She addressed him with as much accusation as she could, making him laugh.

"Well, do not keep your guest standing about, Celeste. She is Lady Blakely now. You ought to offer her a seat." He held up a conspiratorial hand as he spoke as though he were actually being helpful. If she were closer to the settee, she might have thrown a cushion in his direction. Instead, she turned her attention to Bryn.

"Please do sit down and tell me everything," she invited.

Once seated, Bryn began telling Celeste of what had happened from the time she was taken from Whitbury Manor to the present, including her obvious marriage to Lord Blakely. Bryn also explained that Jacob had known of their coming to Town and had invited her and Lord Blakely that evening, but she had wanted some time with Celeste beforehand. Celeste was grateful for that and made certain that Bryn knew that she and Lord Blakely were forever welcome with an open invitation.

As Celeste spent the next few happy hours enjoying the company of her unlikely friend, and every animated moment of her recollections, Jacob came and sat beside Celeste, holding her hand. He laughed with them, and they were eventually joined by Lord Blakely, who made the room come alive, adding less-believable embellishments to each part of the story. Not that Jacob was any better. His tales of learning to manage the estates made him sound positively heroic in the eyes of the tenants. Not that that was so very far from the truth. He seemed to have found his place in the world, and Celeste enjoyed seeing him so happy.

It was not lost on Celeste as she looked around the room that she had always considered as ideally situated for escape, that it was here that this had all begun. And though she might not yet admit it to her mother, she was eternally grateful to have been wrong.

***

About the author

JoJo Hanbury was born with a thriving imagination, enhanced by her childhood discovery of a magical land called *The Library.* As a mother of five, this has only increased with impromptu bedtime stories and turning boring moments into an adventure. She lives with her family in South Australia, which boasts the best chocolate, jam, and honey anywhere (in her humble opinion).

JoJo fell in love with the Regency era at a slumber party where she was introduced to Pride & Prejudice for the first time, and has visited that, and the surrounding eras, many times since.

Acknowledgements

Thank you to Savannah, for being a soundboard, helping me with the title, and letting me generally talk your ear off.

To my family and friends, for supporting my dream to become an author. Also, to Brad for answering my multitude of questions and just being a true friend.

Enormous thanks to all of my beta-readers and supporters for all of the time and encouragement given throughout the years. You have kept me believing that I could do this!

And, most of all, to God for giving me this gift (amongst many other blessings), and the joy that comes with it.